END OF THE LINE

By Robert Scragg

What Falls Between the Cracks
Nothing Else Remains
All That is Buried
End of the Line

END OF THE LINE

ROBERT SCRAGG

Allison & Busby Limited
11 Wardour Mews
London W1F 8AN
allisonandbusby.com

First published in Great Britain by Allison & Busby in 2021.

A CIP catalogue record for this book is available from
the British Library.

First Edition

ISBN 978-0-7490-2705-6

Typeset in 11.5/16.5 pt Adobe Garamond Pro by
Allison & Busby Ltd

The paper used for this Allison & Busby publication
has been produced from trees that have been legally sourced
from well-managed and credibly certified forests.

Printed and bound by
CPI Group (UK) Ltd, Croydon, CR0 4YY

For Nic, the only woman for whom I would walk five hundred miles, and maybe even the same again

CHAPTER ONE

His footsteps echo off stark brick, bouncing off walls that once penned in prisoners, blind to any guilt or lack thereof. No matter how softly he treads, the *tap-tap-tap* of his boots races down the corridor ahead of him. Might as well be a base drum, beating out his approach to any security guards. A shallow trickle winds its way down a back already slick with sweat. He hefts his rucksack squarely back onto his shoulder and steps through the doorway.

The room beyond looks just like the pictures he's seen online. Perfect. Seems so small a space to have seen such serious situations. A row of three chairs to his right where the magistrates used to sit, the central one high-backed, a throne compared to the two that flank it, surveying its wood-panelled kingdom. Twin strip lights dangle down from a glass dome in the centre, sunlight magnified through a thousand glass tiles, lighting the room up like a stage. Apt. That's exactly what it's about to become. A platform to launch his next attack, and this one could be a killing blow.

No time to waste. The court closed down a couple of years back, but there's still a guard who checks up on the place. Not due for another hour, but why leave it to chance? His business here won't take long. He shrugs off his rucksack, sliding out a collapsible tripod, positioning it on the table in the centre of the room. His smartphone fits snugly into the grip at the top, tapping the screen to flip it round so it shows his face. He takes a few steps back, studying the screen. Slides the legs a few feet further, allowing the royal crest on the wall above into shot.

Dieu et mon droit
God and my right

Gold paint is peeling away from the lion and unicorn like sunburnt skin. Like the rest of the building, the crest has seen better days.

That and the rest of the country, he thinks with a shake of his head. What he does today should go some way to righting the ship. He may have started small, but every broadcast he does hits seven figures now. One more glance around, weighing up light and shadow. Can't be faffing about moving the camera once he goes live. Most of what he needs to say is committed to memory, but he mutters one last run-through nonetheless. He lays out his few props by the foot of the central chair. Feels right that he speaks from there. Today's broadcast isn't just getting up on his soapbox. No, he's promised to bring those bastards at the English Welfare Party down more times than he cares to count. Today is more than delivering a judgement. Today he burns the whole fucking lot of them down to the ground.

He slides into the seat, hands dangling from the end of armrests, settling back like a monarch presiding over court. Closes his eyes. Deep breath. Hold for a three count. Out. Three more of the same. It's time.

He reaches into his pocket, clicking the small remote. A switch flicks somewhere in his head. Showtime.

'Evening all, this is Stormcloudz coming to you live and uncensored from right here in London. You folks best make yourself comfortable cos you're in for a treat today. I'll give you the tour later, but we've got quite a bit to get through today. These fools at the EWP have had their day.'

Even just the mention of the EWP makes him grimace. They're everything that's wrong with Britain. He's on a roll and just finished his intro when the man appears in the public gallery. Not there one minute, staring him out the next. Words stick in his throat like a clogged drain, registering not only the figure now but the balaclava hiding his face. Fear sears the moisture from his mouth, and he licks his lips, rising slowly to his feet.

The man doesn't move. Just stands there behind the glass panels. Slits for eyes, impossible to tell anything from them. He's wearing some kind of boiler suit, dark burgundy with a logo on the breast difficult to read from this distance.

'In case you're wondering,' he begins, hearing and hating the wobble in his voice, 'I'm not doing this one solo. Looks like we've got a visitor.'

He clicks his remote again, flipping the camera around to take in the room, viewing gallery and all.

'Say hello to the great British public, my friend.'

The figure is statue-still. Only sign they're even breathing is a slight rise and fall of shoulders.

His own breath is shallow, tongue darting out to lick lips like a nervous lizard. Whoever the fuck this is, he isn't here to sit and chew the fat, and he definitely isn't the bloody security guard. Come to rob the building perhaps? Can't be much of value left. Copper wiring maybe. He squints, trying to make out the logo, but the sunlight streaming in is bouncing off the glass, making an already hard task impossible.

'You one of Winter's boys, then? You don't frighten me, mate. You're streaming live on Facebook as well—' He breaks off, leaning forwards to look at his screen. 'One point three million people and rising. You see, my friends,' he says, taking a half-step forward with new-found confidence. 'This is how they work, Mr Winter and his jack-boot boys at the EWP. They intimidate. They try and silence anyone who disagrees, and not with logic or argument. With force. They're—'

He stops mid sentence. The man has taken a step forward of his own, almost touching the glass now. Raises a clenched gloved fist to his own throat, drawing it across his neck with thumb pointing inwards like a blade. The same hand drops to his breast, tapping the logo, while the other reaches inside the boiler suit. The blade appears like a magic trick, impossibly long, a matt black curve of steel, punctuated by a row of tiny holes.

'Holy shit . . .' It comes out more of a whisper the first time. The figure taps the logo one more time. 'Holy shit!' Halfway to a shout now. He has walked the full building twice, plotting out escape routes in case the guard came early. For the man to reach him, he will have to smash the barriers, or run back out and around. Either way, time enough to grab his phone and make a hasty exit the way he came.

'We'd best finish this up later, folks,' he says, faking a smile to the camera, darting forwards to retrieve it. As he does, the angle of glare against the glass changes, and he sees the logo. The effect is instant. His eyes widen like saucers in recognition, any hint of the smile giving way to abject terror. Not one of Winter's men. He'd happily take a kicking from half a dozen of Winter's men than be here, now, with him.

'Hate to cut and run like this, but something tells me he's not just here for a cuppa.' He's an octave higher now, giving lie to his bluff of confidence. A quick glance over his shoulder as he heads for the door, waiting for the man to make a move that never comes. That's what seals his fate, attention fixed on the immediate threat, his own voice masking the slightest of creaks from the other side of the open doorway that he should have heard.

He sees a hand jabbing towards him, holding some kind of device, but it's too late. Staccato clicks like ball bearings raining on a tabletop. The pain is a thousand lances of shrapnel as the lights go out. He knows he's falling, but any sense of where to winks out before he gets there.

CHAPTER TWO

Detective Inspector Jake Porter had forgotten to breathe for a full five seconds.

They matched the prints we found. Whoever he is, he was also in the car that killed Holly.

Superintendent Roger Milburn's words echoed in his mind on repeat. The worst kind of earworm. A double tap on the window snapped his head back around. Nick Styles looked out at him like a parent trying to figure out what their naughty kid was up to. He must have seen enough on Porter's face though, hint of a smile giving way to concern. Porter looked past his DS, deeper into the house. Styles's wife, Emma, cradling their newborn baby, as Porter's girlfriend, Evie Simmons, pretended to try and extricate her finger from the little Hannah's stubby fist, knuckles blanched white despite having just fallen asleep.

Holly Porter had been killed in a hit-and-run a few years back. They found the car a few miles from the scene. Nothing to indicate who drove, but a decent set of prints on the passenger dashboard. Trouble was, whoever owned them had never popped up for air. Until now.

He felt light on his feet, unsteady. He turned away towards the road, taking a deep breath. Tried to wrap his head round a moment he'd hungered for, but now it was here, it felt surreal. A glance back at the house. Evie's face peered out from half-shadow, smiling but concerned. He flashed one of his own back that felt far from convincing and made his way back inside.

'Everything all right?' she asked, squeezing his arm as he came and stood beside her.

'Yeah, uhm, I ah . . .' Thoughts swirled around his mind, like Milburn's words had pulled a plug and the life he'd rebuilt was circling the drain.

'What did Milburn want? We got a new case?' Styles asked.

'Something like that, but he's not going to let me anywhere near it.'

Three sets of eyes looked at him, waiting for an explanation.

'The prints from Holly's case,' he said, hearing the strain in his own voice. 'They've found him. The passenger from the car.'

The words settled heavy over the room, a wet blanket smothering the domestic bliss, snuffing out the sense of new beginnings. Nobody spoke for the longest of times as Porter looked at each of them. It wasn't until he locked eyes with his partner that the silence was broken.

'What we waiting for then, boss?' Styles asked. 'Let's go and have a chat. Sergeant Rose on the custody desk owes me a favour. Milburn doesn't need to know.'

'If he was in any fit state to talk, I wouldn't give a shit if Milburn knew or not,' said Porter. 'He's in a coma. Burglary

13

gone wrong. Guy whose flat he was trying to rob cracked him one with a baseball bat.'

'Have they got an ID on him?' Evie asked.

Porter nodded. 'Young kid by the name of Henry Kamau. Runs with the Triple H gang apparently.'

'I know them,' Evie said. 'Run by a guy called Jackson Tyler. Nasty piece of work.'

'Well, they don't tend to recruit for their people skills,' said Porter, a little too harshly. 'Sorry, didn't mean to snap like that. It's just . . .'

She stood up, hand resting on the back of his neck, fingers rubbing a gentle circle. 'It's OK, Jake.'

'We should go,' he said abruptly.

'Don't be daft,' Emma said. 'That's some fairly big news you've just had there. Let me top up everyone's cuppas, and you just sit yourself down.'

Porter wasn't great at sitting still at the best of times, least of all now. He felt like he'd been sucker-punched and needed to walk it off.

'Honestly, I'm all good, thanks, Em. We'll leave you to it. You need to take your rest when she takes hers,' he said, nodding at the sleeping Hannah. He started towards the door before she or Styles could reply. Evie followed, looking somewhat stunned, not sure what to do or say.

'If you're sure,' Emma called after him, sounding as convinced as if he'd just told her he was off to play chicken with the traffic outside.

He waited while Evie and Emma gave each other a brief hug. Heard Emma half whispering something about keeping an eye on him. Styles and Emma stood back, framed in the doorway. Well on their way to the two point four children and white picket fence. Family life. The kind he could have had with Holly by now. Should have had. That one gave him a twinge of guilt, thinking what the parallel universe version of he and Holly would be like now, while climbing into a car with Evie.

The journey back to his was predictably quiet. Evie tried to tiptoe around it. Told him it was fine to feel whatever he felt. He wasn't even sure how to describe it to himself, let alone open up to her. They had been an item for around nine months now. Evie had made the first move. She was a copper too, working on the Drugs Squad, but it had taken Porter a while to open up to the idea of being with anyone post-Holly. Even now, as happy as he was, there were moments, only occasional, where he felt like he was living someone else's life.

That initial spike of adrenaline that had come with Milburn's news had sparked off a heat inside his chest, one that prickled all the way up the back of his neck, like goosebumps. Hearing that the guy was in a coma, that he might not regain consciousness, scratched away at that veneer of hope. What if he never woke up? Porter needed to look him in the whites of his eyes. A name. That's all he wanted. The kid could skate on the burglary charge for all he cared. Porter just wanted the name of the driver.

That first flush had faded now, simmering back to an impatience. One he was used to, never one to let a case stagnate. The only direction is forwards. A mantra to live your life by. Did Milburn honestly think he could just stand on the sidelines and watch, as somebody else got to arrest a man complicit in his wife's death? To hell with that – his wife's *murder*? The boss told him not to meddle. Such a subjective term.

'What are you going to do?' she asked finally, as they pulled into a space outside his flat.

'Do?' he asked. 'I'm going to go for a jog. Need some fresh air.'

'Who's got the case?'

'Pittman.'

'Could be worse.'

'Could be better.'

'And I suppose you're the man to make it so, are you, Jake? Come on, you know Milburn will have you trussed up like a turkey if you so much as breathe on that case.'

'Who says I'm going to do anything?'

Evie fixed him with a withering look, shaking her head as they went inside.

'Your poker face needs work.'

'I'm not stupid, Evie. I'm not going to do anything that would jeopardise the case.'

'But you are going to do something?' she pressed him.

'What do you want me to say?' he snapped, skidding his keys across a narrow wooden table in the hallway, striding through into the kitchen. 'That I'll stay at home like a good little soldier while someone else gets justice for Holly?'

'I just meant—'

'It's Pittman's case, but I can't just do nothing,' he said, reaching into the fridge, twisting the top off a bottle of Corona. 'For nearly four years I've not been able to put any kind of face to what happened.'

'He was the passenger, Jake, not the driver.'

'You don't know that for sure. And even if he was, he'll know who was sat two feet to his right.'

Even without seeing Henry Kamau, without knowing what he looked like, anger towards the man coursed through Porter, heat spreading across his cheeks, jaw tightening. Two deep breaths punctuated by a long swig from the bottle.

'Thought you were going for a run?' she said, but her attempt to change the subject and talk him down had the opposite effect.

The confines of the kitchen felt stifling. The call from Milburn had popped the lid off a jar of dark memories he'd not long managed to contain. He gave his best shot at a reassuring smile, hoping it didn't look as forced as it felt.

'Maybe later. Could do with some fresh air though,' he said, clinking the half-empty bottle on the counter.

'Want some company?'

'I do, and don't take this the wrong way, but would you mind if I just had a little wander myself first though? My head's just . . .' He made a swirling gesture by his temple with a finger.

She nodded, lips pressed into a thin line, stepping back to let him past. Porter leant in, kissed her softly, felt her relax into him.

'I know it's all kinds of weird. That was then, me before you. This . . .' he said, waving a finger between the two of them, 'is where I am now, but I can't ignore what's happened today. Just bear with me. Can you do that?'

She looked up at him, smiling, nodding, any tension around the eyes gone now.

'Go on, get yourself away. I'll finish that off for you,' she said, gesturing towards his beer, 'and we can do something when you get back.'

He angled past her, pulling the kitchen door closed behind him as he headed out, taking care when scooping up his keys so as not to jangle. He hadn't lied about wanting fresh air, just hadn't shared where he planned to sample it.

CHAPTER THREE

Nick Styles lay back against his sofa, legs tucked up and pressed together, making the angled platform on which Hannah Styles currently lay. Already, only seven days into fatherhood, anything that predated her arrival had a hazy hue to it, a part of his life he could never revisit, nor would he want to.

He'd been smitten the moment he first held her and, barring a trip to the shops and picking up a takeaway, he'd been happily wrapped up in the bubble of his new family life. Emma sat at the other end of the sofa, head against the armrest at an angle that made him wince, mouth half open. The snore that came out alternated between hibernating hamster and wildebeest. Hannah didn't so much as twitch, even when her mum hit base notes loud enough to measure on the Richter scale.

He split his time between watching a muted recording of *Match of the Day* and glancing at his two ladies. Life felt pretty good right now. Could do with a few more hours sleep, but with

Emma wanting to breastfeed, up God knows how many times during the night while he slept, he could hardly complain.

He had just started to consider a stealthy retreat into the kitchen to snaffle a sly cheese toastie when his phone began to flash. Work. Not a name, just the main station number. Sod that for a game of soldiers. He was due back on duty the next day. Nothing that couldn't wait until then. Styles started the painfully slow process of Operation Toastie. One hand slid behind Hannah's head, the other reaching under, palm against her back, unfolding his legs at a glacial pace, careful movements that a bomb disposal technician would be proud of.

As he edged towards the Moses basket, one tiny fist jerked out like she wanted to bump knuckles, but the eyes remained firmly closed. Lowering her in, he felt like a backwards version of Indiana Jones, returning the treasure to its pedestal.

He made it two steps into the kitchen before his phone flashed again. Milburn this time. Styles toyed with ignoring it. Easy enough to say he'd been busy changing the baby and hadn't seen it until later. On second thoughts, having seen Milburn dish out grief for far less, he tapped the screen to answer.

'Is Porter still with you?'

So much for any preamble, enquiring after the mum and baby, or anything else that might suggest the super even vaguely took an interest in his people's personal lives.

'No, he left about an hour ago. Everything OK, boss? He told me the news about Holly's case. Anything I can help with?' Styles asked, reasoning that if he could get a foot in the door, Porter might trust him to see things were done properly, rather than getting any ideas about sniffing around the case himself, like Styles knew he would. It's what he would do himself if roles were reversed.

'No, thank you, Sergeant. DI Pittman has it covered. Porter's not answering my calls though, and I've got something else I need you two to pick up for me.' The super paused, making Styles wonder if it was something delicate, needing to fly low on the radar. 'Have you seen what I sent you yet?'

Styles frowned. 'No, what have you sent?'

'Just check the email, find Porter, then call me back.'

'Um, sure, boss,' Styles said, more than a little confused, about to remind Milburn that he was on paternity leave until tomorrow, but his super had already ended the call.

He opened his email to see Milburn's message was a link to a Facebook page. The page had a striking cover picture. A 3D perspective of the UK, huge bank of clouds about to roll in from the east, forked fingers of lightning reaching out, striking the south coast. The banner across the top proclaimed it as the home of someone by the name of Stormcloudz. Made Styles picture a moody teenager trying to add attitude by slinging in a consonant that didn't belong.

What the hell was Milburn wanting him to do with this? He dragged a finger downwards, scrolling through the posts, but pressed back down, halting the slide of information as the very first entry made his eyes widen, mouthing a silent *What the . . . ?* as he tapped to expand the video.

The small red box in the top corner told him what he was watching wasn't just a recording. It was live. This was happening right now. The young man sat in the high-backed chair, biting down on a cloth gag held in place with black tape, eyes rattling back and forward in sockets like ping pong balls. Cable ties looped around his wrists, pinning arms to the chair. He was bookended either side by two men in matching outfits. Boiler suits the colour of rich red Merlot, some kind of yellow graphic on the breast. Their faces were obscured by black balaclavas.

Styles grabbed his iPad from the kitchen bench, opening up the same link, freeing his phone up to call Porter. Ten tinny speakerphone rings, then voicemail.

Their captive looked mid twenties at a push, sandy hair flopping around his eyeline as he twisted his head, looking to either side of shot like watching a game of tennis on fast forward. His captors stood stone-still, arms crossed, against a backdrop of wood panelling. Where the hell were they? A mix of sad and angry emoticons bubbled up, floating off over the screen. Comments popped and scrolled down below. Reams of text exploded beneath the images.

Enough's enough

Not funny

You wanna stop, mate, I've called the coppers

Slight wobble to the picture as the camera was slid back, widening the shot, the wannabe cameraman entering stage left. He wore the same boiler suit, face hidden. Half a dozen strides and he was up by the young man, a gloved hand resting on his captive's shoulder. The mouth slit was so small, Styles couldn't even see lips moving behind the black wool when he spoke.

'For too long, Britain has been a club, wielded by America, against our people and our God. Like any other weapon, Britain can be broken. That starts today.'

Styles pulled the kitchen door closed, not wanting to wake Emma or Hannah, turning up the volume a notch as he tried Porter again, but the result was the same. Milburn would do again for now.

'Have you found him?' Milburn questioned, curt as ever.

'Not yet sir.'

'Are you watching this?' asked Milburn, a little more muted, as if not quite believing what they were seeing.

'I am, sir. Do we know the who and where?'

'No, we're busy trying . . .'

Milburn tailed off, and Styles tuned back into the diatribe coming from his phone, wondering what had distracted his super.

The knife looked too big to be real. Not even a knife, more like a machete. The matt black blade blended against the dark wool of the balaclava as the man held it up, middle section of what must border on two feet of steel seeming to disappear like a magic trick.

'This is the first, but not the last.'

Styles saw the slight rise in the man's shoulders, a deep breath, precursor to action. Jesus, was this really happening? The bookends each reached over, clamping the young man's hands to the armrests. A half-step to his right, and he was behind the chair, one hand grabbing underneath the young man's chin, the other bringing the blade around on the horizontal.

The petrified captive strained against his bonds, eyes bulging, rolling, reminding Styles of a spooked horse. Styles watched as the blade neared his throat. Watched as his head was pulled back. Watched as the masked man started to saw. Couldn't watch past that.

CHAPTER FOUR

If you looked up anticlimax in the dictionary, this is what Porter fancied it would look like. Almost four years since Holly had been taken from him. How many times had he imagined what he would say to anyone responsible? What he would do to them? Yet here he stood, looking at the face of a man who at very least knew who killed his wife, but could even be that man himself.

Man? More like boy. Henry Kamau looked like he should still be at school. Actual age nineteen by all accounts. His head and most of the left side of his face were obscured by a surgical dressing. Foothills of dark swelling traced the edge of the gauze. The last time Porter had stood in a hospital ward, watching over someone like this, it had been Evie in the bed, more wires and cables bunched around her than an IED. He'd prayed for her recovery back then but couldn't bring himself to utter the same words for the man before him now. The

'Take it he was unconscious when they found him?'

'This is as talkative as he's been,' said Pittman, slurping a mouthful of coffee.

'Anyone been in to see him? Family? Friends?'

'Nope. Not sure what family he has, and can't see any of his Triple H buddies popping by with flowers, can you?'

'Who else is on it with you?'

'I've got O'Connor, Ayla and Manfredo on door-to-door and taking statements. Guy who clocked him says there were at least two more, but they scarpered after this one hit the deck.'

'What about Jackson Tyler? Who's talking to him?'

Pittman narrowed his eyes. 'For a man who's staying out of my way, you seem to know entirely too much about my case.'

'I know Milburn doesn't want me anywhere near it—' Porter began.

'I don't want you anywhere near it,' Pittman said, prodding a finger at his own chest for emphasis. 'I know that's gonna be hard, because of your wife and all, but that's the way it has to be.'

'All I'm asking is that you let me know as things develop. Don't make me have to wait to see it on one of the super's press conferences,' said Porter.

'I'll see what I can do,' Pittman said, almost reluctantly. 'No promises mind. Milburn's already said he wants this done right, and not just cos of the connection to you. Triple H boys have been on his shitlist for a good while now. When this one wakes up, if he wakes up, Milburn's already given the thumbs up to offer him a deal to talk.'

'He's done what?' Porter asked, unable and unwilling to keep a rasp of anger from his voice.

'We let him walk on the burglary if he gives us the driver of your hit-and-run, plus dirt on Jackson Tyler. Enough to haul him in.'

'Walk on the breaking and entering, but not on Holly?' Porter asked, not liking what he saw on Pittman's face.

'Depends what we get. If he gives us the driver plus Tyler, he walks on the rest. If we don't get Tyler, the rest sticks.'

'I don't fucking believe it.' Porter felt anger fizz in his cheeks, heat on the back of his neck. 'He either drove or helped cover it up. Either way, he does time with his prints in the car.'

'Chances are he wasn't the one who did it,' Pittman said, softening his words. 'His brief will argue his prints were from a previous trip. Walking on the B&E is our leverage.'

'You don't know that for sure,' Porter shot back. 'There's just as much chance he was the driver, panicked, wiped down the wheel but forgot about the bits he'd touched on the other side earlier and just ran off.'

'Look, mate, get yourself away. He's going nowhere for a good while yet,' Pittman said, nodding at Kamau. 'I'll give you a shout after tomorrow morning's briefing, let you know what the door-to-door turns up. How about that?'

Porter knew Pittman by reputation more than from experience. There just wasn't much of a rep either way, that was the problem. Pittman was just a plodder, and if even half of what he'd heard about Jackson Tyler was true, it would take more than the threat of a short stint inside for B&E to get someone to turn on him. That called for some lateral thinking. There had to be a pressure point somewhere, but he wasn't convinced that Pittman was the man to find it and apply any. Still, Pittman was right. Nothing more to be gained from hanging around here. Not until Kamau woke up anyway.

'You're right. I'll leave you to it, then.'

Pittman's half-smile suggested he was far from convinced of Porter's ability to keep out of his way. He'd be right to be suspicious. Porter had no intention of being a spectator. He had to do something, just hadn't decided exactly what that something was yet. He'd sleep on it, metaphorically anyway. He wasn't a great sleeper at the best of times, but his head felt like today's news had gone into a blender with the switch jammed on. Evie would have questions. Milburn and Styles too. How was he feeling? What was he thinking? Wasn't sure he had answers for himself, let alone others. Why couldn't this have happened earlier? Why now, when he'd not long reached a place where the past felt like it was in its rightful place?

He checked his watch as he came past reception. Head back home, take a walk somewhere with Evie, then work out his next steps. A figure unfolded itself from a slouch against the wall by the car park pay station, and he glanced over to see Nick Styles saunter over, hands in pockets.

'Everything all right, boss?' he said, looking borderline embarrassed to use such a cliché, knowing things were pretty bloody far from it.

'All good. Just broke a nail but the doc fixed me up fine.'

Styles grinned. Porter narrowed his eyes. How had Styles known where to find him? Surely Pittman hadn't sold him out already?

'Evie said you'd gone out to clear your head. Didn't take a detective to figure out where you might be. It's where I would have come.'

Porter nodded, sliding his ticket into the parking machine and popping a few coins to cover it.

'Just had to see him for myself, you know. He's just a kid, looks like he should still be in school for Chrissake.'

'He talking?'

Porter shook his head. 'There's a chance he never will again. Anyway, you don't have to worry about me. I'm off home now. Get yourself away back to your ladies, and I'll catch you tomorrow.'

'Sorry to disappoint, but I didn't just get dropped off here out of brotherly love,' said Styles.

'Milburn send you?'

'Yeah, not because of who's in there,' he said, gesturing back at the hospital. 'There's a new case he needs us on.'

'Tell him it can bloody well wait,' Porter snorted. 'You're still on paternity, and I'm . . . well, let's just say I've got a few things on my mind. There's plenty of others on duty who can pick it up.'

'We're not exactly talking a missing cat here, boss. Here' – he tapped his phone screen, reversing it, a video playing – 'you're gonna want to see this, and then you'll probably wish that you hadn't.'

CHAPTER FIVE

Porter watched for the second time as Styles drove. The footage was simultaneously sickening and oddly unreal. The first run-through had left him with a dry mouth and a feeling like he'd swallowed a cricket ball. His mind told him this couldn't be real. Just a clever camera trick to shock. Get people talking and make it go viral. Styles wouldn't have come out for that though. They had tasered the victim as he tried to escape. He'd been out cold as they strapped him to the chair, but he was painfully conscious now.

It took the hooded figure a good sixty seconds of sawing. Porter tried not to fixate on that part of the screen, instead seeing the smaller details. The way the victim's hands scrabbled and scratched at the armrest. Fingers jerked in an irregular dance, playing air-piano. His eyes pinballed in every direction, looking for an escape. The gag in his mouth soaked up most of the sound, but Porter could still hear something between a gargle and a choking noise seeping out. That, and an occasional grunt from his killer were all he could make out, surprisingly loud in the otherwise quiet car.

Porter had never seen so much blood. The victim's T-shirt, once white, had a red carpet running down the centre, spatter speckling either side. His attackers' overalls by contrast, just looked damp in places, the already dark burgundy fabric stained darker by the spurts of blood. The killer centre stage looked to be largely shielded from any spray by the high-backed chair.

By the time the killer had finished, his victim had long since stopped twitching. The men either side moved away as the killer made his final stroke, head parting from body with a slight jerk, like snapping the top off a flower.

'This is the beginning,' said the killer, breathing heavier than before, holding the severed head out to the side by the hair like a trophy, before letting it fall to the ground, out of shot. 'This is the beginning. There will be no end. *Allahu Akbar.*'

'Jesus,' Porter muttered under his breath as he paused it. 'Where are we then? Has anyone claimed responsibility yet?'

'Not yet,' Styles said. 'And not much in the way of information. I only found out the location on the way to pick you up. It's the old Greenwich Magistrates' Court on Blackheath Road.'

'Didn't they close that down?'

'Yep, couple of years back. They still have a security guard who does the rounds there to keep the urbexers out.'

'What the hell is an urbexer?'

'Urban explorer,' said Styles. 'Quite popular apparently. People seek out old buildings, hospitals, prisons, factories. Sometimes to take pictures, sometimes just for the hell of it.'

Porter wrinkled his nose, not exactly his idea of fun. 'And what, we think the poor bugger getting his head hacked off was one of these Urbexers?'

'No, we know who he is.'

'Bloody hell, that was quick.'

'That was the easy part. The live link Milburn sent me to watch was streaming from the guy's Facebook page. Name's Ross Henderson, but he goes by the name of Stormcloudz,' said Styles, whacking plenty of emphasis on the final consonant. 'He's a gamer and political activist, and a popular one at that. More than ten million followers on YouTube.'

'You mean to say ten million people watched that?' said Porter in disbelief.

'Not the full whack, but the viewing numbers were into the low seven figures when I was watching.'

'Oh my God,' Porter muttered. Strangers watching were one thing, but what if the audience had included any of the guy's friends or family? The very thought made him shudder.

'What's Milburn had to say?'

'Other than to find you and get our arses over there, not much so far. You'll have the pleasure of his company soon enough though. He's meeting us at the scene.'

That'd be right. Come out centre stage for the meaty ones. Milburn to a tee. Porter knew exactly why the super would want him on this. Distraction tactics 101. Throw him something big and keep him away from Holly's case.

The sun had just dipped below the skyline as they pulled up on Blackheath Road. The old courthouse was a faded, dirtied version of its early twentieth century classical glory. Flanked on either side by what looked like townhouses, the entrance a slate grey dome that resembled a squashed down copper's helmet. Up on the roof, front and centre, a now bare flagpole, candle on top of an out-of-date cake.

A cordon had been set up across the front of the entire building. Twin double doors either side of the main entrance, and walkways up to them, taped off like mini boxing rings. One lane of the road outside it was closed off too, one officer allowing traffic from either direction to alternate. A gallery of frustrated faces peered out as Porter walked past. All oblivious to the carnage carried out a stone's throw from where their engines idled.

Across the road, a growing gaggle of press shuffled restlessly in the Kwik Fit car park. Never ceased to amaze Porter how quickly they sniffed out a story. One familiar face amongst them already. Amy Fitzwilliam from Sky News. A hungry up-and-comer who he hadn't had the best of experiences with so far. She was good at her job. Too good. She'd buzzed around the edges of his last big case, a missing seven-year-old and a trove of bodies dug up in a London park. Caused him no end of bother, breaking stories live at the scene, using information that the police hadn't released. He saw her clock him and looked away as he and Styles approached the edge of the cordon.

'Detective Porter!'

He recognised her voice, glancing over even as he told himself not to react.

'Detective Porter, is it true that this is the location Stormcloudz was broadcasting from? Are the men who attacked him still inside? Are they in custody?'

He gave her a half-smile, nothing more, and turned his attention to the officer controlling access to the scene. Pointless exercise, hurling questions like that, spitting them out like an involuntary tic. Did any of them honestly expect him to just stroll over and spill his guts, sharing everything they had? Not that they had much at the minute.

He and Styles signed in, walked into the lobby and suited up in disposable Tyvek all-in-one coveralls. The lobby floor was a work of art. Thousands of tiny mosaic tiles, enough to make his head hurt with the thought of how long it would have taken to lay. The wood panelling on the walls was identical to that he'd seen in the courtroom broadcast.

They made their way through a series of short corridors, entering the courtroom from the side. Porter recognised the public gallery that the first masked man had stood in, off to his left. That meant the magistrate's chair the poor bugger had been tied in was behind the door to the right. Even before he stepped through, the smell was unmistakable. A coppery taint in the air, thick, soupy, like an invisible smog.

He followed Styles through the door, his view of the chair blocked by a pair of similarly suited figures with their backs to them. Porter took a moment to survey the rest of the room. A bizarre sense of déjà-vu washed over him. To have never set foot in here until now, but to have watched such a horrific sequence unfold in this room, gave it a surreal familiar quality. The phone that must have filmed every gory moment of it still sat clamped in a tripod on a table bang in the centre of the room.

'Ah, I see you two finally decided to show up.'

Porter looked over at the voice, recognising his superintendent, Roger Milburn, and his holier-than-thou tone that always sounded like he was speaking to an audience. Probably used it even when he was alone at home with his wife. Porter opened his mouth to make up an excuse as to where he'd been, but Milburn just waved him over.

'Come on, come on. Clock's ticking,' he said, making no effort to hide his impatience.

Porter worked his way around to the left, moving across a series of transparent raised anti-contamination stepping plates, so as not to smudge the blood spatter that decorated the floor. Didn't need a scene of crime officer to work out who most or all of it came from, thanks to the live broadcast. Always a chance that one of the offenders had nicked themselves though. Paid to be thorough.

The sight when he got past Milburn's shoulder was every bit as bad as he'd feared. The headless body, still tethered at the wrists to the chair by cable ties, was slumped forward ten degrees or so at the waist. Stains of all shapes and sizes blotted jeans and T-shirt like one big Rorschach test, darker now, drying from red to a rusty brown. Porter made a conscious effort not to stare at the neck, stomach on spin cycle. Behind him, he heard Styles breathing loudly through his mouth.

'Nice to see you again, Jake,' the figure next to Milburn spoke, and Porter smiled as he recognised the voice. Kam Qureshi was one of the best they had when it came to forensics. He'd made a career plucking needles from haystacks. If there was anything to find in all this mess, he was the man Porter would want searching for it.

'Hey, Kam. How you doing?'

'Better than our friend here,' Kam said, cocking a thumb towards the body. 'I was just telling the super that solving a murder is going to be the least of our worries.'

'What's that supposed to mean?' Porter asked, puzzled.

'What he means, Porter, is that our victim here was more popular than Ed bloody Sheeran.'

'I wouldn't say that, sir, Sheeran's got thirty million—'

'Never mind that, Qureshi. This chap has – had – millions of followers online. Seems he spent most of his time whipping them up against people like the EWP.'

Porter wasn't massively political but had picked up enough about the English Welfare Party in the news to know they were the Marmite of English politics. They'd snatched the right-wing baton from UKIP, and from what Porter could see, took every opportunity to bellow out the rallying cry of Britain for the British, or a variation on a theme.

'Bad enough that the EWP are gaining traction by hitching their wagon to the Brexit train,' Milburn continued, 'but that video is a right-winger's wet dream. They'll stuff that down the throat of anyone they can in the hope of dragging a few more into their camp.'

'Nick said we're still waiting for someone to stick their hand up and claim it?'

'Strictly speaking yes, but Kam here thinks he's got us a step ahead.'

'How so?' Porter asked, looking back at Kam.

'If you watch the footage back, you can see they've all got some kind of badge on their suits.'

'Take your word for it, Kam,' said Porter, no desire to watch that back any more than was absolutely necessary.

'I watched the footage a few times and took a screenshot. Bit blurry, but enough to get an idea. I'll show you the picture when we get out of our posh frocks,' he said, patting his paper-thin suit. 'But for now, we're looking at a crescent moon with a single star off to one side.'

'Why do I get the feeling that should mean something to me?' Styles asked.

'Because it should,' Porter said. 'Couldn't tell you if it has a particular name, but those symbols are linked to Islam. That, plus the main fella shouting *Allahu Akabar* was a bit of a clue.'

'Gold star for Porter.' Kam nodded his approval to the first point.

'Jesus, the EWP will lap that up,' Styles said, eyes flitting between the body and the blood on the floor.

'Indeed they will, Sergeant, which is exactly why we need to make sure we're on point when it comes to managing the information flow on this one. Speaking of which, I need to head back and prep a statement. Don't leave until you've spoken with the chap from the Counter Terrorism Unit, Porter, then call me right after that. The guy they're sending is called Taylor.'

True to form, Milburn turned on his heel and left them to it. Never one to stand on ceremony or worry about social niceties like hello or goodbye.

'Well, what a little ray of sunshine our illustrious leader manages to bring to proceedings,' Porter muttered once Milburn was out of earshot. 'What else have you got for us then, Kam?'

Kam didn't miss a beat. 'I can give you an educated guess as to the cause of death.'

CHAPTER SIX

Porter left Kam to it, and with Styles in tow, took the chance while still suited up to walk where the masked men had. The public gallery. The corridor behind the raised dais that the magistrates had sat at, leading to a cluster of holding cells. Tiny, spartan spaces that could make a man claustrophobic even with the door open. Pillar-box panes set into doors several inches thick. If only Ross Henderson could have made it back here. Maybe he could have shielded behind one of these.

'Did we get eyes on our three masked marauders leaving the building?' he asked Styles.

'Not that we've found so far, boss. No eyewitnesses.'

'For a crime witnessed by over a million people. That's almost ironic enough for Alanis Morissette to write a song about.'

'I spoke to the security company who look after this place though. The guard wasn't due on site for another hour, so looks like it was all well timed.'

'By Henderson, or the three blokes?'

'I'm thinking both,' Styles said. 'Urbexing is basically trespass in a lot of cases, so Henderson needed to make sure he wasn't spotted.'

'Got to assume those three followed him here, then?'

'You'd tell me off for using the A-word.'

'Privileges of rank,' Porter shot back.

'Right, we need to get the rest of the team up to speed. See who you can get hold of.'

'Just had a text off Sucheka when you were speaking to Milburn,' Styles said. 'She's waiting outside with Williams and Tessier. Waters is on his way.'

Porter grunted an approval. Styles came across as laidback at times. Any more he'd practically be as horizontal as a limbo dancer, but he had a knack of shuffling pieces into place without being asked.

'Let's get out there and crack on then. We can nab a few of the uniforms to knock on doors. Think it's mainly residential east along Blackheath Road, but I spotted a couple of takeaways, a barber shop, that type of thing. Three masked men in bloody overalls can't have exactly blended in.'

'You'd think, but this is London. There's just as much chance the three of them barged past people who had their heads buried in a smartphone.'

'Wish everyone was as optimistic as you,' Porter said. 'Come on, let's head out and nab the others.'

They made their way back to the tiled lobby, shedding their suits like snakeskin, signing out of the crime scene. Porter exited through the wooden double doors back out to the street. He turned to Styles as he neared the line of police tape, colliding with whoever had just ducked past it. It would have been chest to chest, if they weren't at least half a foot shorter than him. He looked down to see a smartly dressed redhead, hair shaped into a tight bob. She'd practically headbutted his chest. Couldn't be more than five-two at a push. She wore a navy blue suit, shirt so white it could be from a Persil advert, with a join-the-dots cluster of freckles across her nose.

She slapped one hand against his chest for balance, eyes batting out Morse code as surprise turned into what looked like recognition.

'Detective Porter,' she said, and he couldn't work out if it was a question or a statement. Had he seen her out front with the rest of the press, waiting for the feeding frenzy when the body bag came out?

'Yes, but I'm afraid I'm going to have to ask you to wait over the road with the others if you're press.'

She looked up at him with a half-smile, nose wrinkling in amusement. 'I thought you'd be taller from watching your press conferences. Must have just been a high podium.'

'Do we know each other?' he asked, looking over to Styles, seeing no recognition in his face either.

'We do now,' she said, thrusting a hand up and out. 'Detective Inspector Bell, Counter Terrorism.'

'Oh,' Porter said as he shook it. 'Sorry, I was expecting Taylor.'

'Doesn't everyone,' she said, with a roll of the eyes. 'That's still me.'

'Now you've really lost me.'

'DI Taylor Bell,' she said, pumping his hand up and down a second time. 'If I had a quid for every time someone assumed I was a bloke—'

'You'd have about three quid,' Styles chipped in.

'Oh, he's funny,' she said, flashing a full-beam smile his way, still addressing Porter. 'He's a keeper. So, if you're Porter, that would make you DS Styles?' She nodded at them in turn.

'At your service,' Styles said, with a tilt of his head.

'Can I assume your super told you why he's brought CTU in?'

Porter nodded. 'The symbols on their overalls, plus what they shouted, linking it to an Islamic group. Nobody's taken credit for it yet though.'

'That's where you're wrong,' she said, very matter-of-fact.

'The super only left a few minutes ago,' Styles said. 'Where's your intel coming from?'

'I know exactly who did this,' said Bell. 'You would too if you knew what to look for. And it's worse than you think.'

CHAPTER SEVEN

'You're right in that the crescent moon and star combo is linked to the Islamic faith,' Bell said, 'except this one is a little different. There's a crack running through the moon, puts it a little off-centre. That version isn't so much Islam in general. There's a particular radical offshoot. Call themselves the Brotherhood of the Prophet. They use it as their badge—'

Styles cut in. 'I've heard of them. They're the ones behind the bombing in Istanbul last year. That and they beheaded that journalist chap last year in Syria, so they've got form. This is going to have the EWP marching the streets, demanding deportations and God knows what else.'

From what he'd seen of the EWP on the news, Porter fancied their propaganda machine would already be whirring away.

'What else can you tell us about them?' Porter asked.

Bell gave him a serious look. 'As far as UK-based operations go, not a great deal. All their high-profile activity has been overseas so far. We've picked up a few bits and pieces these last twelve months, tracked some chatter suggesting they had plans to recruit over here, but nothing concrete. No actual activity that we've been aware of.'

'Where the hell do we start, then?' Porter snapped frustration creeping into his tone.

'This is still your case, Porter, for now,' said Bell, palms held out in a *cool-your-jets* manner. 'I'm just here to assist, but I can start by getting word to some of our undercover officers in a few other organisations, see if tongues are wagging in the dingy flats they seem to spend most of their time cooped up in.'

Porter started to nod, opened his mouth to reply, then stopped for a second. 'Wait a minute, what do you mean it's my case for now?'

'Exactly that,' said Bell with a shrug. 'Look, this isn't some kind of pissing contest. My height means I haven't got the angle for any kind of distance anyway. But all joking aside, you're good at what you do, and so am I. I know how these people think, how they set up cells, how they communicate, who they like to target. It's a murder, and a horrible one at that, but let's be honest, we're only hours in. The top brass will drop trousers and size up to decide who runs with this, but the smart money's on me.'

'Detective Porter!' A voice came floating from over the road. All three of them turned, seeing the petite figure of Amy Fitzwilliam. 'Are you ready to make a statement yet?'

'Friend of yours?' Bell said, a smirk curling the corners of her mouth.

'Oh, we're BFFs,' Porter said, trying to decide whether Bell's mix of banter and bluntness grated on him or made him gravitate towards her.

'I'll leave you all to it if you don't mind. I want to take a look inside for myself.'

'It's not a nice one,' Porter said. 'Hope you haven't eaten recently.'

'Oh, I'm tougher than I look,' she said as she trotted up the half a dozen steps and disappeared inside. He had no doubt that she was, and that she'd probably had to prove it more than most.

Off to the left-hand side, he saw the rest of his team where they'd been waiting patiently for him to finish the conversation. It suddenly occurred to him that he hadn't thought of Holly, or Henry Kamau, since he got here. Maybe Milburn was right about him needing to be on this one. Keep his mind off things. To an extent anyway.

He still needed to work out how far he could stick his neck out to keep close to Holly's case, without falling afoul of Milburn. If anyone had asked a few hours ago, he'd have gladly told them where to shove this one. Now though, it had already sunk its hooks in. The violence, up close and personal. The sheer audacity to do that to another human in front of that many people, albeit virtually. Porter didn't care who the three men were, or why they'd done what they did. Just that they had to be stopped.

'What now then, boss?' Styles asked.

'Now?' repeated Porter. 'Now, we brief those three.' He nodded to the rest of his team. 'Then we crack on before Bell comes back out.'

'She rubbed you up the wrong way?'

'Like sandpaper on sunburn.'

Porter felt his phone buzz. He glanced and saw Evie's name flash up. As guilty as it made him feel, he rejected the call. He'd promised some time together, and she'd be expecting that to be him unloading the contents of his head and his heart. There was plenty in both to unpack in light of today's revelations, but he needed a clear head. He'd call her back once they left the scene.

'Come on,' he gestured Styles over to where the others stood. To say Gus Tessier stood wasn't entirely accurate. He loomed, towering over everyone except Styles, but he had Styles beaten hands down when it came to width. Half-French, half-Ghanaian, he was the Met's answer to the Mountain from *Game of Thrones*, but with a much nicer temperament. Next to him stood Kaja Sucheka, literally half his size. She'd only been on the job a little over a year, coming in via the fast-track scheme, but had impressed Porter. Not many had the level of single-minded determination she possessed. He wondered where it came from, what drove her to push herself so hard. There was usually a story behind folk like that, but she kept her cards close to her chest. The final member of the team, Dee Williams, stood side on, looking over at the latest news van to pull in over the road. Dee was quiet, often too quiet in briefings, but had a great eye for detail. Still no sign of Glenn Waters.

'You lot look like a B-list version of the Avengers, poised and ready for inaction,' he said, dipping under the tape.

Tessier laughed, a low rumble. Once you got past the intimidating size, Gus was one of the nicest, happiest people Porter had ever met. This line of work tended to rough you up around the edges, but Tessier's mood seemed impervious to anything and everything.

'Don't know about superheroes, boss, but Nick's more of

an Inspector Gadget with arms and legs like his.'

'Don't make me get physical, Gus,' Styles said. 'I mean it, please don't. Wouldn't end well for me.'

'What's it like in there?' asked Kaja. 'Is it as bad as it looked?'

'Let's just say be thankful Facebook doesn't have an option to smell the videos too,' Porter said, still sure he could catch a hint of the slaughterhouse scent from inside. 'You've all seen it, I presume?'

Nods all round, serious faces to match. Just the memory alone was enough to strip away any of the previous humour.

'First things first: Kaja, Gus, I need you two to work your way up both sides of the street. Shops, takeaways, pubs – customers and CCTV. Not often we get an exact time for a murder, so let's make the most of that. Dee, let's get chapter and verse on our victim. Both sides of him as well. This whole Stormcloudz malarkey all feels a bit showy. What was he like when he wasn't in front of the camera? Nick, see what you can find on this Brotherhood. I need to check in with Milburn, then grab our CTU friend when she comes back out. Everyone good with that?'

'Looks like the village idiots have come out to play,' said Williams, looking east along Blackheath Road. Porter turned, saw the group of four men loitering under a street lamp fifty yards beyond the journalists. They'd all clearly gotten the memo, jeans, T-shirts and jackets zipped all the way up. Strung out across the pavement, they were currently blocking the way for a pair of ladies, each wearing a long *abaya* dress, edges brushing the ground, hijabs covering their heads. Porter saw the men's mouths moving, but they were too far away to hear what was said. Body language didn't leave much to the imagination. One man, front and centre, arms out at his sides in a *what's the problem?* gesture. Ladies looking from the ground to each other, then back again. Trying to walk around the men, failing as the barrier of arms shuffled sideways, forcing them out into the road.

'Gus, do me a favour,' asked Porter, 'have a quiet word, will you?'

Tessier's smile was still there, harder around the edges though. 'Thought you'd never ask.'

He clapped hands together that would put a Yeti to shame and strode towards the group. One of them clearly spotted him before he'd even crossed the road, human barrier dissolving, relieved women scurrying through, not realising or caring why they'd been allowed safe passage.

'Right, let's crack on then, shall we?' Porter announced.

'Before we do, boss,' Sucheka cut in, 'while you were inside, I watched the clip back again. Spotted something I missed first time around. Something I think we all did. Look,' she said, pulling out her phone, screen paused on the courtroom scene, the only figure visible, Ross Henderson, already dead. Could be worse, she could have made him watch the actual beheading again.

'Look,' she repeated, tapping play, sliding one finger along the progress bar to fast forward.

'What am I missing, Kaja? He's not moving any time soon.'

'He isn't, but somebody is. There. You see that?'

She paused it again, finger hovering over the table that the tripod had been set up on. Porter and Styles leant in at the same time, millimetres away from a clash of heads.

'Watch,' she said, sliding the footage back and forward, five seconds either way.

46

Movement in shot. Not a person, a shadow. Flowing into shot from the side, ebbing away again just as quick. She pulled it back ten seconds again.

'Now, listen this time as well as watch.'

A few seconds of silence. Rustle of fabric. Laboured breathing, heavy nasal. A heaving sound, someone retching, once, twice. Faintest of scrapes, followed by what sounded like a scuff of shoe on carpet. A voice next. Male.

'Ah, Jesus.' Not a voice he recognised.

'That's the first officer on scene. PC Macken. That's him over there,' she said, pointing to a uniformed constable standing by the cordoned off west entrance.

'Maybe I've got baby brain from lack of sleep, but so what?'

'Macken was first on the scene. First to enter. First copper anyway.'

Styles's eyebrows raised as the penny dropped, same time for him as for Porter.

'So, whose shadow was that?'

'Exactly,' Sucheka said, beaming at the reveal. 'Everyone's been so fixated on the actual murder. There's almost an hour of footage with just Henderson in the chair that nobody had bothered with.'

Porter called Macken over and asked him to talk them through arriving at the scene. Macken had a weathered face, tired eyes, and was probably regretting answering the call that brought him to the scene.

'Wasn't just me. There were four of us, two cars. Three of us went in, one on the front door.'

'And there was no sign that anyone else was still in the building? You didn't see or hear anything else in the courtroom?'

'No, sir. Door was locked when we got here, and no sign of anyone else inside.'

'And whoever was on the front door, you're sure they didn't budge until the place was sealed off?'

'Sure as I can be,' Macken said.

Porter thanked him and sent him back to his post, poor fella looking hangdog, like he'd cocked up the case somehow.

'The three blokes we saw looked calm as you like. Didn't even flinch while that poor bugger got butchered,' said Styles. 'Whoever's shadow that was, I can't see them getting all squeamish once the show was over.'

'Someone else was in the building.'

Porter voiced what they were all thinking. A possible witness. There the whole time. Might still be now.

CHAPTER EIGHT

They went through every room, twice. Checked cupboards, under desks. No sign of the mystery witness, but it did yield one important piece of information. A window at the back of the building had been broken from the outside, studding the carpet with diamante shards. A route in for some, if not all four men captured on camera. Kam Qureshi found matching fragments embedded in the soles of Ross Henderson's trainers, confirming he'd used that route in, blissfully unaware at the time that it was a one-way trip.

'You think they came in this way too?' Styles asked.

'Probably,' said Porter. 'Main door was locked. No other sign of forced entry.'

'Good chance they followed him here then. Feels like a bit of a coincidence that they use the same route and rock up minutes after he gets started. With a bit of luck there'll be some CCTV. Can't be hard to spot three blokes in overalls, even without the masks.'

'Or they knew he was coming here,' said Porter. 'Either way though, building's clear now. Our witness is in the wind.'

'Can't say I'd stick around either if I'd seen that live,' said Styles.

Porter opened the shattered window frame, which led out onto a fire escape. He stepped through, rusty grated flooring ringing out underfoot. He stood still, surveying the ground below, head turning slowly from left to right. Greenwich High Road bordered to the east, running parallel to what used to be the car park when the court was still up and running. Looked like residential flats straight over and a hotel to the west, each with their own car parks slotted together like a concrete jigsaw.

'There's got to be a few cameras down there surely,' said Porter, as much to himself as anyone. 'The killers would have been boxed in on three sides. Funnelled out onto Greenwich High Road whether they were in a car or on foot.'

'Easy enough to narrow the time frame on any footage we get,' Styles said from behind him. 'We know literally to the second when they left the main courtroom, and I can't see 'em hanging round for the hell of it after what they did.'

'You coming out?' Porter asked, sidestepping to make room.

'Nah, I'm OK, thanks. Not too great with heights,' Styles said, taking an instinctive half-step back.

'Bit of a bugger that you're six-four then, isn't it? Must suck to be you every time you stand up.' He leant out over the railings, peering down, feeling that weird sensation some get inches away from a drop, as if the concrete below had some strange magnetic pull. 'Besides, we're only three stories up. Still a good view mind,' Porter said, enjoying Styles's obvious discomfort.

'Beautiful,' Styles agreed, 'but I still ain't coming out.'

Porter suddenly realised he'd forgotten to call Milburn. 'You head back down if you like. I need to call the super. Meet you back out front.'

Milburn picked up on the third ring. 'What have you got for me, Porter?'

Porter ran him through Kaja's find, the discovery of the entry/exit route, and what he'd deployed his team to do.

'This one is big, Porter. Potentially huge, with the kind of exposure it had online. I need you on your game. I know the timing is shitty, what with the news about your wife's case and all. If I had the manpower going spare, I'd suggest you take a few days, but we're stretched thin enough as it is. You might want to think about speaking to Occupational Health again.'

Unless Porter was mistaken, that sounded like genuine concern from Milburn. Porter had been forced into a number of sessions with a counsellor last year when things got heated with a suspect. Ended up with him snapping, laying hands on the guy, all caught on camera. He wasn't one for opening up at the best of times, but those sessions with Sameera Misra had been like emotional waterboarding, attempts to dredge up what he'd rather keep stashed away.

'I'm fine, sir.'

'You might be now, but if you're not, I need to know. Understood?'

'Loud and clear.'

'Right, in that case, I need you here first thing tomorrow. We'll be doing a press conference at nine, so I'll meet you here for seven to prep.'

Porter glanced at his watch. By the time they finished up here, he'd be lucky if he managed more than five hours back home. Not like he'd have slept much anyway to be fair.

'Seven it is,' he replied.

'Did that Taylor fellow find you?'

'Yep, and he's a she.'

'Oh, ahm, all right then, well you can . . .'

The rest of Milburn's words were lost as Porter jerked his head around. A noise from the front of the building. Sounded like something from a football stadium. What the hell?

'Sir, I'm going to have to call you back,' he said, hearing Milburn squawk as he took the phone away from his ear, not happy at the notion that something else trumped him in the pecking order.

Porter stooped back through the window frame, stray bits of glass crunching under his soles. Even inside he could hear it, albeit more muted. What was it? Singing? Chanting?

He took the stairs two at a time, jogged across a surprisingly deserted mosaic-floored reception and burst out into a cacophony of chanting.

Where before four men had stood and hassled the two women, a crowd had gathered, easily ten times that size. Mainly men, but a few female faces peppered their ranks. Several amongst them held up signs, scrawled on card, flexing like wobble-boards. Slogans like *Britain for the British*, and *Your government's looking out for immigrants, but who's looking out for you?*

Some wore T-shirts, sporting a red, white and blue lion that Porter recognised as the English Welfare Party logo. Front and centre, a tall, wiry man led them in their chants, conducting his orchestra.

'Turf out the terrorists!'

'Pack 'em up, ship 'em off!'

Directly opposite, a huddle of press, like kids in a sweet shop, cameras panning from the mini-mob, over to the front of the building, tape and all. Several officers had made their way across the road. Sucheka, Tessier and Styles amongst them. Porter trotted down the steps, ducked under the cordon like a boxer entering the ring and headed over to join his colleagues. When he reached them, he found Taylor Bell, all five foot and change of her, arms folded, addressing the ringleader.

'I'm going to have to ask you to have to move on, sir.'

The man paused mid chant. 'Just exercising our right to free speech, Officer.'

'It's Detective, but we'll let that slide for now. You can all exercise that right, as long as you do it somewhere else.'

Porter couldn't place the accent. Sounded like a mash-up between Scottish and Geordie. The man had a face like a rat sucking on a lemon. All teeth and angles. The lines across his forehead were canyons, carved deep from a lifetime of scowling. Something about the way he carried himself though. An energy about him that worried Porter. Something that could spill over if provoked.

'It's a free country,' snapped a rosy-faced woman off to his side.

'That it is, madam,' Bell said, 'but I'm guessing you haven't applied for permission to protest, and you're blocking a public walkway, so again, I'm asking you all to head home, or anywhere else you prefer, just can't be here.'

'Those savages butchered that boy in there,' said Rat-Face, 'and you're more bothered about hassling us than finding them? That's what's wrong with this bloody country. You've all got your priorities wrong. That's how the likes of them stroll in here and do what they want, and we've had enough! You lot are part of the problem.'

That drew a chorus of agreement from the crowd, a mix of *yeah*s and *too fucking right*s.

'You're the problem here,' Porter cut in. 'I didn't catch your name, Mr . . .'

'Didn't give it,' Rat-Face shot back.

Porter kept his tone as level as possible. 'The longer we're here asking you to leave, the more it distracts us from finding whoever did this.'

'We know who bloody did it, mate,' said Rat-Face, firing tiny grenades of spittle to accompany his angry words. The crowd behind him responded with grumbles and murmurs of agreement. There was an energy to them, something that crackled, emotion ready to spill over. This needed diffusing, and fast.

'Sir, we want to find them just as much as you do,' said Porter.

'Oh, I doubt that very much,' said Rat-Face, mouth twisting into an ugly smile.

'Be that as it may,' Porter continued, 'nothing else is happening until you turn around and leave, all of you.' Behind him, car doors popped open, closed, scuffs of hard soles on concrete. He turned to see a dozen more uniformed officers marching towards them. Cavalry with perfect timing. He looked back at Rat-Face. Saw his eyes narrow, assessing options. Saw his mouth set in a hard line of acceptance.

'We won't take this lying down,' he said. 'Not any more. We have to protect ourselves. Pretty bloody clear you lot can't or won't.' He spat the words out like bullets, holding Porter's stare for a long three count, before turning to walk back into the crowd. Those around him turned to follow suit. Porter felt the tension seep out of the situation.

"Bout bloody time,' Bell muttered.

Everything happened too fast. Truce broken in three words, but Porter was caught off guard, too slow to react. He could only watch as it unfolded in front of him. So much for a peaceful protest.

CHAPTER NINE

Rat-Face turned back to look at Bell. He kept walking, albeit it backwards now, shaking his head like a disappointed parent. A larger man to his left, chubby, not muscular, with a ruddy complexion and shaved head, made a hawking noise, dredging up whatever he could from his throat, reared his head back and spat. The large glob arced towards them, cresting, dropping like a stone right onto the crown of Bell's head. Seemed like she darted forward at the moment of impact. Half a dozen steps closed the gap.

She grabbed his right wrist, pinning it high to his chest, stepping past to the left, planting her right foot behind his left. Momentum made up for the difference in size. Dipping and driving her shoulder into his chest, controlling the spin and fall, until he hit the ground with a meaty thud.

The front line of the retreating crowd stood stock-still, a few mouths hanging open in surprise, but as she whipped a set of handcuffs out to snap on, those that were closest moved forwards. Porter started towards her, but Tessier was nearest. Two steps moved him in front of Bell, like a giant chess-piece sliding into place. He held out a hand the size of a hardback novel.

'You touch her, you're next.'

A half-dozen of them had formed a semicircle a few feet back from where Bell had their fallen comrade pinned. Hands clenched and unclenched, faces set into hard lines. Porter moved to stand by Tessier's right, and saw Styles and the others step up to strengthen the line.

'Don't sweat it, Davy,' Rat-Face called out to the man on the ground. 'We'll have you back by bedtime.'

'I wouldn't count on it,' said Bell, looking up at him, face flushed, faintest hint of a smile. She was enjoying this, a little too much in Porter's book. 'Davy, is it? Well, Davy, I am arresting you on suspicion of assaulting a police officer,' she said, patting his back.

'We'll be taking your friend to Paddington Green police station,' Porter said. 'If you're sorting his brief, that's where he'll be.'

'Whatever you say, Officer,' Rat-Face said, with an exaggerated bow. He backed away, giving a sharp whistle as he went, which seemed to spark the rest of them into action. A sea of scowls backed away, turning to head east down Blackheath Road.

As Bell stood up, pulling a tissue from her pocket to wipe off the saliva, Tessier crouched down, picking up the dough-faced would-be hero. Nothing to it, as if it were just the clothes and not the man inside them. Once upright, the man eyed Tessier with somewhere between contempt and relief, that he hadn't been daft enough to try and get past him. A pair of uniformed constables ushered him away towards a waiting car.

'You all right?' Porter asked.

She arched an eyebrow in a *why the hell would I not be?* expression. 'I'm good.' She cast an eye down the road at the retreating bodies. 'Friends of yours?'

Porter grunted a half-laugh, switching subject. 'What did you make of the courtroom? Any thoughts?'

She brushed dirt from her sleeve, flicking away a few strands of hair that had caught on the side of her mouth. 'Honestly, if this is the Brotherhood, then I'm worried. We all need to be worried. They make what ISIS did look tame.'

'You say "if". What makes you think it might not be?' asked Styles, stepping up beside Porter.

'Don't get me wrong,' she said, 'they've got form for beheadings, bold statements, recording it all to scare the shit out of people on the news.'

'But?' Porter prompted.

'But everything I've seen in the last twelve months says they're not active in the UK.'

'Intel can be wrong though.'

'It can,' she conceded, 'but mine usually isn't, not about the big stuff anyway.'

'How can you be so sure?' Styles asked.

'Same way I know I didn't need your pet mountain there to step in and save me like a damsel in distress.' She looked over at Tessier. 'No offence.' He just shrugged. 'I'm good at what I do. No, scratch that, I'm bloody good at what I do. Don't take this the wrong way, Detectives, but CTU is a different breed to what you do. You do a great job. You catch people who've done bad things, who've killed people. For me, if people are dead, I've already failed them. I stop the bad things from happening. I can't afford to be wrong.'

Every word came out coated with conviction, something Porter could relate to, but there was an edge to them, like a child spitting a dummy.

'All right,' Porter said, keeping his tone more conciliatory than he felt, 'if you're telling us there's a chance it might not be them, then how about sharing your thoughts on who it might be?'

'I'm not saying it isn't them. It's not that they're not active. God knows they've caused their fair share of harm around the world, but they're a talkative bunch. In the build-up to each of their big attacks overseas in the last few years, they've been up on their soapbox before they act. Making demands, release of prisoners, withdrawal of troops, cease and desist on drone strikes, that kind of thing. Most of what they do is retaliation. They call their shots in advance. Not the details obviously, but the nation they're targeting and why. That, and they tell the whole bloody world about it within the hour. I've not seen anything like that yet, have you?'

Porter shook his head. 'Not yet. All due respect though, these guys pinned their colours to the mast with their wardrobe choices today, never mind what they said or did. Over a million people watched today, DI Bell.'

'I know how it looks,' she said with a hint of annoyance, 'but it's not just what they did that bothers me. It's who they did it to.'

'What do you mean?' Styles questioned.

'From what I've seen of Henderson, he's as liberal as they come. Fair treatment for refugees, pro-withdrawal of troops from the Middle East. He's basically shouting for what the Brotherhood want – to leave them be.'

Porter shrugged. 'You said it yourself, they want the whole bloody world to know what they're doing. Who better to pick than someone with as many followers as Henderson? Pretty much guarantees you an audience.'

She stared him out for a few seconds, soaking in the possibility, before dismissing it with a shake of her head.

'Not convinced. Could just as easily be someone looking to make a name for themselves by piggybacking.'

'Hey, I'm open to whatever the evidence points to, but unless you've got a credible alternative, they're staying top of the list.'

She kept her eyes fixed on his, clearly not used to anyone doing anything with her opinion other than following to the letter. 'Well then,' she said finally, 'I guess you've just set me my homework, haven't you?'

Before he had a chance to reply, she strode off back towards the courthouse, leaving Porter shaking his head and Styles wearing a bemused grin.

'Well, she was . . . interesting,' Porter said. 'Not so much a chip on her shoulder, as a full bag of spuds.'

'Oh, I don't know about that,' Styles said. 'I kinda liked her.'

'I'm on the fence,' Porter replied. 'She comes with top billing according to the super, but I'm going to need a little more convincing than "I'm never wrong".'

The last part came out in a gruff voice, more of a crap Schwarzenegger impression than anything even vaguely approaching Taylor Bell.

'Anyway, fun's over,' he said, turning to his assembled team. 'Busy evening ahead. Let's crack on. Nick, you come with me. We need to find out who his next of kin is and pay them a visit.'

That was going to be a shitty one. Talk about a rock and a hard place. He might be the one to have to break the news to them, on the slim chance they were amongst the few people on the internet who hadn't watched the bloody thing live. Either that or try and get through to someone who had it on permanent repeat in their heads after seeing it.

'Already got that, boss,' said Styles. 'Lives with his parents near Old Dagenham Park. Sent a Family Liaison over, so we shouldn't be going in cold.'

Porter could empathise to a degree, at least with the notion of what, if not how. For him, it had been like feeling punch-drunk, to begin with anyway. Like taking a big shot to the head, hearing a rush of white noise like an untuned radio, borderline spaced out. Looking back now that night Holly was killed felt like it had happened to somebody else. Trying to imagine how seeing it happen would magnify that feeling, distort reality beyond repair, fired him back into that same headspace.

The two cases, both emotional overdoses, meshed in his head, coalescing, twin black holes tugging away what little energy he had left.

'Actually can you do me a favour?' he said to Styles, 'Any chance you can handle that one yourself? Milburn wants me in at daft o'clock tomorrow, so I could do with hitting the sack. Long day coming.'

'Um, yeah, no probs,' said Styles, hands in pockets, looking expectantly at Porter, clearly hoping he would share what that something else was.

'Thanks, Nick. Good to have you back, even if it is a day early. I'll, ah, see you at the station in the morning then.'

'No worries, boss.'

Porter saw the concern on Styles's face as he walked past. His lacklustre smile clearly wasn't fooling anyone. His phone buzzed as he reached the car. Evie again. He felt like a bit of a shit for doing it, but he tapped reject again. He'd call her on the way home later, but right now, he had somebody more important to talk to.

CHAPTER TEN

Styles commandeered one of the cars at the scene, and tapped Ross Henderson's parents' address into the satnav. Back over the Thames, and a bit less than half an hour at this time of day. As he drove, the occasional flash of footage from the courtroom popped into mind. It'd be a while before he forgot this one.

His phone chirped as he pulled up outside, Evie's name flashing up.

'Hey, Evie. Everything OK?'

'Yeah, I was just wondering if you knew where Jake was. He went out to clear his head, but that was hours ago.'

So, Porter hadn't told her about the case yet. Safe to assume she hadn't seen the news either. Styles gave her the headlines, leaving out for now the fact he'd found Porter at the hospital. No need to worry her more than necessary.

'Oh my God,' she said when he finished. 'I kind of want to watch it now, but I don't.'

'Your call, but it'll stick with you for a long while if you do,' he said. 'I'd give it a miss if you can.'

'Is he there with you now then?'

'He's on his way home. Said something about a stupidly early start with Milburn tomorrow.'

'Oh, OK. Sorry to bother you then, Nick.'

'Don't be daft,' he said. 'He's the one that bothers me. You're like a breath of fresh air.'

That got a few seconds of laughter, before she got all serious again.

'He doesn't talk much about her, you know. Think he thinks it'd weird me out or something. Truth is it would probably help him if he did.'

'He's a deep one all right,' Styles agreed.

'Look after him for me, Nick.'

'It's my full-time job,' he said, trying to keep things light, but there was no mistaking the shared concern for Porter.

He signed off with a promise to keep Porter out of trouble and stared out at the house.

Without a doubt, this was one of the worst parts of the job, intruding on people's grief, asking questions when all many of them wanted to do was curl up and cry. He didn't envy the Family Liaison Officers one bit.

He recognised the face that greeted him at the door. Aaron Bryant was one of the best FLO's Styles had worked with. He had a knack for keeping people in the here and now, guiding them through their grief instead of watching them fall to pieces.

'They're in the kitchen,' said Bryant. He had the kind of voice that wouldn't be out of place on one of those mindfulness apps, soft and soothing.

'They see it happen?' he asked Bryant.

'Thankfully no, but they've heard, thanks to relatives phoning up.'

Styles followed Bryant though an open door and into a small kitchen. A woman stood at the sink. Mrs Henderson, presumably, canary yellow Marigolds up to her elbows like gauntlets, scrubbing a cup hard enough to wear the floral print off the rim. She must have heard his footsteps on the tiles and turned around, putting on a brave face, but Styles couldn't imagine a sadder smile. Late forties at a guess, the slightest hint of crow's feet in an otherwise smooth face. There'd be a few new lines etched in before she'd come to terms with today's events.

Her husband sat nursing a half-full mug of coffee. Had been for a while by the looks of the tell-tale ring when he tipped it up to take a sip. Brian Henderson looked a good ten years older than his wife, once dark hair now stippled with grey, long since receded like a one-way tide. His jaw worked side to side, as if trying to work something loose from his teeth. He made no attempt to get up, brain still in neutral, knowing but not understanding the news they received a few hours ago.

'Mr and Mrs Henderson, this is Detective Sergeant Nick Styles. He's one of the team heading up the investigation,' Bryant said by way of introduction. Styles stepped forward, offering Brian Henderson a hand, that the other man took in a half-hearted grip.

'So sorry for your loss, sir,' Styles said, turning to repeat the sentiment to Angela Henderson.

'Cup of tea, Detective?' she asked, in a voice balanced at breaking point.

Styles didn't want one, but saw it for the crutch that it was, keeping her occupied, stopping her from dwelling, and nodded his thanks, asking for milk, two sugars.

'May I?' he said, gesturing to a seat opposite Brian Henderson.

Brian nodded, said nothing and turned his attention back to his coffee.

'I know you're still hurting, and talking about it might be the last thing you want to do right now, but the more we know about your son, the better chance we have of figuring out what's happened.'

'Doesn't take a genius to work out what happened,' Brian muttered. 'I told him. Warned him he needed to be careful who he went after, but he was a stubborn bugger.'

'Just like his dad,' said Angela, placing a cup in front of Styles. 'He was passionate about what he did, Detective.'

'He was passionate about getting his bloody face plastered all over the internet,' snapped Brian, voice firmer, like he'd just been prodded awake.

'What can either of you tell me about Ross, about his . . .' Styles searched for the right word, 'causes?'

'I still can't believe he could get that many people watching him,' Angela said, joining them at the table with Bryant. 'I mean a lot of what he does goes right over my head. The streaming, and followers and whatnot, but I do love to hear him talking. Always clever with his speeches, our Ross. Isn't he, Brian?'

Styles noted the use of present tense, common where news like this was still fresh.

'Oh, he had some strong political views, that's for sure.'

Brian nodded. 'I take it you've not caught them yet, then? The ones who did this?'

'Not yet, sir, but it's early days,' said Styles, keen to keep the conversation on track. 'This persona he used, Stormcloudz, where did that come from?'

Brian sat up a touch straighter as he answered. 'He had a rough time in secondary school. He was good mates with two brothers from around the corner, the Chakrabartis. Thick as thieves the three of them were. Some of the local hard cases didn't take kindly to it – a racial thing. Said he should hang out with his own kind.' Henderson looked almost apologetic bringing up race, as if there was a chance Styles might take it personally. Styles had been on the receiving end of his fair share of barbed race-related comments growing up here in London, his family originally from Barbados.

'Made Ross's life hell for a while.' Brian Henderson's knee bounced up and down as he talked, a mix of nervous energy and anger at old injustices. 'Anyway, things got out of hand, and the three of them got jumped one night while they were out on their bikes. Ross needed stitches, so did the younger of the brothers. Dammit, why can't I even remember their names now?' he said, scratching his hand back and forward across his temple, trying to jar something free.

'Dev and Prab,' Angela offered, leaning over, taking his hand in hers, bringing both back to the tabletop.

'That's them,' he said, nodding thanks. 'Prab's face was all busted up. Dev though, poor bugger, was on crutches for months. Took Ross a while to come out of his shell after that. The other lads were arrested, but it seemed to light a spark under our Ross. He hated bullies. Hated racist ones even more.'

67

'That's where that whole Stormcloudz thing started. Silly name, I know, but he was so proud of what he did,' said Angela.

'Had he received any threats recently as part of that?' Styles asked.

'If he did, he didn't share them with us,' said Angela.

'Was there anybody else involved in his broadcasts, or did he work alone?'

'There's a group of them that help out,' Brian said. 'Mates of his. Jason McTeague and Elliot Kirk.'

'Don't suppose you know how I can get hold of them, do you?'

Angela shook her head. 'We don't have numbers for them, but they'll be in Ross's phone, if you have that? If not, Jason works at the Duke of Wellington pub around the corner, and Elliott is a teacher at Saint Aiden's in Hornchurch.'

They had found a phone at the scene, presumably his as the background picture was the same logo as on his Facebook page, but Styles made a note of the two names. He'd make sure someone spoke to them tomorrow.

Something bobbed back to the surface in Styles's head. 'You said before, Mr Henderson, that you'd told him to be careful who he went after. Was there anyone in particular you meant?'

Brian Henderson huffed out a loud breath. 'How long have you got?' he asked, folding his arms and shaking his head. 'He thought I didn't know about the death threats, being as we're not as clued up on the internet, but I'm not totally stupid. I told him as much when I confronted him about them, but he laughed it off. Called them keyboard warriors, whatever the hell that means.'

The sharp intake of breath from Mrs Henderson told Porter that this was the first she was hearing about it. He pressed on before she could interrupt.

'What kind of threat? Who from?'

Brian shook his head. 'Threats I said, not threat. There was more than one.'

'What can you tell me about them? Were they letters, emails, online posts?'

'I can do better than tell you,' Brian said, pulling out his phone. 'I'll show you. Took screenshots in case the lying bastards tried to delete them or deny it. I was going to go to the police, but Ross, he talked me out of it.'

'Talked you out of it?' Angela Henderson finally found her voice again. 'How could you let him talk you out if it?' Her words came out shriller with every syllable.

'You know as well as I do, he always got his own way.'

'Mr Henderson,' Styles butted in before it became a full-scale domestic. 'You said you could show me?'

Brian Henderson scrolled through a ream of pictures on his phone, stabbing a finger at one, and spun the screen around to face Styles. A vaguely familiar set of eyes stared back at him. Took three or four seconds of puzzling over it, a memory finally slotting into place like a game of Tetris. A face he'd seen all too recently.

CHAPTER ELEVEN

Porter pulled up short of the street light that cast a cone of diluted yellow by the main gates. Way past closing time, but that had never kept him out before. A quick glance either way along the road as he locked his car. No traffic, no nosy neighbourhood watch. Plenty of people on the other side of the metal railings, but they wouldn't be grassing him up any time soon. The cemetery was boxed in on three sides by thick hedges, with a half-height wall and railings running the length of the front.

On a previous visit, Porter had spotted a couple of teenagers acting suspiciously along the east side. He'd gone to approach them, but they'd both scarpered, vanishing straight into the foliage from what he could see. On closer inspection, there was a gap in the far corner, where two hedgerows met. They'd looked like they'd ran head first into it. Porter, on the other hand, had to turn sideways and breathe in.

He'd used it a dozen times or so since then, when work stopped him from visiting Holly during more sociable hours. The last of the groundskeepers were long gone. Just Porter and a thousand ghosts. Only one that he was here to visit with though.

Before he and Evie became an item, he was a regular here, visiting every few days. Not even his mum and dad knew how often he'd come to speak with her. These last three or four months though, the visits had tailed off. Not a conscious thing, just that when you started to share your life with somebody new, to spend time with them, other things had to give. He felt between a rock and a hard place. It was unfair to Evie to cling too tightly to the past. Disrespectful to Holly to let it go completely.

He'd come to what he thought of as a happy medium lately. Until today. This afternoon's revelation had set his mind spinning. He picked his way through rows of headstones, lined up like a macabre game of Guess Who?, full moon spotlighting his way, but he knew the route off by heart anyway.

The flowers he'd brought last time had wilted, withered heads drooped from the colander-topped vases either side of her plot.

'I know, I know, I could at least have had a shave,' he said, speaking softly. 'Makes me look more rugged though, eh?'

He set about swapping out old for new, slotting in the new bunch of blooms he'd bought at a twenty-four-hour garage on the way here. The old ones went into a plastic bag, to be disposed of later. He stayed squatting, one hand resting on cool granite, partly for balance, but mainly to be close.

'They found him, Hol. Well, one of 'em anyway. I know I promised you I'd move on, but . . . I don't think I know how.'

Porter felt the emotion balling in his throat, part sadness, but mainly anger. Now that his frustrations finally had a face, he was just supposed to look the other way. He could practically hear Holly's voice in his head, telling him to do exactly that. He'd built a new life, the foundations of one at least. One he thought he could be happy in. It wasn't rocket science. If he went after Kamau, and the Triple H outfit, he'd be on his own. No way would he get any official help, bearing in mind he'd already been told to back off by Milburn and Pittman. Styles would help if he asked. Porter knew he would out of blind loyalty. He couldn't have a wrecked career on his conscience though, so that wasn't an option.

'What do I do, Hol? What the fuck do I do?'

He knew what he couldn't do. He couldn't sit there and wait for Pittman to slither around at a snail's pace. A vague outline of an idea started to form. Not perfect, but a start. Something to play around with. To shape as he went.

Porter's knees cracked like party poppers as he stood up. He pressed two fingers to his lips, transferred the kiss to the top of Holly's headstone, then turned and headed for the hidden exit, working through the first stages of a plan. Coming here always seemed to give him a clarity of thought that he couldn't find elsewhere. Whether that was the proximity to Holly, or just the peace and quiet, was open to debate. Either way, if he was honest with himself, he'd made his decision before he came here. It had been made the second Milburn dropped the news.

SKY NEWS BULLETIN

Monday morning

'I'm Asim Bashara, and these are your morning headlines. Emotions are still high in the wake of the brutal murder of Ross Henderson yesterday at the hands of suspected terrorists. Mr Henderson was killed live on Facebook at the old magistrates' court in Greenwich. We at Sky have taken the decision not to show the footage due to the graphic nature. Reports say this is the work of the Brotherhood of the Prophet, although that's yet to be confirmed. Police Commissioner Agatha Wallace has urged the public to stay calm, but not everyone is heeding that advice. We go live now to our correspondent Amy Fitzwilliam outside Greenwich Magistrates' Court. Amy.'

'Thank you, Asim. You join me here for what is a tense standoff between police and protestors. The English Welfare Party are out in force, unsurprisingly calling for

73

a drastic overhaul of immigration laws. On the other side of the police line, members of the local Islamic Centre have come out as a community to distance themselves from any extremist involvement, with the local imam calling for cooler heads to prevail, saying that the community needs to come together at times like this. With me is Sally Ashbrooke, leader of the British Independence Party. Mrs Ashbrooke, troubling times following yesterday's brutal events. What are your thoughts on what's transpired, and what action the police and the Prime Minister should be taking?'

'Firstly, let me offer my condolences to Mr Henderson's family. Nobody deserves to die like that, much less in such a public fashion. I think sadly though, that this is the sum total of successive governments' mistakes coming home to roost. The Prime Minister's open-door policy to the world, without a proper system of checks and balances, plus his refusal to contribute to the international task force fighting the Brotherhood, is as good as an open invitation to extremists, that not only are our doors open, but that we won't lift a finger to stop you doing whatever you want, to whomever you want.'

'Can the Prime Minister honestly be blamed for the actions of a determined and resourceful group like the Brotherhood?'

'Absolutely. If he isn't able to guarantee the safety of the British people, then he needs to step aside and let somebody else do the job.'

'Latest polls have you ten points behind the Tories but only a point off taking the second spot from Labour. If you were to find yourself in Downing Street after the next election, what message would you be giving to the British people in a situation like this?'

'I'd tell them that every single one of us has a part to play in defending our country. It starts with placing their trust, and their vote, in a party committed to making the tough decisions needed to keep us safe. Now don't get me wrong, I'm not advocating we implement the kind of extreme measures that the EWP would see us have and kick hundreds of thousands of people out of the UK, but something needs to change. If the public see fit to place me in office next year, I will personally oversee a full review of our immigration system and commit to a net zero figure by the end of my first term.'

'Net zero migration? That's a bold statement to make, Mrs Ashbrooke. What makes you think you could control in four years what others have failed to do in decades?'

'It's well documented that my youngest boy was killed in the line of duty. He, and thousands like him, put their lives on the line so we don't have to. His battleground was Afghanistan, mine is Westminster, but make no mistake, we're fighting the same fight. To keep the British people safe, to help them thrive and to build a country that we can be proud to leave to our children.'

'Sally Ashbrooke, thank you. Emotions running high on both sides of the . . . sorry, what was that . . . Asim, I'm afraid we're being asked to move back by the police. Members of the EWP faction have begun throwing bottles into the contingent from the Islamic Centre. Things are definitely heating up. Back to you in the studio.'

CHAPTER TWELVE

'How likely are any repeat attacks?' a journalist from *The Sun* shouted to be heard over the clamour of questions.

Same angle, different words. Asked and answered, thought Porter. This was one of the parts of the job he hated. Why he had no desire to rise any further up the ranks. The politics, and endless press feeding frenzies, only served to make life more difficult in his view, more to wade through, like pouring treacle on ants.

'As I said before,' said Roger Milburn, holding up a palm to quieten his audience. 'This is still at a very early stage. Nobody has formally claimed responsibility yet, but we don't currently have reason to believe that there is an imminent threat.'

'Apart from the threats they made after they hacked his head off?' another reporter piped up from the back.

'This is a highly unusual case,' Milburn carried on, not missing a beat, 'in that many people had the misfortune to witness the crime take place, and we urge anyone affected by that to reach out for professional support and counselling if they need it. I wouldn't normally hold a conference this early on, but due to the public nature of the murder, we wanted to reassure the people of London that we are putting additional measures in place to ensure their safety.'

Milburn ran through a list of numbers, extra boots on the ground, pennies in the overtime coffers, Counter Terrorism on board as part of the team and finished by introducing Porter as the man leading day to day, while stressing the fact that he remained in overall command as SIO, as if that was ever in doubt. No way would a political animal like Milburn pass up the chance to be the face of a case with as much exposure as this would no doubt have. Play the hero if it went their way, palm off the blame if it didn't, most likely Porter's way.

'I'm afraid that's all we have time for this morning, but as soon as there's more to share, I'll let you know. Thank you.'

Milburn ignored the verbal volleys of the impatient audience. Give them an inch to print and they wanted a whole page. Porter followed him off the raised podium and out into the corridor beyond.

'That should hold them for now,' said Milburn, looking far more pleased with himself than he had cause to be. It had been a non-event. Nothing of any substance shared that they hadn't already seen in way too much detail from yesterday's live stream. 'What time are you briefing your team?'

'Now, sir. You're welcome to join if—'

'Sir!'

A woman's voice from the other end of the corridor, brusque, urgent. Taylor Bell hustled towards them, serious, all business.

'Ah, DI Bell, perfect timing. You'll be able to help Porter at his briefing, give your views on this Brotherhood bunch.'

'About that, sir, we may have a problem.'

'What sort of problem?' Milburn asked. 'We've not had another murder, have we?'

Porter fancied the concern on Milburn's face was just as likely to be worry at the fact that he'd just told a room full of journalists that the city was a safe place, rather than for anyone else who might have been hurt.

'Another one? No, not that I know of anyway. That's just it though, sir. I think we've got it wrong. Yesterday's attack, I don't think it was the Brotherhood. I think someone's playing us.'

CHAPTER THIRTEEN

'So, you're saying it isn't terrorists then, boss?' Sucheka asked, her face mirroring the confusion around the briefing room.

'I'm not saying it couldn't be, just that there's enough to cast doubt. DI Bell, can you talk us through what you shared with me downstairs?'

Taylor Bell hopped off her perch on the edge of a nearby desk and walked out in front of the group.

'You've all seen the footage?' she asked. Nods and grimaces all round. 'So, you've all seen their motif, the fractured crescent moon and star. Sometimes things seem too good to be true, and that's what I think we have here.'

'What makes you think they weren't who they say they are?' Dee Williams asked.

'Two things. First,' she said, holding up a finger, 'the absolute lack of any chatter from our network about any UK-based activity. Syria, Afghan, sure, but nothing here. We're not infallible, but we have access to what the Yanks have, and that includes them claiming to have someone inside the Brotherhood. We've reached out to them to confirm or deny, but that could take a day or two.'

'A lot could happen in a few days if we're wrong,' Tessier grumbled from the back.

'You're right,' Bell conceded, 'it could. Second thing though, these guys have a plan and they stick with it. They don't tend to deviate. They don't usually feel the need to wear a uniform,' she said, tapping a screenshot taken from the footage that was taped to a whiteboard.

'So, we're gonna look past them because they changed their branding?' asked DC Glenn Waters.

'That's the point though, they don't need a bloody brand identity. They kill people, they take credit for it by shouting about it to anyone who'll listen. They're not like us, with badges or warrant cards to flash.'

'They haven't though, have they? Taken credit I mean?' asked Sucheka.

'Yes and no,' Bell said cryptically. 'Twenty minutes ago, two tweets were sent from an account professing to represent the Brotherhood, claiming that Henderson was killed in retaliation for the death in custody of one of their own. This has the same hashtags they've used in the past and the same profile pic of the moon and stars. First one is in Arabic, second one in English, but both basically saying the same thing. Problem is that we don't think it was written by a native Arabic speaker.'

'What makes you say that?' Styles asked.

Bell reached behind her, grabbing several sheets of paper, screenshots of the tweets, and holding them up like show and tell.

'Two reasons. Firstly, grammatical errors. See here and here,' she pointed at the Arabic first, then to the corresponding part of the English version. 'Normally, these announcements are worded very formally. The wording they've used here though is more of a slang equivalent. Also, there are a several mistakes, the kind you might make if it wasn't your native language.'

'They recruit though, right?' Styles said. 'Could be someone who just isn't as fluent?'

'Second reason,' Bell said, shaking her head, 'is this comment here.' She pointed to the third one down, left in Arabic from a user with no profile picture. 'This account belongs to a known Brotherhood member. Roughly translates to say "Whatever your reason for joining our cause, you are no stranger but a true friend."'

'So why would they be a stranger to begin with, if they were members?' Styles said, nodding to himself as it sunk in.

'Not cast iron by any means,' interjected Porter, 'but enough to mean we look elsewhere until DI Bell hears back from the Americans.'

'Speaking of elsewhere,' said Styles, 'I had an interesting chat with Mr and Mrs Henderson last night, and if what you're saying about the Brotherhood is true, then I've got another name to throw into the mix. Roland Thomas.'

Porter was none the wiser, nor it seemed was anyone else judging from the blank looks all around.

'You all met him last night.'

'This isn't twenty questions, Nick. Spit it out,' said Porter.

'Thomas is the guy who was trying to flirt with DI Bell last night. You know the one who looked like he'd just smelt a bad fart.'

'Ah, yes. How can I forget him? Face only a mother could love. What about him?'

'Turns out he'd made threats online. Henderson Senior has

a screenshot from Facebook showing comments from Thomas about how Ross should be treated like any other traitor, and that they should bring back hanging. Had a quick look at his online profiles and he's EWP through and through.'

'And he just happened to be a hundred yards away from the very man he thought should be swinging from a noose?'

'There's more threats in the comments on YouTube too. Quite a few actually. Pick of the bunch says that if Ross wanted to be a martyr so bad, he'd be happy to help arrange it.'

'And there was me thinking after last night that he was such a gentle soul,' Sucheka chipped in. 'Worth a look.'

'Consider him on the list of people we need a conversation with. Anything else, Nick?'

Styles added the names of Ross Henderson's two friends to the mix and filled them in on the background he got from the parents.

'Those weren't the only threats he received though,' he said. 'Ten million followers, pages and pages of comments across multiple platforms, Facebook, YouTube, Twitter. All his content was pretty emotive stuff, so they either loved him or hated him. If Roland Thomas doesn't pan out, there'll be plenty more to choose from.'

'By the sounds of it, we'll end up wallpapering the room with mugshots,' said Waters.

'Well volunteered, Glenn,' said Porter.

'Eh, volunteered for what?' Waters looked confused.

'Make a start on cataloguing comments and usernames.'

Waters scowled, opened his mouth to talk his way out if it, but said nothing.

'Kaja, Gus, anything from the door-to-door last night?'

Sucheka shook her head. 'No one saw a thing, boss, least not that they're sharing with us.'

'In that case, I want you on the two friends – Jason McTeague and Elliott Kirk. What was their role in this? If he was the face of Stormcloudz, what did they bring to the table? Nick, you and I take Roland Thomas. Any questions?'

'Mind if I tag along?'

He'd almost forgotten Bell was there, lost in rattling through what needed to be done.

'If interviewing right-wing racists is your thing, you're more than welcome, but I'm sure you've probably got more important things to do.'

'Nope,' she said, pursing her lips. 'I could do with the fresh air, or I might faceplant in my coffee.'

'Late night?'

'Mine never finished.'

Was there the tiniest emphasis on the first word? He couldn't quite figure her out, whether he could trust her or not, or whether she had her own agenda, one that would drag a joint effort firmly into her court. Better then that he keep her close. Besides, the terrorism angle was still their number one pick in his eyes, and like it as not, she was the expert. Anything else hit today, and they'd need her around.

Porter shrugged. 'Ready to go in five.'

He dismissed the others, watching as Bell headed back to the desk she'd been sat at, grabbing her jacket and phone. He could have refused but had the feeling she'd have made sure it cropped up in conversation with Milburn. This changed things though. He had plans for today that didn't include Styles, let alone Bell.

CHAPTER FOURTEEN

Roland Thomas worked as a mechanic at a garage near Dartford. A bored-looking woman glanced up from her magazine, desk cluttered with enough Post-its and scribbled receipts to give a clean freak like Porter's mum palpitations just by looking at it. She squinted through jam-jar glasses as she scrutinised his warrant card, as if searching for small print that wasn't there.

'Roly's doing a job in bay six.'

Porter looked around the warehouse-style building. Must be at least a dozen cars, some up on ramps, some with bonnets propped up like open mouths, only the bottom half of an overalled mechanic visible. No huge flashing number six to guide him.

'Third from the end,' the woman said, sounding put out that she had to take yet more time away from her precious magazine.

'She should work for the Samaritans with a caring attitude

like that,' said Bell, getting a chuckle from Styles as they made their way past a row of cars.

Roland Thomas was preoccupied with whatever he was fixing, mostly hidden from view in a pit sunk into the garage floor, as they stopped short of the vehicle he was working under.

'Mr Thomas,' said Porter. 'Can we borrow you for a minute?'

Thomas peered out, a sly smile of recognition crinkling his face.

'Come to apologise for the heavy-handed behaviour last night, have we?'

He clambered out, wiping greasy palms down overalls that looked as if they hadn't been within a hundred feet of a washing machine in years. He folded his arms across his chest, and Porter saw the tattoo poking out from a rolled-up sleeve.

'You like the ink?' Thomas asked, clocking Porter's interest. He pulled the sleeve up further, flashing the rest of the artwork. A pale shield with an inverted sword running through it, blade coloured in red. The EWP logo, a bastardised version of the Saint George's Cross.

'Beautiful,' said Bell. 'You even managed to keep your crayon inside the lines and everything.'

Thomas made no effort to keep the menace from his expression. Just stared at them, mouth set into a tight smile. Ten seconds into the conversation and Bell was stepping on toes already.

'We'd like to have a chat with you about last night, Mr Thomas. I understand you and Mr Henderson didn't exactly see eye to eye, politically speaking?'

'Mr Henderson?' Thomas looked up to the ceiling as if struggling to place it. 'Ah, you mean that little runt who got himself killed last night. Stormy Daniels, or whatever he called himself.'

'Stormcloudz, yes,' Porter said. 'My colleague here found less than friendly comments you left on some of his earlier videos.'

'Yeah, and?'

'And you don't exactly seem cut up at what happened to him last night, no pun intended. Where were you at four-thirty yesterday afternoon?'

'Oh, I see,' said Thomas. 'You think *I* did this?'

'Stranger things have happened,' said Styles. 'And you haven't answered the question.'

'Sorry to disappoint you all,' he said, spreading his arms out, nicotine-stained teeth nibbling at his upper lip. 'But I was here working, till just gone five.'

'And I'm assuming your lovely lady on reception will vouch for you as well?'

'Better than that, you can even check the cameras. You'll see me finish off a timing belt on a BMW, then head out for a beer with the boys.'

'Wouldn't be the same boys you were out for a stroll with down Greenwich last night, would it?' Bell asked.

'Seems to me my social life ain't the issue here. You know as well as I do what time that boy was killed, and I can prove I weren't there, so how about you all piss off and let me crack on?'

'I suppose you and your mates just happened to be in the area, and in between pubs when we bumped into you?' she pressed him.

'Look, me and him, let's just say we weren't exactly on the same page, but what those bastards did to him, nobody deserved that. Soon as we heard, we headed down to protest. That's all.'

'But you had previously threatened his life?' Styles asked.

Thomas rolled his eyes, shaking his head. 'That was just all, whatcha call it, for show. Can't let him spout his shite and say nothing.'

'So, you've never threatened him in any other way?'

'Me?' he asked, face the picture of feigned innocence. 'Not guilty, Officer.'

'We'll be checking your cameras on the way out, Roland,' Porter said. 'They don't show what you say they should, we'll be turning right around and the rest of this chat happens at the station under caution.'

Thomas looked completely unfazed by the threat. Either he'd been inside enough for the shock value to wear off or he genuinely had nothing to do with the murder. Porter's bet was probably both. Seemed entirely too cocky to have anything to hide, at least as far as this was concerned. Didn't mean to say that the EWP wasn't pulling some sort of strings in the background though, just not ones Porter could see yet.

They left him to climb back into his pit and headed back to the receptionist, who looked even less pleased to see them than the first time. She ran the previous day's footage for them with all the enthusiasm of a stroppy kid being told to do homework. Sure enough, there was Roly Thomas, time- and date-stamped, same mucky overalls.

'One down, ten million to go.' Styles shrugged as they reached their car. 'What now, boss?'

Porter pretended to think it over, this next part having been thought up on the fly on the way here.

'Let's divide and conquer. I promised the super I'd brief him face-to-face, so if I head back and do that, you two can see if you can track down Damien Winter, assuming you're still up for tagging along, DI Bell?'

She shrugged. 'I'm assigned to this until it's done or stops being terror-related.'

'EWP registered office is up near Barnet. I'll just hop out anywhere near the station and you can carry on from there.'

Styles slid into the driver's seat. 'Your wish is my command.'

Porter hated lying to his partner, but what other option did he have?

CHAPTER FIFTEEN

Porter parked up and stared at the block of flats for a full minute before getting out of his car. Still not convinced his idea was sound, but there was no plan B, at least not one he'd been able to think of yet.

Henry Kamau's listed address was a second-floor flat on the corner of Moor Lane, near Cranham. It sat atop a barbers and dry cleaners, although Porter had it on good authority from what little digging he'd done this morning that Jackson Tyler, the leader of the Triple H gang, had bought the whole block outright a few years back, flats, businesses, the lot.

He had no idea what he hoped to do or find here, but Porter had to start somewhere. If there was a good chance Kamau wouldn't wake up, the next person on his list to speak to was Jackson Tyler himself. Kamau had been in the gang back when Holly died, and the fact she was married to a copper had made for more than the usual tabloid inches. That, and the Met pulled out all the stops to hunt down whoever was responsible. Every chance that Tyler had heard about it at the time, and just as likely that he'd know of any involvement from his people. Whether he'd talk about it was another matter entirely. For that, Porter would need leverage or something to offer, and at this stage, he had neither.

Of course, he'd have to find Tyler first. The man was like a ghost. No fixed address. No property in his name, not directly anyway. Places like the flat that Henry Kamau lived in were owned by a shell company. No direct link to Tyler.

There was little traffic as he strode across and up the stairwell at the side. Kamau was the only name listed as a tenant, but that didn't mean he lived alone. He stopped several feet short of the door. A faint whiff of stale urine hit him as he rounded the corner, into a poorly lit corridor, Kamau's door the furthest of three.

He tried the door. Locked. Porter knocked, putting his ear to the door as soon as he'd finished. Nothing. No footsteps, no whispers, not even a television or radio playing. He took a step back, looking at the lock on the door. Didn't strike him as the heaviest of timber from his knock. A couple of well-placed kicks by the handle would do the trick. Question was, how badly did he want to see what was inside? Could be that he broke in and found nothing of any use. What alternative did he have though? Pittman or one of his team would pay a visit soon enough. Could even be on their way as he stood there dawdling.

This was a line he hadn't crossed before, a step beyond getting creative with the rules. This would be breaking and entering, plain and simple. No warrant, no cause. Not his case. The alternative was to sit this one out, and it was the thought of waiting, of inactivity, of Kamau waking up and walking away that swayed him.

He backed up against the far wall. Worst case he'd say he heard noises inside, somebody calling for help. One long, deep breath as he psyched himself up, palms flat against the wall, ready to push off and drive his foot at the door, when something stopped him. A noise from the stairwell. Scraping of feet on concrete. Voices, getting that tiny bit louder with each word.

Instead of hurling himself at the front door, he whirled away, towards the matching staircase that wound its way down the other side of the building, pulling his phone out as he did, tapping the screen trying his best to look nonchalant. From the sounds of the voices behind him, they'd rounded the corner just as he turned his. He flicked the mute switch, holding the phone to his ear, ready to mock-up a conversation if needed to explain his lurking on the stairs. He'd wait until they went into whichever flat they lived in, then reassess.

Two voices as far as he could make out, both male, arguing about which local takeaway was best. Scrape of a key in a lock, closer than he'd expected, but hard to tell exactly how far along the corridor they'd come, which door they'd stopped at. A hinge creaked open, the voices faded, but didn't disappear altogether. Porter risked a peek around the corner and his eyes widened at what he saw.

The door to Kamau's flat stood open now, the briefest of flashes of red footwear, as whoever it was disappeared inside. Whoever they were, they had a key. Could be family, come round to pick up a few bits to take into hospital. Wait, no. Pittman had mentioned they hadn't found anyone to notify when they admitted Kamau.

Inside, drawers opened and shut, footsteps moving deeper into the flat. Going in wasn't an option, not a sensible one at least. If he'd had Styles and Bell with him, maybe. Alone though, with no idea of who they were and why they were there, whether they were armed, that would be reckless to say the least. He couldn't just stay in the stairwell either. What if they decided to go back down via the side he was on instead of the way they'd come?

Porter made his way downstairs, careful not to kick the crushed can or carpet of crisp packets halfway down. No way to call in any backup without alerting others that he'd stuck his nose in where he shouldn't. The joys of working under the radar. Instead, he headed back to his car, glad now that he hadn't parked right outside.

A little over five minutes later, his patience was rewarded. Two figures emerged from the side he had exited minutes earlier. A pair of twenty-somethings, casual dress, jeans with dark lightweight jackets. Unremarkable, apart from the lead man, crimson trainers that could have been dipped in blood and not changed colour.

His partner, wearing a far tamer pair of dark brown boots, had a black bin liner clenched in one fist that swung like a pendulum as they walked. Whatever was in it was heavy. They climbed into a black BMW by the kerb and jerked out into traffic.

Porter let three cars pass, before pulling out to join them. Two options scrolled through his head. Most likely they were members of Triple H, cleaning up Henry Kamau's place before any coppers turned up to search it. He could lead them to Jackson Tyler, or at least one step closer. There was also a chance they could be part of a rival organisation, carrying out an opportunistic raid on whatever Kamau had stashed if word had gotten out that he was hospitalised.

He mixed it up, letting a little more space open up on longer stretches of road, but never more than a couple of hundred yards. They cut down towards the Thames and west along Newham Way. The dome of the O2 poked above the skyline to his left, support struts jabbing into the air like prongs on a crown. On past Canary Wharf, its high-rises jutting up like a half-finished game of Tetris.

By the time they crossed Tower Bridge, Porter was beginning to wonder if they'd spotted him, and were just playing. Finally, after little under an hour of driving, the BMW pulled off Camberwell Road at the Castlemead Estate, just shy of Camberwell Green, doubling back on itself behind a matching pair of buildings. Two parallel blocks of flats, Keats House and Milton House. All sounded very highbrow.

They pulled into the road that bisected the two buildings, Porter making sure to drive past then double back. The nose of his car poked around the corner just enough for him to see them disappear into a doorway halfway along. He waited a long ten count, before getting out and wandering towards the door, pretending to text on his phone, snatching glances either side just in case.

A sign over the door promised access to Keats House, numbers seventeen through twenty-four. Unfortunately for Porter, an intercom and some kind of touchpoint for a key fob told him there was little chance of slipping in unannounced, unless he could find someone to tailgate. He turned his attention to the car instead. Hard to tell whether either man had been carrying the bin liner from where he'd been looking.

One last look around for nosy neighbours and Porter darted forward, peering through the windows. Couldn't hang around too long in case they came back out. It occurred to him yet again that if they did, and if it went sour, he was here alone. No cavalry waiting in a van around the corner. No telling who he was dealing with or what they might do, but it was the price he had to pay for doing this on his own. Worth it.

The interior was clean, conspicuously so. The kind of tidy you got in a new hire car. Or if you were paranoid about leaving anything incriminating around. No sign of the bag. It must have made the journey inside after all. He tried the door. Locked. Wandered to the back next and was about to try the boot, when a shout made his head snap up.

'Oi, you! The fuck you think you're doing?'

A young black guy stood in the now open doorway. Not Red-Shoes. His mate in the boots. Porter pretended not to have heard him properly.

'Sorry mate, what's that?'

'You lose whatever part of you touches that car,' he said. 'That clear nuff for ya?'

'I dropped a tenner,' Porter tried. 'Think it blew under.'

'Ain't your tenner any more then, is it?' Brown-Boots said, coming out to meet him, hands that had been stuffed into pockets now hanging by his side, ready. Behind him, Red-Shoes appeared minus the hat. Porter saw now his hair was dyed practically white-blonde, an Eminem wannabe.

'Who the fuck's this joker?' he asked his mate.

'He's the fella just about to give us his wallet and phone, ain't that right, mate?'

They both advanced towards him, and he obliged by pulling out his wallet, but not quite how they'd intended, holding out his warrant card. Not the first time he'd been in a bit of a jam, but his pulse hammered a loud, excited beat in his ears all the same.

'Think this kind of wallet is the sort you boys would rather keep clear of.'

Something about the way they carried themselves, the sneer on their faces, suggested that his status as a copper might make him a more attractive target to these fools. As they made to close the gap, he clenched his fists, ready for whatever they might be stupid enough to throw, fingers tightening on the mobile he'd forgotten he was holding.

'It's OK, boys, stand down,' he said, raising it quickly to his ear. 'They're not as daft as they look.'

Both faces opposite him creased into frowns, halting their advance as they looked first at each other, then at each end of the street, scanning the balconies on both blocks of flats. Porter pressed him his advantage.

'No, it's fine. I got this,' he continued his one-sided conversation. 'You're not going to make me ask the others to join the party, are you?'

Red-Shoes kept scanning but stayed quiet. Brown-Boots kept up his tough guy act.

'The fuck you want? You got no right sniffing round my motor.'

Porter lowered his phone. In for a penny, in for a pound. 'You two mates with Henry?'

'Don't know no Henry,' said Red-Shoes, turning his attention back to Porter.

He let the double negative slide, new course of action decided. 'Sure you do. That's why you had a key to his flat, isn't it? What you did back there would be breaking and entering if you weren't his friends. We haven't been able to find any family to let them know where Henry is. I was hoping to speak to Jackson Tyler to see if he could point me in their direction.'

'Man, you'd best move on,' said Red-Shoes.

'We just want to know—' Porter began.

'You not listening, bruv?' he said. 'We don't know no Henry, and we don't know no Tyler either. You keep asking, you going to get escorted off the premises, copper or no copper.'

'I'd rather leave the others in their nice cosy vans,' Porter said, holding up his phone again, 'but if you're coming at me, you'd best make it quick to get a few shots in before they taser you.'

He hoped the words sounded a damn sight more confident than he felt, and that they couldn't see the light blistering of sweat he felt pop on his forehead.

'Enough.'

A voice drifted down from above them. What it lacked in volume, it made up for in authority. Porter looked up. Saw a face at a third-floor window. One he recognised from a mugshot he'd seen this morning. Thirty-five and at the top of the Triple H tree for five years now, Tyler had a misleading face, one that looked like it belonged in middle management, not running a criminal enterprise. Short, neat hair, rectangular wire-framed glasses. White cotton shirt, top button undone. Looked like he'd just stepped out from a meeting to see what the commotion was. Porter knew better than to judge this book by its cover though. He'd read enough background on Tyler to know that he didn't need to cultivate the hard man image, when he had his reputation to do that for him.

Headlines that popped to mind included liberal use of violence, one in particular where a suspected informant who Tyler had allegedly used as a human dartboard, numbers drawn around his body in permanent marker, enough puncture wounds to use him as a colander, one dart still lodged deep in his throat. Nothing alleged about the injuries or cause of death, but Tyler had kept a step ahead of them so far. No direct ties to any of the atrocities he'd supposedly carried out. The police had tried and failed to turn a few members of his crew, but his men were fiercely loyal.

Jackson Tyler rested both arms on the window ledge. 'Problem, Mikey?' he asked, looking at Red-Shoes.

'No problem, JT,' he said, chest puffed out, shoulders squared, peacocking for the boss. 'Long arm of the law just got lost is all. You was just leaving, wasn't you?' he said to Porter.

'Mr Tyler,' Porter ignored the posturing. 'DI Porter, Met Police. I was looking for you actually. Hoping to grab five minutes of your time.'

Tyler just stared at him, unblinking eyes boring in, even at a distance. 'I'm a busy man, Detective. Barely have two minutes to take a piss. What makes you think I'm going to waste five on you?'

'It's about Henry Kamau,' Porter said, looking for a reaction but seeing none.

'That supposed to mean something to me?' said Tyler.

'He's living in one of your flats,' said Porter.

'Can't help you. Don't own any. Must have me confused with someone else.' There was a lazy drawl to his words, as if Porter was boring him.

'Wouldn't bother you if we searched all the Moor Lane flats then?'

'Ah, but you'd need cause for a warrant, so I wouldn't worry too much about that.'

Porter took a deep breath, looking down at his feet, then back up at the window. He was aware that the two men here on the

98

street with him had moved a few feet closer. Could feel the energy coming off them, practically vibrating, waiting for a word from above that would let them sort this situation their way.

'I'm not here for you, Mr Tyler. I'm not even here about what happened to Henry.' He chose his next words carefully, ignoring how unpalatable they felt on the way out, but needing to hook Tyler's interest. 'It's um . . . it's personal.'

He glanced at Red-Shoes and Brown-Boots, as much to convey that he'd rather not talk in front of them, as to check how close they'd moved.

Tyler frowned, the ghost of a smile hovering around the edges of his mouth. Porter resisted the urge to keep talking, letting the seed of interest worm its way in. Must have been a full five seconds before Tyler spoke.

'Flat six.'

With that, he disappeared back inside, leaving Porter on the receiving end of a pair of disdainful glares. A buzzing sound came from the door, and he heard the lock click open. Porter gave both the wannabe hard cases one last glance, resisting the urge to wink at Red-Shoes, and went inside. How this would go was anyone's guess. Tyler could have a half-dozen more men upstairs with him. Porter could turn around, walk out and head back to the station. Still up to him, his choice.

He gave a slight shake of the head as he went upstairs. Who was he kidding? It was no choice at all.

CHAPTER SIXTEEN

Styles and Bell pulled up outside the Duke of Wellington pub, perched on the corner of Rainham Road South. Capping off the end of a tired-looking high street, somebody obviously took pride in appearances. Hanging baskets punctuated the front wall, mini explosions of colour. Two tables outside stood clear of any empties, the third occupied by a young couple, leaning in close, as if there was a risk of their sweet nothings being overheard on the practically empty street.

Styles caught a glimpse of his and Bell's reflections in the window as they approached, an incongruous pairing of little and large, him towering almost a foot and a half over her. She must have seen him peering at the image.

'You worried people will think I'm your date or your daughter?'

'I don't look that old just yet,' he shot back.

'More chance of me getting ID'd than you,' she said, quickening her pace to double time it through the door ahead of him.

The lunchtime crowd had made an early start. Pockets of people dotted around, pints in hand, clutching crisp packets. The faint base notes of hops soaked into carpets and furniture made Styles glance over towards the bar, pretty sure Porter would have gone for a cheeky one if he were here, equally sure Bell would raise her eyebrows.

'Your mother teach you no manners?' she said as they soaked in the atmosphere, such as it was. He looked at her, confused. 'You not buying the lady a drink then?'

'Oh, um, yeah, can do. What you having?'

'Nothing for me, thanks, I'm on duty,' she said, heading over to the bar.

He couldn't help but smile, shaking his head as he followed her. The lone member of staff behind the bar glanced up from the pint he was pouring, eyes flicking from them to the rising level of Guinness and back again.

'Be with you in a minute,' he said as Bell tapped out a rhythm against the wooden counter.

'You wouldn't be Jason McTeague, would you?' she asked.

His gaze flicked up again, held hers for a beat. 'Yeah, that's me. Sorry, do I know you?'

He was a beanpole of a man, almost as tall as Styles when he straightened up. Messy dark brown hair and pianist's fingers. Styles pegged him for thirtyish. McTeague leant over, placing the Guinness in front of a grey-haired old man, who returned the favour with enough change to fill a piggy bank.

'DI Taylor Bell,' she said, flashing him a full beam smile. 'And this is DS Styles. Wonder if we can borrow you for a few minutes?'

'I'm not due a break until two.'

Bell looked around, eyebrows raised. 'You're not exactly

101

swamped. I'm sure your friend there has got it covered.'

She nodded towards the far end of the bar where a barmaid had appeared, who couldn't be more than an inch taller than Bell herself. McTeague looked like he'd rather slam his head in the serving hatch, but nodded, and wandered over to mumble something at the unimpressed-looking barmaid.

They settled into a table in the far corner, out of earshot of nearby punters. McTeague looked uncomfortable, as if they'd just ushered him into an interview room at the station.

'This about Ross?'

Bell slipped into a more serious mode than she'd shown at the bar, jumping the queue in front of Styles again. So much for just along for the ride.

'It is,' she said. 'I understand you two were friends?'

'He went to school with my brother,' he said, not answering the actual question.

'How well did you know him then, Mr McTeague? I hear you helped him with his social media channels?'

McTeague sat back, nodding slowly. 'I did, yeah.'

Talkative this one. Like getting blood from a stone.

'Can you elaborate?'

'Have you caught them, then?' he asked. 'The ones who did this. Have you arrested anyone?'

'Not yet, sir,' Bell said. 'That's why we're here We need to understand more about Ross's activities, his background, to help us do just that.'

'I can't watch it,' he said, eyes unfocused, staring over her shoulder at the wall behind.

Don't blame you, mate, thought Styles, but he stayed quiet, waiting the other man out.

'Fucking animals,' said McTeague eventually.

'Who else knew Ross was headed to the courthouse?'

'No one,' he said. 'Wouldn't even tell us.'

'I thought you helped record his sessions with him?' said Bell.

'Nah, he did all that himself. Me and Elliott are . . .' He caught himself, correcting tense. 'Were like general dogsbodies. Admins on his website and social channels, arranging the events he did, sorting merchandise, that sort of thing.'

'Merchandise?' Styles said in disbelief. 'What, like T-shirts and mugs?'

'And the rest. Pens, mouse mats, baseball caps. He was big business. Had some big sponsors on his pages as well.'

'So he wasn't just doing this out of the goodness of his heart then,' said Bell. 'How much money are we talking?'

'Enough to kill for you mean?' said McTeague, shrugging, 'Comfortable six figures last year, but he gave most of it away to charities – homeless, refugees, Help for Heroes, that type of thing.'

'Any idea who would want him dead, Jason?' she asked.

He looked puzzled. 'Apart from the terrorists who hacked his head off you mean?'

'We're looking into a number of possibilities.'

'Cos catching the bastards live on video isn't enough to convince you?' said McTeague, raising it a few decibels, looking around as nosy regulars tried to hide interest behind glazed glances.

'His dad told us about threats from a member of the EWP, a Roland Thomas. Name ring any bells?'

'Huh!' McTeague spat out a laugh. 'How long have you got?'

'You know of more then?'

'Elliott and me, we used to monitor the comments that came in. Traced plenty of the more extreme ones to blokes who didn't exactly hide the EWP link. Most of 'em have the bloody logo as their profile pics or else it's tattooed all over themselves.'

'Don't suppose you could get us a list of the ones you traced?'

'It's all public domain, you can see 'em all yourself, but yeah, think Elliott saved a list of them.'

'And you never thought to call the police before now?' asked Bell.

'And say what? Some middle-aged racist is being mean to me online. Can you make him play nice, please?' No effort to keep the sarcasm hidden.

'Death threats aren't nothing, Jason,' said Styles. 'We would have taken them seriously.'

'We tried. At least Elliott did, back when the first few appeared. They're clever though, they're threats without being directly threatening, most of 'em anyway.'

'What do you mean most of them?' Bell asked. Styles could hear impatience creeping in around the edges.

'Look, this was always more his fight, not mine. It's all very noble and stuff, but it's not worth dying over.'

Styles felt them losing him, seeing the glances back towards the bar. Couldn't shake the feeling that he was holding back though, hanging on to something. Time to apply pressure to shake it loose.

'Look, Jason, we don't want to drag you into anything you don't want to be part of, but look at it this way' – he paused for effect, leaning forwards over the table – 'these men, whoever they were, there's no guarantee they'll stop with Ross. If they targeted him, there's every chance they might come after Ross's associates next, anyone aligned to his cause.'

'What are you . . . are you saying?'

'I'm saying that anything you can share that helps us, no matter how small you might think it is, gets these guys off the street. Stops them from hurting anyone else.'

McTeague sat back into his seat, rubbing his palms up and down his thighs. Nerves? Sweaty palms? Styles could practically hear the cogs turning as McTeague wrestled over whether to share whatever he was keeping back. Deep breath in, out loudly through the nose. Slightest of nods, and he folded his arms, decision made.

'You didn't hear this from me, right? I want my name kept out of it.'

If it was solid info, they'd have to take a statement, but Styles kept quiet, praying that Bell would too. Just let him talk. Styles gave the slightest of nods to encourage him.

'OK, so Ross used to speak at a few political rallies, organised a few of his own too. Few months back though he went to one he wasn't invited to. An EWP bash, not to cause trouble, just to listen to their crap. We said he looked like a shit James Bond. Baseball cap and a week's stubble hardly makes you a master of disguise, does it? Anyway, when he came back he was pretty shook up. Took me a while to get it out of him, but someone had recognised him. Ended up getting dragged off into a side room by two gorillas in suits. They told him what would happen if he showed his face again.'

'And what was that?'

'He said one of them had a cut-throat razor. Held it up to his throat and dry-shaved off some of his stubble. Said if they saw him hanging round again, it wouldn't just be his facial hair they'd cut.'

'Who's "they", Jason? Who said that to him?'

'There was a bunch of them there, not ones he'd seen before, except for one that is. The one holding the razor. He said it was Winter.'

'EWP Damien Winter?' Bell clarified.

'Course Damien bloody Winter. How many other Winters do you know?'

Milburn would have a coronary if they went back and pissed all over the chips of a perfectly good terrorist angle, but this couldn't be ignored. Bringing Winter's name up seemed to have ratcheted McTeague's nerves up a notch, making him fidget in his seat like a naughty child.

'Anyone else vouch for this?' asked Bell.

'You calling me a liar?' McTeague said, a little steel creeping back in.

She shook her head. 'No, but it's your word against his. Can't exactly see him backing up your story, can you?'

McTeague's tongue darted out, wetting chapped lips. 'What if there was a way to prove it?'

'Such as?'

'Ross, he used to wear a body cam when he went to these things. Tiny bit of kit, one of those buttonhole things, with a micro SD card.'

'You're saying he might have recorded it?'

McTeague shrugged. 'I never heard him mention it, but yeah it's possible.'

This was starting to feel ominous whichever way they chased it. Londoners were already up in arms shouting about terrorists, how the government and the Met needed to do more. Going after the EWP without hard evidence would make an even worse feeding frenzy out of it, if that was possible. EWP would call it a witch-hunt. Styles could only imagine the uproar if there was any truth in this new thread. EWP members had already shown a propensity for confrontation. Get this wrong and people would get hurt. No pressure.

CHAPTER SEVENTEEN

'Define personal,' said Tyler. No preamble. No offer of a cuppa or a seat. Straight to business.

Porter had run through a few options of how to position this on his way up. None of them felt appealing. Come across too needy and Tyler would be looking for something in return, a debt that Porter wasn't sure he could bring himself to owe, no matter the stakes. Try and strongarm him and, well, Tyler didn't seem the kind to respond too well to threats.

The gang leader stood propped against a wall, hands in jeans pockets. He wasn't a big man. Similar size to Porter, but he wore his authority like a cologne. The air of a man used to having his orders followed, happy to dish out the consequences to those who let him down. The flat was as minimalistic as they come. Nothing on the walls, one sofa, one chair. Not exactly lived in. Probably not even a cup in the cupboard or a knife in the drawer. The two men stared at each other. Felt like Porter's entire body was thrumming with energy, fight or flight waiting to make a decision.

'My wife,' he said eventually. 'She died a few years ago. Killed in a hit-and-run.'

'Condolences, Detective, but this concerns me how?'

'The car that hit her was ditched a few miles away. Never found the driver, but your boy Henry, his prints were in the passenger side.'

Porter paused, waiting, looking for a reaction. Nothing from Tyler, not even so much as a twitch. He'd be a nightmare to play poker against.

'Like I said, I'm not here for you, or anything to do with your business, but one of your boys was in that car. I need to know who else was with him.'

'Ask him,' he said with a shrug.

Porter gave a wry smile. 'I'm guessing you probably know already there's no telling when he'll wake up, if he even wakes at all.'

'Nothing I can do about that.'

'No, but you strike me as the kind of man who knows his business inside out. The kind of man that would know if one of his people killed someone, accident or otherwise.'

'You're saying I've known about this all these years and kept it to myself, Detective? A pillar of the community like me?'

'A case like this could bring a lot of unwanted attention to you, to your business. If you gave us a name, there'd be no need to dig too much deeper into anything else.'

'So we're negotiating now, are we?' asked Tyler, pushing off the wall, strolling over to where Porter stood in the centre of the room. 'What you offering me in return then, hypothetically speaking, if I did know anything?'

'This isn't a negotiation, Mr Tyler,' said Porter. 'We don't dish out favours.'

Tyler stopped three feet away now, smallest of chuckles. 'Hmm, funny that.'

'What's funny?'

'You say the Met don't do favours, but it's not the Met standing in my living room, telling me it's personal. Tell me, Detective, you sure they're actually letting you work this case?'

Porter tried his best to keep a straight face, but clearly had let something slip in his expression.

'That's what I thought,' said Tyler, leaning inches closer, studying Porter, like a scientist with a specimen. 'Here's my offer for you. I'm going to let you walk out of here. I'll even call off the dogs downstairs.' He gestured towards the window he'd leant out of. 'Even though they're itching to have a dance with you. Call it a mark of respect, seeing as you're a grieving widower and all.'

Tyler folded his arms, showing Porter a sea of rippling ink poking out from beneath rolled-up sleeves.

'This doesn't just go away when I leave here,' said Porter through gritted teeth, feeling the mood shift.

'We'll see about that,' said Tyler.

'How far would you go,' Porter asked, 'if it was your wife?'

Sod any attempt at diplomacy, Tyler wasn't going to budge willingly. Truth be told, Porter would have been suspicious if he had. Fine line though, between baiting and pushing over the edge. If he could push the right buttons, Tyler's next move could be to reach out to whoever Porter was looking for, to warn them or discipline them. He'd likely send Dumb and Dumber downstairs. Porter would follow them wherever they headed.

'Oh, I don't think you want to see how far I would go, Detective. Asking how far you'd go implies limits. That's something not all of us have.'

Tyler took half a step nearer. Porter stood his ground, studying Tyler closely, working out the chances of things getting more than just verbal. Felt himself tensing, weight shifting to the balls of his feet. They stood like that for what seemed like an age, in reality just a few seconds, before Tyler flashed a cold smile, turned and headed back towards the window.

'You know your way back downstairs,' he called over his shoulder.

'I'll go,' said Porter, 'but I'll be back. If we catch enough of you and your lot being naughty boys, I'll get my man eventually. Just going to cost you more that way.'

Tyler turned back to face him, back in his original slouch against the wall. No poker face this time, eyes narrowed, jaw set in a hard line.

'I ain't no old man, Detective,' he said. 'You'll not find me rolling over like Locke.'

Porter couldn't keep the surprise from his face. Alexander Locke had been the head of a criminal enterprise, one that Porter had come up against a few years back. Locke had a man inside the force on his payroll, keeping him a step ahead, until it all unravelled. More bodies than Porter cared to remember by the end of it, Locke being one of them. The void he had left was still up for grabs to a degree. New players had come in, existing ones like Tyler had used it as an opportunity to expand.

'Yeah, that's right,' Tyler said, smile playing around the edges of his mouth now. 'I know you. Knew Locke too. He was old-school. Got sloppy.'

Nothing to be gained by just standing sounding off at each other now. Porter headed back out into the corridor. Just as the door closed behind him, Tyler fired his parting shot.

'You come at me, you best not miss.'

CHAPTER EIGHTEEN

Styles couldn't help but glance at Porter's empty desk and wonder, mind racing as Milburn stood waiting for an answer. Porter had said he was heading back to brief the super, so if he hadn't made it back, where the hell was he? Milburn looked at him expectantly.

'He, uhm, he went to interview Elliott Kirk, sir. Divide and conquer, and all that. Should be back any minute.'

Truth be told, Styles and Bell had struck out with Kirk. He hadn't been at the address they had for him, but tomorrow was Tuesday, and being a teacher, little chance he'd be anywhere other than the school. They could catch him tomorrow. Important thing now was letting Porter know where he was supposed to have been before Milburn collared him.

As if on cue, no sooner had the words left his mouth, Styles saw Porter bump the door open, head down over his phone. Time to jump in before his gaffer dug a hole.

'Guv, we were just talking about you,' he called over Milburn's shoulder. 'How did it go with Kirk?'

Blank looks from Porter, and as soon as Milburn turned to look the other way, Styles raised both eyebrows, tiniest of head tilts towards Milburn, sending his best play-along vibe with it.

'Hmm?' Porter looked confused. Had every right to be, but then again, so was Styles, wondering what Porter had been up to, and why he hadn't wanted to share.

'Kirk? Did you track him down?'

A split second later he saw Porter catch on. 'Ah, Kirk, um no. No sign of him. He'll have to keep to tomorrow. What about McTeague?'

For Milburn's benefit Styles gave a rundown of Roly Thomas first, then sharing McTeague's twin revelations about Winter and possible footage. Porter was hearing this for the first time too, and Styles saw the same uncertainty on his face that he felt in his own gut. What looked like a straightforward if gruesome case was sprouting more legs than a centipede.

'He have any idea where Henderson might have stored this footage?' Porter said when he finished.

Styles shook his head. 'All he knows is that he was paranoid about keeping things on his hard drive. Preferred cloud storage, or something more portable, like a flash drive.'

'We need to go back and see his folks again,' said Porter.

'DI Bell, what's your take on this?' Milburn cut in. 'All sounds a little too convenient for my liking. All these death threats and nobody says a word until now?'

Bell looked first at Porter, then Styles, before she answered. 'Honestly, sir, I don't think we can ignore it. Group like the EWP, as far as I'm concerned, they're one step away from domestic terrorists. Tends to be disgruntled masses with a militant core. Some nasty characters in there with not a whole load of morals to share between 'em. Wouldn't be a great leap to think they would engineer this to whip things up, bump your average punter off the fence and onto their side. I think we have to at least do what we can to rule this out.'

Milburn had a look about him that suggested he was picturing conflicting printed press inches. Stuck between gems like *Police ignore genuine terror threat to chase after patriots* and *Met allowing the proverbial pressure cooker to simmer after getting fooled by the EWP*.

'What do you suggest then?' he asked her.

Styles shared a glance with Porter, one that asked why the hell she was getting put in pole position. This was still their case.

'Give me twenty-four hours to hear back from the Americans. I'll try and put a rush on it, but that will give us as close to a confirmation as we can around whether this was the Brotherhood.'

'And in the meantime?' Milburn asked.

'I'm happy to be an extra pair of hands for your team.'

Milburn mulled it over for a few seconds. Styles could practically hear the wheels turning, knowing how Milburn operated. SIO centre stage when things go right, with an option to palm off blame for somebody else's plan gone wrong. That someone could well end up being Taylor Bell, she just didn't realise yet.

'Fine,' he said finally. 'But not a word of this EWP business to the press, not until we know more. Make sure your team know that, Porter. Anyone who leaks will answer to me.'

'Of course, sir,' Porter replied, irritated by the inference that any of them would be sloppy enough to do that in the first place.

Milburn's threats were like the man in general. Mostly for show.

The super's attention span had clearly run its course, and with promises to come to the next team briefing, Milburn strode off towards his office, leaving the three of them to their own devices.

Styles saw Bell's glance flick between the retreating Milburn and Porter. She knew there was something at play she didn't fully understand. Curious, but enough smarts about her to pick up on Styles's play and not drop them in it with the super. Whether she'd ask for a favour in return or not remained to be seen.

'I'm going to grab a coffee. Get you boys anything?'

Styles and Porter declined in stereo, and she disappeared off downstairs. Just the two of them now. Styles waited a beat, giving Porter the chance to explain, but Porter just glanced back down at his phone.

'You're welcome,' Styles said eventually.

'Hmm? For what?'

'Covering your arse with his lordship.'

'Covering for what?'

'Don't know what happened to coming back here to brief him, but he was busy grilling me about where you'd disappeared to.'

'And?' said Porter, sounding put out.

'And if you'd gone off on a tangent related to the case somewhere, I'm assuming you'd have mentioned it as part of that little debrief, which makes me wonder, if you've been skulking around on something else, what that something else could be. Wouldn't have involved another trip to the hospital by any chance?'

'What? No. Course not,' Porter protested, with something approaching a laugh. Too forced though. Something he wasn't sharing. Maybe not the hospital, but Styles knew his boss better than most. No way could he let things lie and leave Pittman to it.

He leant in, lowering his voice just above a whisper. 'You know I've got your back, right?'

Porter hesitated, conflict of some sort rippling across his face. 'Course I do. It's nothing, honestly.'

Styles held his gaze, eyebrows raised, offering another chance to come clean.

'What?' Porter laughed out loud this time, but again, it rang a little hollow. 'You're being paranoid, mate.'

He gave Styles a double shoulder pat as he walked past him to his desk. Styles took a deep breath, shoving hands deep into pockets. He knew two things for sure. One, his boss had just lied to him. Two, he needed to find out why, before Porter got himself into a hole too deep to haul him out of.

Sucheka burst through the doors before either man could sit down.

'Boss,' she panted at Porter, as if she'd just sprinted up the stairs. Probably had. 'It's all kicking off. The EWP has clashed with a group of Muslims at a local mosque. Couple either side in hospital. There's been a fire at the South London Islamic Centre as well.'

All Styles could think of was one of the toys Emma's mum had bought for Hannah. A musical mobile dangling above her crib, one of the many tunes it tinkled, more prophesy than lullaby.

London's burning, London's burning.

CHAPTER NINETEEN

Angela Henderson's face, framed by the gap in the doorway, was full of hope when he introduced himself. Must think they'd made progress already, maybe even an arrest. Porter quashed that in a few short sentences.

'Sorry to bother you again quite so soon, Mrs Henderson' said Porter, introducing himself as Styles's partner. 'Nothing major to report, I'd just like to have a look in Ross's room if that's all right?'

Her smile drooped, face flat again. 'Ah, yes, of course, come on in,' she said, stepping back to let him past. 'Is there something in particular you're looking for?' she asked. 'I might be able to help you find it.'

He debated sharing specifics but decided against it. Actual footage of a death threat was going to be sensitive enough if it existed, the fewer outside his team that knew about it, the better. Instead he kept it pretty generic.

'My colleagues just asked me to take another look around, fresh pair of eyes and all that,' he said with an apologetic shrug. 'We took a couple of laptops with us then, but just wanted to have another look to see if he had any more devices he might have used to run his social channels.'

'Help yourself then. His is the door at the end of the hallway,' she said, gesturing upstairs. 'Think he just had the two that you took, but I'll ask Brian if he knows about any more.'

A once-over on their first visit had yielded a pair of MacBooks, currently being scrutinised closer than an MP's expenses, by the tech team at the station. Aside from those, and a sheaf of papers and letters, there'd been nothing else to speak of. Different now though, knowing what he was looking for. There was every chance he'd find nothing, that Henderson had everything stored in the cloud.

McTeague had mentioned a micro SD card, portable storage smaller than a postage stamp. Even if Henderson had uploaded it anywhere, if he hadn't used the device again since, the footage might still be there. Digital dynamite waiting to be discovered.

Henderson's room was the kind most mothers with kids still at home would relate to. Clothing scattered on the floor like someone had spontaneously combusted, duvet rumpled at the foot of the bed as if it had been kicked off, bedside table littered with paperbacks, Post-its and a trio of empty cups. A massive wooden desk dominated the room. Solid mahogany and must have weighed a ton. The dark green leather top poked out from under messy piles of paper, faded, scuffed and worn in places, from the resting of a thousand elbows. Two matching pillars of four drawers either side, with a long thin one dead centre. Porter snapped on a pair of latex gloves.

All nine were unlocked. Porter slid each one out, running fingers underneath. Bit of a cliché hiding place, but Henderson could have taped something under one of them. Nothing. He bent down, picking up T-shirts, socks, jeans, with thumb and forefinger. Unfolding, checking pockets, seams, even making a half-hearted effort to fold things and put them on the bed as he did. One less thing for Angela Henderson to pick up. Obvious spots under the bed, behind the desk, yielded nothing. He worked fast, and in silence for another ten minutes, clearing a path through the debris that remained of Ross Henderson's life. He was beginning to wonder if he should have brought Styles instead of sending him to pay a visit to the EWP's main office. No, he needed this time alone without distraction to sift through his meeting with Jackson Tyler, consider a next move.

Tyler's confidence had bordered on arrogance, suggesting enough layers of insulation against anything incriminating him personally. Truth be told, Porter would have been more surprised if he'd given up any information full stop, let alone an actual name. Wouldn't play well for him to be seen to help the Met. In that world, reputation was everything. Plenty lurking in the shadows behind him, waiting to step up and take their shot any time a crack showed.

No, Tyler wouldn't budge unless he was forced. And what would that take? Catching him in the act of whatever he was up to these days? Nah, no way would he get his hands dirty personally when he had men to take that risk for him. What would back him into a corner, and how far was Porter willing to go to apply the pressure?

120

That idea of reputation hovered in his mind like a fly waiting to be swatted as he stepped back, hands on hips, eyes doing a slow sweep. How comfortably Tyler sat on his throne relied on his ability to control his men, make things happen, bring in the money. What if that was threatened? If his business was so affected that giving up a name was the preferred option? Under normal circumstances, if this was a case Porter led on, he'd have his team to back him up, to squeeze the life out of Triple H's cash flow, shutting them down one arrest at a time. He wasn't naive enough to think others hadn't tried though, and the reality was that his team here consisted of him. Anyone else in their right mind would say no to going against chain of command, and anyone that would help him, Styles for example, Porter wouldn't want that on his conscience.

Perception is reality.

The words came to mind like subtitles on a screen. A mantra an old boss had sworn by. If Tyler believed the threat to his livelihood was real, that might be enough, but he had to *believe*, not just suspect. He filed that thought to return to, gaze coming to rest on a white rectangle resting against the wall to the side of the desk. It hadn't been there before. Must have been sandwiched between some of the detritus in the desk, fallen out as he shuffled through things. The back of a photo by the looks of it. He squatted down, one knee on the carpet, turning it over to reveal a picture of Henderson, looking at the camera, wincing as a woman in side profile poked the tip of her tongue in his ear. Both his arms were by his side, one of hers extending out into the picture. A selfie by the look of it. The Hendersons hadn't mentioned a girlfriend.

He made a mental note to ask them when he went downstairs and was about to stand up when something caught his eye. A furrow cut into the carpet running almost parallel to the desk. A quick glance at the other side of the desk revealed a matching groove in the carpet pile. The desk had been moved. Recently by the looks of it. Maybe Henderson had hidden something underneath it? He tried pushing it with his shoulder, but the weight, combined with a deep pile carpet, meant it only moved a few centimetres. He stood up, grabbing the front and back edges, knees slightly bent to take the weight in his legs rather than back, and grunted as he lifted, dragging it away from the wall until it sat at ninety degrees to its original position. Nothing left behind on the carpet except a couple of coins and a paperclip.

He had another thought, tipping it gently backward, feeling it grow heavier as it tilted, until the rear edge rested on the carpet. Both sets of drawers, the chunks at either side that Porter thought of as the twin pillars of the desk, were exposed, the bottom of the last drawer sitting an inch above the floor. This created a space about the size of two hardback novels.

Porter peered at the first pillar, running his fingers around the edges. Nothing. He reached into the second side, breath catching in his throat as his fingers brushed against something standing out from the grain of the wood. He dipped his head, looking under the top edge, seeing a strip of tape with a bump in the centre. He picked at the edges with his thumbnail, tugging the tape free. It came off in one piece, and he saw the lump, still stuck in the centre of the strip, was a plastic case the size of a large stamp, tiny black SD card held safe inside.

CHAPTER TWENTY

The English Welfare Party headquarters wasn't so much an office as a warehouse. The drab unit was on Canterbury Industrial Estate, near Peckham. With its half-brick, half-corrugated metal front, it could have been mistaken for just another wholesalers or mechanics, if it weren't for the inverted sword logo plastered across the door.

Styles had deliberately not called ahead, figuring the EWP had set its stall out well enough yesterday as not exactly cooperative. If Winter was here, no sense giving him time to compose himself, if he even waited around for Styles to arrive. No, Styles preferred to catch people on the fly, see real-time reactions, micro expressions, tics they didn't even know they had. All in the moment, no time to rehearse a response.

He pulled into the space closest to the door and scanned the rest of the area. The unit sat back from the road, surrounded by a gunmetal grey fence, easily eight feet high, tips of each strut split into three sharp points like a mini-trident. Not exactly the home you'd expect for a political party. The Tories and Labour usually pitched their tents on a main road, big glass windows plastered with a collage of propaganda. This was more like a compound.

He'd barely swung his legs out from the car, when the door to the unit opened, and a man stepped out. No mistaking the fact he'd come out to see Styles. He stood there, arms folded, face set into something approaching a sneer. Somewhere in his fifties, hair barely long enough to pass for stubble, well-cultivated beer-belly spilling over his belt, grubby fleece zipped up to under his chin.

''Fraid this is private property. Gonna have to ask you to park somewhere else,' he said, giving Styles a once up and down as he climbed out and straightened up to his full six-four.

'What if I'm here to join up?' said Styles, pointing up at the logo.

'Here to . . .' A flicker of something between disbelief and confusion flickered behind the man's eyes. 'We're not accepting new members at the moment. Not the likes of you anyway.' He puffed his chest out, rounding his shoulders, trying to look the big man.

'Likes of me? What, you mean you don't allow Sagittarians?'

'He means you can only join if you're British,' a second voice came from inside, soon followed by a second man, shorter than his tubby friend, but wiry. Styles clocked a tattoo on his left arm that matched Roly Thomas's, wrapped around a forearm braided with muscle, the kind you get from a life of hard graft.

Styles made a show of patting his pockets. 'If I'd known you did ID checks I would have brought my passport.'

'How 'bout you do us all a favour and piss off?' said the new arrival. 'There's a good lad.' Those last words were sickly sweet with sarcasm, hint of a West Country accent creeping in around the edges.

'Sorry, I didn't catch your names, fellas.'

'You don't want Jimmy here to have to ask twice,' said the first man. 'That'll just make him angry. Now do like he said and piss off back to wherever you came from.'

No mistaking the racial undertones now. Nothing Styles hadn't heard before. He'd learnt enough self-control not to react long before he joined the Met, but he'd had enough of the verbal sparring.

'Jimmy, is it?' he said, cocking his head as if checking for understanding. He pulled out his warrant card as he spoke. 'Well, don't you worry, Jimmy, I'll be heading back to Paddington Green soon enough, but not before I've had a chat with Damien Winter. DS Nick Styles by the way.' He flashed a *how-do-you-like-them-apples?* smile, enjoying the frustration on both faces as they realised they weren't going to scare him off with a little casual racism.

'You not going to invite me in then, gents?' Styles asked.

'He ain't here,' said Jimmy.

'You mind if I take a look inside to check?'

'You got a warrant?' Jimmy snarled.

'Ah Jimmy, I thought we were all mates here. You, me and . . . I didn't catch your name,' he said to the first man.

'It's Pat, and that badge you flashed don't make us mates.'

'OK Pat, how about I take you at your word and believe you when you say Mr Winter isn't here. Do you know where I might find him?'

Pat checked his watch and smirked. 'He's going to be pretty much everywhere, any minute.'

Something about the way he said it set Styles's nerves jangling. Whatever the dunce in front of him was hinting at, odds were it wasn't going to be good.

CHAPTER TWENTY-ONE

Porter rummaged in his pocket for the adaptor he'd nabbed from Styles, that would let him slot the card in and view any files on his phone. He slotted the micro SD card in, aware his breathing had become shallower. Menus popped up, and he tapped through them, anxious to see the contents. One file. No name, just a date. Porter tilted his head towards the door, convinced he'd heard a creak. No sound other than a car driving past outside. He sat on the edge of the bed, hunching over the screen, and pressed play.

The footage opened fast and jerky, as if Ross had been putting on his jacket. Porter recognised the very room he was in, looked at the scroll bar and saw the clip was over two hours long. He'd get one of the team to sit though the full thing later, but for now, he just needed the highlights. He dragged a finger across the bar and the picture leapt forwards like stop-motion animation.

After a minute or so of trial and error, he left it playing at a point where Henderson was outside, walking towards a large group of people. The soundtrack so far was mostly Henderson's footsteps, occasional rustle of fabric for good measure, but as he drew closer to the crowd, Porter could make out raised voices, some kind of chant. The footage wasn't high definition, but eventually what had been white blobs in the distance melted into focus. Placards. Some kind of protest? Slogans crept into view.

One race – the human race

Root out racism

Dotted around the edges of the protestors, splashes of luminous yellow. A dozen officers set against a backdrop of a hundred or more people. A token safety net if ever there was one. Henderson veered off right before he reached the throng of people, hugging a wall that ran down the side of whatever the building was they'd gathered around. He stopped by a set of dark green double doors and stayed there. Porter waited him out for a minute before scrubbing ahead again. Bodies popped into shot from nowhere only minutes later, and he dragged it back and forward until he had the moment the doors opened and whoever it was exited the building.

Porter recognised Damien Winter straightaway. Could have been a poster child for the Third Reich back in Nazi Germany. Tall, smartly dressed, blonde hair bordering on white in the sunshine, rocking the Aryan chic look, with cheekbones you could sharpen a knife on. Flanking him either side were burly twin minders, cut from the same cliff face, craggy features and bulging biceps. Winter barely gave Henderson a glance as they went to breeze past where he stood. 'Mr Winter? Mr Winter?'

It was the first time Porter had heard Henderson's voice other than on the footage of his murder. He sounded younger than he looked, borderline nervous, little of the steel Porter had heard in the opening minutes of his final Facebook appearance.

Winter turned to face him, stopping mid sentence. No mistaking the recognition on his face, quickly turning to irritation, slightest of eye-rolls, like a parent about to explain something to a child for the fifth time.

'Well, well, if it isn't storm in a teacup,' he said. 'I haven't got time for your shit today.'

Winter turned to walk in the opposite direction. Slightest of tremors to the picture, Henderson huffing out a loud breath.

'You got time to talk about the delivery driver a couple of your men put in hospital last week?'

'Don't know what you're on about,' Winter called over his shoulder, six feet away now.

'So, if I said I had proof, you'd not have time for that either?'

Winter stopped and wheeled around. Looked like he was staring straight into the lens.

'You had proof, you'd be speaking to one of those fine officers of the law up there,' said Winter, pointing over Henderson's shoulder. 'Not having a cosy little chat with me.'

The perspective twisted slightly, making Porter wonder if Henderson was looking back at the officers, wishing they were a little bit closer right now. A rustling noise muffled the next few words. Next thing Porter saw was a phone in Henderson's hand, different from the one he had seen in the courtroom. An older model, camera on, mini version of Winter on screen, timer ticking forward showing it was recording.

'. . . to see what you had to say. Might not be enough to put you behind bars, but it'll be enough to make them dig. What are they going to think about your little trips to Peterborough as well?'

Winter glanced down towards his feet, half-smile, shaking his head. He turned towards the slab of muscle to his left, muttered something Porter couldn't make out. The man smiled, all the warmth of a snowball, and moved faster than someone of his size should be able to. One minute the phone was in Henderson's hand, the next it was gone, presumably getting pulverised under the big man's foot, from the way he was stamping a boot down.

Henderson jumped back a few feet. 'Hey, you can't—'

'Can't what?' the big man growled, a meaty hand the size of a shovel reaching out, grabbing a handful of jacket, pulling Henderson back in close.

The two men were close enough that all Porter saw on screen was the white of the other man's shirt, bookended by black edges of jacket. Winter's voice, when it came, was calm, flat even, no trace of emotion. The polished edges to his pronunciation slipped off, leaving behind the North London boy. That made what he said all the more menacing.

'You'd best stick behind your keyboard, son.'

Breathing came in hurried, shallow bursts. Had to be Henderson's.

'The world's a dangerous enough place already with those bleeding-heart liberals up there, begging to open the floodgates to any Tom, Dick and Abdullah who wants to come and help themselves to some dole money. Let's not go stirring up any more trouble than we need to, eh?'

'Get off me,' Henderson said, picture wobbling as he wriggled, but the grip on him held firm. For all Porter knew, he had the other man-mountain's hands on him now as well.

'You might have a few million fools following you online, but they ain't here now, are they? Now, you listen up good. You crack on and preach all you like, but you cause trouble for me or any of my boys, and you're gonna find yourself taking a long walk off a short pier. Freddie and Leo here would be happy to help you with that, wouldn't you, boys?'

A series of grunts, what probably passed for laughter from the two big men. More laboured breathing.

'First and only time I'll tell you this,' one of the big men said. 'There ain't no second chances with me. You try me, it won't end well. Tell me you understand that.'

Few seconds of silence. 'I asked you if you fucking understand that,' he roared, voice like a revving engine.

'Yes, yes, I hear you, for God's sake, I just wanna—'

More muffled words, Winter and his men exploding back into view as Henderson was presumably released and pushed away in one movement.

The three men turned, oddly synchronised like soldiers on parade, and left without another word.

'Jesus,' Porter let go a breath he hadn't realised he was holding.

'Jesus,' Henderson's own voice mirrored his own, making hairs stand up on the back of his neck.

They had Winter, well, enough to bring him in for questioning anyway. Not even Milburn could ignore a death threat caught on camera. Clever of Henderson to pull the phone out, goading Winter into letting his guard down when he thought the chance of anyone else hearing the conversation had gone. Well, maybe not clever as such. Could have cost him his life ultimately.

He checked his watch, an hour to go before he'd agreed to meet Styles back at the station. Milburn needed to hear this now though. He popped the cable out, slipping the micro SD card back into the case, and sliding both into his inside pocket. As an afterthought he reached out and plucked the photo up off the duvet. Quick check in with the Hendersons to see if they knew who the girl was and he'd be on his way.

Styles's name flashed on his phone.

'Nick, I'm heading back now. You're not going to believe what I've just watched. I—'

Styles cut him off. 'I've got something you need to watch right now, boss. It's Winter. He's broadcasting live.'

CHAPTER TWENTY-TWO

'I thought long and hard about what to say today,' Winter began, 'or whether I should say anything at all.'

Porter's phone connected to the car as he started the engine, and Winter's voice boomed out, like he was there in person. He dropped his phone into the passenger seat, along with the items he'd taken from Henderson's room, and pulled out to head back to the station. It was surreal, hearing a different version of the man he'd just seen threaten Ross Henderson's life. This, his public face, was all charm. Measured, articulate. Easy to see how he swayed a certain type to his cause.

'And it came down to this: how could I not?'

He couldn't help an occasional glance down as he drove, seeing Winter stare at the camera for a beat, as if expecting an answer to his own rhetorical question. The irony that he was broadcasting using the same Facebook Live feature that had screened Henderson's murder wasn't lost on Porter. Looked like he was sat at a dining table. Porter saw what looked like turned down photo frames on the shelves behind him.

'Ross Henderson and I sat on opposite ends of the political table, but he was still just another human being. What happened to him was deplorable. Those responsible need to be punished, but so do those who let them into our country in the first place. Our Prime Minister hasn't just gone for an open-door policy, he's taken the bloody door off the hinges. You mark my words a storm is coming.'

A flash of passion now. Porter could sense him building. Was that an intended play on words with the storm reference?

'He needs to go, and he needs to go now. Someone in authority needs to pay for what happened to Ross Henderson, and that man is Prime Minister Joseph Banks. He needs to, if you'll pardon my expression, fall on his sword. The time has come for new leadership, and I for one propose a vote of no confidence in him and his government.'

Winter radiated a peculiar mix of anger and energy. A dangerous man at the best of times, let alone if he conned enough disillusioned voters. He had stood for election three times that Porter knew of, beaten each time by one of the larger party candidates, but narrowing the gap inch by inch.

'Now, we at the EWP are growing, make no mistake about it.' He stabbed a finger at the tabletop. 'We are here to stay, and to you, the British people, I say this.' Winter paused for effect. 'Let us put aside our differences and grieve for the young man who lost his life. Let us punish those who killed him. But once that is done, you need to demand more. You need to put a government and a leader in place that puts you first, that stakes our claim to being the world power we know we are. Neither the Prime Minister nor the leader of the opposition are that person. It's time for a new party to rise, be that mine or any other, and give you the country you deserve.'

Winter signed off with a nod to whoever was working his camera to end the broadcast, and Porter drove the rest of the way back in silence, mentally chewing over what he'd just heard. Styles's was the first face he saw when he strode out of the lift back at Paddington Green.

'You catch it all, boss?'

'Yeah, I saw it. Fancies himself as a bit of a Churchill-type figure, doesn't he? Trying to stir up the Great British public and all that.'

'They're a dangerous bunch, the lot of 'em,' Styles said, and filled Porter in on his visit, and the warm welcome from his new friends Jimmy and Pat.

'And they didn't give anything away on Winter?'

'Nope. They were too busy worrying that having a black man on site might lower the property value. Only thing missing from the reception I got was a burning cross and them breaking out their white hoods for me.'

'I'll be amazed if he doesn't know we were there by now,' said Porter. 'He doesn't know what we do though. Take a look at this.'

'Playing show and tell?' a voice over by the door said, and Porter turned to see Taylor Bell striding towards them, hands in pockets. 'I've got something to share if I can join in.'

'Ladies first,' said Styles.

'I kicked a guy in the balls once for calling me a lady,' she said, deadpan.

Porter flicked from a stunned Styles lost for a witty comeback to Bell's face just in time to see her crack a smile.

'I'm just kidding,' she said, patting him on the shoulder as she slouched into a neighbouring chair.

Styles went to hit play just as she finished with, 'I didn't kick anyone in the balls, I just punched him.'

She reached forwards and tapped play herself before either of them could respond. Porter couldn't help but smile as he walked away to grab their coffees. Despite his better judgement, he was warming to her. Hard not to. She gave as good as she got. He'd admired the way she'd handled the EWP crowd yesterday too. Plenty would have relied on safety in numbers, not stepping forward and dealing with it from the front like she had. He fired off a text to Evie while he waited for the cups to fill.

Gonna be a late one tonight. Case picking up pace. Will explain later.

Not a lie as such. There was momentum in cases like this, a current that carried you with it like a river. Sometimes you hit shallows, but this felt significant, speeding towards something. The equivalent of a waterfall, knowing his luck. He would be late tonight, just not because of the case. Well, not this one anyway.

SKY NEWS BULLETIN

Monday afternoon

'Breaking news in the wake of yesterday's terrorist attack at the old magistrates court in Greenwich, we're receiving reports of a series of racially motivated attacks across London. A contingent from the English Welfare Party has maintained a presence at the scene since yesterday. We go live now to Amy Fitzwilliam in Greenwich. Amy?'

'Thank you, Asim. Yes, we're hearing reports of a number of attacks within the last few hours. Mainly damage to property, but we've also had a serious assault confirmed. The victim has been identified as Zain Kassab, a Deliveroo rider, who was badly beaten in central London today by a group of men who dragged him off his bike. Mr Kassab was taken to hospital, where we understand he's in a critical condition. Witnesses claim to have heard a number of racial slurs as the group attacked Mr Kassab.

I'm here with EWP spokesman, Jeremy Hodgson. Mr Hodgson, what do you say to allegations that the EWP is using yesterday's killing of Ross Henderson as an excuse to whip up hatred against certain ethnic groups?'

'I'd say if people are reacting, it's because they're scared. I mean who wouldn't be after yesterday?'

'And what do you say to reports that EWP members assaulted a Deliveroo rider earlier today?'

'Don't know that they were any of ours what did that, but I'd say whoever they were, I'm sure they had their reasons.'

'What about the racial slurs that witnesses heard the men shouting? What about the fact that three men beat one man bad enough that he's in a critical condition?'

'Like I said, miss, people are afraid. People will do all sorts to protect what's theirs.'

CHAPTER TWENTY-THREE

Styles and Bell had finished by the time he made it back upstairs with the coffees, Porter clocking the concentration on Styles's face, like a kid trying really hard to pay attention in class.

'Boss, you're going to want to hear this,' he said, taking a coffee from the cardboard cup holder Porter offered.

'Hear what?'

'This,' Bell said, pointing to the laptop they'd just watched the clip on, 'is your best bet right now. I spoke to my guy in American Intelligence, and he says this wasn't the Brotherhood. No way.'

'How can he be so sure?' Porter asked. 'Did he just sit down at dinner and ask them outright?'

Bell ignored his sarcasm. 'First off, yes, he's sure, and if he is, then so am I. Intel from his sources in the last year alone has prevented a dozen credible threats. And if that's not enough for you, his contact has heard first-hand from the Brotherhood that they wish they knew who it was so they could thank them for their contribution to the cause. Normally these fuckers are crowing from the rooftops. Take it from me, if this was terrorism, it wasn't the Brotherhood.'

'Why would one group of terrorists let somebody else claim their glory?' asked Styles.

'Oh, this one's sharp,' she said to Porter. 'They wouldn't, Boy Wonder. That's why Winter needs putting under the microscope.'

'Does that mean you're moving on, then?' Porter asked.

'You want rid of me already?' she said, raising an eyebrow.

'Hey, you stay as long as you want,' he said, and meant it. 'More the merrier.'

'Well, I'm thinking your super would almost rather this was a terror attack than the shit show it'll become if it turns out Henderson was murdered by one of his own countrymen. Milburn seems the sort to worry about the optics as much as the outcomes, am I right?'

'More than you know,' mumbled Porter. 'Right, if you're sticking around, let's get the others together and bring everyone up to speed. Something tells me no one's going home any time soon.'

CHAPTER TWENTY-FOUR

As if there hadn't been enough riding on the case before this, the sea of concerned faces told Porter they all understood the gravity of the situation. Any hint that they were even looking at Winter, rumours like that were fumes waiting to catch a spark, and the EWP had shown themselves as not the type to back away from conflict.

'Gus, Kaja, anything from CCTV?'

'Nothing concrete,' Sucheka said, sounding disappointed in herself, like it was her fault.

'But not nothing?' Porter asked, reading between the lines.

'Nobody came in from the front, we know that much. Doors were still locked when first officers arrived on the scene, so our suspects have to have used at least the same side, if not the same method of entry as Henderson.'

'We have Henderson walking past the front about half an hour before he started broadcasting,' Tessier chipped in. 'He turns right, up Greenwich High Road, but we've got no coverage back there.

You go far enough along and there are a few bars and a chippy that have cameras that catch passing traffic out front. Trouble is we don't have a timeframe for the killers entering. Could have been waiting for him for hours, and hundreds of cars go past in that time.'

'Question is though, if they were waiting for him, how did they know where he'd be? His mate Jason said that he didn't even tell him or Elliott Kirk where he broadcasted from, so how would they know?'

'He could have told someone,' Dee Williams chipped in. 'Just because he didn't tell Jason, doesn't mean he didn't tell anyone else.'

'So, who would he trust more than two of his closest friends?'

Porter reached into his jacket, an afterthought, and pulled out the picture he'd found of Henderson and the girl.

'I found this in Henderson's room,' he said, holding it up for his team to see. 'His folks never mentioned a girlfriend when we spoke. Meant to show them this but completely forgot when Winter started broadcasting, but she could just as easily be an ex. Either way, I'd like to speak to her. Well volunteered, Dee.'

Williams accepted the task with a sardonic smile.

'It's a valid question though,' Porter said. 'They had to know where he'd be, so did they have a heads up, or did they track him there somehow? Glenn, can you have a word with Tech? I want to know if there's anything going on with his phone, any way they could have used that to track him without his knowledge.'

'On it, boss,' said Waters, 'anything else for me?' he asked, ever the keen one.

'Yeah, you find anything worth sharing in the comments from the other Stormcloudz videos?'

'Only that the guy had almost as many haters as supporters. All his content was taking potshots at the far right. He was all about human rights, freedom of movement, equal opportunities, those sorts of things. Calling for a second referendum, so he's got the Brexit brigade gunning for him as well. Most of the nasty stuff is about his stance on immigration though.'

'Any standouts we need to look at?' Styles asked.

'Yeah, if you've got nothing better to do for the next few months,' Waters said, laughing a little too loudly at his own attempt at humour. 'I haven't even finished yet, nowhere near, and I've got over two hundred that threaten to at least hurt if not kill him in one way or another.'

'That's racists for you,' said Tessier.

Somehow Porter couldn't imagine anyone threatening Tessier full stop, never mind being stupid enough to do it to his face.

'I've split 'em into a few lists,' said Waters. 'Some of them are EWP members. Easy enough to spot. They're the ones with the badge splashed all over their profiles or flashing their own tattoo. Then there's a load whose profiles are set to private. Can't see anything except their profile pic, and some of them don't even have a face on.'

'It's a start. Stick with it, Glenn. The video of Winter isn't enough on its own. He might have shot up our list, but we can't rule out that this was inspired by him, rather than carried out by him. Not that he'd need to get his hands dirty personally anyway. More likely some of the idiots that follow him.'

'Good place to start might be those two meatheads with him on the video,' said Styles.

'Good shout, Nick. Chances are we find them, we find him, and vice versa.'

'So, we're sacking off the terror angle altogether then, boss?' Sucheka asked.

Porter paused for a beat. 'I don't think we can just yet, but based on what DI Bell has already shared, it's looking less likely that's where this is headed.'

'What did the super make of that?' she asked.

'He doesn't know yet.'

Porter didn't think Milburn would take exception to having Winter and the EWP on the table as suspects, but he'd want something pretty bloody concrete before he went public with that. The threat on tape wouldn't be enough on its own. They needed to get Winter in an interview room and see what kind of alibi he threw their way.

'Kaja, was there anything else about the CCTV? We went off on a bit of a tangent.'

'Yes actually. I'd already been thinking about how they knew he'd be there, so we went back a bit with the footage. A week in fact. Got a few others to help scan through it, and we saw two things. Firstly, Henderson had done a couple of previous passes.'

'He'd been in the building already?' Styles asked.

'Don't know about inside,' she said, 'but he'd taken that same route. His phone data backs that up. Probably just scoping it out, checking security, that type of thing. Second though, and this one is a bit more interesting, is who else we saw.'

'Not Winter?'

'No,' she said, 'but somebody else we already know. Here,' she said, pulling her phone out, holding it screen out for the rest to see.

Jason McTeague.

CHAPTER TWENTY-FIVE

Could be nothing, but Porter wasn't a big believer in coincidences. He'd seen too many being the end of a thread, that when pulled, unravelled people's stories. For McTeague to walk past the site of his friend's murder forty-eight hours before it took place, in a city the size of London, when he lived fifteen miles away on the other side of the river, felt more than just chance.

'Nick, I want you and Kaja over to his pub now. No cosy chat over the bar this time. I want him down here, sweating in a room when we ask him why he went for a stroll past a murder scene. Gus, Dee, have a second crack at finding Elliott Kirk for me. Glenn, you stick with the social media. I know it's a ball-breaker, but it needs doing, and not much gets past you on that front.'

Waters perked up at the compliment, and Porter made a mental note to give the guy a break and throw him something more exciting the next chance he got. That kind of data trawling was the part they left out on shows like *Line of Duty*.

'Everyone happy with that?' he asked, avoiding looking at Waters in case the reality of yet more hours scrolling through angry rants had set back in.

'What about me?' Bell asked.

Truth be told, she'd been uncharacteristically quiet these last few minutes and he'd forgotten she was even there. Porter intended to have a pop at tracking down Damien Winter, and was toying with a second visit to the hospital to see if Kamau was showing any signs of recovery yet. Maybe even spend a little time looking into Jackson Tyler. She could help with the first but would be in the way with the second and third. No plausible alternative to her tagging along popped to mind though. He'd get creative when he needed to branch out on his own.

'You can come with me, see if we can find Winter.'

'I always knew you'd ditch me for a younger, better-looking model,' said Styles, with a mock pout.

'Nothing to do with your age, mate. She's just got better banter than you.'

'Harsh but fair,' Styles conceded.

'Porter!'

A loud voice cut across the office. Only one man bellowed like that in here. Porter saw Milburn in the door to his office, beckoning him with a finger.

'DI Bell, you as well, please.'

Porter dismissed the rest of the team, sending them scurrying off to their allotted tasks.

'My gaffer couldn't be louder if he swallowed a megaphone,' Bell said as they wandered towards Milburn's office. 'Yours has him beat though. Who needs hand driers in the loos when you've got hot air on supply?'

Porter smiled at that one.

'Careful,' she counselled. 'That's twice I've caught you smirking at one of my jokes. Any more and people might start to think you like me.'

She walked into Milburn's office ahead of Porter, and a thought flashed briefly through his mind as she turned to look at him. Was she flirting with him? No, Styles always said he was crap at reading people outside of a work context. If he thought she was, chances are she was trying anything but. All the same, he felt warmth in his cheeks. Could just as easily be anticipation of updating Milburn, seeing how his boss reacted to news that might not fit his current world view.

He had the super pegged as basically a good guy at heart, just one who lost sight of what really mattered at times. Politics over people. Porter wasted no time, keen to get away from the station, to see what he could shake loose. He'd have to shake Taylor Bell loose first though. He ran Milburn through Bell's intel about the Brotherhood, watching his boss's face with interest, seeing a surprising lack of reaction. Bell echoed her assurances about the validity of her sources, and Milburn stayed uncharacteristically quiet until after Porter showed him the footage of Winter and Henderson.

Milburn sat back, hands folded, resting on a paunch that seemed to grow bigger every time Porter set foot in the room.

'What have you got in play at the moment then, Porter?'

Porter ran him through the assignments he had just dished out, emphasis very much on Winter and McTeague now, adding in Bell's offer of staying with them. Unlikely as it now

147

looked that the Brotherhood were behind this, Porter wasn't one to dismiss possibilities, no matter how small. If this took a turn back in that direction, for whatever reason, they'd need her expertise. If it didn't, she'd be a useful extra body until she got pulled back by her own chain of command.

'So, here's what I'm thinking,' Milburn said finally. 'The press is expecting daily updates thanks to the terror angle. If we don't give them that, they'll fill the void with their own speculation. If we discount it completely, that won't satisfy them without knowing who we're looking at now, which we can't share yet. I'll schedule the next one for tomorrow morning, say the usual stock statements about pursuing all leads, can't comment further at this stage, etc. What we can't do yet is take the terror part off the table.'

'Sir, with all due respect, people are panicking out there. Overreacting. We've already had the EWP marching on a mosque, and the Islamic centre that went up in flames. There's no telling what might happen if Winter keeps whipping up his halfwits with his stupid sermons.'

'If we confirm it wasn't the Brotherhood, we might as well tell Winter we like him for this,' Milburn said, sterner edge creeping in.

'And if it was just one man, working alone, you might be right, sir, but Winter calls the shots for too many men who'd like nothing better than to drop a match in a mosque. Risks of us saying nothing massively outweigh those of him thinking he's in the frame. If he thinks we suspect him, he's less likely to do anything stupid or order anyone else to do it for him, and if it was him, we'll get him some other way.'

'And what about the risks of taking terror off the table and it turning out that you've got this all wrong?'

You've got it wrong. No *we* in this equation if things went tits up.

'Sir, for what it's worth, I agree with DI Porter's assessment, and my intel is reliable, so . . .'

Milburn sat forward quickly in his seat, no mean feat for a man of his size, belly pressing up against the edge of his desk.

'Is it one hundred per cent, DI Bell? Would you be willing to stake your career on it, because rest assured that's what you'd be doing. We go public with what you're saying, both of you, and it goes the other way? I'd be looking for another job, and I'd make damn sure I dragged the pair of you out the door with me.'

There was no such thing as a veiled threat from Milburn. Porter knew he would do exactly that, but he also knew it wouldn't come to that. Simple fact was that Milburn wasn't asking their opinion. He'd decided a course of action, and it was more a case of them being in the room while he talked out loud. Porter also knew trying to change his mind at this stage was like arguing with a stubborn toddler. With what he had planned over the next few days as far as Holly's case was concerned, there was every chance of a run-in of epic proportions anyway. Nothing to be gained in adding fuel to a fire he had zero chance of putting out.

Milburn's threat hung heavy for a few seconds, followed up by one of his toothiest *we're all friends here* grins.

'Now, unless there's anything else, I've got a speech to write for a charity gala tonight.'

'Nothing from me, sir.'

'Good,' said Milburn, turning his attention to his laptop, no hint that he expected an answer from Bell. She looked at Porter, one eyebrow raised, and followed him back out to their desks.

'Is he always so charming?' she asked in a tone that dripped sarcasm.

'Oh, he's worked hard to get it to that level,' said Porter.

'Every day must be a joy.'

'You have no idea. Anyway, on to far more exciting things, let's do a bit of digging on Winter, see if we can't figure out where he's holed up.'

Bell looked at her watch. 'Could do, or, bearing in mind it's been a hell of a last twenty-four hours, we could just catch up with him tomorrow and grab a drink instead. Could have murdered one when I was in McTeague's pub.'

'I don't think that's such a good idea,' said Porter. 'We need to—'

'You're not going to give me the whole "let's keep this on a professional level" speech, are you? Wouldn't be too hasty to flatter yourself. A drink's just a drink.'

'I never . . . No, what I meant was that we need to find him, and if anyone sees us slinking off to the pub before we do, there's a good chance the super will spontaneously combust.'

'You blushing, Detective Porter?' she asked.

He hadn't been until she said that, but now she had, he was pretty sure the warm glow in his cheeks wasn't just good health.

'How about if I told you I know exactly where he'll be tomorrow at noon?'

'And how the hell would you know that?'

'Good old-fashioned police work,' she said with a flash of wide-eyed innocence. 'Well, with a little help from Officer Google.'

She clicked her phone to life, screen showing the EWP logo

at the top. An events page, promising a speech not to be missed from the one and only Damien Winter.

If he hadn't been blushing before, he definitely was now.

'So, sure you don't fancy that drink?'

He laughed, quick glance around the room, a reflex action, but now one he worried would make it look like he was checking for eavesdroppers.

Jesus, man, get a grip. She's only suggesting a drink. One can't hurt.

Just the one though. He'd need a clear head for what he had planned tonight.

CHAPTER TWENTY-SIX

Even as Evie picked up her phone to make the call, she hated herself for it. She'd known about Holly from the start. Jake wasn't the best at reading women. She'd made a pretty bold play for him at a colleague's retirement bash, and he hadn't seen it coming at all. She'd turned him into a stuttering Hugh Grant spin-off, and thought she'd scared him off for good.

Patience was the secret sauce. She hadn't pushed too hard after that. Had let him travel those last few feet himself, to the point where he was ready to give it a go. Give them a go. The revelation about Holly's case had clipped the edges of her world like a drink-driver. Not enough to cause a crash, but she definitely felt a wobble. These last six months had been pretty much perfect. The fact that he still came across awkward at times, feeling his way back into a relationship, was endearing. Made her want him all the more.

Now here she sat, wondering where he was. Truth be told,

Holly still cast a long shadow. It had been the memory of her, still tugging at Porter's heart, that had made him hang back as long as he had. Only natural he felt that way, and there was no statute of limitations on grief. All the same, there was still that small seed of doubt that burrowed its way in like a tick, that whispered she would always be a plan B.

These thoughts that occasionally marauded around her mind weren't helped by episodes like last night. Nick had said Jake was on his way home. Shouldn't have taken more than half an hour at that time of day, but it had been coming up on two hours by the time he'd crawled into bed. Evie wasn't stupid. The nature of the job meant odd hours, best laid plans constantly changing. He'd mumbled something over breakfast though about leaving Nick to it so he could get some shut-eye, but no mention of anything else that had kept him up later. The beauty of them both being on the force was that she understood the demands of the job. The flip side was she was good at what she did, meaning she had a better than average bullshit meter, and there was something pinballing around that head of his that he wasn't sharing with her.

She stared at the double blue tick of another read message. Read but not replied to. She tried to put herself in his position. She couldn't imagine the emotional tailspin he must be going through right now. Self-preservation kicked in, telling her to batten down the hatches. Let this run its course. Let him get his closure, and they could put it all firmly back in the rear-view mirror where it belonged. From what she'd been told, Holly sounded like an incredible woman, but this was *her* time now. Her chance at happiness.

Even as she told herself to sit tight, to do nothing, her finger tapped at the screen, calling Emma Styles, instantly cursing herself in case the baby was asleep.

'Hey, Evie.' Emma's voice drifted down the line before she could change her mind and hang up.

'Sorry to bother you, Em,' she said, words she'd prepared in her mind sounding like an insecure teenager. 'I'm just trying to track Jake down. Don't suppose Nick's around to see if he knows where he is?'

'Yep, he's just in the shower. Hang on, I'll go ask him.'

Bump of footsteps, a rustling noise. Muffled words that she couldn't make out.

'He says Jake was out trying to find Damien Winter, the EWP leader, for a friendly chat.'

'Oh, OK, never mind. I'll let you—'

'Everything all right? Hannah's flat out and he takes for ever in the shower, so I don't mind swapping the peace and quiet for a good gossip,' Em said. Had Evie's mood been so transparent in just a few sentences, desperate for someone to offload to?

A few seconds of silence while she composed her thoughts. 'I'm just worried about him, Em,' she said finally. 'He's never been one to open up much at the best of times, but this' – she sighed, searching for the right words – 'this has really knocked him. More than he'll admit, well, to me at least. I just . . . I'm just worried that's all.'

'It's OK to be worried for him,' Emma said. 'But that doesn't mean you should worry about the pair of you.'

'What? No, I didn't mean—'

'Take it from me, as someone who's known him a good few years now. I saw what he was like with Holly. I see what he's like with you, and I saw what he was like in between. That last version of him wasn't half as much fun as he is now.'

Evie let a quiet laugh escape.

'He's a stubborn one. If he didn't want to be with you, he wouldn't be. He just needs to wrap his head around this and move on. Just give him a little time. It's only been a few days.'

Framing it like that, less than forty-eight hours since he was brought a step closer to knowing the truth about Holly's death, made her worries feel ridiculous. He had lied to her though, about where he was last night. And he was missing in action tonight as well. She opened her mouth to share her suspicions with Emma about last night but stopped herself. Enough. Give the man the benefit of the doubt, she told herself.

Somewhere in the background, a high-pitched wail, punctuated by pauses.

'Sorry!' Emma said. 'I'm being summoned by she who must be obeyed. Let me get her settled and I'll call you back.'

'No, no, it's fine, honestly. I need to pop out to the shops for a few bits anyway. Go sort Hannah out then enjoy your peace and quiet.'

The crying grew louder, a door opening. Emma heading into the nursery.

'OK, well, if you change your mind and you need to talk, you know where I am. It'll all be fine. You'll be fine.'

Evie signed off with promises to pop by one night during the week. She hadn't felt comfortable sharing with Emma about Porter going off somewhere last night, any more than she wanted to share the text he'd sent her a few hours back.

Another late one. Don't worry about dinner. I'll just grab a burger with Nick on the road.

He wasn't with Styles. He wasn't at home. Where the hell was he?

CHAPTER TWENTY-SEVEN

Porter didn't have a clear plan, truth be told, when it came to Jackson Tyler, except that he needed to apply pressure. He didn't have the level of intel on Tyler or his gang that he'd usually have access to, and couldn't get it without leaving breadcrumbs for Pittman or Milburn to follow. Best he could hope for would be the illusion of a net closing in. Make Tyler think giving up a name was his preferred option. What exactly that looked like in practice, he hadn't yet decided.

The one drink with Bell turned out to be just that. One pint of Guinness, and she made her excuses before he had to think of a way to ditch her, so he could turn his attentions to the Triple H gang. First stop was the hospital, get the latest on Kamau and see if he'd had any visitors. Porter approached cautiously, pretending to be on his phone as he neared the door, tailgating in behind an old couple, presumably shuffling in for visiting hours.

He walked past Kamau's room at first, in case Pittman or any of his team were there. Empty, save for Kamau looking no healthier than yesterday. Eyes closed, rise and fall of the blankets barely noticeable. His skin had a matt look to it, like no one was home, as if his body had shut down all but the essentials while he fought to wake up. Porter huffed out a loud breath, ramming hands deep in pockets, worrying at his bottom lip. If Kamau died, that was no more of a resolution that he had before. Less, if anything.

'Excuse me,' a polite but firm voice came from behind him. 'Can I help you?'

He whirled around to see a nurse staring at him with a mixture of curiosity and impatience, as if she didn't have enough to do without spotting potential trespassers. Her hair was pulled back in a bun so tight it almost gave her a facelift. She wore the navy uniform of a ward sister, white piping around the collar and sleeves.

'Sorry,' he said, not sure what he was actually apologising for. Force of habit. He reached into his pocket, flashing his warrant card, whipping it back out of sight as she squinted to read it.

'I'm with the Met. You've probably met my colleague, DI Pittman.'

'Sorry, I didn't catch your name?'

Giving his own name could come back to bite him if she mentioned this to Pittman.

'DS Rose,' he said, making one up on the fly, holding out a hand. 'Just come to see how our patient is doing. Any developments?'

She shook her head, lips pursed. 'Could be days before the swelling goes down enough for us to know for sure the extent of any damage.'

'So, there's still a chance he'll not actually wake up?'

She sighed, a sound that spoke of maintaining a level of compassion despite God knows how many back-to-back shifts.

'I'll tell you the same as I told his brother, he's suffered massive head trauma and—'

'Wait, sorry, you said his brother?'

'Yes,' she said, frowning like he'd just asked if the earth was round.

'When was this?'

'Just about half an hour before you showed up. Why?'

'We haven't been able to find any family to contact for him. Did he show you any form of ID?'

'We don't usually ask to see visitors' passports or driver's licences, Detective,' she said, folding her arms across her chest.

'Did he say when he'd be back?'

'Didn't say much to be honest. I did ask if there was anybody else that would be coming, to let them know about limits on visitors, but he said there was nobody. Mum and Dad passed a while back it seems.'

'What did he look like?'

She shrugged. 'Like an older version of him,' she said, gesturing at Henry Kamau, 'except without the bandages.'

'In the last half hour you said?'

'Yes, that's right. Is everything OK?'

'Yes, yes, just that it would have been useful to speak to him that's all.'

'Would you like me to call you if he comes back?'

Porter would love nothing more, but if he left his number, that was one more inch of noose to hang himself with if anyone caught wind he was sticking his nose in.

'That's OK, we'll manage to get hold of him I'm sure.'

A germ of an idea took hold, grew into something he could use. He made his excuses and headed back out towards the front entrance. The security office was set back from reception. He tried the door. Locked. Three quick knocks, then stepped back and waited. When it opened a few seconds later, the face that peered out reminded Porter of Penfold from *Danger Mouse*. Lenses that must be half an inch thick. One ropey strand of hair flopped over the top of an otherwise bald head, more of a tassel than a hairdo. Porter's chin was level with the guy's head, so the glasses were staring straight up at him.

'Help you?' said Penfold, in a snappy impatient voice that suggested he had better things to do.

Porter got a reaction when he showed his warrant card, again careful to not leave it hanging out there too long, using the same made-up name. A thought flashed through his mind as he explained what he needed. Here he was, a police officer guilty of impersonating a police officer. Hadn't occurred to him in the moment he gave a different name to the ward sister, but he'd slid one foot over a line. What side he was left on remained to be seen.

Ten minutes and a hasty trip through CCTV footage later, Porter watched as the man who claimed to be Henry's brother left the ward, exited out into the car park and got into a dark-coloured car. Ford Focus maybe? Penfold came through for Porter in a big way, when he dropped in that the car park worked on a number plate recognition scheme instead of paper tickets. Porter scribbled down the plate, thanked the man and left the office, keen to run a check on the plate.

The way out was through a double-wide set of revolving doors, and he was halfway through revising his order of priorities. Track down the brother first, see what he had to say. Could even be a member of Triple H himself for all Porter knew. Build what intel he could, then make his next move against Tyler. He almost walked out without noticing. One of those blink-and-you-miss-it moments. Turned just in time to see the flash of colour on the man walking in the opposite direction. Correction: two men. Young, white, matching haircuts like they'd got a two-for-one deal, short back and sides. The colour wasn't the clothing. The tattoo on the arm of the closest one, three overlapping capital Hs, blood red.

He felt the instant spike of adrenaline hit. Should he call for backup? He would have to explain his presence as well, but that would be a small price to pay. It boiled down to simple logistics though. If they were here for Kamau, it would all be over before the first car arrived.

Not as if Penfold would be much use either. Porter gave them a five count to clear the door, then looped back around inside. Just him then.

CHAPTER TWENTY-EIGHT

Porter slipped his jacket off, scrunching one hand around the middle and carrying it down by his side. Popped an extra button on his shirt. People often said you could tell a copper a mile off. He didn't believe that applied to him, but the more like a tired relative on his way to visiting he looked like, the better.

The two men in front of him sharked off left, towards the lifts. Porter kept his head down, looking at his phone and veered right, towards the stairwell. He knew his way to the ward from the previous two visits. No sense chancing it by stepping into a lift with them, even if they didn't know who he was. What if Tyler had told his men to be on the lookout for an angry copper, given a description? Hell, all he'd have to do would be to google his name to get a picture thanks to a few of the high-profile cases he'd worked on. The crazy notion that they could be here for him flickered to life. That they could have followed him here on Tyler's orders.

Porter took the stairs two at a time, pausing for a moment on the third-floor landing to suck in a few deep breaths, steadying himself. The lifts were at the far end of the corridor as he peered through the glass pane set in the door. A muffled ping as it slid open. They'd have to walk past the entrance to the stairwell to get to the ward, which from memory was another twenty feet or so in the other direction. He stepped to one side, pressing his back against the wall, pulling his phone out again, partly for show, partly with 999 on screen ready to dial.

The drag of soles on the hard rubber floors as they strode past the door. He counted to five before daring to nudge the door open a centimetre. Just enough to hear one of them arguing with a voice coming through the intercom. Sounded like the same sister he'd spoken to, and they'd missed visiting hours by minutes. Unfortunately for them, sounded like she was a stickler for the rules.

'Tomorrow,' she said, and Porter pictured her with the same crossed arms and determined set to her expression. 'Hours are on the wall beside you.'

'He's my brother, i'n't he,' said the one closest to the speaker.

'Doesn't change the fact I can't let you in. Break the rules for you and I have to do it for everyone.'

'Took us an hour to get here, man. We'll only stay five minutes.'

'You can stay as long as you like, but it'll be on that side of the door until tomorrow,' she said. 'Now, if you'll excuse me, I've got patients to see to.'

The crackle from the intercom stopped. The guy jabbed the button again.

'You serious? You just hung up on me!'

'She's not on a phone, bruv,' said the second one. ''S go. We can come back tomorrow.'

'What a joke, man,' said the first, slapping a palm against the speaker. 'Joke.' Second slap, harder this time. Porter eased the door back into place and shot down the stairs, jumping the last four. No need for stealth now. Seeing these two here gave him the seed of an idea. Get to his car, follow them wherever they went next. If he couldn't access most of the existing info on the Triple H gang, he'd start building his own file. Henry Kamau wasn't going anywhere, nor was Jackson Tyler. Could be a long slog to get the answers he wanted. Needed. He'd waited this long; he could wait a little longer. One tiny line crossed tonight already. No idea how far he would push it. The lines between what was allowed and what might be necessary were starting to converge. No telling where that movement might stop.

He checked his watch. Evie would most likely be in bed by now. How would she react if he told her what he had planned? Risking everything here and now, to avenge a memory. It wasn't that he didn't trust her. More that he wanted to protect her if it went pear-shaped. That, and the symmetry of his girlfriend helping bring down his wife's killer, felt off.

He hunkered down low behind the wheel of his car, eyes not leaving the hospital entrance. Sure enough, less than two minutes later, the pair emerged. They fiddled with the buttons at the payment station, before finally climbing into a black BMW, a carbon copy of the one he'd followed to Tyler earlier today. Seemed like a lifetime ago.

Porter let them get near the exit before he pulled out, tucking in behind, but keeping a respectable distance. They could be heading home to call it a night for all he knew. No guarantee tonight would go anywhere, but worst case he'd follow them to another Triple H location, a flat, a shop, one of dozens that Tyler allegedly owned. Another pin to stick in a map. Porter swallowed down his natural impatience, reminding himself the longer this played out, the more the likelihood of Pittman moving on, the case on Kamau being left in limbo while he languished in his coma. That played into Porter's hands. Made it easier for him to work his own angles on Jackson Tyler. All about the long haul.

After a little over ten minutes, the BMW pulled sharply to the left, into a parking space outside a pizza shop. Porter kept his eyes fixed front as he passed them, pulling in another hundred yards past and creaking the rear-view mirror a half inch for a better view. The driver got out, wandered over to a moped parked up outside the shop. Looked like he was rooting round in his pockets for something. Porter took a chance and twisted round. The man bent down over the storage box at the back, went through the motions of unlocking it, taking something inside that got shoved into his jacket, before lifting up a carrier bag Porter hadn't noticed in his other hand and placing it inside.

Porter turned to face front again, doing a mental coin toss. Who to follow? No intel to base a decision on. He'd stick with the car. Less chance of losing that than the more manoeuvrable moped that could zigzag through traffic. To his surprise, instead of the two splitting up, he watched the man get back in the car, leaving the moped where it stood. A minute later, they'd pulled out again and cruised past him.

He signalled to pull out. Quick traffic check in the rear-view, when movement caught his eye back outside the shop. A man exited the shop and bent down to insert what could only be a key in the same moped. Flick of the eyes back to the road and the gap to the BMW was fifty yards ahead and growing. Behind him, the man reached in, took out the bag Porter's new friend has deposited and headed back inside.

Five minutes later, outside a Chinese takeaway, the same scene played out. Another moped, another carrier bag. Another man appearing to take custody of the bag after the car had pulled away. Had to be a dead drop of sorts. Of what, Porter could only guess, but chances were it was nothing legal. He smiled in the dark of his car as he resumed his quiet pursuit of the BMW. He'd committed the licence plate to memory when they drove past him on the way out from the hospital. The two locations were fresh in his mind as well, and when they pulled up outside a third takeaway, he changed tack.

Instead of sitting tight, he jumped out, dodging into a corner shop, grabbing a pay-as-you-go SIM and tapping his card against the terminal. He slid back into his seat, just as the BMW pulled away again. He fumbled the back off his phone, popping his SIM out in favour of the new one. Time for one quick call that could start to swing this in his favour.

CHAPTER TWENTY-NINE

Porter watched from a safe distance as the pair stood with their legs spread, hands on top of the car. He could see the arresting officer leaning in, talking. They'd be asking whether there were any sharp objects in the pockets, anything to declare in the car. While Porter didn't know the exact contents of the bags they'd been dropping off, he could hazard a guess at some form of drugs. Evie had said that was one of the gang's main sources of income, and being on the Drugs Squad, she'd know better than him.

They might not have any left in the car, but worst case, they'd have whatever payment they'd undoubtedly picked up along the way. Any large sums of cash would be seized and not returned unless the men could show it had been obtained legally. With a bit of luck, they'd still have some product with them as well.

Porter had given all three drop-offs to the 999 operator, as well as the licence plate. He had included one small embellishment, saying he'd seen one of them holding what looked like a gun, knowing the call would get taken more seriously. He'd tucked back in, a few cars behind and watched minutes later as the first of what would soon be several cars with uniformed officers picked up the trail. They didn't pull them over immediately, waiting for a firearms team to act as their cavalry.

From the direction they were travelling when they were stopped there was every chance they could have been heading to the same block of flats Porter had visited earlier that day. Could have been a nice double whammy if Tyler had been caught accepting cash or product from them.

He watched as one of the officers emerged from the back seat of the BMW, holding two, maybe three, bags in a clenched fist like a trophy. Perfect. No chance of these two making good on their promise to visit Kamau tomorrow. Nothing to stop Tyler from sending two more though. He needed some way of warning Pittman. Anonymous Post-it note on his desk with a message from the hospital, worried about an aggressive man claiming to be a relative should do it.

Porter stayed put until the pair were guided into the back of a car, a helping hand from the officer to shove their heads down. Five minutes later he was stood at the entrance to Jackson Tyler's block. No guarantees anyone was home, let alone the main man. Porter jabbed a finger at the buzzer, leaning on it for a ten count for good measure.

He took a step back, peering up at the window Tyler had appeared at earlier. Curtains drawn, an unblinking eye reflecting the street light back at him. No sign of life.

No noise except muted traffic from the street and the whisper of his own breath. He turned to look along the back lane, half expecting the same two fools he'd followed here earlier to be advancing towards him. A crackle cut across his thoughts, and he whipped his head back to the speaker.

'Mr Tyler?'

Faint hiss of static. Was that breathing he heard?

'Mr Tyler?' he tried again. 'It's DI Porter.'

He was beginning to wonder if he'd imagined the noise coming from the intercom, when the reply came.

'I warned you. Shouldn't have come back here.'

Every word packed with ill intent.

'And I warned you,' he said, matching the understated grit with his own voice. 'I told you your boys would start getting picked up. Two of 'em just got pulled over, a mile or so from here. Interesting what we found in their car.'

'Mm, that right?'

No surprise or shock at the news. Had they called him the moment they saw blues and twos flashing in their rear-view?

'Just these two for now, but you can be sure there'll be more to follow. How many is up to you.'

'Let's say for the sake of argument that I knew what you was talking about. You're saying you picked up two of my boys. Two's the magic number. Know why?'

Porter didn't answer.

'Cos I ain't ever had to give two warnings to anyone. You know why?'

'I've got a feeling you're about to tell me,' said Porter, trying to sound bored.

'Cos most people know what happens if the first one gets ignored.'

'Give me a name and this goes away,' said Porter, silently

promising that he'd make a point of keeping Jackson Tyler on his shitlist no matter how this turned out.

'I'll give you two,' said Tyler. 'Fozzie and Slim. Those two boys should be with you right about now. Enjoy your second warning.'

Porter took a step back from the door, looking up through the glass pane. A black metal railing ran up the side of the stairwell. If he leant forwards he could see through a gap up to the next landing. A sound. Not the intercom now, that was dead. Something more solid, a beat. A pair of feet rounded the first-floor landing, a second close behind them.

Porter hesitated, half a breath, no more. Didn't wait for a second look. Something told him Tyler wasn't one to make empty threats, not even to a copper. He turned, ran back along the fifty yards of back lane to where he'd parked his car. Heard a door burst open as he fumbled with his keys. His finger found the key fob, slid over the button, indicators flashing a promise of safety.

Shouts blurred with footsteps as he slid into the driver's seat, engine roaring to life. Two shapes barrelled down the road towards him. He tried to focus on making a hasty exit, not to fixate on them, but as he slammed the car into reverse, looking into the rear-view mirror, he couldn't help but look at his pursuers. Unfamiliar faces contorted into cartoonish masks. Eyes wide, mouths working overtime to spit streams of obscenity his way. He saw some kind of weapons in their hands, long, thin. Could be bats, pipes, hard to say, everything moving at a hundred miles an hour. He wasn't sticking around to find out.

They'd covered half the ground now. Something about their faces, overlaid across the testosterone-fuelled fury.

Anticipation. They lived for this. He half twisted round, looping one arm around the back of the passenger seat, and floored it, lurching backwards, praying nobody would pick this moment to step out behind him. He was committed now, and something told him that not even that would put these two off their stride. The widening gap seemed to spur their shouting on to new heights.

As the rear bumper drew level with the corner of the building, Porter pulled the wheel down hard with his right hand, swinging his front end around ninety degrees. Quick one two on brake and accelerator, and he shot towards the main road. That last manoeuvre had helped them close the gap, almost but not quite. Something slapped hard against the boot, a hand maybe. Just a token gesture though, and he saw in the mirror they'd slowed to a trot. His luck held and a gap in traffic meant he swerved out into the left-hand lane without clipping anyone or anything. A loud thud from outside, somewhere between a crack and a crunch. They'd thrown something his way, whatever weapon that had been meant for him. No way that hadn't damaged something back there, but rather a cracked taillight than cracked head. Wasn't until he could no longer see the road he'd shot out of in his mirror that he relaxed back into his seat. Deep breath. Sweat stuck the cotton shirt to his back like a second skin as he leant against the leather. He took one hand off the wheel, made a fist, flexed it, straightening fingers. The tremor was slight, but it was there.

Tonight had been about sending a message, and he'd done exactly that. He'd received one of his own though. Jackson Tyler wasn't about to roll over any time soon. That meant Porter had to either hope that Kamau woke up in a talkative mood or up the ante himself with Tyler. Most leaders of gangs like his weren't leaders in the true sense. They ruled by fear. They ruled by keeping others far enough below them on the pecking order. Fought with their fists, not words. There wasn't room for inspiring speeches. Actions were the measure of the man. He'd acted tonight without hesitation. Porter couldn't help but feel that despite the arrests and whatever had been seized, Tyler came out of this the winner. He'd laid down a marker, daring Porter to take a step closer.

What he'd give for a half-dozen officers, squashed into two cars, dragging Tyler out kicking and screaming. As it was though, his entire team on this one was here in the car with him now. Porter considered again the risks of involving Styles, or any of the others for that matter. It wasn't that they couldn't handle themselves. More that there was already a huge target on his chest. He didn't want to involve anyone else, dragging them in front of him like a human shield. Couldn't live with himself if somebody else got caught in the crossfire.

Keeping Styles in the dark went against every instinct, but it was the only option that kept him out of harm's way, made sure he went back in one piece every night to Emma and Hannah. Home. His mind wandered to Evie. To the unanswered message he had received on his way here. None of this was fair to her either. Wasn't her fault that it had taken him so long to lay down the baggage from his life before her. A little voice somewhere deep down told him off for lying to himself. He hadn't lain it down, just moved it out of sight.

How would he feel in her shoes? He'd never been a good liar and he was pretty sure she didn't believe him last night.

Truth was if he'd told her where he'd actually been, he was pretty sure she'd understand. Why had he lied then? God only knew. These last forty-eight hours it felt he'd stepped off a ledge. It was only a matter of time before he hit the bottom.

CHAPTER THIRTY

She heard the car pull up. The ticking of the engine and footsteps on the path. He tried his best not to wake her whenever he came in late, but he wasn't quite the ninja he thought he was. Evie heard the key in the door, soft padding of feet on stairs, followed by the tell-tale creak of the third from the top. She was on her side, facing away from the door when he came in, a thick wedge of light splashing on the wall beside her, winking back to black as he eased the door closed.

Silence, as if he'd paused, maybe watching, listening for her breathing. She waited him out, not wanting him to know she was still awake. Not yet. Didn't want any suggestion of suspicion that she'd waited up. Better to give him a chance to talk, to explain. She knew him well enough now to know that he didn't respond well to being put on the spot if he wasn't ready. She heard the rustle of clothes being shed and felt the mattress dip as he slid in behind her, slipping an arm over her hip.

Evie breathed deeply, quietly grumbling, stirring from a non-existent sleep and turning to face him.

'Sorry,' he whispered, even though there was no one left to wake. 'Tried my best to sneak in.'

'Mmm, 's OK,' she said, turning into him, nestling her head into the gap between his shoulder and cheekbone, one palm flat against his chest. 'Good day at the office?'

His chest swelled under her hand, deep breath, long and slow, out loud through the nose. About to share, or just stalling for time?

'Long.'

She waited for him to elaborate, but he said nothing.

'Wow,' she said, 'the way you tell it really brings the day to life.'

He laughed. 'You know how it is. One of those you get to the end of and you're no further forward than when you got out of bed.'

'Tomorrow'll be better,' she promised. 'What've you and Nick been up to that's kept you up past your bedtime?'

'Damien Winter.'

'Ah, our friendly neighbourhood right-wing megalomaniac. What's he had to say for himself?'

'Plenty, all online anyway. Haven't managed to track him down for a proper chat yet. Pretty sure we'll manage tomorrow though. He's doing a live event, so we'll pay him a visit.'

'Ah good,' she said, as sure as she could be that he wasn't giving her the full story, working through how best to dig without the appearance of digging. 'We'd best be buying Emma a bottle of something nice if Nick's getting dragged around London at all hours instead of doing a stint on Dad duty.'

Just tell me the truth, Jake. At least tell me Nick wasn't with you.

'Ah she's probably glad of the break from him. Hannah's got better craic than him already anyway.'

Male distraction tactics one-oh-one. Deflect with humour.

'That may well be true, but a new mum needs her rest. You can't be sending him back at this time every night, or they'll be divorced before the month's out.'

'I'll go easy on him,' said Jake, raising the shadow of a double-finger salute to his temple. 'Scout's honour.'

That was his second chance to come clean. Half of her wanted to slap him, tell him she deserved a bit more respect. The other half whispered that he had his reasons, that the last few days had hit him hard. That he might be drifting, but he'd come back to her. She didn't in her heart of hearts believe that he was going behind her back with anyone. Only other explanation was to do with Holly's case. Porter should have more sense than that, operative word being 'should'. He'd gone his own way before though, finding shades of grey in orders from an SIO, asking for forgiveness later, rather than permission in advance. Even for him though, this time, it was something that could blow up in his face faster than a dodgy firework. Either way, she had to know, for her sake as much as his. Had to protect him from himself if it was option B. The words came out before she could stop herself.

'Thing is, Jake, I was on the phone to Em earlier, a couple of hours back. She mentioned Nick was in the shower.'

She left it hanging. Felt him shift slightly, uncomfortable with what she'd laid out there. She lifted her cheek from his shoulder, looking up at him in the half-light, waiting for an answer, getting none. She felt him take another deep breath. Which way would he go? Share or stonewall?

'It's not what you think, Evie,' he said finally.

She pushed up and away, propped up on an elbow, any pretence of sleep gone. 'And what do you think I think?'

'I'm not . . .' he sighed. 'I haven't been, you know, up to no good.'

She reached over, snapped her bedside light on. Looked at him, searched his face for any hint of deceit, but all she saw was worry. A trio of crinkles above his nose where he frowned, his eyes searching hers for a sign she believed him.

She breathed out an exasperated sigh. 'Then what are you up to?'

Watching him chew on his bottom lip, she found herself mirroring the gesture. He sat up now, scooting his back up the headboard, running both hands through his hair. Any other time there'd be a wisecrack from one of them about him auditioning for a shampoo advert or something equally as silly, but not tonight, not now.

'Pittman's about as much use as an ashtray on a motorbike,' he said eventually, a pleading edge to his voice.

'Jake!' she said, louder than she'd intended, but knowing now that best case he was meddling, worst case flirting with professional suicide. 'Milburn will crucify you if he finds out. What were you thinking?'

'What was I thinking?' he said, a little louder now. 'I was thinking he couldn't find his own arse with both hands and a map.'

'And you steaming in is a recipe for success, is it?'

'Tyler knows who did this, Evie. He's protecting them.'

'You don't honestly expect him to give up his own people just because you ask nicely, do you? You can't make him do anything he doesn't want to do.'

'Not first time of asking, no, but everyone's got a breaking point.'

'Will you listen to yourself?' she said, sitting upright, sheet wrapped around and tucked under her arms. 'Breaking point? You're going to break him now? And how are you going to do that on your own, without any help, on a case you shouldn't be within a hundred miles of?'

'This is why I didn't tell you,' he said, reaching over to take her hand. 'I didn't want you to worry.'

'Worry?' she said with a derisive laugh. 'Why would I worry? You're taking time off from chasing some homicidal bloody maniacs to go and rattle the cage of a man with a reputation for swinging a hammer round like he's Thor.'

Jake looked confused. 'Eh? You've lost me.'

'Oh, you didn't know about that?' she said, in full flow now, taking the tiniest bit of pleasure from putting him in his place. 'Where do you think the Triple H name comes from?'

He shrugged, bit of a pout not liking her having the upper hand.

'You haven't even read up on him properly, have you?'

'Not yet, but—'

'But you can't in case Milburn finds out. Triple H. H, H, H.' She popped a finger up for each one, counting them off again as she explained. 'Hard. Hitting. Hammers. That's what he made his name with before he formed his own gang. Used to walk around with one hanging off a belt loop, like a bloody DIY-style gunslinger.'

'You sure he's not just a West Ham fan,' Porter said weakly.

'Jake!' she snapped, saw him blink and flinch at the sharp tone. She pushed up and out of bed, turning back to face him, arms folded across her chest. 'This isn't a bloody joke. You could lose your job if Milburn finds out, or a damn sight worse if you get on the wrong side of Jackson Tyler.'

She paused, studying his face, seeing something there she didn't like. Look of a kid standing next to a smashed lamp.

'What did you do?'

'Nothing really, I just . . .'

'What did you do, Jake?'

'I went to see him, OK? I went to see Tyler.'

'And . . . ?'

'And he wasn't exactly helpful. He wouldn't say if he knew anything, never mind give me a name.'

'And you expected anything different?'

'I just thought—'

'You didn't think though, Jake, did you? I know this must be hard, and I can't begin to imagine where your head must be at right now, but diving in head first isn't going to fix this. You kicking off with Jackson bloody Tyler won't help arrest anyone. You're not avenging Holly this way. You'll end up joining her at this rate. Maybe that's what you want.'

Even as the last five words left her mouth, she knew she'd gone too far. Saw the hurt etched on his face, frown ploughing lines across his forehead.

'Jake,' she started, 'I didn't mean that. I'm sorry, I—'

'That's what you think?' he said, voice low and flat.

'No, I'm just worried about you, that's all.'

'I can take care of myself, Evie.'

'Easier said than done when you're doing this by yourself,' she said. 'Does Nick know?'

He stared a moment, before shaking his head.

She couldn't decide if that was a good thing or not. Styles would have his back no matter what. That was just the kind of bond they had. Whether it was fair on Emma and Hannah to let Nick get mixed up in this was another matter.

'You have to stop, Jake. Let Pittman do his job. How would you feel if somebody was going behind your back, trying to undermine your work?'

'Difference is I know what I'm doing.'

'And so does he, Jake. He's not a bad copper.'

'But he's not a great one either, and this case can't be done half-arsed.'

He lapsed into silence, and she sat there wishing she knew the words to get through to him. He was usually all about the logic, but he was way too close, blind to seeing how that might lead to some bad decisions. Jackson Tyler didn't sound like a wait-for-you-to-throw-the-first-punch kind of guy.

'Why do I get the feeling you're still not telling me everything?' she asked, narrowing her eyes.

He looked for a second like he was weighing something up. 'You'll probably hear about it tomorrow anyway, but there was one more thing.'

He told her about spotting Tyler's men, following them from the hospital, calling in their little delivery service. His story ended with their arrest, but she couldn't escape the feeling this had been a redacted version.

'You can't tell anyone it was me that called it in though,' he said. 'Too many questions.'

'You better hope for your sake they don't try and track down the mystery caller,' she said. 'They ask for any CCTV footage from along that route, are they going to see your car lurking in the background?'

'I was careful,' he said, shaking his head, looking almost hurt that she thought he'd make such a schoolboy error. 'It'd be easier to work my angles if I had somebody to check up on a few bits for me,' he said, giving her a sideways glance.

'Oh no, no, don't you drag me down with you.'

'Thanks for the vote of confidence.'

'This isn't about whether you're a good copper, or whether you can stick up for yourself, Jake. We'll get whoever did this, but it has to be done right.'

'It'd just be some background on Tyler,' he said, 'maybe a few of his guys, information on his operation. Anyone asks, you could just say you were looking into a tip about his drug business.'

'No,' she said, feeling her already paper-thin patience vibrate at breaking point.

Jake sat, sulking for a second like a huffy teenager. 'I thought if anyone would understand, it'd be you,' he said.

'I get why you feel like this, but I also know it's not the way to fix it.'

'You keep on talking about fixing things. How do I fix a dead wife, hmm? Tell me that?'

That stunned her into silence. Kind of proved her fears that he wasn't as healed as he made out. That there was still something, a part of him deep down that had a hairline fracture running through. Invisible, but still there. He jumped up off the bed, paced over to the window, kept his back to her as he spoke.

'I have to do this, Evie. I couldn't live with myself if I didn't try.' He turned now, fixing her with earnest eyes. 'Are you with me, or not?'

It took a lot for a man like Jake to ask for help. She wanted to, more than anything. But what if all she did was help put him in harm's way? Could she live with that? Would she punish herself if anything happened to him, the way he had with Holly?

'Jake.' Her throat felt like it was closing, choked with mixed emotions, letting down the man she loved, not that she'd told him that part yet, or risking both of their jobs, not to mention safety. 'I can't' she said finally, words coming out quiet, timid almost. 'I just can't.'

She saw his face run from disappointment to frustration to hurt. He glanced towards the window, then back at her, looking like a lost child.

'At least I know where I stand then,' he said, bending to pick up his clothes, carrying them out the door, footsteps fading downstairs. She heard the front door close behind him and his car start up. She wanted to run after him, tell him to come back, rewind to before the conversation started, but she stayed where she was, until the soft purr of the engine faded.

She sunk back into the dent on her side of the bed, a hollow, scooped-out feeling in the pit of her stomach. First proper fight they'd had. Just a spat, or a crack that would only get wider?

CHAPTER THIRTY-ONE

It was still dark when Porter slipped out of bed, head fuzzy from a flurry of blurred dreams. To call it a bad night's sleep would suggest there'd been a full night of it. But it couldn't have been more than four hours by the time he'd drifted off, if that. No time to stick the coffee machine on thanks to an early start arranged over text with Styles. Instead, he heaped two spoons of instant into a travel mug, flashes of last night's argument scrolling through his mind.

He felt pretty shitty for storming off home now the dust had settled. He knew she was right, that he should stay clear of Jackson Tyler, Henry Kamau and anything to do with Holly's case. At the same time, he couldn't help himself. The case had its own gravitational pull, dragging him along with it, into it.

Last night's encounter with Tyler and his men had shaken him, but not so much so that he was ready to down tools just yet. More than one way to skin a cat so to speak. If he

183

could bring some heat Tyler's way, to the point where he gave up whoever it was, it didn't have to be direct to Porter. That's what had put him in harm's way last night. Ego. The need to be up close and personal when Tyler cracked. The gang leader knew what they wanted. The right kind of pressure could have his toes curling over the edge of a cliff, ready to talk, but that could just as easily be to Pittman. If it came down to it, Porter could even tolerate the inevitable crowing Pittman would do about how he'd landed a big win. Rather sit on the bench of a winning team than a starting line-up for the losers. Not his usual philosophy, but it would do here.

Quick check of his phone on the way out the door. One text from Evie, timed around half an hour after he'd stormed off.

I'm sorry. This isn't easy for me either. Free tonight to talk it through over a takeaway? x

He started up the car, went to pull away, but thought better of it and fired back an answer.

I'm sorry too. Sounds perfect. Call you later to sort a time x

As much as he would have valued her help, he understood why she couldn't. That's why he hadn't asked her in the first place, same reason he hadn't asked Styles. He didn't want to compromise those he cared about, so by extension, he had no right to bear a grudge if they did the right thing. Easier to say now, not so much in the heat of the moment.

By the time he reached the station to pick Styles up, the combination of caffeine and the blast of fresh air through his window had perked him right up. One thing he hadn't decided yet was whether or not to share his Tyler run-in with Styles, now that Evie knew. Probably should. Evie had gotten closer with the Styleses, Emma in particular in recent months. Wasn't a huge leap to imagine her worry might make her reach out for help in persuading him to step back.

'Morning, boss,' said Styles, sliding into the passenger side, legs long enough they could have been stolen from a giraffe, folding up, knees pressed against the dash.

'You got the address for Kirk?' Porter asked, punching the postcode into the satnav as Styles rattled it off. Elliott Kirk had evaded any attempt at contact so far. Gus Tessier and Dee Williams had turned up both at the school he worked at and his home address yesterday, but no joy. The headmaster at St Aiden's said he'd taken a few personal days, trying to come to terms with Henderson's death. If everything went according to plan, they'd catch him before he had a chance to leave the house. Dee and Gus would be picking up McTeague to bring him in for questioning to time it with Porter getting back to the station. He'd not been at work the previous day when Nick and Kaja paid a visit to the pub, but his boss had assured them he was due in for a shift today.

'Look, mate,' Porter started as they zigzagged through the early morning commuters heading east on the A13. 'Something I should probably tell you, but before I do, you know nothing, right?' Porter glanced way from the road, one eyebrow arched.

'I know less than Jon Snow,' said Styles.

'Who the hell is that?' said Porter.

'Jon Snow? Seriously?'

'Have I arrested him?'

'We playing twenty questions?'

'Look, I'm trying to be serious here,' said Porter, none the wiser, wishing Styles would stop dancing around it.

'Oh, you know how much I love explaining my jokes,' said Styles. 'Really adds a whole other layer of humour to them.

Fine, it's a *Game of Thrones* reference. You really haven't even heard of him? That's the catchphrase – "You know nothing, Jon Snow",' said Styles, voice going up an octave.

'Was that supposed to be a woman saying that?'

'Like you could do a better impression. You don't even know who I'm talking about. Anyway, you were saying?'

Porter gave the slightest of headshakes and started filling Styles in on his extra-curricular activities, even including the second visit to Tyler and the near miss with his two thugs.

'Jesus, boss, you can't go after him on your own.'

'No,' said Porter, stern like a teacher putting a naughty kid in their place. 'You're not helping. Emma would have me hanged, drawn and quartered, and if she didn't, Evie would.'

'Well then, doesn't that tell you something about how bad an idea it is?'

'What would you do, if it was Emma?'

'Whatever it took,' said Styles, no hesitation.

'And there you have it.'

A few seconds of silence, save for fingers drumming on the wheel.

'Let me at least do some digging on Tyler for you, maybe help bounce a few ideas around with you,' said Styles eventually.

Porter knew his DS well enough to know that if he didn't give him something, Styles would start using his own initiative to try and help in some other way. He couldn't have that. Better to steer him in a direction that had as little risk as possible.

'One condition,' he said. 'Information only. You go nowhere near Tyler.'

'Promise,' said Styles.

'I need to know more about his business,' Porter began a download of his idea, such as it was. 'There has to be a sweet spot somewhere, something he's into, that if he loses that, it cripples him, or at least makes life a damn sight harder than it needs to be. Something big enough to drive him into Pittman.'

'I'll see what we've got already, maybe put a few feelers out. I can always say we got an anonymous tip that some Triple H members are linked to the Henderson case if anyone asks. Might not fool Milburn if he caught wind but couldn't prove otherwise.'

'Nick, don't get yourself on his shitlist for me, you hear? If he gets you in a corner, you tell him I made you do it.'

'Snitches get stiches,' said Styles in a poor man's Ray Winstone impression, pulling a thumb across his throat, executioner-style. 'I ain't a grass, copper.'

'See what you can get, but don't push it.'

They tossed ideas around the rest of the journey, pulling up outside Elliott Kirk's house a little after seven.

'You think he's been avoiding us then?' Styles asked as they got out.

'Your guess is as good as mine. I'd have said McTeague was on the level until he popped up on camera, so who knows.'

Kirk peered out through a six-inch gap in the door, chain strung at face height, just the right level to act as a metal moustache on an otherwise youthful face. Sandy hair and freckles. Looked like he and Ross Henderson could be related, cut from the same cloth.

'Mr Kirk?' Porter asked.

Kirk's eyes flitted between them, suspicious, no move to open the door any further.

'DI Porter and DS Styles, sir. We're with the Met. We need to speak to you about Ross Henderson.'

The distrust dropped away with an embarrassed half-smile. Kirk popped the chain off and stepped back, pulling the door open.

'Sorry, it's just that I had reporters round here yesterday. Bastards were camped outside like I was a bloody A-list celebrity. I had to slip out the back just to go to the shops.'

He led them through a narrow corridor, into a poky kitchen. Not a house for the claustrophobic.

'Can I get you a cuppa?'

'All good, thanks,' said Porter, answering for them both. They sat on opposite sides of a table stained with splodges of varying colours. Kirk clearly clocked Porter's glance, launching into an unnecessary explanation.

'I look after my sister's kids sometimes. Both gonna be famous painters when they grow up. Messier the better at that age.'

Far too early for small talk, Porter launched straight in. 'I understand you and Ross Henderson were close, and we're hoping you can fill in some blanks for us.'

'I . . . um . . . yeah, sure. Whatever I can do to help.'

'Thanks. So, we spoke to his parents, and his dad shared some information with us about threats he'd been receiving. Are you aware of those?'

Kirk's gaze drifted down to the table, no surprise registered. Nodded twice.

'What can you tell us about them?' Styles prompted.

'I saw a fair few, but I'm pretty sure there were plenty more he kept to himself.'

'What makes you say that?'

'Stuff he said. Fact that he handled the inbox for the

Stormcloudz website himself. Wouldn't share the password. Said there were plenty of bored white middle-class men with too much free time on their hands, bad enough that it filled it up like spam sometimes.'

'No other reason he wouldn't want you to have access?'

'Not really, no,' said Kirk. 'Apart from the fact he wouldn't tell us the broadcast locations, he was a pretty open book.'

'When you say us, you mean Jason McTeague as well?'

'Yep. The three of us have been doing this for almost four years now.'

'And how would you describe the relationship between the three of you?'

'Relationship? We were mates. I was in the same year at school. Jason was a few years ahead. His brother was in our year though, so I've known him since I was about ten.'

'And you all got on well?'

'Yeah, course we did,' he said, looking puzzled. 'Sorry, but what does this have to do with what happened to him?'

'Just background,' said Styles. 'The better we know someone, the more it helps us sift through what's relevant and what's not.'

'What do you mean "relevant"?' Kirk said. 'How's whether we got on or not relevant to him having his head hacked off by a bunch of bloody terrorists?'

'I know this has been a hard few days for you, Mr Kirk, but—'

'Hard? If by hard you mean worried that they might pay me a visit next, then yeah, it's a bit hard.' Kirk's stress levels were showing.

'What would be really useful,' Porter said in a neutral tone, 'is to just get a sense of how you guys all worked together. Whoever did this to him knew where to find him.

189

There has to be something in what he did, how he did it, that allowed them to do that.'

Kirk leant back in his chair, palms rasping over a Brillo pad's worth of stubble. He looked exhausted, lost, like a man who'd just woken up in a different room to the one in which he closed his eyes.

'Don't know how they could, I honestly don't. He told us nothing. Literally nothing. First we'd know of it was when we saw the streams. Had to be live as well. He wouldn't pre-record. Said it made it more authentic.'

'And there were only the three of you on the project?'

Kirk scoffed. 'Project? A project is a collage you make for GCSE art. People's civil liberties isn't a project, Detective.'

Touched a nerve there, thought Porter.

'Nobody else was involved, then?'

Kirk shook his head.

'And the threats, what can you tell us about those?'

He shrugged. 'Just par for the course these days. There are lots of keyboard warriors out there who'll happily dive onto a Twitter thread with a death threat. Price of doing business online.'

Keyboard warrior. There was that phrase again. Made Porter picture a pasty-faced teenager, huddled over a keyboard in a dark room, streaks of camo paint on his cheeks.

'What about run-ins with the EWP?' Styles prompted.

'Those soulless bastards,' Kirk said, face screwing up like a toddler who'd been asked to eat their vegetables. 'They like to try and flood our comments, start arguments with our fans. If they had their way, we'd have a whitewashed Britain. I'd love to see those twats take a DNA test and see all the random bits pop up. I'd pay for the lot of 'em just to see them top themselves

190

when they find out they've got a couple of per cent from Kenya.'

'Anyone specific?'

Kirk shrugged. 'We used to trace a lot of 'em back through their profiles. There's some worse than most though. Worst one is a guy called Leo Finch. One of Damien Winter's lapdogs. Ross used to do most of his stuff online, but we did a couple of street protests too. Finch turned up at a couple with his boot boys. Didn't get physical. Too many witnesses most likely, but he was up in our faces. One time, he was literally this close.' Kirk held up his thumb and forefinger a few inches apart. 'Leaning right in, whispering something to Ross. I was too far away to hear, but I tell you what, that's the only time I saw Ross shook up. Whatever Finch said put the shits right up him.'

Porter was about to head off on a tangent with his next question, when something fired up a connection. He pulled his phone out, flicking to the copy of Henderson's micro SD card footage he'd saved on there, pausing on a particular frame.

'Don't suppose you recognise any of those faces, do you?'

Kirk's face was the one kids make when the rabbit pops out from the magician's hat. 'That's him,' he pointed at the men flanking Damien Winter. 'His babysitters. This one's Freddie. Freddie Forrester, and that,' he said, leaving his finger pointing at the second face, 'that's Finch.'

CHAPTER THIRTY-TWO

'What do you mean he's gone already?' Porter asked. 'Why did you let him leave?'

'Didn't have much choice, boss,' Tessier said, looking every inch the scolded schoolboy, not a sight you saw often with a man of his size. 'His brief was here by the time we got back. Smarmy little sod, looked like he should still be in school, but McTeague's story checks out so the solicitor started making all sorts of threats if we didn't let him walk.'

'Why was he wandering past a murder scene then?' Styles asked.

Porter didn't bother to correct him. Technically it wasn't a murder scene when he did, but that was just splitting hairs.

'Says he was pitching for work. He's a graphic designer by trade. Only works at the bar cos there hasn't been much work coming his way. Gave us details of a job he was quoting for that day and it checked out. Just a coincidence.'

'You know I hate the C word, Gus.'

'Yeah, I know, but what can you do? We sent a car to the address he gave us. They even still had his business card.'

'You've met him before, Nick, what do you think?'

Styles weighed it up for a few seconds before he answered. 'Do I think he's told us everything, probably not, but him, Kirk and Henderson, they're up in arms against the establishment. Hardly likely to bare their souls. Besides, his story checks out, and we've got bigger fish to fry with Finch and Winter. What time does his thing start?'

'Kicks off at noon.'

'Who's kicking off?'

Porter spun around at the sound of Evie's voice, hating the heat rising to his cheeks.

'Me,' said Styles. 'They've started charging for those sachets of sauce down in the canteen. Disgraceful. Thinking of writing to my MP.'

She gave him her best sarcastic smile. 'You poor baby, Nick. How will you cope?'

'It's Damien Winter,' Porter said, cutting through the flow of banter. 'He's speaking at an EWP rally at lunchtime. Plan is to bring him in for questioning after that.'

'And there was me about to offer to take you for a burger at The Lockhouse, but I can't compete with a wannabe white supremacist.'

Her poker face held for a second longer, then broke into a smile that melted any residual tension away like warm water on an icy windscreen.

'Rain check?' he asked. 'How about we grab a drink after work?'

'I'm sure I could squeeze you in. How about The Green Man?'

Definite peace offering from her. Porter's favourite of the pubs nearby, with an extensive selection of real ales. The very bar he'd stopped off for one in last night with Taylor Bell.

'Oh, boss, did you have a try of that one I told you about?'

Porter hadn't even seen Glenn Waters arrive. Popped up out of nowhere like a bloody genie, and for someone who you normally wished would shut up, had made an uncharacteristically quiet entry.

'One what, Glenn?'

'The ale I mentioned. Haymaker. Best I've found this year so far. Did you try one last night?'

At the mention of his one drink with Bell, Porter felt a tiny prick of guilt. Hated that it felt like a betrayal, when he knew there was nothing in it, not from him and he was pretty sure not from Bell either. All the same, he hadn't mentioned it to Evie, and the thin ice that had reformed over last night's cracks felt like it might be a test too far. Their spat had left him with a pretty clear view of how his choice not to share, even for what he saw as the right reasons, could twist like a tree root, taking on a totally different shape from the one he intended. Evie's eyes had narrowed ever so slightly. Confusion or distrust? Hard to say. No sense in lying, wasn't his style anyway.

'No, Glenn, I'm saving that for when you put your hand in your pocket.'

'What about DI Bell? I reckon she's more the white wine spritzer kind.'

'She'd drink you under the table, Glenn,' said Tessier with a chuckle.

'Sounds like quite the woman,' said Evie. No mistaking the tension in her words now, not for him at least.

'You'd like her,' he said, slipping into damage control, trying to keep any hint of discord from the others, dirty laundry out of sight so to speak. 'We've got her from CTU on the Henderson case.'

'Mmm,' said Evie. 'Well, I'll leave you boys to it.' She turned on her heel, heading back out to the lifts. A call of 'See you when I see you' over her shoulder was all he got. Next chat would be interesting, and not in a good way. He toyed with tearing a strip off Waters for dropping him in it, saw in the young copper's face that he expected something coming his way. What was the point? he thought. He was the one who'd dug this hole. Dug? Who was he kidding? He was still waist-deep holding the shovel.

CHAPTER THIRTY-THREE

From the footage of previous events Porter had seen, these gatherings were never quiet. Plenty on both sides wanted their voices to be heard. This one, it seemed, had been arranged at short notice, presumably because of this week's events, and was an attempt to politicise Henderson's death, use it as a recruiting tool even.

A fine balance, then, between walking in exposed and piling in heavy-handed. There would already be a police presence outside for the expected protest, but last night's run-in with Jackson Tyler had left Porter with the uneasy distrust that people would even move on a copper if they were backed into a tight enough corner.

They'd parked up a few hundred yards down the street. Styles and Bell in with him. Waters, Tessier, Sucheka and Williams in a second car behind. Plan was for Porter to slip into the audience unnoticed to listen to Winter's rhetoric. There were two fire exits and a back door. The other six would split into pairs, marking each door by the end of the event, ready to catch Winter slipping away like he had when Henderson had collared him. The team huddled in the gap between cars for a last-minute check-in.

'Right, you all know where you need to be. Nobody leaves their spot unless I say so. Everybody clear?' he said.

Nodding heads all round. He set off ahead of them, creating a gap wide enough that nobody would think to link them as he approached. Granted there was every chance that all seven of them gave off the scent of a copper like a heavily applied aftershave. Ten minutes until the start, and already there was a healthy counter-gathering out front. Porter guessed at between thirty and forty, herded off to one side by a line of uniformed officers. The protesters were an eclectic mix, young and old, all ethnicities. Home-made placards bounced up and down in time with chants. Some of them crude, one of them with an acrostic EWP down the left – *English Wanker Party* scrolling out to the right. Others more heartfelt, one catching Porter's eye that read *National pride knows no colour*.

A steady stream of attendees filtered in, some shouting back at the anti-EWP chants, but Porter couldn't make out what was said. He tucked in behind a pair of young lads, somewhere in their twenties, checking the officers as he walked past, seeing no familiar faces. Inside, it reminded him of his old school hall. Rows of hard plastic seats designed to guarantee numb cheeks after twenty minutes. Quick guestimate put the count somewhere near two hundred, rows of ten either side of a centre aisle, with an old-fashioned wooden lectern front and centre, raised up a few feet on a boxy platform.

Porter had to pick his way along a row to nab one of the few remaining spaces. Five more minutes and it would be standing room only. A pair of cameras sat on tripods at the front, ready to plaster Winter's face and pipe his words far and wide. Quick scan of the room and it wasn't hard to get a sense of where the core of Winter's following lay. White, working class, forties and above, made up the bulk of the faces.

Porter checked his phone was on silent, seeing texts from the others confirming they were in position, and settled down to wait for the main event. Winter kept them waiting, like the rockstar he probably thought he was, striding out ten minutes later than advertised. Jeans and shirt, no tie, going for the man-of-the-people look. Porter recognised the man he now knew as Finch, as well as minder number two, flanking him either side, scanning the room, playing secret service with earpieces. They, like Winter, had an image they wanted to project, and the crowd lapped it up. Chair legs scraped back, applause, and even a few whistles echoing around the room.

Winter took his place at the podium, Finch and his counterpart standing a few feet to either side, pumped up golems, taking fashion tips from their boss. Nothing relaxed or informal about them though. Pair of them gave off a fizz of energy, waiting for an excuse to spring into action.

Winter held up his hands to dampen the applause. 'Thank you. Thank you.' His smile looked photoshopped from a catalogue, definitely there, but it looked forced to Porter. Like many things about the man, all for show.

'Lovely to see so many of you sacrificing your lunch hours to join us,' Winter said when the clapping had faded. 'And that's a word you're going to hear me talk about a lot today. Sacrifice. Ross Henderson paid the ultimate sacrifice for free speech this week.'

A wave of grumbles, half-whispered comments rippled through the room.

'Make no mistake, he and I weren't friends. When it came to politics, to beliefs, we were chalk and cheese, but that doesn't mean I don't mourn him.'

Winter paused for effect, looking down at non-existent notes, making out that he didn't already know exactly what he wanted to say. He was good in front of an audience, Porter had to give him that.

'I listen to what the fine officers of the Met are saying, that horrific as it was, they have this under control. That those responsible will be brought to justice. That we shouldn't panic. To them and to you I say this: the enemy isn't at the gates.' Another pause. 'The enemy, our enemy, came through those gates a long, long time ago. They're still coming through now, hundreds of thousands every year, and our government doesn't just let them. They hold the gate open, and say have a nice day as they waltz in.'

Another wave of discontent washed across the crowd. The whole thing felt weirdly co-ordinated, timed for effect to keep step with Winter's speech, everyone assigned a role and playing their part. Speaking of which, Porter was conscious he was the only one that was not weighing in with a clap or a comment. Couldn't bring himself to, even though he'd blend in better. He settled for nodding, arms folded, as Winter hit his high points.

'Now, am I suggesting that everyone not one hundred per cent British should pack their bags and be on the next boat out? No, I'm a reasonable man. There's a place for those who follow the rules, who add value to society.'

Undertone being that they should know their place. Winter wasn't stupid. He'd attract a much larger following than if he went full racial purge. This was aiming at a sweet spot, hinting at wanting what was rightfully theirs, playing on a sense of who'd been here first, where their place in the queue should be. Porter wondered if Winter believed his own hype. If he ever stopped to think about what being British truly meant. Conquered by the Vikings, ruled by the Normans, all the richer for the multicultural mix you saw every day in London in his book.

'You get what you vote for,' Winter continued, 'Every illegal who slips past our borders, every so-called refugee who syphons our benefits. Benefits you, and you, and you' – he pointed at faces in the crowd – 'have funded with your taxes. Taxes that should be paying for more police on our streets, more doctors and nurses in our hospitals.' Emphasis on the *our*, a sense of shared ownership, bonding them together.

'And the only people who can change this are the likes of all of you in this room.'

Cheers this time. Shouts of encouragement. Cries of *Spot on* and *Damn right*.

'How do we do that?' he asked, tilting his head as if expecting answers. Porter looked around, a sea of faces hanging on Winter's every word. Grim nods, an energy in the room that you could practically reach out and grab a fistful of. Dangerous in the wrong hands.

'We don't just vote with ballot papers. Why wait two more years for that? We vote with our feet. We vote with our voices. We get out there and show this excuse for a government that they we won't take this lying down. We push back against the dark tide that's flowing in.'

Porter's phone buzzed, a text from Styles.

What a prick.

They must have found the stream and were watching it from outside.

Porter slipped it back in his pocket, not wanting to run the risk of firing one back, exposing his screen for anyone nearby to see.

Winter kept the pace up for another half an hour, and practically every word he uttered made Porter's skin crawl. The guy was basically advocating taking matters into your own hands, without going the whole hog and asking for outright violence. That was the gist of it though. Making people believe that it was their right to act, that they could stop atrocities like Ross Henderson's death by standing up for their country.

London already felt like a tinderbox waiting for someone to drop a match. If even a fraction of those here and everyone watching online answered this call to arms, the few incidents Porter knew about so far would be eclipsed by a bonfire big enough to be seen from space.

Winter was drawing to a close now. 'I can't tell you how much I appreciate the show of support. I'm going to let you all head off for a bite to eat now, but I'll leave you with this.'

One final pause, hands gripping either side of the lectern. A preacher delivering his sermon.

'In the words of our greatest playwright, William Shakespeare, once more unto the breach, dear friends, once more. Each and every one of you has a part to play in fixing this, and don't let anyone in Westminster tell you different. If any party leaders are brave enough to call for a vote of no confidence in the PM, I for one would throw my weight behind them. I'm talking to the likes of you, Sally Ashbrooke, and you, Marcus Davidson, leader of the so-called opposition. My door is open to anyone brave enough to step through it.'

Winter stepped back from the lectern as the room erupted. It had been loud enough when he'd walked in, some even shouting for more, like it was a gig, and he'd run back out with the band and play an extra set. The two minders tucked in either side as Winter strode down the centre of the room. Rows of faces turned as he passed, like a congregation at a wedding watching the happy couple breeze past.

Winter could easily have snuck out through one of the side doors, but he, and his organisation, needed coverage like oxygen. He'd want his moment on the steps. Once he was out there, it would be harder to control the conversation. Two sets of opposing views, his loyal followers in here, die-hard protesters outside. Better to have a word inside, even with a throng of Winter supporters keen to get back to work, lunch or whatever else they had on; the more appealing of two crappy options. No guarantees that Winter would come back to the station with them willingly on the spot. Worst case they'd have to arrange a time for him to call in.

Porter had taken up residence in the second row from the back, bang in the middle, and started pushing his way past those to his right. He figured best to exit to the side and circle around, catch Winter in the reception area, rather than step out, centre aisle like a one-man roadblock. Looked like he'd timed it well, Winter was midway through the crowd, as Porter walked around, behind the back row. All going according to plan. Until it wasn't.

CHAPTER THIRTY-FOUR

Porter heard the man coming before he actually saw him. His attention was fixed on Winter, visible from the head up between his standing supporters. Shouts from somewhere in reception, the words lost in a barrage of noise, chanting from outside dominating the soundtrack now. Doors must be open. A figure burst through the doorway, moving fast, jeans and jumper, too quick to make out a face. Looked like one of the home-made signs, nailed to a two-by-four, raking the floor where he dragged it behind him.

Winter's face was framed between two rows, beginnings of surprise on his face, jaw changing from slack confusion to disbelief. Porter charged along the remainder of the row, shouting to be heard above the noise.

'Police, out the way. Move! Move!'

He rounded the last seat, cornering like a ten-year-old Ford Fiesta in need of a MOT, catching a foot against a metal chair leg and stumbling against an outstretched arm that came from nowhere, like a clothes line. Twenty feet away, minder number two was manhandling a scruffy-looking man to the floor, egged on by the crowd, several of which had jumped into the aisle to help.

Over the melee, Winter was being guided away by Finch, a slight stoop in his gait as if expecting something launched their way. Porter fished his radio out as he shouldered his way into the growing throng, seeing a kick connect with the man on the floor, but unable to see the boots' owner for the other bodies.

'Winter's heading for the back,' he barked into the radio, no time for preamble, and to the crowd, 'Police, back in your seats. Step back, now!'

His voice must have carried. Finch glanced over his shoulder, met Porter's eye, face as sour as spoilt milk. No question of following them, not with the lynch mob kicking seven bells out of the guy on the floor. He'd have to hope the others would collar Winter on his way out. Both Finch and Winter disappeared from his view as he shoe-horned his way between two more bodies, clamping a hand on the minder's shoulder, where he knelt on top of the protestor.

Fresh shouts from behind him, back towards the door. He twisted around to look, even as he identified himself again.

'Police, back off. Hands off him. I've got this.'

A second figure had raced through the door, several crowd members at the back alert to the new threat. Those further forward sensed it, surged in a wave that caught Porter, bearing him down. Through a tangle of legs, a flash of high-vis yellow, cavalry arriving. Something solid connected with his temple, fireflies bursting across his vision, dragging him down, down.

CHAPTER THIRTY-FIVE

A buzzing filled Porter's head, white noise, expanding, filling every corner of his world, like tinnitus on an Olympic level. He had fallen sideways, the upper half of his body now in one of the rows. Pushing up on one arm, he saw people scattering in every direction. Strands of sound started to separate out. Shouts from somewhere in the room. A flash of colour to his left, neon yellow. The officers from outside. His head clearing fast, vision un-fogging like a windscreen, he pulled himself up against a seat. He saw the man still pinned to the floor by Winter's hired help, the minder slipping in sly blows to the trapped man's ribs.

'Get off him,' he said, feeling the steadiness flood back into his legs. 'Police, I said off him now.'

The minder looked up, sneered, held Porter's eye as he hammered home another punch. Porter took a step towards him but jerked back into the row as two uniformed officers burst past, grabbing an arm each, hauling the minder off his victim.

Quick sweep of the room, and most of it had cleared now. Porter slipped his warrant card from his jacket and showed it to another pair of uniforms who came down the aisle towards him.

'DI Porter, where's Damien Winter?'

Split-second cynicism as they clocked the ID. 'Haven't seen him, sir. Didn't go out front, I know that much.'

Porter left them to it, trotting past the protestor, complaining of police brutality as his hands were cuffed, even though they'd saved him from a far worse beating. The minder might as well have had 'bully' tattooed on his forehead. The kind of guy who pulled wings off flies as a kid.

'Tell me someone has him,' he barked into the radio.

Styles's voice crackled back. 'Rear left fire exit, boss. Everything OK in there?'

'Never better,' said Porter, grimly.

He pushed the bar down on the door and winced as he stepped out, sunlight hitting him like a flashbulb. A quick press against his temple and a lance of pain shot through him, edges blurring for a fraction of a second. Not quite one hundred per cent back online yet.

'Boss, over here.'

Styles's voice came from the other side of the door, and Porter stepped out, letting it swing closed behind him, to see Winter and Finch, Styles and Bell on one side, Sucheka on the other. Finch was face to the wall, one arm wrenched up behind his back courtesy of Tessier. Finch might look like he lived in a gym, shirt like a second skin over his biceps, but he might as well be a skinny kid who'd never been in the same room as a dumbbell with the ease with which Gus held him there.

'Ridiculous,' Winter said. 'Those idiots attack us, and you're out here pushing us around instead of locking them up.'

A sheen of sweat glistened on Winter's forehead, not quite as composed as he had been two minutes ago. Porter raised his eyebrows at Tessier.

'Gus?'

'He tried to swing for me, boss.'

'Tried being the operative word,' said Bell, fighting back a smile. 'Looked like he was trying to swat a fly.'

'You let go of me, and we'll see just how hard I can swat. Knock you back to your own bloody country,' Finch snarled through lips smushed against brick.

Tessier gave Porter a look that said he'd be game for that, but Porter ignored it.

'We're not here for you, Finch. We're here for your boss.'

As he said it, he saw an ugly expression ripple across Winter's face, one of a man constantly looking down his nose at others. 'And since when is exercising your right to free speech a crime?'

'When what comes out is as bad as yours, I'd say all day, every day,' said Styles.

Winter fixed him with a cold, unblinking stare, like he was something to be studied.

'Your winning personality gets you through though, I'm sure,' said Styles.

'Sorry, I didn't catch your name, Constable . . .'

'Detective Sergeant Styles' he said, enunciating the first two words to hammer them home.

'So that affirmative action stuff really works then? Good for you, both of you,' he said, inclining his head towards Tessier as well.

'About as well as the Hitler Youth programme has for you,' Styles said, deadpan.

Porter caught Winter's micro expression. Slitted eyes, clenched jaw. Nick had made an enemy here for sure.

'Enough of the small talk,' he said, cutting across the pair of them. 'Mr Winter, this isn't to do with your little get-together in there. We need to talk to you about Ross Henderson. You too, Mr Finch, isn't it?'

Finch looked surprised at the mention of his name.

'What about him?'

'Not really a street corner kind of conversation,' said Porter, seeing Waters and Williams appear around the corner, beckoning them to join the party. 'If you've got no lunch plans, you can join us at Paddington Green.'

'Afraid I've got places to go, people to see. Some other time perhaps,' said Winter, nice as pie, like Porter had invited him around for dinner and drinks.

'Up to you, but it's going to happen sometime in the next twenty-four hours whether you like it or not,' Porter chanced his luck, no way to force him in such a short timeframe. 'Either way, we'll keep hold of Mr Finch here. DC Tessier looks a little shaken by the attempted assault. We need to speak to him about Mr Henderson as well, so you can have him back when we're done with him.' He paused, enjoying the silent anger radiating from Finch, but especially the realisation from Winter that he wasn't the alpha here, not now at least.

'Fine, but you might as well have a revolving door on there, for how long my solicitor is going to let you keep me.'

'You see, mate,' Styles said, leaning in, as if sharing a secret with Finch, 'you soon learn who your friends are. He's watching his own back already. I've put away a few over the years that are gonna love you when you're inside.'

Finch tried to twist around, but Tessier's grip was a vice only a few could break, and he wasn't one of them.

'They want a reaction, Leo. Don't give them the satisfaction. I'll take care of everything.'

'You take care of Ross Henderson?' Bell asked, stepping forward, two feet away from Winter now. 'Or you have one of your Gestapo like Finch here handle it?'

Winter didn't rise to the bait, just slipped his phone out and started scrolling through his contacts, looking for his solicitor presumably.

'No need for a brief if you've got nothing to hide, Damien,' said Bell, feeling around for which buttons to push. 'You don't mind if I call you Damien, do you? Loved *The Omen*. Great film.'

As much as Porter was sure Winter's brief would have something to say about this kind of needling, he sensed where she was going. Men like Finch in particular, those with fuses shorter than the seven dwarves, could be herded into a corner, prodded until they bit, overshared in anger. Winter looked a little too composed to fall for it, but it was worth a try.

'Yes, hello, can you put me through to Gene Rafferty, please? It's Damien Winter.'

Porter recognised the name. Rafferty was the marginally less obnoxious half of Rafferty and Nath, a firm renowned for representing some of the most polarising public figures to grace the red top gossip columns.

'Boss, you got a sec?' It was Dee Williams, she and Glenn Waters having finally caught up.

'What is it, Dee?'

She was a little out of breath from trotting around from the other side of the building, but Porter's eyes widened as he took in what she had to say.

'Right,' said Winter, ending his call. 'He's on his way. Let's get this over with, shall we?'

'Don't think it's going to be quite as quick as you think, Mr Winter. You might want to cancel any afternoon plans as well.'

'And why would I do that?' Winter said, dripping with contempt now he had the cavalry on the way.

'Because, Damien Winter, you are under arrest for conspiracy to murder Ross Henderson.'

Porter rattled through the rest of his rights, motioning for Tessier to take Finch, and Styles to escort Winter back to the cars.

'What the hell just happened?' Bell asked, as Porter ran a hand through his hair, wincing as the pain flared back up from his forgotten blow to the head.

'Dee got a call just as all hell was breaking loose in there. Apparently, we've got him on tape agreeing the hit on Henderson.'

CHAPTER THIRTY-SIX

'No,' said Bell, drawing the vowel out for a three count, sounding almost disappointed. 'Who'd he ask to do it?'

'No idea yet. Seems we got it via email. Audio file of a call, don't know who else was on with him. That new lad – what's his name? One that looks like Harry Potter – he listened to it and called Dee.'

Porter kept his voice low as they trailed six feet behind the others, not wanting to tip his hand to Winter just yet. He needed to listen to the file first. Arresting Winter had been an in-the-moment call. Could have still taken him in, checked the audio and arrested him after it was all out on the table. It had been the comment to Nick that tipped it though. Casual racism, passing as polite conversation, and Porter knew from Winter's reputation that there was nothing casual about his beliefs. To hell with him. Milburn wouldn't be happy about not being looped in before the arrest was made, but bollocks to bureaucracy and the bullshit that came with it. Besides, it had felt good.

'Calls for a celebration then,' said Bell. 'Same time, same place, my round.'

'I, um, I don't think I can tonight,' he said, flashing back to Evie's reaction earlier. Bridges to build.

'Your loss,' she shrugged. 'You change your mind, you let me know.'

He looked across at her, trying to read her, but was none the wiser. What did it matter whether it was just a friendly drink or not? Wasn't like him to overthink, but regardless, he had some making up to do with Evie.

When they reached the front corner of the building, Porter saw several handcuffed men being loaded into a van. Hard to tell which side of the fence they'd been on. He could see their unmarked cars where they'd left them parked up. Ahead, Winter was still arguing the toss with Styles. Porter caught the odd word, Winter trying to figure out what they had, what had changed things back there.

A muted rapid-fire sound reached his ears at the same time he heard footsteps. Three people, all press, converged on them. The photographer, snapping off shots, camera clicking like a Geiger counter. Following close behind, an all-too-familiar face.

'Detective Porter, Amy Fitzwilliam, Sky News. What can you tell us about the men you've arrested? Are they protestors, or . . . ?' She tailed off, expression freeze-framing for a split second as she processed who it was being led away.

'Is Damien Winter under arrest, and if so, can you tell us what for?'

'Jesus,' Porter muttered under his breath, before turning, giving her a polite smile and a bland answer.

'We can't comment at this stage. Excuse me, step back, please,' he said as her own cameraman edged closer, positioning himself ahead of Porter but walking backwards, then panning forward to catch a shot of Winter.

'Have you made any progress on the Ross Henderson case, Detective? Is this linked in any way?'

Winter, ever the one to seize an opportunity, twisted around, calling over his shoulder. 'People dying on our streets, terrorists free to come and go as they please, and I'm the one they arrest? Speaks volumes as to this government's priorities.'

What a load of crap, thought Porter. As if the Prime Minister had called in a favour from him, asked him to pick on Winter. There may well be politics at play, but this arrest was anything but politically motivated.

'Please, Ms Fitzwilliam, any more questions, you can ask them at the next press conference,' said Porter, holding his arms out to the sides, trying to shepherd them away, or better still, stop them in their tracks entirely.

'Next conference?' she said, eyes lighting up at a loose thread to pull on. 'So, it is linked then?'

Porter clenched and unclenched his jaw, said nothing,

'Doesn't pay to make assumptions, Ms Fitzwilliam,' Bell chimed in. 'I'd stick to facts, and if it's facts you're after, there have been a number of arrests after a disturbance at an EWP rally today. That's all we can say at the moment.'

Fitzwilliam raised one eyebrow. 'And you are?'

'Leaving,' said Bell, tapping Porter on the shoulder as she walked past. Fitzwilliam stayed where she was, for now at least.

'I owe you. Nicely done,' he muttered as they jogged to catch up with the others, practically at the cars now. Milburn

213

would shit a brick when that aired, regardless of how little he'd actually given away. 'Made it sound like we'd been called out for that, instead of just being here for him.'

'Not just a pretty face,' she said. 'Does that mean I get to sit in on Winter then?'

Porter considered it, whether Styles would have an issue missing out. Then again, he may well prefer to play some more with Finch.

'All right then, you're on.'

By the time they got back to the station, Porter had the bones of an interview mapped out in his mind. Of course, a plan rarely survived intact by the time you finished these things. Winter's solicitor, Gene Rafferty, was waiting there for them when they arrived. A nervous man, he looked like an owl, behind thick-rimmed glasses and hair that couldn't have had more than a passing acquaintance with a brush for a few weeks at least. He was softly spoken but Porter got the impression that in itself was one of his weapons. Rafferty asked for some time with his client, and they were ushered into interview room four.

Porter tracked down his Harry Potter lookalike, Alistair Hobson, a young PC who'd only been on the job a few months. Hobson pulled out a spare chair and offered Porter his headphones. He clicked play and settled into his seat as the ringing began. The first voice he heard gave nothing away with a barked one-word answer.

'Hello?'

'Damien Winter?' When the second person spoke, it was metallic, words twisted together by some kind of voice changer.

A few seconds' pause.

'Yes?' he asked, low, bordering on a whisper.

'Ross Henderson has footage of you threatening his life, few months back. You and Leo Finch. He's also got proof of who did the delivery driver, and he knows all about your trips to Peterborough.'

'That right?'

'Yes. If you wanted to talk to him about it, he'll be doing one of his live events on Sunday, alone, somewhere quiet.'

Three seconds of static.

'If you wanted to have a chat with him about it, I could tell you where to find him.'

More silence.

'Somewhere nice and quiet,' the voice echoed.

'I'm listening.'

'Old Greenwich Magistrates' Court. Sunday at noon.'

'Why? What's your angle?'

Static. Shallow breathing. A sigh. 'Peace and quiet. You'll do it then?'

'I'll take care of it,' came the reply.

Porter stood up as the call ended. 'Who sent it in?'

'Just some Gmail address, no name attached. I tried replying to them, asking where they got it from,' said Hobson, eager to please. 'They haven't replied yet.'

'Nor will they,' said Porter. 'Bit pointless using an anonymous email address if you're going to write back and spill the full story like a Bond villain.'

'You think they used it just for this then?'

Porter leant back towards the screen. 'I'd say so, unless their parents were cruel enough to christen them *helpful2020@ gmail.com*.' Hobson blushed. 'I'm just messing with you. Let me know if you get anything back, and do me a favour, ask someone in tech to take a look at the file, see if there's anything to learn from that,' he added, more to throw the lad a bone.

Porter forwarded a copy to his own email address, then headed back to where Styles and Bell stood chatting outside the interview room that Winter and his solicitor occupied.

'Any good?' Styles asked.

'Mmm. Not as smoking a gun as I'd hoped. Quality's not great either. He's practically whispering all the way through.'

He summed up the call for them, feeling a niggle working its way deep, something about it felt out of sync, sticking against edges of his thoughts like a door against a warped frame.

'Question is then,' said Bell, as if she was reading his mind, 'if Winter was the nail, who was the hammer? Who wanted him dead? Who made the call?'

Jackson Tyler flashed to mind. Triple H. Hard. Hitting. Hammers. He huffed out a loud breath blowing away any Holly-related cobwebs, for now at least.

'Apart from every member of the EWP?'

'If we're lucky we might get something from the email address, or even the audio file,' said Styles.

Before Porter could answer, the door to his left opened, Gene Rafferty peering out.

'Ready when you are, Detective,' he said. Couldn't have sounded more impatient if he had a plane to catch. Didn't even wait for a response, ducking back out of sight as quickly as he'd appeared.

Porter turned to Bell. 'You want a listen before you head in?'

'The call? Yeah, go on then.'

He passed her his phone, grabbing the door handle as she listened, making sure Rafferty couldn't pop back out and eavesdrop. Porter wanted the first time either client or brief heard it to be in there, on the spot. Wanted to watch Winter's reaction. Whole thing took a minute, give or take. He watched as she listened, saw the same uncertainty on her face as he had felt himself.

'Lead the way,' she said, nodding at the door.

'Finch is next door with one of Rafferty's lackeys,' Porter said to Styles. 'Play it for him as well. Should be in your inbox now.'

Styles nodded, disappearing through the neighbouring door.

'Right, let's do this,' said Porter, holding the door open for Bell.

Rafferty and Winter were huddled on the far side of the table, but conversation stopped like an old Wild West saloon. Porter ran through the formalities and started the recording.

'How would you describe your relationship with Ross Henderson, Mr Winter?'

'Relationship?' Winter chuckled. 'Makes it sound like I used to wine and dine him.'

'Longer you dance around it, the longer we sit here,' Bell said, clearly in no mood to mess around.

'In that case, let's just say we had differing views on what's wrong with the world.'

'You hold some pretty strong views, don't you, Mr Winter?'

'Can I ask what relevance my client's views, political or otherwise, has to the charges, Detective Porter?' Rafferty asked, somehow managing to make a basic question sound like he was questioning Porter's intelligence.

'Goes to potential motivation for seeing any harm come to Mr Henderson,' Porter answered with a curt nod. 'How many times did you meet Mr Henderson face-to-face?'

'On purpose? Never,' Winter scoffed. 'Turned up at a few of my events, trying to disrupt things.'

'Any of those occasions get heated?'

'Define heated.'

'You don't deny that you met then? Good, we'll let's say heated would be anything from cross words to a punch in the face.'

'I'm not going to pretend I liked him, but I've never laid a finger on him.'

'How about someone else's finger?' Bell asked.

Rafferty rested a hand on Winter's arm. 'Detectives, if it's all the same, rather than dance around this, can I suggest we stick with more direct questions, or we'll be here all day?'

Porter resisted the urge to tell Rafferty where to shove his suggestion, opting for a polite politician's smile that Milburn would be proud of.

'OK then, direct it is. Did you, or did you not, threaten Ross Henderson's life outside one of your events at a community centre in Enfield a few months back?'

Winter opened his mouth to answer, but Rafferty leant in, whispering into his ear.

'It's fine, Gene,' said Winter, squaring his shoulders, seeming to fill out, puffing up for effect. 'Yes, we've had cross words in the past. He was spreading lies about me and my people, but that's it. Why the hell you think I would have anything to do with this is ridiculous.'

'For the benefit of the recording, I'm showing Mr Winter the video obtained yesterday in a search of Mr Henderson's home.'

Porter hit play on the tablet he'd brought with him, spun it round and slid it across the table. Curiosity on Winter's face turned to dread, knowing what was coming next, not being able to stop or change it.

You're gonna find yourself taking a long walk off a short pier.

Winter's expression soured, as if the sound of his own voice repulsed him. 'I didn't . . . I mean that's just . . . just me trying to tell him to mind his own business.'

'Really?' Bell said. 'Because if that's the case, then I'd have expected you to say mind your own business, Ross, not threaten to kill him.'

'I didn't bloody kill him, all right.'

'Glad we agree on one thing then,' said Porter, reaching out, spinning the tablet back around, leaving both Winter and Rafferty looking as confused as if he'd just given them a piece of paper with PTO on both sides.

'For the benefit of the recording, I'm now playing the audio file of a call between Damien Winter and an unnamed individual.'

No waiting for Rafferty to interject with a question. The audio filled the room, pauses between sentences feeling oppressive, weighted by the decisions being made. Winter started muttering under his breath, too low to hear, brow pinched like folded fabric. He turned to Rafferty, speaking louder this time.

'Not me.' A shake of the head. 'That's not me.' He hammered home each word on the table with his index finger. 'This is a set-up, that's what this is. A bloody set-up.'

'Who's the other voice on the call, Damien? Who were you talking to?'

No answer. Another whisper from Rafferty to Winter, more urgent this time, almost audible.

'You said you'd take care of it, Mr Winter. What exactly are you referring to?'

'I wasn't referring to anything cos that isn't my bloody voice on that tape.'

'Detective,' Rafferty cut in, finding his voice again, 'we'll need to know the source of this information and access to the originals to conduct our own analysis. These things can be faked with an app on your phone these days. This is just as likely to be a forgery to implicate my client. The sound quality on that recording in particular is subpar, most of it is practically whispers. Really, if that's all you've got, then this is tenuous at best.'

'You call a death threat on video and a corroborating phone call tenuous, Mr Rafferty?'

The solicitor puffed out his cheeks, making a show of it. 'You might not, Detective, but I'll be surprised if the Crown Prosecution Service don't side with me. Until any of this is verified, that won't be enough for you to charge my client and I think you know that.'

There was a knock at the door before Porter could reply. He gave a painful smile. *This better be bloody good*, he thought. Nothing worse in an interview than having someone barge in when things were heating up. Threw the rhythm right off. Great for a solicitor, pain in the arse for the interviewer.

'I'll go,' said Bell. 'You stay and crack on.'

Porter nodded his thanks, announcing her departure for the recording.

She got up and opened the door, and Porter saw Hobson in the corridor, wide-eyed excitement hard to miss.

'Sorry to interrupt, ma'am. Have you got a minute?'

Bell slipped outside, letting the door click behind her. Porter looked across the table. Winter looked shell-shocked. Either he was putting on a great front or this genuinely had caught him off-guard.

'All I know,' said Porter, picking up where he'd left off, 'is

220

that your client had motive and was gifted an opportunity by some deep-throat wannabe. He's admitted the threats are part of genuine footage. Violence seems to follow you around, doesn't it, Mr Winter?'

'What's that's supposed to mean?' Winter sounded indignant.

'The delivery driver Henderson referred to in that footage, the one he alleged your men put in hospital. Two EWP members are currently awaiting trial for it.'

'And my client has already gone on record in that matter, confirming they acted independent of the party, and that he did not endorse their choice to take things as far as they did.'

'But you did endorse them verbally abusing the man, isn't that right?'

'We're not going to be commenting on an ongoing case, Detective,' said Rafferty, 'and quite frankly I still don't see the foundations for a strong evidential case, unless there's something fairly significant you haven't shared. Is this your roundabout way of saying that you don't believe the death of Mr Henderson to be a terrorist attack?'

This was a question Porter had hoped Rafferty wouldn't throw his way. They were on the record, an answer confirming that could have a ripple effect. Deny it, and it weakened the very reason they'd dragged Winter in here. The door opened and Taylor Bell came back in, sheaf of papers held against her chest. She peeled them off, showing the contents to Porter. He couldn't hide the smile this time. *Gotcha.*

CHAPTER THIRTY-SEVEN

Porter reread the printout Bell had handed him, making sure he hadn't misunderstood. He peeled off a copy and handed it across the table.

'Now sharing a preliminary report on the audio file,' said Porter. You had to hand it to Hobson, he worked quickly and came up with the goods. 'You'll see from the underlined sections that in addition to a source providing this file, they've since replied with additional information.'

'Do you recognise this landline number, Mr Winter?' said Porter, rattling off the digits.

'This a trick question?' Winter screwed his face up.

'No tricks, just one that needs answering,' said Bell.

'Well,' Porter asked, 'does it sound familiar?'

More shakes of the head, so slight they could pass as a muscular twitch. 'It's my number at the office.'

'The office being the EWP main London location?'

'Yes.'

'And whereabouts in the building is the actual phone?'

'In my office.'

'Anyone else have access to it?'

Winter shook his head. 'It's locked when I'm not around.'

'That's a no then?'

'No.'

'What about this number?' Porter recited a second one.

'No idea.'

'What if I was to tell you that this is the number that made the call to your office, the call we listened to the audio of a few minutes back?'

'I'd tell you that you can say that all you like. Still doesn't make that me on the call.'

'What if I was also to tell you that we've been able to verify that a call was made between those two numbers on Thursday, three days before Ross Henderson was killed?'

'My client has already stated several times that he is not one of the voices on that recording, Detective.'

'True,' said Porter, frowning as if that had derailed his train of thought. 'Here's the thing though, your client also told us that the phone is in a private room, one he keeps locked when he's not there, and that nobody else has access to that phone.'

Winter's face dropped like a man who'd just heard rifles cock on the firing squad.

'S-someone must have broken in,' he stammered, usual composure long gone. 'Snuck in when I wasn't looking.'

'Snuck in to take a call they weren't expecting, from a person they didn't know?' Bell asked. Winter's face was a picture. Porter suspected that Winter lost for words wasn't something you saw every day.

'I think we're at a bit of an impasse here, Detective. If you were going to charge my client, I suspect you'd be doing it around about now. This is—'

Winter shot up straight in his chair, like somebody had just plugged him back in.

'Wait, that call, you said the Thursday before he died. What time?'

'Why do you ask?' said Bell.

'What time was the bloody call?'

Porter checked the notes. 'Came in at two thirty-two, lasted for sixty-four seconds.'

Winter's confidence was back, wicked smile curling up at the edges, a bully about to kick over a sandcastle. He nodded, savouring whatever he was about to share for a second more.

'Three days before Ross Henderson died, I wasn't even in London, never mind my office. I was in York and I can prove it.'

SKY NEWS BULLETIN

Tuesday evening

'Hello, I'm Asim Bashara, and here are your headlines this evening. Tension mounts in the capital as police make multiple arrests in clashes between the English Welfare Party and a number of locals at multiple mosques across the city. The EWP have been out in force following Sunday's brutal slaying live on Facebook, of activist and vlogger, Ross Henderson, also known as Stormcloudz. With me now in the studio is British Independence Party leader Sally Ashbrooke. Mrs Ashbrooke, you met with the Prime Minister and the leader of the Labour Party, Marcus Davidson, earlier to discuss how to tackle what are becoming borderline riots in some areas. Shops have been trashed, buildings set alight. We've had reports of a mosque in Wood Green being the subject of attempted arson. What do you say to people out there who are taking matters into their own hands?'

'I'd say I feel their fear and I feel their pain, but we need cooler heads to prevail. We need to find those men who killed Ross Henderson and bring them to justice. Then, after that, we can put the rest of our house in order.'

'Damien Winter, head of the EWP, made a speech earlier today where he called for a vote of no confidence in the Prime Minister and said he'd throw his lot in with anyone who would challenge the government on their immigration policies. Is that something you'll take him up on?'

'Look, Asim, I'm all for open debate, but the EWP are a little too far to the right for my tastes. I thank Mr Winter for his offer of support, but I'd need to see some tempering of views before I'd have a serious conversation with him, and I think we both know that isn't likely to happen. At the same time though, the Prime Minister's views are not strong enough. He's condemned the Brotherhood in Parliament, and on Twitter, but where is the decisive action? Where is the personal leadership needed to reassure Londoners that this will not happen again on his watch? When will he put his money where his mouth is and throw the time and resources needed at fixing the unchecked, unvetted flow of illegal immigrants into our country? The people won't stand for this much longer, I can assure you. The tidal wave of public opinion will wash this government away within a year, you mark my words.'

'If you were in his shoes, how would you put your money where your mouth was?'

'I've already shared my proposals in an open letter to the Prime Minister, but as far as money goes, I'll do one better. The *Daily Mail* has offered a reward of fifty thousand pounds for information leading to the capture of these men. I've been approached by a long-time party supporter, who has asked to remain anonymous. They have offered to add the same again, to help bring these men to justice.'

'Another fifty? That's a very generous offer indeed!'

'It certainly is. Someone out there knows something, and if this helps to persuade them to come forward for the good of the country, to help us move past this and heal, then I'd say that feels like money well spent.'

'You heard it first here, folks, the reward is now standing at an even one hundred thousand pounds.'

CHAPTER THIRTY-EIGHT

'A phrase involving a piss up and a brewery comes to mind,' said Milburn, looking between Porter and Bell like an old-school headmaster deciding who to cane first. The super wore a line in the carpet, pacing behind his desk.

'Bad enough he and his brief make you look like a fool, waltzing out of here smiling like they'd just won the police raffle. Now I've had Sky bloody News on the phone, asking for a comment on his arrest and links to the Henderson case, which we now know is about as shaky as an alcoholic trying to go cold turkey.'

Milburn paused, and Porter could swear it was purely to appreciate his own little turn of phrase.

'Three television vans outside already, door-stepping anyone that looks even vaguely like a copper for a quote. Winter threatening to sue for wrongful arrest. You couldn't pick a low-profile case to screw up on, could you?'

'With respect, sir,' said Bell, 'We only got the extra info on the call once we were already in the room with him. It was a fair call to make at the time. I'd have done the same thing.'

'And you'd have jumped the gun as well,' said Milburn. 'You could have brought him in for an interview under caution without an arrest. You could have chosen somewhere less public to approach him than one of his bloody rallies. You could have even held off questioning him about the audio file until you'd done your due diligence.'

Milburn counted each smackdown out on his fingers. Nice that Bell had tried to stick up for him, but he could have told her it would fall on deaf ears. Much as he hated to admit it, Porter knew there was a grain of truth in Milburn's words. He'd let himself get too invested in putting a bigot like Winter in his place. The way he'd spoken to that crowd, to Styles even, had left him with an urge to score points. Couldn't blame Hobson either. As the more senior officer, Porter should have seen the risks, taken a step back. Too late now.

'What about his man, Finch?'

Finch had been an arrogant bastard. Sat there and grinned his way at Styles through a barrage of *No comments*. Left the room with the same smile fixed on his face, like the Joker from Batman.

'Gave us nothing, sir. Barely spoke,' said Porter.

'Think it's best if the pair of you steer clear of the next press briefing,' said Milburn, grabbing his jacket from the back of his seat. 'I'll take care of that woman from Sky. You,' he said, pointing at Porter, 'try not to waltz around in front of her camera too much more. And you, DI Bell, I expected a little more from you, what with your reputation. Until we have proof that this wasn't an act of terror, I expect that to still be a line of enquiry. Understood?'

'Sir.' She nodded in acknowledgement.

They left him struggling to get into a jacket that probably fit him three stone ago and made their way back to Porter's desk.

'I expected more from you,' she said, aping Milburn, amping up the pomposity levels. 'Jesus, is he always that big a prick?'

'You caught him on a good day there to be fair.'

Styles and Tessier were dissecting the day when Porter and Bell arrived. Styles glanced at Bell, picking up on the cloud of irritation still hanging over her.

'Guessing you've been Rogered?'

'Excuse me?' she said, not sure how to take that.

'Rogered. Roger Milburn. As in had the pleasure of seeing what a nob he can be first-hand.'

She shook her head. 'He even has his own verb? Yes, in that case I have, and yes, he's a nob.'

'She can stay,' said Tessier.

Porter filled them in, recapping a second time for Sucheka, Waters and Williams who joined halfway through.

'Where does that leave us now then, boss?'

Porter had been asking himself this since Winter sauntered out of the interview room.

'That bloody reward they're offering isn't going to help for starters. We'll have the usual tidal wave of calls that have us running around like headless chickens. I can't see any of Winter's people giving him up, even for an easy payday. All a bit too fanatical for that, so we're just going to have to pin him down the old-fashioned way. We know part of Winter's York story checks out. He showed us his e-tickets. Doesn't mean he got on the train though, but we should be able to get eyes on him at King's Cross if he's above board.'

'We know the call happened as well,' Styles chipped in. 'Could be the audio file isn't kosher though. What if someone made a call, then recorded that conversation to match the length?'

'No way to verify the content,' said Sucheka, 'but someone answered that line.'

'Can't see Winter airing his dirty laundry in public,' said Bell. 'He knows someone on his side is involved, maybe not how deep, but if I was him, I'd be looking for whoever answered that call and asking some pretty direct questions.'

'Or get Finch to do it for him?' Waters chipped in.

'Agreed, he's probably more likely to start advocating for open borders than he is to help us now,' Porter said, 'but we need to ask, whether it's the man himself or just his minions. Taylor, I want you to be blunt with us,' Porter said, turning his attention to her. 'Are we leaving ourselves open by sidelining the terror angle altogether?'

She shrugged. 'I get why your gaffer is nervous. He'd be the one facing the mob with torches and pitchforks if it went that way and we'd been blind to it.'

'But?' he prompted, pretty sure he'd read the subtext.

'I told you when we met that I can't afford to get things wrong, that I stop bad things from happening. I just don't see that here. I don't see the next big thing coming. Usually these bastards crow from the rooftops, especially with something this big, this public. Here, nothing. Then there's the grammatical errors in the tweet, plus zero chatter from our Intelligence community. I've got one of my guys fiddling around with the footage, see what else he can pull from that for us.'

'It's OK,' said Porter, 'we've already had someone take a look at that.'

'Has your guy hacked the Pentagon before?'

Porter saw Styles looking as bemused as he felt. 'Hacked the Pentagon, and he can still get a job on this side of the law?'

She gave him a look like he'd just asked if she was sure Santa didn't exist. 'You want the best, that's where they learn their trade.'

Porter held his hands up. 'OK, OK. Any idea when he'll have anything for us?'

She checked her watch. 'I emailed him the link and the audio file about an hour ago, so I'd say we'll have an answer before you slope off home for *Coronation Street*. I need to check in with my gaffer, so I'll ask while I'm there and leave you lot to it.'

She bustled out, promising to call the moment she had anything. Energy on legs, that was the best way to describe her. Porter chopped up what tasks there were between them, beckoning for Styles to sit as the rest of the team dispersed.

'You had a chance to do any digging yet?'

'Ah, you mean about our nudge, nudge, wink, wink, secret project?' Styles said, tapping his nose, looking around like he expected Milburn to jump out like Kato from a Pink Panther movie.

'You'll be wanting a bloody codename next,' Porter said.

'I've always fancied myself as a bit of a double-oh something or other,' said Styles, going for a Roger Moore eyebrow arch. 'Who says Bond can't be black?'

'Anyone who's ever seen you do that.'

Styles pretended to look wounded, but lowered his voice a touch, all serious now.

'Little bit, yeah. Lots of fingers in lots of pies. Drugs,

knock-off gear, even a bit of good old-fashioned protection racket. Mostly the drugs though. Expanded a bit since we took care of Mr Locke, but still small in comparison to the bigger players.'

Alexander Locke, the head of the organisation they'd helped dismantle in the not-too-distant past, had been one of the largest importers of class As in the UK. His business fell apart like a Jenga tower when he died, and men like Jackson Tyler had taken full advantage. Nature abhors a vacuum. Seemed that the London gang hierarchy was no different.

'No firm intel on how he brings it in. Half a dozen of his low-level dealers got scooped this year so far. His reputation does the job though. They all took heavier sentences rather than turn on him.'

No surprise there. A quick google showed up the few stories that had made it into the press. Attacks attributed to Tyler, or his gang at least, never proven. Blunt force trauma, hammer suspected. No arrests made.

'So, bugger all then?'

'That's about the size of it. He's smart. Big enough to earn serious money. Small enough that he's never been number one on our list. His people just don't talk.'

'So how the fuck do we get him to give us the name of the driver?'

'Can I be honest, boss?' Styles asked, not waiting for an answer. 'I don't think we can, not just the two of us flying solo. Not what you want to hear, I know, but they've already run you off once. What's to say you don't run fast enough next time? Not as if you're letting anyone watch your back.'

'With bloody good reason in your case.'

'Whatever your reasons, this isn't a one-man job.'

'Maybe, maybe not,' Porter mused, 'but that's the way it has to be.'

'Sorry, DI Porter, hi.' Alistair Hobson stood off to one side, holding a piece of paper like he was about to ask for an autograph.

Porter glanced at Styles, then back at Hobson, and wondered how much the young constable had heard.

'What's up, Alistair?'

'Had Francine from reception on for you, sir. Somebody popped in downstairs and left a message for you at the front desk, she just asked me to pass it on.'

Porter took the half-torn page, squinting to decipher Hobson's spidery scrawl.

'Who left this?' Porter asked, a little sharper then intended.

Hobson had started to turn away, but froze, full on deer in headlights. 'I, ah, I don't know, sir. Francine rang me, and I wrote it down. I didn't . . .'

'What's up, boss? Everything OK?' Styles asked.

'It's fine,' Porter said, hearing the strain in his own voice. 'When was this?'

'Just now, sir. I just . . .'

But Porter didn't hang around to hear the rest. Across the office and through the door to the stairwell, note crumpled in his hand. He'd confided in Nick about Jackson Tyler, trusted him enough to share pretty much anything. But not this. Not all of it anyway. Not if this was what he thought. What else could it be though?

Taking the stairs two at a time, he burst through the door

to the ground floor. No time to speak to Francine just yet, she could wait. Out onto the steps leading down to street level, almost colliding with a solicitor whose face he vaguely recognised. Down the steps, scanning the street. He clocked the man straightaway. Action-Man-style bristle haircut. Boxer's nose, dent chiselled in the centre. Jaundice yellow nicotine-stained teeth.

Porter never had caught the guy's full name. Knew him only as Józef. Last time he'd seen him was a few weeks ago, when he had popped up as part of a previous investigation.

Józef worked for Branislav Nuhić, a fellow Slovakian with a dark backstory that had followed him from his homeland like a bogeyman's tale, and another player in the drug trade. Bigger operation than Tyler by far. Unlike Tyler, Nuhić had a legitimate business to hide behind. Wasn't as if he needed the illegal side of his empire for the money. For men like him, it was what he'd always done, always known. The kind of guy who could no more walk away from that part of himself than he could his own shadow. Nuhić's words from a fortnight ago echoed in his head.

You owe me, Detective, and one way or the other, I will collect.

The Slovak saw his previous intervention with Graham Gibson, a suspect in multiple murders, as a debt to be repaid, even though Porter had told him where to stick it. Józef pushed up and off the black railings that lined the road, as Porter walked towards him, checking over his shoulder that nobody had followed him down the station steps. A cigarette dangled from Józef's mouth, bouncing up and down like a conductor's baton when he talked.

'Mr Porter.'

His accent emphasises the vowels, making it sound more to Porter's ear like *Meester*.

'What are you doing here?'

'This is no way to talk to old friend, yes?'

'What's this supposed to mean?' Porter said, holding up the paper balled in his fist, smoothing it out again to read back to Józef. 'White-van man? Giving yourself codenames now, are we?'

Józef shrugged. 'Is what I do. Is there, you see,' and pointed to the van.

'I know you drive a bloody van,' Porter snapped, doing a sweep of the street every few seconds. 'But you can't drive it here. You need to leave, now.'

Porter went to turn away, but Józef reached out a hand, clamping on his shoulder. Porter felt the strength in the grip, pincers digging, somehow knowing that Józef was barely trying.

'I have for you,' he said, reaching into his jacket with his other hand. 'You must talk.'

He pulled out a phone. Porter reached up to the hand gripping his shoulder, prising it off. Józef tapped the screen, holding the device out to Porter with his other hand.

'You must hear what is to be said,' he ordered. 'May be much help.'

'Help? Help with what? What do you mean?'

Porter took the phone, seeing a number on screen, no name. He put it to his ear, turning his back to Józef, glancing up at the station steps, mercifully deserted, doors closed.

'This is DI Porter, who is this?'

He asked the question, even though he was sure he knew who it would be.

'Ah, Detective Porter. How wonderful to speak again.' Branislav Nuhić's accent was almost as strong as Józef's. 'I hope you will forgive this intrusion. I know you are a busy man.'

Porter moved away from Józef, veering off to the Harrow Road side of the building, adding a little distance to reduce any chance of association.

'Mr Nuhić,' he said grimly. 'To what do I owe the pleasure?'

'Maybe I'm just calling to see how you are.'

Nuhić chose that last word carefully, a man used to watching what he said over the phone.

'Maybe, but I doubt that.'

'And this is why you are such big shot detective, yes? So perceptive.'

'Busy big shot detective, Mr Nuhić. Are you calling to report a crime, because if not, then I'll have to cut this little chat short?'

'As a matter of fact, my call does concern the criminal element, yes,' he said smoothly, as if he wasn't one of them. 'Jackson Tyler, you know this name, yes?'

That one caught Porter by surprise, leaving a gap that Nuhić slid into.

'Mr Tyler is a . . .' pause while he searched for the words, 'person of interest to you, yes.'

Was Porter mistaken, or was there emphasis on the *you*, stressing him personally, rather than the Met as a whole?

'Who?' said Porter.

'You do not know the man you visited yesterday then? How odd.'

That one hit him hard, a cold wave washing over him, goosebumps popping like Braille on his arms. How the hell could Nuhić know that? The Slovak spoke, a hint of amusement in his voice.

'There is not much that doesn't reach me, one way or the other,' he said.

'If you know everything,' said Porter, 'then why do you need me for anything? That's why you're calling, right?'

'I'm just a concerned citizen, who sees things happening, things that the police may wish to take interest in.'

'I told you back then, and I'll tell you again now. The Met isn't in the habit of doing favours for criminals, and don't tell me you're just a humble baker.'

Porter had visited the Nuhić family bakery on a previous case, down on Creekmouth Industrial Estate. A front for everything that lay behind it, the tip of a shady iceberg. He looked around, saw no familiar faces except for Józef, leaning against his van, cigarette down to a nub.

'And who says this is a favour for me?' Nuhić countered. 'Regardless of whether any of my business interests overlap with Mr Tyler, could this not just be a gesture of goodwill?'

'Something tells me you don't share anything for free.'

'What in life is ever truly without cost?'

Porter was about to answer, when something registered in his peripheral vision. Movement back towards the station. Taylor Bell emerged, cradling something in her hand. She hadn't seen him yet, and he glanced over to Józef, signalling with a slight jerk of the head to get lost, but the stocky Slovak was lost in his phone screen.

'Detective, are you still there?'

'Hmm, yes, I . . . look, I have to go.'

'And Mr Tyler?'

Porter wavered, just for a moment, a toes-on-the-edge-of-the-cliff moment. He wanted Tyler so bad it was a physical ache, to force the bully to give up the goods. Not like this though. That last step would be a fall he didn't know if he could recover from. He'd known coppers, good men at heart, guilty of one bad choice that forked their road onto a less than righteous path, for what they told themselves was a just reason. Never was though, not in the end. There had to be another way, one that didn't end up with him in Nuhić's pocket.

'I have to go,' he said again, and ended the call.

Bell was at the foot of the steps now, rummaging in her pockets, pulling out an e-cigarette, and now she clocked him. Confused creases in her forehead were visible even from here. She started towards him, and he was about to meet her halfway when he remembered the phone still in his hand. That realisation made it double in weight, palms instantly slick against the edges.

Józef's eyes were on him now, flicking between Porter and the approaching Bell. Couldn't let her see the Slovak, or at least not pick up on the connection between them. A bin stood by the railings to his left, and he made a show of scrunching up a receipt from his pocket, tossing it in with one hand. Seeming to grip the railing with the other, while sliding the phone onto the top railing, just out of sight below the level of the bin.

'Didn't have you pegged for a smoker,' he said, turning to face her.

'Reformed, please,' she said, holding out the chrome tube. 'Tried going cold turkey, but with a job like this, you know, sometimes the little vices get you through the day. Speaking of little vices, what brings you out here? That wasn't a butt of your own you were chucking away there, was it?'

'What? Oh, that, no, just some chewing gum.'

'What's yours then?'

'My what?'

'Little vice. Everyone's got something, right?'

Over her shoulder, Józef stood out like a penguin at a polar bear convention, angling his head, clearly watching them even though he had zero chance of hearing what was being said. Porter forced himself to focus on Bell, to the point he was worried she might think he was staring a little too hard. He needed to steer this his way, get out of here without his white-van man entering into the equation.

'Vice? Coffee, if you can count that. Drink enough of the stuff to keep Sleeping Beauty awake. Speaking of which, I was just going to grab one. You want anything?'

'Mm-mm,' she mumbled, taking a long draw on her device. The breath out was more of a billow, like someone had just thrown water on a blaze, except this cloud smelt fruity.

'I'm all caffeined out, thanks. I'll make do with a hit of wild berry,' she said, holding it towards him like a baton.

'I'll, um, I'll see you back in there then.'

She shook her head. 'Nope, got to see my gaffer, remember?'

'Ah yeah, course. Let me know what your guy comes up with then.'

He left it there, moving past her, back towards the steps. Józef gave him a quizzical look, clearly expecting a second half to their conversation. Porter couldn't even risk a glance back towards Bell or the bin. Had to make do with an exaggerated eye-roll to one side, hoping it was a clear enough warning.

Whether Józef had seen the move with the phone was anyone's guess. Didn't matter to Porter if he couldn't find it. Thank God Bell didn't smoke anything that needed a bin.

He quickened his pace, saw Józef let his stump of a cigarette drop, grind it into the pavement with his heel. How had Nuhić known about the connection to Tyler? Was Józef following him? He'd done it once before at his boss's request. If he had been, would he have stepped in if Porter had been caught by Tyler's two thugs?

Nuhić's call buzzed around his head like a mosquito. Nothing for nothing. The Slovak would want something in return for whatever information he had. If not now, then down the line. Porter couldn't set foot in that bear trap. There was no telling when it would snap shut.

'Porter!'

The shout came from behind him. He turned, Bell walking towards him through a haze of scented smoke.

'Yours?' she asked, holding out the phone handset.

The grin he fixed her with felt as fake as a politician doorstepped by the press. He fought the urge to see if Józef was still there, still watching. Deny it, and he risked her going through it, no idea what might be on there besides the number Nuhić called from. What if she called it to identify the owner?

'Old age,' he said, trotting back down the steps to meet her. He held his hand out and she slapped it into his open palm. 'I popped it down when I was wrapping my gum up.'

'You're working too hard,' she said.

'Par for the course,' he said, still smiling, expression feeling like it'd been stuck on with glue that was starting to give.

241

He saw her glance right, over to Edgware Road.

'Help you with something, sir?'

Shit. Józef.

Porter saw the burly man act confused, look around as if surely, she must be taking to somebody else. Not a soul within twenty feet. He put a palm to his chest.

'You are meaning me?'

'Yes,' she said, angling off towards him. 'You were staring. Do I know you?'

'I do not think so, no.'

'Then why were you staring?' She didn't give him time to answer. 'That your van, sir?'

He nodded. 'Yes, it's—'

'It's parked in a bus stop. I'm going to have to ask you to move.'

His gaze flicked between her and Porter, but he said nothing. Just shrugged and pushed off the railings.

'No problem, Officer.'

She watched him go, before turning back to Porter. 'For a man who wasn't staring, he managed to clock the fact I was a copper. You seen him around before?'

Porter gave what he hoped was a nonchalant shake of the head.

She turned again, watched him drive off. 'Bet he wouldn't have given us a look in that van if we'd asked.'

'What makes you say that?' said Porter, pocketing the phone he realised he was still holding before she could ask any more questions about that.

'I can smell a wrong 'un a mile off, and that one, my friend, had a stench about him.'

'Now who's been working too hard?'

She tapped her nose. 'When you know, you know.'

She turned and left without another word, leaving him stood there wondering. Was that last part about Józef or aimed at him? He didn't have much time to consider, as he turned back towards the station and saw Evie holding the door open. He tried for another convincing grin, but the tank was empty.

'Evie, I was just—'

'Was that her then?'

Bollocks.

CHAPTER THIRTY-NINE

'She's been assigned by CTU, Evie. I can't just refuse to work with her because she's a woman.'

'Oh my God,' she said, jabbing a finger at the lift button. 'You really think that's what this is about? That I can't handle you working with another woman?'

'Well, what then?'

She stabbed at the button again, twice more. Gave it up as a bad job and strode back towards the door leading to the street. He put a hand on her shoulder as she passed, stopping her, and she rounded on him with a stern look.

'I've been worried sick about you, about everything that's going on, and you can't even be honest with me about where you are or who you're with.'

'It was one drink, Evie, for Christ's sake, nothing more. And I didn't tell you because I didn't want a scene like this.'

'Oh, it's a scene now, is it?'

'Come on now, I didn't mean it like that.'

'How did you mean it then?'

'I'm not trying to make excuses, really I'm not, but this . . .' He looked around, as if they were surrounded by visuals of everything bouncing around his mind right now. 'All of this, not being able to work Holly's case, not properly anyway, it's killing me, Evie. Imagine if someone had done that to your mum, your dad, and you were benched. That, and Winter ran rings around us today.'

'I heard,' she said, a little of the heat taken out of her words. 'Nick told me. Be honest though, Jake, if this had been a few weeks back, you probably wouldn't have arrested him on the spot, would you?'

She was right. He knew it, hard to admit, but couldn't deny it. After a pause, he shook his head.

'And that's why you need to stick inside the lines on this one, babe. You're as good a detective as anyone in there, but this is throwing your judgement.'

'And you could just stick it all in a box, could you? Ignore it and hope for the best?'

'Honestly? I don't know. But this isn't about me, it's about you, and—'

'Exactly, and I need the likes of you, Milburn and anyone else telling me how I should feel like I need a hole in the head right now.'

The words landed hard. He caught the moment they registered, saw her blinking in disbelief. She reset just as quick though.

'I know I pushed for this Jake, us. I chased after you. First you lie to me about where you were the other night. Now I find out you were off having a drink with someone else.'

He went to speak, but she held up a palm to stop him.

'I trust you, Jake, really I do, but that needs to be a two-way thing, and if you can't give that . . .' She paused, swallowed hard. 'Well, let's just say we'll be doing this dance again over something else somewhere down the line, and there's only so many times . . .' She tailed off.

'What? What are you saying, Evie?'

'I don't even know,' she said. 'I'm tired. Haven't slept much these last few nights. I'm going home. You do what you have to do, and I'll see you . . . soon.'

'Evie, wait—' he started, but she had already brushed past him, out of the door and halfway down the stairs now. 'Evie!' he called one last time She glanced over her shoulder as she stepped out onto Edgware Road, as sad a smile as he'd seen, and disappeared as a bus hid her from view.

'Shit,' he spat out. 'Shit, shit, shit.'

As weeks go, there hadn't been a worse one since he lost Holly. Now, here he was, watching any hope for justice slip through his fingers, halfway to cocking up the best thing that had happened to him in the last few years and dropping more balls at work than a narcoleptic juggler.

Way to go, Jake.

CHAPTER FORTY

Evie chanced another glance, but the 332 bus to Bishops Bridge had cut off the view of the station. She was breathing fast and shallow, a hangover from the conversation with Jake, more so than the hightailing it over the road. She'd felt a few seconds away from tears when she'd spun on her heel and left him. More frustration than anything else. Wanting to help so badly, that needing to support him in every sense, but afraid of the consequences if it all fell apart.

Milburn would have a coronary if he knew what Jake had been up to. Correction: was still up to. The super would likely find out eventually, but it couldn't be from her. That would act like ice in the cracks that were appearing, force them apart. Only way she could think to get through to him was via Nick. The two of them were tight, a stream of sticky situations and complex cases had given them something not far off a brotherly vibe. She'd speak to Nick, two heads better than one. Just the thought of it lifted her mood, and even just that fraction was a tangible difference in weight.

She merged with the flow of people squeezing into the crimson tiled doorway of Edgware Road Tube station, grabbing an already read copy of the *Evening Standard* for the journey. The lift down to the platform was pin-your-arms full, and as it dropped, so did her mood as her mind wandered.

Holly felt like a silent partner in the relationship at the best of times, but these last few days, Evie could swear it was like a physical presence in the room. Jake's ties to her, to that part of his past, were what drove him to take risks. Risks though that affected the here and now. None of this changed how she felt about him, but she couldn't just sit there and say nothing when his decisions affected her, their future.

The lift was a full-on sensory experience, not quite muffled strains of Beyoncé drifting from headphones to her left. Someone a little too keen on garlic, with weaponised breath nearby. Enough to turn anyone claustrophobic if they spent more than a few minutes inside. The knot of people poured out in front of her when the doors opened, and for once, her timing was perfect. A train glided in as she stepped onto the platform. Barely anyone got off, leaving those waiting the task of inserting themselves into any gaps that looked vaguely people-shaped.

Evie didn't mind the commute. Didn't mind standing either. People-watching on the Tube was like a real-time version of *Gogglebox*. Depending on the time of day, you could sit back and relax, soaking in anything from domestics to drunken nights out. There was even a guy who frequented the Bakerloo line, busking on the carriages with his battered guitar. Never made much in tips, but damn he could bash out a tune.

Two stops made the difference, and by the time they pulled into Baker Street, she'd worked out how to broach it with Nick, how to suggest he played it with Jake assuming he was on board. And why wouldn't he be? Any cock-ups Jake made would leave a mark on Nick too. Guilt by association, even if he was nowhere near any of it.

Baker Street faded away, replaced by Regent's Park a minute later. The doors opened, old faces replaced by new. She was staring at a poster on the platform, the kind of glassy-eyed trance typical of weary travellers, when the boy approached her. He couldn't have been older then eleven, twelve at a push. Cocky strut to him, rolling of the shoulders as he walked down the centre of the carriage, weaving between people intent on ignoring their surroundings. Evie paid him no mind. He didn't properly register on her radar until he'd pulled a hand from his pocket, thrusting it towards her, something clenched in his fist.

She felt something press against her jacket, looked down, puzzled, what she saw not computing. Her hand reached out instinctively, grasping at whatever he'd produced. Cold, metallic. The second she touched it, he darted out through closing doors, leaving her staring after him. Nobody else seemed to have noticed the exchange. Standard for the Tube. She looked down again, at her hand now pressed against her stomach. The object didn't register at first. Took a second, the realisation crept over her, mind clearing like a sea fret blown away by the breeze. When it clicked, her hand opened of its own accord, the object tumbling to the floor. She barely managed to bite back a scream.

CHAPTER FORTY-ONE

'Where are you now, right now?' Porter asked, a sensation like cold water trickling down his back.

'Marylebone Road, just outside Regent's Park Tube station.'

Might have just been the background bustle of London traffic, but she sounded quiet, and in that instant all the frustrations of the last few days' conversations were washed away. He just wanted to reach through the phone, wrap his arms around her.

'Is there a transport police officer there?'

'What? I . . . I don't know.'

'Wait, Regent's Park? Albany Street station is a few minutes' walk away. Head up the east side on Albany Street. It's up there on the right.'

'Jake, I'm fine. Whoever it was, they've gone. It was only a kid anyway.'

'A kid who could just as easily have had a knife, or God

knows what else, and who's to say he was alone? These fuckers could be stood watching you now.'

Even as the words left his mouth, he debated the wisdom of using them. Didn't want to shake her up any more than she already was, but at the same time, snapping her back into focus, to be painfully aware of her surroundings, of potential eyes on her.

'Seriously, Evie, get to the station. I'll be there in five minutes.'

Four minutes and thirty-two seconds later, Porter bumped the borrowed squad car up onto the kerb, not bothering to lock it as he jumped out and raced up the ramp on the side of the building. Evie was leaning against opaque glass panes by the front door.

'W-what are you doing? W-why are you not inside?' he stammered.

'I'm fine, really. Even if there's anyone following, they're not likely to try anything right outside a cop shop, are they?'

'You should have gone inside.' Stern parent scolding a stubborn child.

'You said it yourself, you were minutes away, and I didn't want to make a fuss.'

He opened his mouth to hammer home his point again, but something about the way she looked made him stop. He wrapped both arms around her, pulling her in close, cradling one hand behind her head.

'I'm sorry,' he said. 'Sorry for being a prick lately. This is all my fault.'

He felt her melt into him and stood like that for what seemed like an age, but it couldn't have been more than ten seconds. She puffed out a loud sigh into his chest.

'Yes, you have,' she said finally, 'but then you get that whole kicked puppy look, and it's hard to stay mad at you for long.' She pulled back a few inches, looking up at him. 'We do need to talk though, about the case, whatever else you might have planned.'

He nodded. 'Fine, but not here.'

A quick glance around. Nobody heading their way on the street, but no telling who might pop their head out of the station.

'Where is it? Show me.'

Evie reached into her bag, pulling out a postbox-red toy car. A Mini Cooper, complete with shiny new alloys. Couldn't be more than a few inches long. Letters scratched into the roof made his teeth clench so tight, it felt like they might buckle and pop out.

Déjà vu

Any doubts as to who was behind this disappeared as his eyes traced the silver lines scored into the top of the car. Same make and model as Holly had been hit by. Stolen from a nearby house, abandoned a few miles away from where she'd been left crumpled on the pavement.

Tyler's third warning. Keep coming after him and history would repeat. Holly replaced by Evie.

'What did he look like? The kid?'

'I don't know,' she said, 'it all happened so fast. He was gone, off the train before I even realised what he'd given me.'

Given. As if it was a gift, not a threat. Enough. A tornado bounced round inside his mind, drawing up all the anger and frustration of the last few days, thoughts battering his head like debris. Enough of the threats. Threats talked about what you *might* do. Time to stop talking and act.

CHAPTER FORTY-TWO

The drive back to Evie's was long. Stuck in traffic that flowed like quicksand, there was no escape, and she took advantage to grill him on what he'd done, where his mind was at now.

'Can't help but think the less you know the better,' he said.

'Those twats tried to scare me, Jake. Worked pretty well too. But if I can't stop you, at least I can try and figure out a way to help get you what you need. Sooner you get a name, sooner you stop winding Tyler up. If he'll threaten a copper, he might be willing to go a lot further.'

'Nick's helping with background, but Tyler looks pretty watertight.'

'No weak spots at all then?'

Porter shrugged. 'We can keep picking up his street level guys, the ones doing the selling, see if anyone will break the trend and turn on him.'

'We already know they won't.'

She was right of course. Tyler's set-up was as tight as he'd seen. Wasn't that he was some kind of megalomaniac villain, quite the opposite. From the looks of it, he didn't want to take over the world, just milk the patch of London that he had. Whatever Porter could threaten any of his men with, unless it included taking a hammer to parts that weren't meant to be tenderised, they'd just take their chances in prison.

Tyler was right about one thing. Threats didn't work if you never followed through. Word got around that you were all mouth, and you might as well not waste your breath.

'What do you suggest then?' he asked her.

She thought for a minute. 'There's got to be something that matters more to him, something important enough that it would leave him no choice.'

'If I knew what that was, I'd have used it already.'

She paused, weighing up what to say next. 'You're right. It has to be bigger than just sweeping a few of his guys off the street. Something that hits him harder, costs him more. I could maybe make a few discreet enquiries with a couple of informants we've used in the past.'

This was a big step for her, after the stand-off they'd had the other night. He opened his mouth to say something, but she stopped him.

'Before you say anything, we don't have anyone directly inside his organisation. I would have told you already if we did. There are some guys I know who work for his rivals though. Stands to reason they might have heard something.'

'Evie, that's . . .' He tailed off, opting instead for a simple, 'Thank you.'

'Don't thank me until you've heard my terms,' she said. 'First, you tell me everything from here on in. No more secrets. Agreed?'

He nodded, pretty sure there was more to come.

'Second, whatever we find, we take to Pittman.'

Porter was slowing to a stop as she said it, and her suggestion made him stamp a little too hard on the brake, bunny-hopping the last few feet.

'Uh-uh,' he said. 'If I take anything to him, Milburn finds out where it came from.'

She arched her eyebrows at him. 'You really think Pittman would pass up a chance to be a little diva in the spotlight by telling the super whose homework he copied from?'

Valid point. Pittman would most likely take whatever he was given and run with it. It was more the sense of responsibility he felt, what he owed to Holly to see it through himself. If he didn't agree though, chances are Evie would revert to being a conscientious objector.

'Fine,' he agreed, unable to resist the childish crossing of fingers down by his side.

That seemed to appease her and she nodded, shoulders dipping a fraction as she relaxed away from the fight she must have been expecting. She reached over, squeezing his hand, and he wondered if she could feel anything but honest vibes. Promises sometimes came with small print. He hadn't promised to share with Pittman immediately, or that he couldn't make a few moves to verify the information first.

'Any idea what time you'll be done?' she asked. 'I was thinking you could come back here afterwards, Chinese, glass of something?'

'An hour, two tops,' he said. 'We've had someone taking a look at the original Facebook footage, pulling apart the sound, frame by frame checks, see if we missed anything.'

He left out the fact that Taylor Bell was the one who'd arranged it, or that she'd texted him saying it would be worth his while heading back to the station for the results, the preview pane open on his screen, peeking out from where the phone lay wedged between his legs.

'Call me when you're on your way so I know when to ring the order in.' She reached over, cupped a hand against his cheek. 'We'll get him, whoever he's protecting. One way or another.'

As she leant over, planting a soft kiss he felt his phone vibrate again. She smiled, lips still pressed to his, pulling away a second later.

'Go on then, go play with the other kids.'

He grinned, afraid to pull the phone out in case it was Bell again. Stupid, he knew. There was nothing in it, not from his side at least. Still, things felt brittle despite the warmth of the kiss. Finely weighted, like snow on a rooftop that a slammed door could bring piling down to bury you.

She blew him a kiss from her front door and disappeared inside before he pulled away. Safe now to look at the phone. A notification sat waiting for him, not Bell though. His sister, Kat. He frowned, seeing a thumbnail preview, but not able to make out the detail. He clicked it open to read as he slipped the car back into gear, and what he saw made his foot slip off the clutch, bouncing the car forward, barely daylight left between his bumper and the car in front.

You been leaving your toys lying around again?

A photo. Outstretched hand, Kat's presumably. Palm open. Small red Mini Cooper with *Porter* scratched into the roof.

Tyler. Motherfucker.

CHAPTER FORTY-THREE

Shopfronts and traffic lights glided past in a blur as Porter's blue lights blazed all the way to Kat's house. Twenty minutes and three near-misses later, he raced down her street, bumping up the kerb hard enough to rattle teeth. Her face when she answered the door was a cocktail of confusion and cynicism.

'You going to tell me what this is all about?'

'Where are the boys?' he asked, wanting to make sure his nephews were safe, and preferably oblivious to any of this. Tom and James, six-year-old mirror images of one another, had been targeted before by someone else out to get Porter's attention. It had only been a few weeks since Graham Gibson, a man living out his own warped view of the world in which his own family, killed in a crash he caused, were still alive, had snatched them to force Porter's hand. That hadn't ended well for Gibson, who had later died from the injuries sustained by Nuhić's man slamming a van into him.

On the day, Tom and James seemed to have coped in that way that kids can, popping back into shape as if it had all been a game. Kat had confided though that Tom hadn't slept well this past week. James had been clingier than usual, and both were nervy in general if they didn't have line of sight to Kat.

'They're fine. They're upstairs watching a film in their room. What's going on, Jake?'

'Nothing, everything's fine. It's just—'

'Hang on a sec, you practically teleport over here after telling me to stay inside and keep my door locked, and you expect me to believe everything's fine?' She stood in the doorway, arms folded, eyebrows in a *Yeah right* arch. 'What's the thing with the car as well? Why have you scratched your name on it? What are you, like five years old?'

'It's not mine,' he said, still mentally testing out the best way to broach this without freaking her out.

'You're not coming in till you start to make some sense.'

'Where did you find it?'

'Jake, just tell me what's wrong.'

'Just tell me where you found the bloody thing,' he snapped, louder than intended, and her face hardened. He swallowed hard, breathed deep. Reset. 'Sorry. I'll explain everything, I promise. Just please tell me where you found it first.'

She stared him out for a second, making him work for his forgiveness. 'Come on, in you come.'

He shook his head. 'I can't stop.'

The first signs of worry crept in around the edges as she studied him. Finally, she threw up her hands. 'Fine, have it your way. Tom found it. It was on the doorstep when we got back from doing the shopping. He thought you'd been and left it cos of the name. That's when I texted you.'

Her doorstep? They'd been to her house? How had they known where she lived? The news coverage of the boys' abduction. Cameras had flocked around the house and the street sign was fixed onto the wall outside her house. Not exactly Sherlock Holmes territory to figure that out via a quick google. Shit.

How could he tell her? After what she'd been through, having the boys snatched from her doorstep so recently, this would be a stick of dynamite lobbed into a still-fragile household. He had to say something though. He couldn't ask for anyone extra to watch over them without alerting Milburn to his personal agenda. Threads of a plan started to weave together.

'Look, Kat, I promise I'll tell you everything, OK? I just need to take care of something first.' He turned back towards his car. 'I'll pop back soon as I can, yeah?'

'Jake? Jake? What the hell's going on?' she called after him, but he just turned, blew a kiss and slid behind the wheel.

She shook her head, disappearing inside with a face that warned him this wasn't over. He drove east, not as fast this time, but with urgency. Gambled on amber lights, tailgated closer than he knew he should. Another text from Bell lit up his screen. He took advantage of a few seconds at a red light to fire off a quick reply, saying he was on his way. Innocent enough lie. He'd get there eventually.

The visit to Kat was a match put to petrol already poured by the kid on the Tube and his little gift to Evie. He'd kept a

261

lid on it in front of Kat, but he could feel the mercury rising, muttering to himself as he drove.

'You don't fuck with family.'

One quick pit stop to make on the way to the station. Jackson Tyler. What he'd do when he got there was anybody's guess.

CHAPTER FORTY-FOUR

No sign of the BMW from his previous visit amongst the half-dozen cars parked around the back of the flats. Porter reversed into an adjoining back street, killed the engine and climbed out. He popped open the boot, rummaged under an old folded blanket. Felt as much as heard a dull clank of metal on metal as his fingers closed around what he was looking for.

The matt black baton he pulled out was around a foot in length when retracted. It would double when he flicked it out, but he kept it close to his side for now. A quick three-sixty glance, but nobody was watching, least not that he could see. Porter strode with purpose towards the doorway, jamming a finger on the buzzer. He pulled out the wad of chewing gum he'd been softening up for just this purpose on the way over, pushing it onto the lens of the fish-eye camera, spreading with his thumb.

The speaker crackled into life. Breathing from somewhere inside. Silence. Porter went for round two, keeping it pressed for a full ten count. No static this time. He didn't stand on ceremony, spinning around and using a drainpipe to hoist himself up onto the small flat roof that covered the doorway. He flicked his wrist, baton magically doubling in size. Long enough to reach down and hit the buzzer again if needed.

It wasn't. He'd barely scraped his trailing foot over the edge when the door below clicked open. A man's head appeared below him, twisting left and right. Porter clocked the baseball bat clenched in his right hand, hanging low, tapping out a rhythm against his leg. Porter's heart hammered so hard he was sure the guy would hear it, look up and take a swing.

'Fucking kids,' the man muttered, taking a step further out of the shadow of the doorway. His head swivelled both ways again, pausing in the direction of Porter's car. The bat came up, resting on his shoulder now. Two more steps to the right. Porter licked dry lips as rough as sandpaper, a shadow of doubt flickering. He knew this wasn't the path, that it was a step closer to people like Jackson Tyler, but you didn't mess with family. These bastards, one of them, had already taken Holly. If he let today slide, what did that say about the kind of man he was? People feared Tyler because he wasn't all mouth. He acted. A man of action would only respond to action.

Porter knelt, one hand gripping the edge of the roof for balance, the other scything the baton down on the man's wrist, landing clean against the ulna. The crunch was sickeningly satisfying, and the bat spun from the man's hand. Keeping his weight on the hand against the roof, Porter swung his legs round and over the edge. Both soles connected between shoulder blades, and the guy went down like the proverbial sack of potatoes, head bouncing off tarmac with a dull thud. The scream of pain he'd started to let loose was cut off before it peaked.

Porter spun around on the off-chance there'd been more than one, but the open doorway was empty. No time to admire his handiwork. He pulled out a four-loop polymer restraint, fed the stunned man's wrists through and pulled tight. Not one of Tyler's lapdogs he recognised. He would be expected back upstairs soon though. No time to waste. Porter dragged him to his knees, all glazed eyes and chin sagging to chest. He half hauled, half pulled him through the doorway, letting him flop against the foot of the stairwell.

Porter bounded up, two steps at a time, retracing his steps to the flat he'd met Tyler in. The door stood open a few inches, muffled conversation drifting out. He paused, listening for a beat. Satisfied there was only one voice, he peered into the flat, nudging the gap wider. Tyler stood dead centre, back to him, talking quietly on his mobile phone. The door was on mercifully quiet hinges, and Porter stepped inside, adjusting his grip on the baton handle, zeroing in on Tyler's knee, going for a chopping motion.

Something alerted Jackson Tyler. Could have been a reflection in the window, scuff of shoe on carpet. Whatever it was, he spun around, saw Porter closing the gap. He swung for the kneecap, but Tyler's turn meant the blow landed against the back of his thigh with a meaty thump. Tyler cried out as Porter advanced on him.

'You like your warnings? Well, this is one of mine. You stay the fuck away from my family. I find out you've been anywhere near them, I'll be heading to B&Q for my own hammer. You hear me?'

The strangest thing. The twisted grimace of pain Tyler wore, took on a slyness, bordering on a smile.

'Didn't think you had it in you, Detective. Good for you. Shame though.'

What the hell was that supposed to mean? 'I asked you if you understood.'

'Let me tell you about what I understand,' Tyler said, rubbing the spot on the back of his leg. 'I understand you want your head read, coming in here all Rambo-style, one man fucking army.'

'People like you make me fucking sick,' Porter said, reaching into his pocket, pulling out the Mini Cooper he'd taken from Kat. 'Here,' he threw it overarm at Tyler's head, but only managed a glancing blow of a protective arm. 'Bad enough you peddle your shit on the street, but you honestly think there's any lengths I won't go to, to get you to give me a name? You and your crew, you killed my wife. My wife!'

He swung again, this time aiming for Tyler's arm. For a man with an injured leg, Tyler moved faster than Porter had bargained for. He moved towards Porter, stepping inside the arc of the blow. It still landed, but Tyler took it on the bicep. A stinger but not incapacitating, and he bowled into Porter, ducking in, driving his shoulder into Porter's midriff, launching them both towards the wall. Porter pushed down on the back of Tyler's neck with one hand, while hammering the butt of the baton down between his shoulder blades. Tyler grunted in pain by the third blow, tried to let go and stand up. Downward pressure from Porter's left arm made that a non-starter. A fourth blow landed. Fifth. The rhythm felt good, years of grief flowing through the baton and finding the spot his anger had been searching for what felt a lifetime.

Tyler's arms, previously searching from blows of their own to land, slid down Porter's legs, the rest of him following suit a beat later. Without a thought, Porter rotated his angle of strike, ready now to whip it down full force against the back of Tyler's neck. It hovered there, top of the arc. Breath ragged and hoarse. Fingers gripped as tight as a man hanging over a cliff edge around the hilt. And still the blow didn't come.

'Gahhhhh!' he bellowed, pushing Tyler away, watching as he toppled back into a messy heap, back arched as he tried to hold the spot Porter had repeatedly slammed into. The world snapped back into focus and Porter grimaced at his own lack of self-control.

His panting and Tyler's combined to mask the approaching footsteps until it was too late. A cannon exploded against the side of his head, room fuzzing around the edges, tilting on its axis. Sliding down the wall. Falling. Falling. Something dark whooshed towards his face. Blinding flash of light, clearing into a swarm of fireflies across his vision.

Rough carpet rubbed his cheek now, and through the haze, Tyler began the slow process of rising to his feet. How had . . . ? Who . . . ? Thoughts like dots he couldn't join. A low laugh cut a path through the white noise filling his head.

'You finished now? My turn,' followed by a harsher, 'What took you so fucking long?'

No idea who else was even in the room, Porter tried and failed to blink himself back into gear. Saw Tyler walking slowly towards him. Started pushing up from the floor, only making it as far as a half-press-up position. Saw Tyler's foot draw back. An instant later, a grenade of pain detonated in his ribs. He slumped back down, face to the floor again, what little breath he had in hammered out.

Porter felt breath against his cheek as Tyler loomed into view, slapping something against the floor, so close it took Porter a few seconds to focus and realise it was the Mini Cooper.

'You keep this up, you're gonna wish you'd been in the car with her.'

CHAPTER FORTY-FIVE

'Try him again,' said Bell. 'He's not answering me.'

Styles sighed, tapped Porter's number again. Five rings then the click into voicemail. He shook his head. 'Might just be driving,' he said hopefully.

Bell shook her head. 'Not unless he's going via Southampton. Should have been here an hour ago. What about trying his missus?'

Styles hesitated. With what Porter had been up to lately, last thing he needed was dropping him in it with Evie again. 'Let's give him ten more minutes. I'll try him a few more times, then worst case, we crack on and he can just catch up.'

Bell looked less than impressed, but with no real recourse, she slumped back into a seat and started tapping away at her own phone. Seconds later, a name flashed up on Styles's phone. Not Porter though, Evie.

'Evie, hey. What's up?'

A loud sniff, followed by noisy breath. 'Nick. It's Jake. He's hurt.'

Styles was up on his feet, moving towards the door as he spoke.

'What's happened? Where are you?'

He spoke low so as not to alert the others, but he caught Bell staring at him. He signalled that he was just going to the loo and stepped out into the corridor, checking both ways, like he was crossing the road. Right, left, right again. He listened to her speak, punctuated by loud breaths, pausing as she tried to process what had happened. His own stomach did a flip an Olympic gymnast would be proud of as she offloaded.

Styles wasted no time, climbing into the car, double-timing it over to King's College Hospital. The A&E waiting area was a large open-plan, atrium-style space, and standing room only. He jogged to the desk, cutting in past the guy just about to step forward. The man had a nose that could double as a ski slope and couldn't have looked less pleased if Styles had just spat in his face.

'Wait your bloody turn,' he said, waving a hand that had a pack of frozen peas gaffer-taped to it.

'Sorry sir, police,' he said, holding up his warrant card. 'I just need a few seconds.' He felt the tiniest twinge of guilt pulling rank, but he ignored the angry mutterings and turned his attention to a now curious receptionist, who heard him out, before pointing him through double doors to his left.

Porter lay half propped up in a bed, curtains pulled either side. One side of his face looked like it had a run-in with a cheese grater, splotches of drying blood raised like Braille. Evie sat on one side, leaning in, holding his left hand in both of hers. His other rested across his stomach, little finger through to middle was a thick bundle of dressing. Porter turned his head towards Evie, spotted Styles approaching and went to scoot up a few inches.

He tried to hide the pain, but Styles saw it ripple across his face. Evie clocked him now as well, and he saw her swallow hard, trying to hold it together. Pink tinge to her eyes and the double sniff as he pulled up a second chair told a tale though.

'Don't tell me you tried running out of Maccy D's without paying again?' Styles said.

Flicker of a smile from both.

'They tried to give me full fat Coke, and it all kicked off after that.'

A laugh escaped Evie, more nerves and bottled tension than humour.

'What the hell happened?' Styles asked.

Porter looked at Evie, back at Styles, somewhere between sheepish and full-blown embarrassment. 'So stupid, I just . . . I was on my way in, and thought I had a flat. I pulled over to take a look and these guys came up. Started off by asking if I needed a hand, then one of them asked to borrow my phone. Next thing I know, there's a third one, and they all just . . . swarmed. Didn't even get a chance to tell them I was a copper.'

'What did they look like?'

'Average height. Average build. Apart from that, it's all a bit . . . fuzzy,' he said, touching a finger lightly to his temple. 'One of them caught me good here.'

'Jesus, how'd you get away?'

'Ah, another car pulled up, few blokes got out and the others just scarpered.'

'Where'd it happen?'

'Just up the road, near Walworth.'

Why south of the Thames? No reason for Porter to cross over on his way to the station. Styles's bullshit meter had already been twitching, but this sent it off the charts. King's College Hospital was miles off the route that he should have been taking. No chance they brought him here as first choice. There were three or four back north that they'd practically have to drive past to get here.

'How'd you get here? You all right to drive?'

Porter shook his head. 'My head, I could barely see straight.'

'They think he might have concussion,' Evie chipped in.

'Someone called an ambulance. My car will still be sat there somewhere. And I haven't got concussion.'

'Busted up?' Styles said, pointing at Porter's bandaged fingers.

His boss nodded. 'These three, plus two ribs. I'm fine though.'

'Oh yeah, you look peachy,' Styles said. 'We got anyone out there yet looking for the guys?'

'He hasn't even called it in,' Evie said, 'maybe you can talk some sense into him?'

Styles gave him a *what-the-hell?* look. 'Here,' he said, pretending to reach for Porter's hand. 'Give me five minutes alone and extra bandages to wrap the other two fingers, and I'll see what I can do.'

Evie let go of Porter's hand, smoothed tendrils of hair back from her temples and stood up.

'You've got two, I'm off to the ladies.'

Styles scraped his chair back to let her past, watched as she disappeared through the double doors and back out to reception. He turned his attention back to Porter.

'Right, that gives us one minute and fifty seconds for you to tell me what really happened.'

CHAPTER FORTY-SIX

Two hours, and a dose of strong painkillers later, Porter walked slowly through the doors and out into the car park, flanked by Styles and Evie. He'd given Styles a quick run-down of what had actually transpired, leaving out the part about him wading in first with the baton. That part stung his pride too much. He was better than that. Emphasis on the 'was'. Used to think he had the self-control that those he arrested lacked. Today had shown that to be a lie.

Styles promised to get someone from the team to keep an eye on Kat's house for a few days, a rotation of Williams and Waters. Any more than that and Milburn might get suspicious. He'd also made another promise. More of an ultimatum really. Full disclosure on anything to do with Holly's case. Anything less, any repeats of charging off to be the lone hero, and Styles swore he'd make the call to Milburn himself.

Porter insisted on riding back to the station with Styles,

much to Evie's irritation. Styles had shared Bell's news though, and Porter was keen to get more detail. Her guy had come through with the audio analysis, and was ninety-nine per cent sure that the main guy, the one who wielded the knife, was not a native Arabic speaker. Something about the one phrase, *Allahu Akbar* not being pronounced properly. They'd also gone as far as to say that the accented English used throughout the rest was most likely forced, and fake.

Evie extracted her own promise from Styles. He wasn't to let Porter out of his sight, until he dropped him back home later.

'If he needs the loo, I expect you to go in and watch.'

Styles raised one eyebrow. 'This could take our relationship to a whole new level.'

The journey back across the Thames to Paddington Green was a grilling, Styles after every last detail about what had happened.

'Look at it this way, boss,' Styles said, as they pulled into the car park. 'Could have been worse. He could have got his hammer out.'

Porter pursed his lips, nodding, saying nothing but picturing the moment when the round hammer end of the tool had cracked his little finger. Ring finger and middle were worse though. He'd known what was coming. Unable to move, the weight of the second mystery man on his back, leaning over holding his hand flat against the carpet while Tyler swung the hammer. Echoes of the gang leader's promises.

Third warning. One finger for each. Only thing saving you is the fact you're a copper, but I know why you ain't here mob-handed, so listen up. Any more shit from you, and it's that pretty sister of yours who gets warning number four. You can't watch her for ever.

Protecting Kat meant walking away from Holly. Damned if he did. Damned if he didn't.

Taylor Bell was halfway through a Krispy Kreme when they walked in.

'It's only my third,' she said, licking a splodge of frosting off a finger. 'Don't you dare judge.' He caught her staring at his fingers, seeing the bloom of bruising between scabs on his temple.

'Walked into a door,' he said, no time for long-winded explanations.

'A revolving one?'

What smile he managed made him wince, one side of his jaw still tender from being rammed into the floor.

'Nick told me the headlines from your guy, said there was something more about pronunciation being off.'

'That's one way of putting it,' she said. 'More takeaway than terrorist.'

Porter wasn't sure he'd heard that right, or what the hell it would mean if he had.

'So it's pronounced Alaw-hu-ak-bur, meaning God is great. Our guy says it like more like *aloo akbar*. Aloo is Urdu for potato, so he's literally saying potatoes are great. Not the greatest poster child for the Brotherhood.'

Styles stifled a laugh. 'So, we're looking for a vegetarian extremist?'

'More likely that than anyone from the Brotherhood.' She nodded. 'Had some more input from our undercovers too. The Brotherhood are actively seeking out our mystery men. They want them just as bad as we do. Difference being, they want to recruit them. Their words, not mine. Why would you be trying to recruit someone unless they were nothing to do with you as it stands?'

'And why would you put a claim on what they did in the name of the Brotherhood, if you weren't a part of it already?' Porter added.

'Exactly,' she said. 'Still probably not enough for your gaffer, but I'm telling you, these guys were not part of them.'

'You're sure?'

'Sure as I can be. I'll know for certain by tomorrow.'

'Tomorrow? What happens tomorrow?'

She bit down on her lower lip. 'I'd rather not say, not just yet. In case I'm wrong.'

'Thought you were never wrong?' Styles said.

'Everyone gets it wrong sometimes,' she said. 'Even God. You think he meant to create a platypus? Must have had a heavy session on the Communion wine that night.'

She had a knack of throwing conversations in directions that left Porter lost for how to respond, and he saw Styles loving every minute of it. She promised to rock up early tomorrow morning, give him a heads up before Milburn poked his nose into the briefing. She drifted off, leaving just the two of them, the rest of the team having disappeared off home while Porter was still in A&E.

'No one else knows I ended up in hospital then?' he asked.

Styles shook his head. 'Didn't see the need to share. Although you should probably have a think what you'll say tomorrow. You look like some kids on a sugar high used you as a piñata.'

'I'll think of something. Where does this leave us with the EWP then? Anything else happen while I was . . . ahm . . . away?'

'Nothing yet, although I've asked Dee to have a look for

any CCTV around the EWP office the day of the call, see if we can at least narrow down who was in. Sucheka's picking up the York angle for Winter, make sure that checks out. I was thinking of sending Gus back to Greenwich after the morning briefing, hit the few businesses we didn't get an answer from around security camera footage as well.'

Porter nodded his approval. 'See, you didn't even need me around today anyway. On a serious note though, my head's pounding. Any chance you can run me to get my car?'

Styles frowned, ridges magically appearing across his forehead, deep enough to scream disapproval.

'I'll be fine to drive.'

Styles gave him a once up and down as if to say, *Look at the state of you.*

'Honestly, I'm fine. If you run me home, I'm just going to get a taxi and pick it up myself.'

'You are one stubborn bastard, you know that?'

'I'll take that as a compliment coming from you.'

'Fine, but I'm following you back.'

'Seriously?'

'Promised Evie, boss.'

Porter held his gaze, both eyebrows arched, but Styles just shook his head.

'Gah! Fine. Pointless, but it's your time you're wasting.'

It was getting on for midnight by the time they got to Walworth. Porter rested an elbow against the door frame, propping his head against one hand, rubbing gently at the spot where he'd been caught. Pretty sure it had been a kick, although he was too dazed by that point to know if it was Tyler or his helper.

'Whereabouts on the high street?'

'Keep going,' said Porter, fingers of a headache starting to curl around the edges, a sure sign the painkillers were wearing off.

They hit the edge of Burgess Park and rolled over the intersection with Bowyer Place. Every approaching headlight was a fresh lance of pain. Porter fumbled in his pocket, popping a couple of tablets from a blister pack, crunching them like Smarties.

'Why don't you take the morning off tomorrow, boss?' Styles said. 'I can handle the briefing, call you if anything big happens.'

'Yeah, let's see how we go,' said Porter, sliding the remaining tablets back into his pocket, brushing against something solid, something forgotten. 'Hang a left here, just before William Hill.'

Porter saw the nose of his car poking out from the alley behind the flats.

'That where he lives?' Styles said, nodding up at the block of flats.

Porter grunted an acknowledgement.

'Which one?'

'Uh-uh,' Porter shook his head slowly, the painkillers yet to kick in. 'I know you're keen to drop him off some flowers, a thank-you card, that sort of thing, but you've been telling me to leave it, so we leave it.'

He opened his door, but turned back, hearing Styles do the same.

'What are you doing?'

'In case they're watching,' said Styles. 'You're in no fit state. Once you're back in your car, I'm back in mine.'

Porter nodded, leaving Styles to head towards his car, smiling at the overprotective little brother his DS had become. All the more reason to keep him out of what would come next.

Porter couldn't help but glance along the lane as he climbed into the driver's seat, déjà vu washing over him. No charging thugs this time, only shadows. He started the car, flicking the Bluetooth off on his phone to stop it connecting, reaching into his pocket. Swallowed back a nauseous swoop in the pit of his stomach. Whether it was injury-related or guilty conscience at what he was contemplating, who knew? Contemplating? Balls to that, he was doing this. No other choice he could see.

The second phone, long-term loan from Józef was Android to his Apple, but only took him another thirty seconds to pair it to his car. Empty call log, save for one number, no name against it. Pressed to dial as he pulled away, turning towards where Styles sat parked. The ring seemed amplified in the otherwise silent car, as if it was conspiring to be heard, loud enough for Styles to catch any conversation as he rolled past him.

Up to the third ring by the time he pulled onto the main road. A click. Few seconds of silence, as the person on the other end waited him out.

'It's me,' Porter said at last. 'We need to talk.'

'Then let's talk,' said the heavily accented voice.

CHAPTER FORTY-SEVEN

Porter was used to having to fight for every scrap of sleep, but last night had been ridiculous even by his standards. Two hours tops, chunks of the night spent staring at the ceiling, working through a dozen other ways this could go. It boiled down to one simple question. What mattered more, his job or seeing his Holly's killer behind bars? Being a copper was all he knew, but in the absence of Kamau waking up, or Jackson Tyler having an epiphany and developing a conscience, he was at a dead end, staring at the only way forward. He just hoped Evie would understand if it all went pear-shaped.

Nuhić had been very specific about this morning. His bakery at Creekmouth Industrial Estate had squatters from the Met outside last time Porter was here. They hadn't been spotted for a few weeks, but no sense taking any risks. Approach from the back he'd been told. A fire escape would be left open for him. Seven o'clock sharp. Evie had still been flat out when he left, and he'd had to fight the urge to plant a gentle kiss on her head as he left, for fear of waking her and having to answer the inevitable questions about where he was heading so early. He didn't want to lie to her any more than he had to. Than he already had.

Porter popped another pair of painkillers as he approached the door. Didn't even have a chance to try the handle himself. It opened when he was still six feet away, a young man in overalls that might have been white once upon a time stared and beckoned him in. No words were exchanged. Porter followed him down a long corridor, into the belly of the bakery. He recognised the layout from his previous visit, the scent of warm, fresh-baked bread teasing his taste buds.

The young man pointed to a door up ahead, but let Porter past him, clearly not on the list for an invitation only. Nuhić rose from his desk as Porter entered, skirting the edge to meet him halfway, extending a hand like old friends. Porter kept his firmly in his pockets. Nuhić had a face hard to date, somewhere in his fifties, although which end was anybody's guess. Expression slightly soured, a look that could curdle milk. Even when he smiled, it looked like an effort. Not a physically imposing man to look at, but like Tyler, who needed bulging biceps when you had an army of them on payroll?

'We are not quite there yet I see,' he said, heading back around his desk with a shrug. 'Please, sit.'

Even the act of sitting down, accepting an invitation from this man, ran down Porter's spine like icy fingers, reminding him just how big a step over the line this was.

'I'm not here for a cuppa and a cosy chat, Mr Nuhić,' he said, sitting uncomfortably upright. 'You said you had some information about Jackson Tyler. Anything you've got that can help prosecute him, you'll have the gratitude of the Met.'

Nuhić gave a slow nod, running one hand over a chin that Kirk Douglas would be proud of.

'So, you're looking to arrest him now? My understanding was that your interest in Mr Tyler was a little more' – split second pause – 'personal, no?'

'He's a criminal, Mr Nuhić, plain and simple. We want him off the streets. You said you had information that can help us do that.'

'I do?' Nuhić looked confused. 'I don't remember telling you that.'

Porter sighed, bored. 'I shouldn't have come here. I haven't got time for this.'

'Yet still you sit there. You have other places to go, be my guest,' said Nuhić, leaning back in his chair.

Porter had a hundred places he'd rather be, but none of them would give him what he needed, what he was here for.

'Look, whatever you called to tell me, I'm here now, so tell me.'

'You are wanting information about Mr Tyler, yes?'

'Yes,' said Porter, no attempt to hide his exasperation.

'You believe he knows about your wife, about what happened to her?'

'I do.'

'He is not a man likely to co-operate with you unless he is forced. Was this,' he pointed to Porter's bandaged fingers, 'an attempt to force him?'

'Something like that.'

'Men like us, me and him, we cannot afford to be seen working with men like you.'

'And yet here you sit,' Porter mimicked Nuhić's words from moments ago.

'Let us just say that a prolonged clash with him would be . . . problematic. If you were to disrupt, maybe even stop, his business, this may force his hand to talk to you.'

'And clear a nice gap for you to step into, just like you did when Alexander Locke died.'

'I'm in a competitive industry. I waste an opportunity, somebody else steps in. No good for either of us.'

'Don't even pretend that we're on the same side,' Porter spat out. 'Or that we're doing this for the same reasons.'

'Now, now, Detective, your motives here are not exactly altruistic, are they? Tell me, if you had five minutes alone in a room with the man who did this to your wife, would you spend that time reading him his rights, or . . . ?'

He let it tail off, Porter's imagination doing the rest. Not a question he would answer out loud, but inwardly, admitted to himself it might well depend on whether it was in Paddington Green station or somewhere quieter. Nuhić nodded, a sly smile suggesting silence was all the answer he needed.

'Tell me, Detective, what do you think it would take to force Mr Tyler's hand? You think it would be enough to just disrupt his business? I could tell you about such things as a warehouse he uses in Camberwell. I expect you have probably already tried this tactic though?'

Porter nodded. 'We picked up a few of his guys. About twenty grand's worth of gear on them, but Tyler didn't budge.'

'Reputation,' Nuhić said, tapping a finger against the desk. 'For me, for him, it is everything. Speaking to you, cooperating in any way, this would cause his reputation to suffer. His men would not trust him to have their backs. He, like me, would do anything rather than that. What is it then, I wonder, that he would fear, that could damage his reputation more?'

Nuhić folded his arms, one hand scratching non-existent stubble.

'I don't know. You tell me,' said Porter.

So Nuhić did. Porter grimaced as he listened. Not what he expected, but definitely what he needed.

CHAPTER FORTY-EIGHT

Porter's mind whirled the whole way back to the office like a hamster on steroids hammering its wheel. What Nuhić had shared with him, if it was true, would leave Tyler with a straight up choice. A walk-the-plank moment. Jump and take his chances that Porter went after whoever he gave up in a way that hid the source. Stay put and end up impaled on the sharp end of the secret Nuhić had shared.

He called Evie when he was five minutes out. She wasn't on shift until lunchtime and had that fuzzy quality to her voice suggesting she was either not long up or still in bed.

'Didn't wake you, did I?'

'Hmm, no. I was just trying to find the will to crawl out from under the duvet. What time did you wake up?'

'Never really fell asleep in the first place,' he admitted. 'Thought I might as well make an early start.'

'Any chance of an early finish as well?'

'I could always play the wounded soldier card,' he said, slipping into his best poorly voice. 'I can feel the migraine coming on already.'

'You should have stayed off, you know. Nobody would have thought any worse of you for it.'

'Anyway,' he said, selective hearing kicking in. 'I was thinking, this weekend, we need to blow off a little steam. You free for dinner and a vat of wine on Saturday? I think I've got some making up to do.'

'Why, Detective Porter,' Evie said, 'if I didn't know better I'd say you were flirting with me.'

'Powers of deduction like that, I've got to wonder if you're after my job.'

'I'll say yes on one condition. You take it easy today. How's the head?'

'Attached.'

'Ha, ha, very funny. I mean it though, take it easy.'

He promised to do just that and drop her a line later with an ETA. Walking into the office, he was surprised to see he wasn't the first in. Kaja Sucheka sat staring at her screen, tired eyes that looked like she'd had even less sleep than him. So engrossed, she mustn't have sensed his approach until he was feet away. When she realised it was him who'd snuck up behind her, her tiredness dropped away, words tumbling out at a hundred miles an hour. If the day had started with a bang thanks to Nuhić, then Kaja's revelation was just as explosive, and Porter felt both cases in danger of pulling away from him at breakneck speed.

'You're sure?' he asked.

'See for yourself.'

He pulled up a chair, watching as her screen flicked between a half-dozen camera shots. Visual only, no audio. Black and white, shades of grey and shadows everywhere, but clear enough where it counted.

Porter drummed a fist on the desk, squeezing Kaja's shoulder with the other hand, feeling a bit stupid when he realised only two of his fingers were up to the job. She sat back, smile fading to confusion, flickering to concern.

'Long story. I'm fine.'

The look on her face suggested she'd have believed him more if he'd said he was a closet fan of One Direction, but she said nothing, letting it slide.

Porter spent the next hour rewatching the footage, jotting down notes, making follow-up calls. Only on a five-minute wander to the canteen did he allow his mind to drift back to the conversation with Nuhić, and how best to use the information.

One by one the team drifted in, every set of eyes settling on Porter, flicking between his bandaged hand, bulbous wrapping next to his one free finger making it look like a giant white crab claw. Took another ten minutes or so until they'd all grabbed a drink and settled into seats, the low murmur of conversation stopping as Porter strode to the front of the incident room.

'Don't try taking candy from a baby,' said Porter. 'Vicious little bastards don't take too well to it.'

More smiles than laughter, as if they knew he was deflecting.

'Dee, let's hear from you first. What have we got on our lovely friends at the EWP?'

'Part guesswork as to who our mystery man on the phone was if it wasn't Winter. I found two cameras that help us. One traffic, one private.'

She stepped up beside Porter, connecting her tablet to the screen on the wall, swiping through a series of stills. Cars entering and exiting the EWP car park, plus a few men coming in on foot.

'We've got a list of eleven inside at the time of the call. Winter isn't one of them. Couple of our favourites are though,' she said, pausing on two faces Porter recognised. Leo Finch and Freddie Forrester.

'Whoever it is,' said Styles, 'They could just as easily be acting on Winter's orders as flying solo. I don't trust that guy as far as I could throw him. Second thoughts, might just supervise and outsource the actual throwing part to Gus.'

'We'll come on to Winter in a minute,' said Porter, unable to help a glance at Kaja. 'How much do we know about the other nine, Dee?'

Williams rattled through a list of names, most of which were new to them, superficial profiles only, the exception being Roland Thomas. His name triggered a memory of the confrontation at Greenwich with the EWP-fuelled crowd, Thomas squaring off against Bell, falling short and skulking away. Where was she this morning?

'Keep digging, Dee. I know it's easy to get tunnel vision on the ones we know and love, but we, and by we I mean I, have already come a cropper from making assumptions on this one.'

'If you need to go down there, Dee, don't fly solo. Give me a shout first,' said Styles. 'They're not the friendliest bunch.'

'Gus, Glenn, need you back out Greenwich way this morning. Mop ups on CCTV for the places we didn't manage to speak to already. Not gonna be enough to just have motive. We need to place them at the scene, whoever *they* are, whether it's Winter, some of his boys or someone we haven't got up there yet,' Porter said, nodding towards the collage of photos, printed sheets and Post-its that wallpapered that side of the room.

'That brings me nicely on to the guest of honour,' Porter continued, walking over to tap Winter's face. 'Kaja, let's share your little find, shall we?'

Kaja Sucheka stood up, wandered over to borrow Dee's tablet, fingers tapping away as she joined Porter at the front.

'So, we know Winter travelled to York the day before Henderson was killed. We've got his e-ticket and CCTV puts him at King's Cross.'

A black and white still popped up on the wall-mounted screen. Winter, travelling light, satchel slung over his shoulder. Jeans, white shirt, looking for all the world to be just another guy off out for a trip, rather than the biggest of a bunch of bigoted pricks. Something bothered Porter about the image. Couldn't quite place it, like seeing a face in a crowd, wondering if you used to go to school with them, nothing firm enough to hang your hat on.

'That's all we had time to check out yesterday before he walked thanks to his brief having a tantrum like a hungry toddler. This is where it gets interesting. We know he got on, but far as we know, he never got off.'

A sea of befuddled faces stared back.

'This gonna be one of those riddles I used to hate at school?' Waters asked. 'A train leaves London at ten, travelling a hundred miles an hour. What colour were the driver's boxers?'

'More of a question than a riddle really, Glenn,' said Styles, never one to pass up a chance to correct the young DC. 'Question isn't whether he got off. Course he bloody did. How else do you think he was sat in room four yesterday?'

'Why didn't he get off in York, and if not there then where?' Williams thought out loud, staring at the screen.

'Gets weirder,' said Kaja. 'His phone records say he was at the office all weekend, and I mean all weekend. Like he slept there, but we know from Dee that he's not on the list of people at the office, least not that came in through the front.' She rattled off stops on the East Coast Main Line the train had pulled into, all the way to Aberdeen and back.

'What's the first confirmed sighting back in London?' asked Tessier.

'That'd be the broadcast he did the day after Greenwich,' Kaja confirmed.

'Where the bloody hell was he in the meantime?' Styles said, leaning forward in his chair.

Kaja held up her hands. 'That part, I'm still working on. Waiting to hear back from British Transport Police about footage from the stations and cameras on board. For now, though, that drags him back in the picture and proves he's lied to us.'

'You think the super will let us bring him back in for that?'

All heads turned to Porter. He puffed out a breath, painfully aware of the consequences of calling it wrong.

'We'll get a lot less grief if we fill in the blanks first,' he said finally. 'Wouldn't hurt to have eyes on him in the meantime for when we do. Kaja, that's priority number one for you today.'

'Boss, how about seeing if we can blag a favour from DCI Agarwhal?' she asked.

Another reminder for Porter that he was off his game. Should have thought of that himself. DCI Amara Agarwhal ran a team of so-called super recognisers. People whose ability to recognise or remember faces was off the charts. They spent their lives scouring CCTV for known suspects and had an impressive strike rate.

'Great shout, Kaja. Tell her I'll owe her one if she comes through for us.' He turned his attention to the others. 'Gus, Glenn, you get yourselves away to Greenwich as soon as we're done here. Dee, you know what you've got. Nick, you and I are going to pay another visit to the parents. I got side-tracked last time watching Winter up on his soapbox and forgot to ask about the girl in the photo. Henderson had plenty of followers, but not many friends. They look pretty close, and yet his folks didn't mention anything about a girlfriend, and she hasn't popped up anywhere mourning him.'

Styles waited until the team had dispersed before he spoke.

'I called the hospital this morning. Kamau's still out cold, but the nurse did say he's responding well after the surgery. Could wake up any time.'

'Shit, that reminds me,' Porter said, snapping his fingers. 'With the EWP mess and everything that happened last night, I forgot to follow up on his brother.'

'Wait, what? He has a brother now?'

Porter filled him in, cheeks reddening at how thick and fast these little cock-ups of his were becoming. Getting out of hand, failing faster than a black-market kidney.

'If you've got a note of the number plate on you we can check it now before we head to the Hendersons'. Maybe swing by on the way back. Two birds and all that.'

Porter rummaged around in his pocket, pulling out a scrunched-up paper ball, smoothing it against his desktop.

'Bingo.'

The Hendersons' house was a forty-minute drive, and while Styles drove, Porter used the time to dig up what background they could on Henry Kamau's brother. Benjamin was two years the elder and, unlike his baby brother, had no criminal record. Didn't mean he was squeaky clean, just that he'd never been caught. The address they had for him was the Willowbrook Estate and a quick google of his name yielded some interesting results.

Seems like he and Henry were flip sides of the coin. Benjamin worked at a community centre not far from there. The website said he was the on-site activities leader, whatever that involved. The place popped up in a few local press articles over the last couple of years. One article about an outreach programme to combat gang culture and another about a knife amnesty they headed up, collecting in over two thousand blades across a bank holiday weekend. Those same blades now stood outside, melded into a sculpture. One figure helping another to climb a step, giving them a help up. Title of the piece was *Leg Up*. It formed part of the mission statement of the centre, offering everyone and anyone who needed it just that.

'Wonder if Benjamin ever ran with Tyler's crew before this,' said Styles when Porter relayed the info. 'Turned over a new leaf, that type of thing. Would have made for a bit of tension at the dinner table growing up, what with him and Henry batting for different sides.'

'Should only be a five-minute job at the Hendersons',' said Porter. 'You can ask him soon enough.'

Brian Henderson looked as good as Porter felt when he opened the door. Baggy pouches under his eyes like he hadn't slept in days. Looked like a man who'd been stripped of his reason for being, like life had kicked the shit out of him and he was just waiting for round two.

'Mr Henderson,' Styles took the lead, as the man Henderson recognised from his first visit. 'DS Styles again, this is my boss, DI Jake Porter. Can we come in for a minute?'

'Has something happened? I saw you arrested that Winter chap yesterday. Has he been charged?' The prospect of any news sparked Henderson to life, only for a moment though, when Styles brought him crashing back down to earth.

'No, sir, no charges, and nothing major to report at this stage I'm afraid.'

Brian Henderson closed his eyes for a second, breathing deeply. 'Then now's not a good time. We've had a fresh wave of reporters at the door after you arrested that Winter fella yesterday. Angela's had to go to the doctor's today to get something to help her sleep. Starting to wonder if I should pop a few myself to be honest.'

He gave as sad a smile as Porter had seen, and he wondered how you even began to cope with the loss of a child, let alone in these circumstances.

'I understand, Mr Henderson, and we'll let you get back inside to your wife. There was just one thing actually,' Porter said, pulling out his phone, showing Henderson a scanned copy of the photo he'd found upstairs two days ago. So much had happened since then, felt like a parallel universe.

'We're just wondering if you recognised this lady here with your son?'

Henderson's rheumy eyes filled up at the sight of his son, and he blinked back the tears as he reached out, taking the phone from Porter, a wistful smile tugging at the edges of his mouth.

'Yes, that's Penny. Where did you get that from?'

'It was in his room. Who's Penny?'

'Penny? She's an old girlfriend of his. Not seen her in, ooh, three years, maybe four. What's she got to do with this?'

'Probably nothing,' said Porter, smiling, feeling the skin around his scabbed temple stretch. 'Just being thorough. Don't suppose you have an address for her, do you? And a surname for that matter?'

Henderson puffed his cheeks out, slight shake of the head. 'It's Penny Trainor. No idea where she lives. Last I heard though she was still working at the Asda just off the A13. You could always ask there.'

They thanked him and turned to leave.

'Detective, sorry to be a bother, but I was wondering if there's any chance I could get the original back when you're done with it? He looks so happy there, so . . .' He trailed off, swallowing hard.

Porter promised to have it dropped off in the next day or two, and they left him to trudge back inside to a house full of memories. He texted Dee Williams about checking up on Penny via Asda before he pulled away. The drive to Willowbrook Community Centre felt like salmon swimming upstream, glacial traffic crawling through a series of roadworks. Porter was quiet for the first half, Nuhić's words like loose marbles rolling around in his head. Styles had started off chattering into the silence, but that dropped off, as if he sensed Porter was struggling with something.

Decision finally made, Porter started talking, problem shared, problem halved. Started with Nuhić's man outside the station. Didn't stop until he dropped the same bomb Nuhić had on him earlier this morning. Styles kept quiet throughout, but even he couldn't stifle a *woah* as Porter finished his download.

'How you going to play it then?'

'Haven't quite figured that part out yet. That place of his at Castlemead is like walking into a bloody rat trap though. Not strolling in there solo again in a hurry.'

'Doesn't have to be solo next time.'

'I've already told you, no way you're on the front line for this.'

'Hmm, we'll see.'

'That's an order, Sergeant,' Porter said, only half serious. He would be exactly the same if roles were reversed.

CHAPTER FORTY-NINE

They pulled up outside the Willowbrook Community Centre a little after eleven. It was a stocky two-storey block of concrete and brick, squatting halfway along a residential street. The whole thing looked like it had been whitewashed once upon a time. The side facing out to the main road was punctuated by a series of large murals. One in particular stood out, bright, with a freshly painted look to it. Olympic rings, faces peering out of each. Different colours and genders, kids and adults. One big show of unity.

Furious footfall and urgent shouts drifted across from a five-a-side pitch off to the left. Porter and Styles headed through open gates and into a reception area. A large black woman eyed them up as they walked in, filing a set of nails that wouldn't have looked out of place on Freddie Kruger. Her purple polo shirt seemed to be part of the branding. Matching seats and noticeboard headers, alternating a Cadbury's Dairy Milk wrapper shade with teal accents.

'Help you, gents?' she said in a happy sing-song voice.

Porter approached the counter, pulling out his ID, introducing them both. 'We're after a quick word with Benjamin Kamau. He around?'

'Ben? Yeah, he's out back refereeing a game. Shouldn't be more than a few minutes,' she said, glancing at a clock on the wall. 'You can wait here if you like?'

They took a seat by a vending machine. Just the sight of a row of salt and vinegar crisps made Porter's mouth water. Ella, he'd spotted her name tag, didn't have a great poker face. Porter could tell she was itching to ask what they wanted to speak to Ben about. She fought the good fight, holding out for a full minute before she caved.

'What is it you need to speak to him about? Maybe I could help?'

'Afraid I can't share details, miss. He's not done anything wrong though.'

A few minutes later, a door burst open down a corridor to Porter's left, a stream of sweaty teenagers, crowd dotted with fluorescent bibs, charged halfway along and into the changing room. Bringing up the rear, Porter clocked Benjamin Kamau, build and gait recognisable from the hospital footage. He stood, meeting and holding Kamau's glance along the corridor. Fixed on Porter and stayed there for a beat. Must be giving off blue vibes, as Kamau came straight to them.

'Can I help you?'

Porter introduced them both again. 'Sorry to rock up unannounced like this, sir, but it's quite important we speak about your brother. Have you got a few minutes?'

Kamau dragged a backhand across his forehead, smearing more sweaty drops than he cleared, and gestured for them to join him in his office, across reception and down a mirror-image corridor. The office itself could have been an IKEA display. It was so bloody neat, looked like all it was missing were the tags. Two big corkboards on neighbouring walls. One dominated by a huge year planner, handwriting so bad it looked like scribbles all over as if kids had been doodling. The other wall was just as busy, but this one was covered with letters. Porter snuck a closer look as he grabbed a seat. Letters and cards from kids. Kamau must have seen what had caught his attention.

'Just a few from the kids who use the place. We try and teach 'em a few things here before they head off to ignore most of it.'

He smiled at his own wisecrack, one that planted deep crow's feet either side. He was the older brother by two years but looked another five on top of that. Not a big guy, but wiry, compact. Buzzed haircut that was closer to stubble. Two-inch scar cutting a furrow through the fuzz above his left ear. Porter couldn't decide what must have been harder: growing up around here, Triple H influence leeching into the lifeblood of the community, or making the decision to stick around, try and turn kids away from that life.

'They wouldn't tell me what happened,' he said, smile slipping slowly away. 'Wouldn't even say what they reckon he's done this time.'

'This time?' Styles prompted, although they'd already read up on Henry's priors. More a case of get Ben talking, use this as a temperature check of how honest he'd be, how much he'd share.

'How long you got?' he said with an eye-roll. 'What kind of brother am I, that I can keep all these out of trouble' – he waved a hand towards his fan mail – 'but I can't keep my own brother safe?'

'Don't sell yourself short,' Styles said, 'looks to me like you're doing more than most round here.'

Kamau gave a mirthless laugh. 'Yeah, for all the good it does. Every one I keep off the streets, there's two think the grass is greener with one of the gangs.'

'Your brother is with Triple H,' Porter said. 'How long's that been going on?'

'Too long. Three years, maybe four,' he said.

'Daft question maybe, but I'm assuming you tried to keep him away, just like you do these other boys?'

'More times than I can remember,' Kamau said, every word laced with regret.

Porter changed tack. 'They never tried to recruit you?'

'They don't recruit. More of a press gang. They want you, you're in, one way or another.'

'And what, they didn't want you?'

'Something like that, yeah.'

Some kind of backstory there, but Porter didn't press it.

'Do I get to know what happened then?' he asked. 'I tried calling up yesterday, but they wouldn't give me anything over the phone. Said someone would call me back. Pullman? Pittman? Something like that.'

Porter shrugged, swallowing down the frustration of Pittman turning out to be every bit as average as he feared. Why the hell had he not followed up yet? No harm sharing the charges and allegations behind them in the meantime. Might be a few questions when he eventually did reach out if there was mention of officers having already visited.

Kamau sat stony-faced, water off a duck's back. Nothing he hadn't heard before. Henry had done a stint in juvenile detention for assault, picked up twice for handling stolen goods, but those hadn't stuck. Nothing major, least not on his record anyway. Time to go digging.

'To be honest though, sir, that's not why we're here today,' Porter said. 'Henry's prints popped up as having been at an older crime scene, one going back a few years.'

'Don't know that I'll be much help. He's his own man. We're not as close as we used to be. Yeah, we have a beer every now and again, but our two worlds don't really mix.'

'This was quite a serious one,' Porter said, 'hit-and-run. A car he was in ran another one off the road. The driver of the other car, a young woman, she . . .' His throat felt tight, emotion wrapping bands around it, squeezing. 'She died.'

Kamau's mouth opened a touch, closed again. Repeated twice more. Baby brother graduating to big time.

Porter realised he was gripping the armrest hard enough for tiny white blotches to blanch his knuckles. Styles clocked him looking, saw the same, and stepped into the silence the other men had left.

'The car he was in was found a few miles from the accident. Did he ever mention anything about it?'

Kamau looked almost affronted at the suggestion. 'What, you think I could have just sat on that for a few years, said nothing?'

'Family loyalty's a strong tie, Mr Kamau, even if you weren't close. We're not saying he would have just come right out with it, but I'm sure you hear a lot said in this place. Maybe even just a throwaway comment. I'm betting there's a few passed through here who've been Triple H?'

301

Kamau shook his head. 'Couple tried, but Tyler doesn't exactly let you just walk away, unless he wants you gone.'

'What can you tell us about him?' Porter asked. 'Have you met him? Do you know him personally?'

Three quick-fire questions. Too eager to get answers, letting heart rule the head. He needed to take a step back, reset. Easier said than done though.

'Everyone round here knows Jackson Tyler, Detective. Best if he doesn't know you though.'

'What do you mean by that?'

'Pfft.' Kamau made a noise like a tyre deflating. 'Everyone knows what happens, you get on the wrong side of him. I just keep my head down, do what I can for the kids that'll let me.'

'What about Henry's friends, life outside Triple H, anyone he hung around with? Anyone else we could speak to?'

'They've pretty much brainwashed him. That gang *is* his life. Look, I wish I could help you, I really do, but whatever shit he got up to with that lot, that's his business.'

Kamau had started picking at one thumbnail with the other, worrying away at a ragged edge. 'Look, I appreciate you coming here, filling in the blanks for me with Henry, but I've got another game to ref in five minutes.'

Something about Kamau bothered Porter. Maybe the nerves, but then again, he'd just found out his brother was involved in a fatal accident. Felt like he was bobbing and weaving through the questions. Giving enough to appear helpful, without actually giving anything. Time to try a not so subtle prod.

'You're sure there's nothing else you can think of that might help us, Mr Kamau? Henry's already facing some time for the

B&E. Be a shame to let him get dragged down by this for longer.'

'What do you mean? You can't do that. How's that his fault? That's like me buying you a beer and getting the blame for you being drunk.'

'He was there, Mr Kamau. We've got witness who saw it happen and his prints in the car. He fled the scene.'

'But the driver's the one you want though, yeah? He's not a bad kid, even with everything he's done. Man, it's bad enough we're losing kids to gangs hand over fist, and you're trying to pin this on him when he can't even speak up for himself. Look, I really got to go,' he said, grin more polite than warm now.

Kamau stood, moving around the desk, opening the door. Porter gave Styles a *he'll keep* look and stood up to follow.

'Just one quick one before you go,' he said as he walked past Kamau. 'You said the driver's the one we want. How do you know that wasn't Henry?'

Benjamin Kamau's grin fixed in place, but the eyes widened. Just a touch, a blink and you'd miss it, but Porter spotted it. Waited him out for the split second it took Kamau to start back up again, like someone had given him a jumpstart.

'That's what you said before, innit? That he was on the other side.'

'Don't think I did,' said Porter, slow shake of the head. 'Didn't even say if his prints were in the front or the back.'

'I'm telling you, you did. Look, I've got to be on the pitch in' – he checked his watch – 'three minutes. You'll be OK to find your way out, yeah?'

Kamau didn't even wait for a reply, trotting off along the corridor and out of sight. Porter turned to Styles, arching his eyebrows.

'He knows,' Styles voiced what they were both thinking. 'He knows what happened.'

Porter's head was already a step further. Leap of faith, but one that felt like a Tetris block slotting into place.

He knows because he was behind the wheel.

CHAPTER FIFTY

Porter jogged around to the five-a-side pitch. Kids pinged half a dozen balls at either end, hammering a constant barrage into empty nets, waiting for goalies to step into the firing line. No sign of Benjamin Kamau though. A few of them stopped what they were doing, looking over at him as he poked his head through the gate, stepping onto the pitch on the off-chance that Kamau was behind the boarding. Styles circled around the edge, heading for the second pitch that sat alongside.

Noise and movement hit Porter together, head whipping around. The top half of a Ford Focus cruised past the hoardings. Same one Porter had seen on the hospital CCTV. He called over to Styles, but by the time they'd both reached their own vehicle, the Focus was nowhere to be seen.

'What do you want to do, boss?' Styles asked, breathing a little heavier from his jog.

'Let's get someone round to his home address. Let's check before we leave here as well if he's got an emergency contact listed, anything like that. Might be way off the mark, but he couldn't have looked more uncomfortable in there if he'd just followed through.'

Styles nodded. 'Could just be that folks round here don't have the best experiences with us. These places don't exactly run their outreach programmes to support your average Tarquin or Tabitha.'

He had a point. Still though, you developed a feel for these things, and Benjamin Kamau had hit every tripwire in Porter's subconscious up to the point he made a hasty exit. Next conversation he had with Ben would be in a boxy room at Paddington Green. Styles offered to head back inside to speak to the receptionist, and while he disappeared, Porter used the breathing space to turn his mind back to Jackson Tyler.

No matter how keen Styles was to be in the mix, there was no way Porter could allow it. Going back another time to the rat trap that was Tyler's block of flats didn't exactly appeal. Might as well punch himself in the face a few times for good measure. Had to be some other way, some place less secluded, to deliver what he hoped would be a knockout blow.

Tyler's men, the two scooped up night before last. The control freak that he was, he'd want to speak to them when they got out, if they got out. One quick call filled in the blanks he needed. One released, one with an extension, meaning he was still in custody thanks to his prints having showed up at a burglary three months back. Likely he'd be out on bail later today though. Every chance he'd scuttle straight off to Tyler, and in the event he didn't, it was just as likely that Tyler would find him.

Styles came out of the centre, holding a piece of paper like a ref brandishing a card. He'd just popped the door open when Porter's phone buzzed. Kaja.

'Hey, Kaja. Everything OK?' he asked, starting the car up.

'More than OK,' she said, excitement making the words tumble out faster. 'It's Winter. He lied about York, and I can prove it.'

CHAPTER FIFTY-ONE

'So, let me get this straight,' said Porter. 'He gets on a train with a ticket for York, but gets off at Peterborough?'

'And we've got him coming back into King's Cross around four hours later, over a full hour before the call comes into his office and a few days before Henderson died.'

'Show me.'

She clicked to open the first of a string of files the British Transport Police had emailed over. A new window popped to life packed with platforms and passengers.

'Here,' she stabbed a finger at the screen. The quality wasn't exactly HD, but there was no mistaking Damien Winter, striding through throngs of people like he owned the place, leather satchel slung over his shoulder. 'He gets on the eight-oh-three with his ticket to York' – she toggled to a second window – 'but here he is jumping off at Peterborough.'

Porter squinted for a second, about to correct her, but stopped.

The man she picked out had a jacket on, unlike the Winter he'd seen at King's Cross, baseball cap pulled down low. Same satchel though, same imperious *out-of-my-way-peasant* strut.

'You owe DCI Agarwhal a drink by the way. Couple of her team checked every stop the train made. Pot luck that this was one of the first, but they spotted it way before I would have.'

'Do we know what he was doing there?'

'Not yet, but I'm on it. He grabs a black cab from outside. I know a DS there. She's tracking down the cabbie for us, see where he dropped him. Far as we're concerned though, what matters is that he's back a little before one.'

'Which gives him time to get back to his office, take the call and chat with our mystery man,' Styles finished.

'Only hole in that is the office CCTV,' said Kaja. 'He didn't appear anywhere when I checked, but then again it's his own system. He could easily have paused it, slipped in, then set it going again.'

'We need him back in here,' said Porter.

'Glenn and Gus are on their way to bring him in now.'

'If I hadn't already done a course on sexual harassment in the workplace, I'd hug you right now.'

Kaja gave him a shrug. 'If I was into guys, I'd probably let you.'

Porter was toying with the idea of updating Milburn. Nah, that could wait until after they'd grilled Winter. Couldn't run the risk of him vetoing the whole thing for appearance's sake. Before he could decide, Dee Williams came bustling through the door.

'Hey, Dee,' Styles greeted her. 'You're not gonna believe the latest we've got on Winter.'

'Go on then, we can play Top Trumps,' she said, drawing a deep breath, always a sucker for the stairs than the lift.

'Wait, what've you got? Ladies first.'

'Just had a nice chat with Penny Trainor,' she said. 'Turns out she wasn't his ex any more.'

'They were back on then,' said Porter, not seeing the significance. 'And?'

'When she stopped being his ex, she started being somebody else's.'

'We doing this twenty questions style, then?' asked Kaja. 'Am I a man? Am I an animal?'

'How about am I Jason McTeague?' Dee said, with a sly grin.

CHAPTER FIFTY-TWO

Jason McTeague looked as guilty as a kid next to a smashed lamp when Porter and Styles walked into the interview room. Dee's revelation was just the first layer. Turned out she'd wasted no time, doubling back through phone records. His didn't move from his house, tying in with his alibi. Different story for the second number she'd checked, the one that had made the call to Winter's office.

'This,' said Porter, sharing a photo via tablet to the wall-mounted screen, 'is footage from Starbucks at Lewisham Shopping Centre. 'And this,' he pointed at a figure outside, back to the glass, 'is you.'

'Detective,' the duty solicitor began, 'I hardly think that's basis for an identification, and even if it was—'

Porter cut over him, continuing as if he hadn't said a word. 'This is from a camera opposite Starbucks. I'd say that's a pretty good likeness, wouldn't you? You can continue to deny it, and we can run through the other dozen or so we have of you on your way there.'

McTeague's eyes were glassy, looking straight through the pictures. He mumbled something Porter didn't catch.

'Can you speak up for the recording, please, Mr McTeague?' asked Styles.

'I said yes, it's me, all right.'

'And that phone in your hand, that's yours, yes?'

No response this time, just a movement of the head, chin down low towards his chest.

'For the benefit of the recording, Mr McTeague is nodding,' said Styles. 'Except that's not your usual phone, is it, Jason?'

McTeague didn't look up. The muscles in his jaw knotted as he clenched and unclenched his teeth. His solicitor, a relative newcomer to the profession, bent in, whispering into his client's ear. No response.

Styles slipped in a sucker punch, sliding the next picture into view. 'And she isn't your girlfriend any more, is she, Jason?'

McTeague swung his head up, and Porter saw the rawness in his eyes as he stared at the image of Penny Trainor.

'I only wanted to hurt him, like he hurt me,' he said softly. The solicitor placed a cautionary hand on his arm, but McTeague shrugged it away. 'He didn't want her back at school, not for long anyway. Got bored and cheated on her with one of her mates.'

He sat a little straighter, folding his arms, staring at Penny.

'What happened between you two, Jason?' Porter mirrored him in voice and posture.

One arm stayed across his chest, the other reaching up, rubbing at his forehead, as if McTeague could massage it all

312

away. His eyes started to fill as he kept fixated on Penny.

'I knew she was seeing someone else. Just knew, you know. Late shifts at work all of a sudden, keeping her distance, hiding her phone when I came in the room. I just knew. Then I smelt her on him, the perfume she wears. Borrowed a jacket off him a few months back, and I fucking smelt her.'

Porter had dozens of questions, but instinct told him the floodgates were open. Let him talk and pick through the bones of it when he was done. McTeague sniffed and swallowed hard.

'I even asked her one night. Just flat out asked her. Denied everything, but what else was she gonna do? I wanted to be wrong, I really did. Thought if I could prove to myself I was just being a dick, I could let it go. That's when I put the button cam in his jacket. Hers were all too flimsy, would have stood out, but he liked those big puffer jackets. Recorded the two of 'em a few days later. Was all the proof I needed. Too much.'

'So, he didn't know it was there?' Porter asked, thinking back to the Winter footage.

McTeague shook his head.

'Then how did that micro SD card get in his room?'

'I put it there the day after he . . .' McTeague couldn't bring himself to say the words. 'Went round to pay my condolences and said I needed the loo so I could head upstairs. Winter was only supposed to rough him up. I never . . . They were just . . . Oh God,' he said, burying his head in his hands.

'And it was you that emailed the audio of that call?'

He nodded again. 'You have to believe me, I had no idea they would go that far. I couldn't just let them get away with it, but I couldn't exactly stroll in and tell you what I knew without getting arrested myself, could I?'

'How did you know where he'd be broadcasting from?' Styles asked. 'I thought he kept that secret?'

'He did. I slipped an old phone in his bag and used Find my iPhone when he first went to scope the place out.'

'That's the mystery number we had show up at the court?'

Another nod.

'But the only one we recovered at the scene belonged to Ross,' said Styles.

McTeague squeezed his eyes tight shut, bracing for some kind of impact, and Porter realised where Styles was headed.

'It was you, wasn't it? Our mystery footsteps after they left and before we found him. You went in and got your phone back.'

McTeague shook his head, but it wasn't a denial. 'I can still see him now. Have done every night since.'

'Have you had any contact with Winter since then?' Porter asked.

'Are you fucking kidding me?' said McTeague, in his highest octave yet. 'After what they did to him, you think I'm going to ring for a chat?''

'He'll be looking for you though, won't he?'

'Bloody well hope not.'

'What about the footage you promised him? Can't see him hoping for the best that it doesn't surface, can you?'

'I put a copy of the micro SD card in Ross's bag,' said McTeague. 'Like you say, figured if they went away empty-handed, they'd keep looking.'

'Any idea who the three men were, Jason? Did you see them on the way in or out?'

'They were long gone. I never planned on going inside myself. Would've just got the phone back later, or the next day.'

'Winter has a copy of the micro SD card then?' Styles said. 'We get that, we tie him to the scene.'

Porter suspended the interview, leaving McTeague with a thousand-yard stare, duty solicitor angrily whispering to him, clearly not happy about being kept in the dark.

Kaja's was the first face he saw.

'Any word from Glenn or Gus yet?'

She shook her head, and Porter felt the first twinge of worry. They should have been back by now. An image of the old Greenwich Magistrates' Court flashed to mind. Blade sawing. Speckled spatter soaking into the carpet. Porter grabbed his keys and bolted for the door.

CHAPTER FIFTY-THREE

Styles rode with him up front, Dee and Kaja squeezed into the back. Porter had insisted on stab-proof vests all round, although how much use they'd be against a slashing machete was anyone's guess. He hit the button to redial Glenn, third time unlucky, ringing out to voicemail. A heavy silence settled over the car as they raced south, over the river. Anything happened to them, it would be on him. Jackson Tyler was more than just a distraction, he was a set of blinkers, blinding Porter to the true level of danger once they got close to their three masked men.

His gut told him Winter hadn't been one of them. More of a general up on a hill, than front-line, hands dirty. Plenty who'd do it for him. These last few days he had seen an uglier side surface in people, some just scared, others revelling in the permission to act as they thought this gave them.

Fourth time lucky, as Waters answered his phone.

'Glenn, I'm on my way to you now. What's happening?'

'Just about to go in, boss.'

'No, stand down till we get there. Where the bloody hell have you been anyway? You've had time to drive there and back twice by now.'

Waters sounded more than a little defensive. 'Not our fault, boss. It was all kicking off when we came through Bermondsey. Couple of right-wing wankers harassing a bunch of teenagers, the usual go-back-to-your-own-country bullshit. Didn't go down well with everyone and a few blokes stepped in, punches thrown, you know the drill. Anyway, kicked off as we came past, so we ended up getting involved. Had to wait for a van to come and take a few of 'em away. What's up? You sound stressed.'

Porter got him to switch to speaker, filling both him and Gus in, getting an update in return. Gates closed, couple of cars in the lot, no eyes on anyone. They pulled up behind Waters and Tessier ten minutes later. Winter's lie about York, together with McTeague's statement, might not be solid enough for Milburn, but Porter's mind was set. No way Winter would come willingly, not after last time. Leaving him to drift in under his own head of steam would give him time to dispose of the micro SD card, if he hadn't already, as well as concoct an excuse about the York trip. No, this was happening now, today, hastily obtained arrest warrant in hand. He'd deal with Milburn later.

'Aim of the game is Winter,' said Porter, as they gathered between two cars. 'We don't have enough to bring anyone else along with him, unless they try anything stupid.'

'What about Finch, boss?' asked Tessier.

'Not even him, not yet. Extra brownie points for whoever finds me that micro SD card though.'

They advanced on the gates, three pairs. Porter had checked Winter with the DVLA and recognised a silver Mercedes GLA by the front door as his. Williams and Waters went left, Tessier and Sucheka right, with Porter and Styles approaching the front door directly.

The door opened with ten feet left to cover. The man who poked his head out looked like he hadn't been within five miles of a gym, dark fleece with even darker stains, flabby half-inch ring of flesh poking out from underneath.

'Ah, Jimmy,' said Styles, like he was greeting an old friend. 'No need to have gotten all dolled up for me.'

'You two know each other?' said Porter with a half-smile.

'Jimmy here was kind enough to deny me entry and ask me to go back to my own country a few days back, weren't you, Jimmy?'

Jimmy couldn't have looked less amused if Styles had unzipped his fly and peed all over his shoes.

'Answer's the same today,' Jimmy said, crossing his arms, chin tilting up, aiming for his best bouncer pose. 'Boss man ain't in, and you ain't welcome. Don't care if you brought a mate neither. Don't change the fact the likes of you don't belong here.'

Jimmy hadn't ventured past the threshold, and Porter doubted he could see either of the other pairs who'd fanned out to the left and right. Might as well have had a neon sign saying 'Racist' around his neck the way he spat out those words at Nick.

'What about the likes of Gus here?' said Styles, nodding at Tessier as the big man lumbered into view. Jimmy took a half-step back, eyes widening as Tessier folded arms that could squeeze most men like a tube of toothpaste. 'You want to tell him he needs to leave the country too?'

'Don't care how many you bring,' Jimmy said, all conviction leeched from his voice now, 'you still can't just walk in here, not without a warrant.'

'That's where you're wrong, Jimmy,' said Porter. 'We've got an arrest warrant for your gaffer, and that's his car over there, so we have reasonable suspicion to believe he's on the premises. Now, I suggest you step back and let us past before Gus here has to move you.'

Jimmy huffed and puffed, jaw working overtime, but he stepped back a few seconds later, waddling off down a corridor faster than Porter would have expected him to move.

'Mr Winter, sir,' he called, glancing over his shoulder as he pushed through a door. 'Police are here.'

Porter strode in with Styles, closely followed by Gus and Kaja, Dee and Glenn working their way around the sides to cover the rear of the building. Gus and Kaja started worked their way through a series of rooms either side, while Porter and Styles followed in Jimmy's footsteps. The door opened out into a gaudy office, Winter seated behind an old-fashioned leather-topped desk that put Porter in mind of the one in Ross Henderson's room. Bookshelves either side of the desk, mostly older leather-bound ones that Porter would bet were for effect. Photo frames acted as bookends. Winter with a handful of politicians and sportsmen. Winter speaking at an event, hands gripping either side of the podium. All about vanity and validation.

Jimmy was leaning over the desk, talking low and fast. Winter rose to his feet as they entered, chest puffed out, eyes blazing with indignation.

319

'This is harassment, plain and simple,' he said in a haughty voice, picking up his phone. 'Wait till my solicitor gets through with you.' He started tapping away at the screen.

'You were in Peterborough, not York,' Porter snapped. 'You were back in London in time to take that call. We've got you on camera.'

Winter paused, phone halfway to his ear. 'What . . . ? How did . . . ? I'm not saying another word without my solicitor.' His bravado faded, giving way to what Porter was pretty sure was fear.

'Have it your way. Damien Winter, you're under arrest.'

Porter rattled through his rights, seeing Winter's eyes flick nervously around the room, as the others set about searching the office.

'What the bloody hell do you expect to find?' Winter spat as Styles worked his way along a bookshelf, running his hands around the edges, opening some up and riffling the pages.

'Let you know when we find it,' said Styles with a wink.

Porter cuffed Winter's hands in front, manoeuvring him towards the door. Behind them, desk drawers rattled open and closed, and Winter twisted around. Porter thought for a second he was trying to break loose, but there was no move to run.

'You damage any of my stuff, I'll be going to the papers about this harassment. Probably will anyway.'

'Somehow I doubt that, Damien.'

Sucheka had finished with the drawers now, crouching on her hands and knees, contorting to look under the desktop, running gloved hands into dark corners. Porter saw her expression change, brief pause, then she reached further under, going shoulder-deep. A scraping sound as something, whatever she'd got her hands on, came away. She held up her find like a trophy.

'What the hell is that?' said Winter.

'That, Mr Winter, is a memory card, and you, sir, are well and truly buggered.'

CHAPTER FIFTY-FOUR

Winter scowled as Porter entered the interview room. What with the railway footage and the memory card, not to mention the taxi driver's input from Peterborough that had come through, Winter looked and felt like a fish in a barrel ready for the taking. Porter relished the thought of popping Peterborough on the record in particular. The driver had given them an address, which had given them a name. One that was already known to the local coppers, but one Winter would want kept between these four walls.

Don't get lazy, Jake. Assume nothing.

Gene Rafferty sat in to represent Winter again for a touch of déjà vu, but the ten minutes he'd had with his client hadn't exactly left him looking brimming with confidence.

Porter wasted no time, quickly rattling through the footage from both stations, laying out the timeline, the glaring window of opportunity Winter had to be back in the office to take the call from McTeague. Cherry on the cake was the micro SD card, already cued up and ready to play. Porter ignored the screen, studying Winter as the footage rolled. Curious at first as he watched himself appear, flicker of recognition as the conversation sparked a memory, turning to grim determination as he whispered something to Gene Rafferty.

'How about we start there then Damien?' asked Porter, friendly, unassuming. 'What did you mean by that? "Taking a short walk off a long pier"?'

'Look,' Winter began, holding up a hand, 'that's not what it looks like.'

'Really?' said Styles. 'Looks to me like you're making a threat against a man who was murdered three days ago. How would you describe it?'

'It's a figure of speech for God's sake. Doesn't mean I'm actually going to do it. I'm not a savage.'

'Any reason you gave my DS here a once up and down when you said that?' said Porter.

'Eh? What?'

'If we can stick to the questions related to the charges, please, Detective,' Rafferty cut in.

'Just an observation.' Porter shrugged. 'But it is linked, isn't it? No secret that you're not a fan of anyone who doesn't share your shade on the Dulux colour chart, now, is it?'

'You're grossly oversimplifying what the EWP stands for.'

'Because of course it's so much more nuanced than that, isn't it?' said Styles. 'Britain for the British? Includes me last time I checked my birth certificate, but you wouldn't know it to hear the reception I've had twice at your place now.'

'Feelings can run a little strong amongst some of the party when national pride is at stake, our safety, the fact we're in danger of becoming a minority in some of our own cities.'

Porter made a show of looking around the room. 'There's no crowd for you to play to here, Damien. You'll probably be glad of that by the time we're finished though.'

'Detective, if can we cut to the chase instead of throwing out childish threats?' Rafferty, the dictionary definition of pompous.

'No problem.' Porter shrugged again. 'You want short and sweet. Tell me what happened on Sunday. Were you one of the three men on camera, and if not, who were they?'

'How many times?' Winter was borderline shouting now. 'It wasn't bloody me.'

'Then how did this memory card get under your desk? A card that had been in Ross Henderson's backpack at the time of his murder.'

'I don't know.' Each word forced out, through gritted teeth. 'Someone else must have put it there. Whoever took that call.'

'Let's move onto that, shall we?' said Porter, lapping up every ounce of discomfort from across the table. 'Whoever put it there was either at the scene or part of it. If it wasn't you, who was it?'

'How many times? I have no bloody idea. Why don't you get them all in and ask them?'

'I'll be honest, Damien, I don't think you were there when it happened. Don't think you'd have the stomach to actually watch, let alone do it.' Porter leant in over the table. 'I do, however, think after listening to all that hate you spew dressed up as national pride, that you'd let someone else do your dirty work to get your hands on that footage. Only way this gets any easier for you is if you tell us who.'

'Asked and answered, Detective,' said Rafferty.

'Your call, Damien, but I'm pretty confident we've got enough to satisfy the CPS as it is. We've got you threatening the life of a man who was brutally murdered, we've got evidence tying you to the scene, and we've got you on tape saying you'll "take care" of him,' said Porter, making air quotes for two of the words. 'Only question is whether you go down alone.'

'This is bollocks,' Winter snapped. 'All of it. You think that by stitching me up, you can silence the thousands who feel the same way I do about the state our country is in?'

'I think those thousands of people would have a different view of what you spout if they knew why you were in Peterborough, don't you?'

'What's that got to do with anything?' Winter said, trying to sound nonchalant, failing badly.

'Cabbie gave us the address you went to. Flat belonging to a Mr Gareth Wood. Tenant by the name of Suzi Adeyemi.'

'Never heard of her,' said Winter, but the denial came to fast, too forceful.

'Funny, she's heard of you. Turns out not only is Suzi an escort, but she's not meant to be in the country. Should have been back in Nigeria long before you crossed paths with her, but her parents were killed by Boko Haram militants and she's scared to go back. Been working off the books so to speak to stay here. It's fine though. We've offered to help her claim asylum in return for testifying when you go in the dock.'

Porter paused for a beat, watched Winter fix on a spot over his shoulder, slight tic twitching away in one eyelid, nostrils flared.

'Wonder what your hardcore supporters will make of that? Their glorious leader shacked up with a Nigerian hooker,' said Styles, perfect poker face revealing none of the satisfaction he must be feeling of slapping Winter back down. 'Kind of undermines your stance on immigration, doesn't it, Damien?'

'No comment,' Winter said after a pause, still looking beyond Porter.

'Your call,' said Porter, 'but if you don't give us the three names, then Suzi testifies. You give us them, and we don't need her story.'

Winter looked at him now, desperation in both face and voice. 'So I paid her. So what? There's bigger crimes committed every day by the thousands who come here looking to leech off us. Stitching me up does nothing but harm our country.'

'I think you're grossly overestimating your own importance, Damien,' said Porter. 'And we don't need to stitch you up, when we have evidence and witnesses.'

Rafferty leant in, whispering, but Winter recoiled, shoving him away. 'I'm not making any bloody deals for something I didn't do!'

Pretty convincing, thought Porter, but then again Winter was used to spinning a line for the masses, Pied Piper whipping up the crowds, pointing them in the general direction of anyone who wasn't white, and slipping their leash off.

A quick-fire triple knock had the effect of hitting the pause button, all eyes on the door. Porter bit down on his lower lip, already prepping a verbal volley for whoever stood on the other side.

The face he saw was Taylor Bell's. 'I know, I know,' she said, 'I'd hate me too if I were you, but you need to hear this.'

He stepped out, pulling the door shut behind him. 'This had better be good.'

'Our main man, the one who did the cutting. We've got an ID. My guy that picked apart the Facebook feed, I gave him a few other samples too.'

'Eh? What other samples?'

'He compared the audio from Facebook footage to the stuff from the memory card and the call. Same man, all three of 'em. It's Leo Finch.'

CHAPTER FIFTY-FIVE

Winter couldn't have looked more confused if Porter had just spoke to him in Russian.

'What? Bullshit.'

'Not according to the audio analysis,' said Bell, having pulled a third chair alongside Styles. 'You won't have much more luck than I did if I try and regurgitate what's been poured into my head about acoustic parameters and verbal probability scale. Most of it just leaked back out the other ear. Suffice to say, bigger brains that yours or mine have deemed it so.'

'Not Finch. Can't be. He literally saved my life last year. Stepped in when some drunken bum tried to glass me at a rally. Why would he do that if he was just going to set me up for this?' Winter kept shaking his head as he spoke.

'If we find him we'll be sure to ask,' said Porter. 'If I were you though, I'd see this as my way out of this. If Finch did it, if you're being straight with us about being in the dark, that puts you in the clear.'

He left that hanging for Winter to chew on for a few seconds.

'There were three men there, Damien. Who would Finch trust to have his back?'

That seemed to spark something in Winter. 'He's ex-forces. Used to be in the Marines. He . . . oh my God . . . him, Freddie and Dominic. They used to serve with him. He brought them on board when he took the job as head of security.'

Never mind a penny dropping, Winter's face looked like the whole piggy bank had just cracked over his head.

'Leo, he has a master key for the whole building. He could get in my office any time he liked. I just . . . why would he do this though?'

'We know Freddie Forrester. Who's Dominic?'

'Dom Twyford.'

'Any idea where we could find them?'

'No.' Frown lines ploughed deep furrows in Winter's forehead. As much as Porter disliked the guy, this was either worthy of an Oscar or he'd genuinely played no part in this.

'Anything else you can tell us about any of them?' he asked.

Winter sighed, gaze skittering around the room like he was tracking a fly. 'Makes no sense, none of it. He was meant to be in Southampton.'

'Southampton? Who? Finch?'

Winter nodded. 'Some army reunion thing. I spoke to him Thursday afternoon after I came back. Said he wouldn't be in on Friday, and that he'd see me Monday.'

Gene Rafferty had sat quietly like a shop mannequin during this last exchange, but he whirred back to life.

'Detective, in light of this new information and your new persons of interest, can I suggest we pause proceedings and let you track down Mr Finch and his friends? I'm sure my client will be happy to co-operate and answer any more questions you have once you do.'

He looked at Winter, eyebrows raised, and seeing his client lost in his own fog of questions, placed a hand on his arm that snapped him out of his trance. He repeated the suggestion for Winter's benefit.

'Yes, yes, of course,' said Winter. 'Whatever you need. Does that mean I can leave?'

Porter looked at Styles, then to Bell, finally back at Winter. 'For now, yes, but RUI, released under investigation. You'll definitely be back here with us at some point.'

Even as he said it, something pinged deep in the shadows. Took him a second to make the connection. Winter wasn't the only one being released today. Tyler's man. Could be out already. Dammit, why hadn't he let Styles handle this one? Because he was a perfectionist, he thought, but it might have cost him.

To say Winter looked relieved as he walked out was an understatement, like a man who's just found out his terminal diagnosis was all a paperwork mix-up.

'We've already done background for Finch,' he said when the door closed behind Winter and Rafferty. 'Need it on the other two, like yesterday.'

'On it, boss,' said Styles.

'Why disappear days before?' said Bell.

'Hmm?'

'He took the call from McTeague Thursday. Not like he

330

didn't have time to prep. Why disappear a full forty-eight hours before?'

'Maybe he was just too busy? Maybe he just couldn't get away from Winter?'

'Yeah maybe, but they knew exactly where Henderson would be. What if they'd been at the court waiting? Since Friday I mean. That would explain why nobody saw them enter or leave.'

'Worth a look. I'll get Glenn on it.'

'Give me a shout when we've got any info on Forrester and Twyford, and let's get Mr Finch back in here,' Porter said to Styles, and went to wander off.

'Where you going?'

'Need to pop and see Kat,' he said, the weight of the lie squatting heavy on his chest. 'Shouldn't be more than an hour.'

CHAPTER FIFTY-SIX

His luck had held. Marlon Hawkins had still been in custody, and Porter watched him now, walking out of the station. Hawkins was a young black kid, looked barely out of his teens, and had definitely got the same dress code memo as Tyler's other hired help. Trainers so white they practically glowed. Jeans riding low enough to see the logo on his boxers. Cookie-cutter gang fodder. While Porter had waited, a more appealing option had presented itself. Hawkins stood for a minute or so, listening to whatever his brief was telling him. The suited solicitor towered above him by almost a foot. Looked like a kid getting a dressing-down from a teacher.

They broke off their separate ways, and Hawkins waited until the taller man was out of earshot, before pulling out his phone. Porter slipped out of his car, passing the solicitor as he double-timed it to close the fifty-foot gap. Porter fell in ten feet behind Hawkins, pulling out his own phone as camouflage, waiting for enough distance between them and the station.

Hawkins hung a right at the first corner, talking low, hard to make out more than a mumble. Porter picked up the pace, jogging out slightly in front of Hawkins, warrant card already in hand.

'Steady on, Marlon. What's the hurry?'

Hawkins screwed up his face, then spotted the ID, giving a *what now?* roll of the eyes.

''S OK,' Porter said, pulse quickening as much from the risk he was taking as the jog over the road. 'I just need you to deliver a message for me.'

'I look like your errand boy?'

'Oh, your boss is gonna want to hear what I've got to say. Tell him Porter said so. One hour, by the river outside the Tate Modern. I'll be there alone. You tell him,' he said, backing away. 'He's not there and the information goes to a bakery in Creekmouth instead.'

Porter disappeared back around the corner, heart beating so fast it felt like he was coming off a hundred metre sprint. This wasn't so much rolling the dice, as chucking them into a fan and hoping they didn't get spat back in his face. But he was out of options.

CHAPTER FIFTY-SEVEN

Late afternoon footfall outside the Tate was light. Steel wool clouds drifted above the skyline, scraping rooftops in the distance. Porter checked his watch. He'd been gone from the station for almost an hour now. Wouldn't be long before Styles would wonder where he'd disappeared to, if he wasn't already.

He scanned faces as people drifted by. A group of a dozen or so, led by a tour guide waving a cherry-red umbrella like a conductor, herding them past like cattle. The Millennium Bridge stretched across the Thames like a steely tightrope, the dome of St Paul's squatting in the background. Porter sauntered over to the railings, peering over as the wind dragged its fingers across the river's dirty grey surface.

Porter spotted Jackson Tyler as he emerged from the wooden drinks shack to the west of the gallery's entrance. On his own, as far as Porter could tell. Dressed as he was the first time Porter had laid eyes on him. White shirt, jeans, only difference being a three-quarter-length coat that flicked out behind him in the breeze. Seemed to have a bubble around him, space that people just didn't want to share, as if he radiated menace.

Tyler gave a soft shake of the head, turning his back to the river and resting against the railings six feet along.

'You're a worse stalker than some of my exes' he said, looking ahead at the gallery, arms folded. 'Thought you might have got the message by now.'

'Yet here you are.'

'Here I am,' he agreed. 'I've got to be honest with you, I'm still leaning towards plan A, having Ty and Reece here slip a little something between those broken ribs of yours and tip you over these railings.'

Porter jerked his head around, spotting two men that had materialised twenty feet to the other side, wincing as the twist tugged at his still tender midriff.

'You didn't really think you were just going to walk away from this, did you? Only reason you got me here is Creekmouth. What business you got with the old man?'

'None yet,' said Porter, 'but if I don't check in with a friend of mine, information's going to be leaked to him that you'd probably rather stayed quiet.'

The fact that the source was Nuhić wasn't something Tyler needed to know. Porter glanced at the pair to his left again, back to Tyler.

'What can you possibly have to say that keeps you out of that river?' said Tyler, still yet to look directly at him. 'And don't think for a second that they won't do it. My men are loyal, Detective. They've got my back, I've got theirs. How long you think that lasts if I let you walk all over that bond?'

'This isn't going away, Tyler. Yeah, it's personal for me, but whether I get to the bottom of it or the guy leading the case does, coppers and their families die, it's bad for business both sides.' He shot a sideways glance down at the choppy surface of the Thames, turned back and scouted out options either side. He'd make a run for it if they moved on him, but his ribs jarred even just walking down the stairs, never mind trying to make like Usain Bolt.

'You don't even have to give me the name now. Save face in front of your boys and call me at the station later.'

'You know what, fuck saving face. Time's up. You're done.'

Tyler pushed off the railing, finally looking Porter in the eye. Only for a second though, glancing over his shoulder, presumably to signal his men. Porter braced himself, ready to push off the railings, make for the Tate. Lock himself in somewhere and call for backup. Shouldn't have come here, much less alone. Should have done it over the phone, but he wanted to look Tyler in the eye and watch it hit home.

He chanced a quick look to his left, needing to gauge when to move. Took a split second to make sense of what he saw. Two new figures approaching Tyler's pair. Styles, Tessier a pace behind him, Nick with a taser held just inside his jacket, hidden from general view, but no mistaking his intentions.

'Everything all right there, boss?' Styles called out, stopping ten feet short of Tyler's men, both staring at Tessier and not fancying their chances from their expressions.

'Come alone, eh?' Tyler said, laughing with all the warmth of a snowball.

'Just as alone as you,' Porter shot back. 'All good thanks, Nick. Didn't have you pegged as an art lover, Gus.'

Tessier cracked a knuckle that popped like a firecracker. 'All about the culture, boss.'

'You mind keeping Mr Tyler's boys company while he and I take a short walk?'

Porter left the four men in an uneasy two by two stand-off and motioned for Tyler to follow him.

'I want you to remember, I'm doing you a favour here. This part, you don't want them to hear.'

'The fuck you think you have on me?'

'Not what I have on you. These boys, however, they do have something.'

Porter handed over a single sheet. Photocopied but good quality. Watched Tyler as it hit home. Knew from the way his face dropped it had gone deep. Bangkok Police Department Header, arrest sheet dated three years ago. Solicitation charges. Boy involved barely in his teens. Jackson Tyler's mugshot a bleary-eyed shadow of the man here now, looking like he'd been out on a three-day bender.

'Now, either you give me who was driving the car that killed my wife or every man that works for you will get a copy. Won't matter how much you paid the Thai Police then. Starting with those two. You've got ten seconds.'

'How the f—?'

'Nine, eight, seven—'

'OK, OK,' Tyler growled, giving Porter a glare that could kill an elephant at ten paces. 'You win, all right. You win.'

'Well?'

'Not here though.'

'Six, five—'

'Look, they see us talking, then you storm straight off

and pick someone up, you don't think they put two and two together? Give me until tomorrow, noon. Make some space between now and then. You'll have a fucking name.'

Porter met his angry glare with one of his own, fuelled by nearly four years of bitterness and grief. He reached inside his jacket, pulling out a business card, shielding it from Tyler's men as he passed it over.

'I don't have a name by twelve-oh-one, I'm going to do a leaflet drop that'll make your streets look like a blizzard.'

CHAPTER FIFTY-EIGHT

Porter had taken the Tube to the Tate, so he hitched a lift back with Nick and Gus.

'I know,' said Styles, 'You're pissed cos I followed you.'

'What if something had happened to you? How do I explain that to Emma?'

'Same way I'd have to with Evie if you keep breaking promises to not run around like you're Batman cleaning up Gotham.'

'Gus, I . . . Thanks for tagging along. Better if you don't ask too many questions in case Milburn gets wind, but thank you. Both of you.'

Tessier shrugged. 'I don't need to know, but fuck Milburn all the same.'

Bursts of nervous laughter all round.

'How did you know to follow me?' Porter asked. 'Am I really that bad a liar?'

'Let's just say you should never join the office poker game.'

'Look, boss,' Tessier said, 'whatever you've got going on ain't none of my business, but you, the team, you're family. You need anything, we're here.'

Gus was a man of few words, so his sentiment caught Porter off-guard, ramming home what a fool he'd been to charge around like this on his own. He'd do it for them, every last one of them, yet he'd taken that choice away from them. Nearly the end of this particular road now though. Hours, not days.

'While you've been playing Lone Ranger, Glenn's come up trumps. Home addresses on Twyford and Forrester, both empty though. No sign of Finch either, but you're not gonna believe this next bit. Dom Twyford's phone pinged a mast right next to the courthouse the day of the murder, two hours after to be precise.'

'They were still there? Where the hell were they hiding out?'

'He was in a hotel around the corner. One of those Hilton DoubleTree ones. Turns out he checked in the night before, checked out the morning after.'

'What about Finch and Forrester?'

'Glenn spoke to the manager. No rooms booked under any of their names, but he picked out Twyford on their CCTV. Checked in as Stephen George. Manager recognised Finch and Forrester as well. Reckons he saw them all having a drink in the bar Sunday night, then the other two were there having a coffee in the morning. We reckon they all dossed in one room. No cameras behind the hotel, so easy access to and from the rear of the courtrooms.'

'They sat there supping a bloody pint while we were around the corner.'

They sank into silence, letting that percolate, before Porter spoke again.

'Let's think this through then. If you're Finch, you do this to try and scare people, play on their fears and drive them towards the EWP. Why would you do it independently of Winter? They're all ex-forces, used to following orders. Why strike out alone, why now, and why plant the memory card in Winter's office?'

'That version doesn't add up for me, boss,' said Styles. 'Finch does the wet work, but Winter is the one who benefits from it all. Course he knew, I just don't see it any other way.'

'If he knew, he put on a bloody good performance,' said Porter.

'Wouldn't be the first,' Styles warned. 'Could even be their contingency plan. Things unravel, Winter puts on a show, and Finch falls on his sword to keep his boss out of it.'

'Maybe. Either way, Winter is still a person of interest until I say otherwise. What do we know about their military service history?' Porter asked.

'Bugger all at the moment,' Styles admitted. 'Work in progress. Nothing on their whereabouts at the moment either, but you've got to assume they know we picked up Winter again, maybe even that we found the micro SD card. Can't see them sat with a cuppa waiting for us to turn up, can you?'

'Finch doesn't strike me as the kind of man who wouldn't have a plan B lined up,' said Porter. 'At least we've got faces against this now, regardless of whether Winter's one of them.'

They lapsed into comfortable silence for a few minutes.

'Is it bad that I'm looking forward to seeing Milburn's face when he realises he has to backtrack on the whole terror angle?'

'Still a win for him though, isn't it? He spins it so he solved the case, while not just paying lip service to the terrorist angle. Slippery bugger is our super.'

'Speaking of slippery buggers, how was our little friend at the Tate? You get what you need?'

Porter shook his head. 'Not yet, but it did the trick. I'll know by tomorrow, or I air his dirty laundry.'

'You not tempted to air it anyway?'

'Course, but he doesn't need to know that yet.'

'Sarge, you there?' Kaja Sucheka's voice crackled out from Styles's airwave radio.

'Yep. On my way back in. With you in five. What's up?'

'We've had a tip off about Finch and his buddies. SCO19 are en route now.'

'Give us the address,' Styles said, and Porter felt that unerring sense of momentum, the tipping point, where a case started to rush head first at you. Even with SCO19, the Met's Specialist Firearms Command on board, taking down three trained soldiers, ones who'd already shown how far they'd go for their cause, wouldn't be an easy task.

Kaja fed them the address. Victory Services Club, a prestigious military members club on the edge of Hyde Park. Stone's throw from Buckingham Palace. Milburn's blood pressure would be off the charts even if it all went to plan. If.

CHAPTER FIFTY-NINE

A pair of armed response vehicles had beaten them to it, out of their cars and prepping on Stanhope Place when Styles pulled up onto the kerb. Six AFOs, Authorised Firearms Officers, head to toe in black, Kevlar helmets in hands, running one last weapons check on their Glock 17s. One of the six detached, coming over to meet them, gloved hand outstretched.

'DS Holt, sir. We'll be good to go in sixty seconds. Spoke with one of your team on the way over and sighting confirmed now with the club manager. All three targets located in the main bar area. Approximately three dozen civilians and staff present. Orders are to hold our position until numbers thin out.'

Milburn had already stated that position when Porter had called him on the way over. No way of knowing if the three men were armed, so steaming in guns out wasn't the play, not yet anyway. Porter checked his watch.

'It's early evening,' he said, turning to Styles. 'Only going to get busier for the next few hours.'

Styles nodded, picking up on Porter's meaning. 'I'll go in with you.'

Porter shook his head. 'Only needs one of us.'

The look he got back was loaded. 'You remember the chat we had by the river just now, yeah?'

A moment's hesitation, then Porter relented. 'Fine, but if Emma asks, I tried.'

'Gus, you up for keeping the doorman company and watching the front while we go in?'

Nod and a grunt from the big man. DS Holt didn't look convinced. 'That puts you at least thirty seconds from us if things go bad, sir. My advice would be to hang back, see how things play out, just for a while.'

Porter walked past him, peering both ways up Seymour Street. 'Over there, that entry to the back lane behind Lanchester Court,' he pointed to what looked like the opening to an alleyway down the side of the building opposite the club. 'You could take up position there, cuts your distance in half.'

Holt walked forwards, staring for a moment. Shrugged. 'Your call, sir.'

Porter nodded, feeling the buzz as adrenaline started to do its thing. The three of them strapped on their stab vests, Tessier's big enough that it would look trench-coat-size on someone like Kaja.

They turned the corner, heading towards the club entrance, hearing the dull drumbeat of boots on tarmac behind them as the AFOs moved into position. The red-brick and sandstone front made for a Battenberg effect, Union Jack hanging limp on a flagpole jutting out above the entrance. A bored-looking doorman glanced their way, doing a double take as they crossed the road towards him. Porter held his warrant card out, keeping his voice low.

'DI Porter, Met Police. I need you to keep anyone else from entering, can you do that?'

'Yeah, of course, I . . . um . . . What's going on?'

'DC Tessier will stay out here with you for now.' Porter ignored the question. 'Where do I find the lounge bar?'

The bemused doorman gave him directions, Porter breezing past and into the reception area. Marble effect floor didn't make for the quietest entry, waist-high desk, a couple of inches of hair and forehead poking over the top of a pair of monitors. Skirting the edge of the desk, he and Styles followed the doorman's directions, corridor opening out into the bar. Low slung bucket seats clustered around polished metal tables. Finch stood at the bar over to the left, his back to Porter but enough of his face visible in the mirrored wall behind it.

'Two o'clock,' said Styles. 'Over by the pillar.'

Porter chanced a glance, seeing another familiar face. Forrester. He recognised Twyford from the pictures that had been circulating. All three of them variations on a theme. All with short back and sides, jaws you could use as a spirit level. The three of them had served together in Afghanistan. Left under a cloud, but exactly how dark a one had been beyond the limits of what his team could dig up at short notice.

'Stay here and keep an eye on those two while I have a chat with Mr Finch.'

Porter picked his way between tables, weaving past the few that had chosen to stand, zipping his jacket up to hide the Kevlar body armour. Finch was shooting the breeze with one of the bar staff, a young brunette, smiling at whatever joke he'd just cracked like he was the first guy to ever try and come on to her.

She placed three bottles in front of him, wedging chunks of lime in the necks. Finch had just tapped his card to pay when Porter leant an elbow on the bar beside him.

'Finch, didn't know you drank here.'

Finch whipped his head around, instant recognition, eyes flicking past Porter, sweeping the room. Styles was out of sight, behind a pillar from where they stood, and Finch seemed to relax a little.

'I could say the same,' Finch answered, turning back to his bottle, stuffing the lime inside with a thick sausage finger. 'Where did you serve?'

'1st Battalion Coldstream Guards. You?'

'40 Commando. You get out to Helmand?'

Porter nodded. 'Only did the one tour back in 2010. Wasn't it 40 Commando that turned the lights off on the way out of there in 2013?'

Finch nodded, taking a long pull on his beer.

'How long you been out?'

'Too long.'

'Are you being served, sir?'

The brunette was back, looking at him while pouring a pint for someone else.

'No, I'm OK, thanks.'

'Another Corona, please, darling,' Finch said. 'This one's on me.'

'Thanks, but I'm fine, honestly.'

'House rules. Nobody turns their nose up at a free beer. You wouldn't be turning your nose up at me, would you, Detective Porter?'

Porter paused a beat, before smiling at the barmaid. 'Corona'll be great, thanks.'

'What brings you here today, then?'

'You actually, Leo.'

'It's Leo now, is it? We mates all of a sudden?'

'You generally buy a beer for people you don't like?'

'Oh, you don't want to know what I do for people I don't like.'

'That's where you're wrong, Leo. I already know what you do to them. What you did to Ross Henderson. I'm here to give you a choice, to walk out of here with me now, the three of you.'

'Let's say I don't like that option,' Finch said, 'what's behind door number two?'

'Oh, you don't want that one, Leo, trust me. I've got armed response teams with itchy trigger fingers just dying to pile in here.'

'You think they can pile in fast enough to save you?' Finch asked, in a voice that might as well have been asking what was for dinner. 'Looks like you need your battles fighting for you anyway,' he said, nodding at the strapping on Porter's fingers.

'Don't you worry about me, Leo,' Porter said, pinpricks of sweat popping across his back, eyes fixed on the bottle the barmaid set in front of him, trying to look nonchalant, feeling anything but.

'Ah, I'm only messing. Besides, we've already done this dance down at the station. You should be out there looking around a few of the mosques instead of bothering men who've fought for their country. Keep following me round, I'm gonna have to ask my solicitor to apply for a restraining order.'

'You sure you can afford him on your own? Can't see your boss picking up the tab this time. Not with what he knows now.'

Finch chuckled, tipping his bottle skywards again. 'Come on then, I'll bite. What exactly do you think you know that I don't?'

'There's no *think*,' Porter said, turning away from his untouched bottle. 'I *know* you killed Ross Henderson. I *know* you took that call in Winter's office. I *know* we've matched your voice on both to the clip of you manhandling Ross. I *know* what that'll look like to a jury.'

Finch smacked his lips, placed his own bottle on the bar, cradling it between bricklayer's hands.

'Go on, call him,' Porter said. 'Don't take my word for it.'

Finch's eyes flicked off right, and Porter risked a glance over. Twyford and Forrester were still seated but staring across. Finch gave an almost imperceptible shake of the head.

'You're full of shit,' he said, pulling out his phone, but Porter sensed more than just irritation in his voice.

Finch's reflection stared back in the mirror, waiting for Winter to answer the call. Finch suddenly stood up a touch straighter.

'Boss, it's Leo, I—'

Finch listened, stared so hard at his drink Porter half expected the bottle to shatter from the weight of it. The bodyguard's mouth twisted into an ugly sneer.

'Yeah, well, fuck you too.'

He slapped the phone back on the bar, picked up one of the two remaining beers and necked half of it in five thirsty swallows.

'What time's your solicitor getting to the station, then?' Porter asked, not trying too hard to keep the smile from his face.

'You're a laugh a minute, aren't you?' Finch said, looking his mirror image in the eye. 'You've served. You must have seen stuff, things you wish you hadn't.'

'Some,' Porter agreed, no elaboration.

'Then you know.' He nodded. 'You know that in a war, you sometimes have to do things you don't like, that civvies would refuse, if you want to change the world for the better.'

'That what you were doing in Greenwich, Leo? Changing the world?'

Finch gave a wistful smile. 'We've each got our part to play, Detective. There's a tidal wave coming that'll wash all this shit away, let us rebuild from scratch. I've done my bit. Doesn't much matter what happens to me now.'

'You think the EWP is going to survive this?' Porter asked. 'You're dead in the water.'

'They may well be,' Finch agreed.

'Why try and make your boss take the fall though? That's what I don't get.'

'Hmm? Oh, him? He wanted this as much as anyone. Just never had the balls to do anything about it.'

Finch drained the second bottle. The background hum of countless conversations seemed to ebb away.

'What now, then?' he asked.

'Now? You and your boys come outside, we head back to Paddington Green, and it'll be what it'll be.'

Finch turned to face him, elbow resting on the bar. 'You got a favourite film, Detective?'

Porter stared him out, no idea where he was taking this.

'For me, it's got to be *Butch Cassidy and the Sundance Kid*. Always saw myself as more Butch than Sundance.'

'Didn't end so well for either of them though, did it?'

'Depends how you look at it,' Finch said, another glance at his men. 'Lot to be said for going out on your own terms.'

Porter shook his head. 'Not worth it, Leo.'

Finch's gaze bored into him, the kind of hard stare that had likely backed plenty of men down before. Only for a few seconds though, then he surprised Porter by letting rip a loud laugh, like Porter had just slung a punchline his way.

'Ah, the look on your face. I mean, it's not like I'm armed or anything,' he said, pulling back his jacket to show nothing but a white cotton shirt. He lifted up the hem, rotating clockwise. Nothing tucked into the small of his back either. Porter felt the tiniest release of tension. Finch looked back across at Twyford and Forrester as he continued his slow-mo twirl, shrugging as if to say *What can you do?* Porter glanced at them again, surprised they hadn't made their way over already. A sign of Finch's authority perhaps? Hold your position unless summoned.

He was still looking at them when everything sped up, as if someone had pressed fast forward. Finch became a blur, arm whipping round, holding an object. All happening too fast to see, whirling towards his head. No Kevlar vest to protect that. No way to stop it.

CHAPTER SIXTY

Whether through blind luck or pure instinct, the blow caught a forearm he hadn't even realised he had raised, the rest of his body twisting away. The impact still hurt like hell, whatever it was, and he carried on his spin, putting distance between him and any follow-up, moving through a full three-sixty. Didn't have much time to refocus as Finch flew towards him, wielding his empty bottle like a cosh, aiming at Porter's temple.

Unlike the first blow, he knew this one was coming. No need to block this time, just a half-step back, watching it slash the air, inches short of his nose. Finch reversed it, readying a backhand strike towards the face again. Porter stepped into this one, surprise showing on Finch's face, as Porter's left hand clamped onto Finch's wrist. He tucked his injured right hand into his chest, scything the point of his elbow into Finch's cheek, feeling it land with a satisfying crunch.

Finch's eyes fluttered, but only for a second. Porter sensed, rather than saw, a knee drive up. Only just managed to twist his hips, taking it on the thigh. They were close now, Finch's teeth bared, straining to break Porter's grip on the hand wielding the bottle. Little grenades of spittle peppered Porter's cheeks, and he pulled back a few inches, readying a second elbow, but this time it was Finch who stepped in closer, his one free arm snaking around Porter's neck, pulling him in close like a dance partner, pinning his own arm across his chest, but taking away any leverage Porter had to swing the elbow.

Pain exploded in his foot, sharp and hot. Again, then a third time. Dirty bastard was stamping on him. Porter tried to glance down, anticipate the next heel coming down, but realised too late that the stomps had just been a distraction. Finch's head, rearing back like a snake ready to strike. The headbutt came in like a steam train. He tried to free himself, to pull away, but they were practically conjoined, each hanging on to the other. Best he could manage was a token dip of the head.

It caught him on the ridge of bone just above his eyebrows. Jarring, disorientating. He staggered back, room tilting, one hand scrabbling at the bar for balance. Slipping off polished wood, counter falling away from him as something hard bumped against his back. Not heavy enough to stop him heading downwards. He hit the ground, backside first, hard enough to jar his spine, pain shooting up the line of discs like dominoes. The stool he'd collided with rattled against the hard parquet flooring where it lay beside him like a fallen comrade.

Finch looked impossibly tall from this angle, blinking away the impact of his own headbutt. Styles flashed to mind for a split second. Was he halfway across the bar to step in, or was he facing off against Twyford and Forrester? No time to check.

Finch shook it off, started moving forward, reaching to grab another bottle from the bar. Porter pushed backwards, trying to crab-walk away. Finch brought the bottle down hard against the edge of the bar. Tiny diamonds bursting, raining on Porter's legs, leaving a jagged mouth of gaping glass.

Finch's mouth twisted into a maniacal grin, enjoying this way too much. Had he done the same behind his mask in Greenwich? Porter went to roll sideways, bumping against the stool. Finch came at him now, switching the bottle to an overhand grip, ready to drive down like an apple corer into Porter's chest.

Porter grabbed for the only thing within reach, the stool, swinging it up and out, as much a barrier as a weapon. The pain in his broken fingers was molten, lighting his hand on fire. He gritted his teeth and fought through it, gripping the seat in both hands as it passed his face, both palms planted against fabric, pushing it up and out as hard as he could. Felt, rather than saw, the impact, Finch's eyes bulged cartoonishly, bottle spinning from open fingers and clattering harmlessly by Porter's head. Finch backed up a pace, doubling over, withdrawing from the stool leg that had just hammered into both testicles with enough force to send them into orbit thanks to his own momentum.

Porter stayed seated, scooting forwards on his backside, jabbing the stool out again, striking first shin, then knee. Finch folded to the floor, still clutching at his groin. Porter pushed up onto his feet, using the stool as leverage. Less than ten seconds, start to finish. Finch was foetal, so Porter risked a glance towards the door. One man belly down, Styles cuffing wrists behind him. Porter did a double take when he clocked Tessier, no longer by the front door, pressing Forrester up against the wall, the EWP man's hands pinned practically up under his shoulder blades. Tessier couldn't have looked more relaxed if he was just propping up the bar. Forrester, on the other hand, looked like if Tessier pushed any harder, he'd merge with the wallpaper.

Porter drank in a deep breath, puffed out hard. Felt all eyes on him. Managed to fumble out his warrant card to fend off any questions.

'You all right, boss?' Styles called out.

Porter ran a hand over his scalp, nodding as he surveyed the room.

'Yeah, I think so,' he muttered, watching Finch try and rise to his knees, realise it was a bridge too far and collapse back to lying on his side. Porter walked over to where he lay, stepping to one side so as to be behind him, ignoring the temptation to accidentally dig a toecap in on the same spot the stool had hammered home. He pulled out his cuffs and snapped them onto Finch's wrists.

'Leo Finch, you're under arrest. You do not have to say anything. But it may—'

A stampede of boots rumbled down the corridor, shouts of 'armed police' echoing from reception. They came through in two rows of three, Glocks out, fanning left and right, scanning the sea of shocked faces. Porter recognised the officer stepping around tables, moving towards him, as DS Holt.

Porter nodded towards the bar. 'You getting a round in, Sergeant?'

CHAPTER SIXTY-ONE

Three interviews, three stubborn silences. No matter. They had Finch bang to rights thanks to the voice print analysis. The other two might try and argue their presence in the hotel that day was circumstantial, but Porter knew how that would play to a jury.

Turned out they'd all served together in Helmand, all been dishonourably discharged, allegations of taking part in a fight that saw two local men hospitalised. None of them were on Winter's payroll directly. He'd contracted them in from Sentinel Security, a firm offering everything from risk assessment through to personal protection. Can't have been cheap, but then again, there were still far too many people who fell for Winter and his snake-oil sales pitch 'Britain for the British', lining his pockets with donations.

Still no word from Jackson Tyler. This morning's meeting with Nuhić seemed a lifetime ago, and Porter was starting to wonder if Tyler would just dig his heels in, refuse to give up a name. Shout fake news and dust off the hammer for anyone that dared to give Porter's claims an ounce of credibility.

Today had felt like a week, and the weight of it all laid heavy across his shoulders now, like a concrete cloak. He rubbed at a knot of tension by the base of his neck. Evie across the desk from him, lifting another slice of pizza, bungee cords of cheese escaping either side. Something about this, about her being here now, anchored him to the present. Who better to share your life with than someone who understood the pressures, the weight of expectation, the drive to see things through? Someone who got changed back out of their PJs to bring you dinner when you called to tell them it would be a later than planned finish.

The urge to wring a name from Tyler like water from a sponge, hadn't faded, but yesterday's scare, Tyler's threats, had snapped him out of his stare into the rear-view mirror. Holly was beyond danger, untouchable. Evie was here, vulnerable, a target thanks to him. Milburn strode across the room towards them.

'Right that's the press conference arranged for noon tomorrow. You did good today, Jake. Still want to throttle you for storming in there before the bloody AFOs, but never mind.'

'You and me both, sir,' said Evie, shooting mock daggers at Porter.

'Both of you, get yourselves home,' Milburn said, 'especially you. And take the morning as well. Styles can handle the second run at our three new guests. Don't expect we'll get much more out of them yet, but not to worry. Would be nice to have them charged ahead of the press conference.'

He left them to it with nothing more than a nod and a smile, short and sweet.

The aches from the bar, combined with the broken ribs and fingers Tyler had left him with, were making a persuasive argument to do exactly what Milburn said. Technically, he could even say it was an order. Before he could change his mind, Evie snapped the lid closed on the pizza, scooping it up.

'Come on. Way past your bedtime. You can come and play with the other children again tomorrow.'

Several goodbyes later, they left the others to it, promises of being in no later than ten. They headed out to the car park, Evie munching a second slice. Porter had barely managed to press the button on his key fob when Evie snatched them from his hand.

'Not tonight, Detective. You're riding shotgun. Kick back, relax and grab a slice. This is a door-to-door service.'

He started to protest, but she was at the driver's side and behind the wheel, so he slid begrudgingly into the passenger seat. Not that he'd admit it to her, but it felt nice, having someone looking after him for a change. He leant back into the headrest as they pulled out onto Edgware Road, wondering if tonight would be the night he managed more than five hours, and was asleep before they hit the first traffic lights.

CHAPTER SIXTY-TWO

The fuzzy edges took a few seconds to clear. He rubbed at his eyes, rolling over to check the time, but his view was partially blocked by a mug. The note propped against it explained the empty space beside him.

Didn't want to wake you. Just popped to shops. x

Rising to one elbow, he peered at the black coffee, pressing fingers against the mug for a temperature check. Lukewarm at best, so she must have been gone a little while. The clock showed a little after nine, a lie-in by his standards, and a surprisingly good night's sleep. No point loafing around, and five minutes later, he ambled into the kitchen, feet dragging across cold tiles to sling a few slices of bread in the toaster, while he totted up a list of what today had in store.

The press conference would be a feeding frenzy. The arrests wouldn't be the end of it. Those who'd answered the EWP war cry wouldn't apologise any time soon, regardless of who'd killed Henderson. That type of next level ignorance and hatred wouldn't be washed away by the simple truth that one of their own was responsible. What still bothered Porter was where Winter factored in. Could he really have had nothing to do with an act that, on face value, was done with the intent of furthering his cause? Porter's gut said no, regardless of how convincing Winter had been. If Finch and the others wouldn't talk though, proving that might be damn near impossible.

As for Tyler, less than three hours to go. If this latest play didn't work, he was out of ideas. He was still turning that thought over when his phone buzzed.

'Hey, Nick, what's up?'

'Morning, boss.' His DS sounded almost apologetic. 'I know you're not in till later, but I figured you'd want to know.'

'Know what?'

'Henry Kamau. He's awake.'

It was as good as a splash of ice water to the face, blasting away any tiredness.

'Is he talking?'

'Yep. Has been since yesterday apparently.'

'Sorry, what?'

'I overheard a couple of Pittman's team talking this morning. They reckon he came around yesterday afternoon and is doing really well.'

'What's he said?' Porter's mouth felt dry, chalky.

'Not much. Nothing to start with. Then when he heard we had his prints, he admitted to being in the car, but reckons he saw it abandoned and just went in to see what there was to lift.'

'Bullshit.'

'Maybe so, but that's all he's saying for now.'

'Can't believe Pittman didn't call me. What a prick.'

'I wouldn't normally stick up for the guy,' said Styles, 'but word is that Milburn warned him not to. Didn't want you distracted apparently.'

'Oh, he's all fucking heart,' said Porter, through clenched teeth.

'Anyway, just thought you'd want to know. I'm heading in with Finch in fifteen minutes. Anything you want me to try?'

'Nah, just run it your way, Nick. I'll be in by eleven, so we can catch up then.'

Porter signed off, halfway back to the bedroom to get ready when the toast popped, forgotten.

CHAPTER SIXTY-THREE

No guarantees he'd get any quality time with Henry if Pittman was there. Even if he managed it, Milburn would almost certainly find out, but Porter was past caring. Besides, yesterday's arrests had to count for something. What was the use in earning brownie points if you didn't cash them in?

He recognised one of Pittman's team leaning against the counter of the nurse's station, a young DC by the name of Sean O'Connor. The look on the young staff nurse's face suggested he was wasting his time with an obvious attempt to flirt. Him laughing enough for both of them at his own joke. She, by contrast, managed a tight smile, attention more focused on a patient file. He straightened up, slipping on a serious face when he saw Porter approaching.

'Is he awake?'

'Yes sir, but I—.'

'Pittman in with him?'

'No, sir, DI Pittman had to step out to take a call, but he should be back any minute.'

Perfect. Easier to ask for forgiveness later than wait for permission now. Porter kept walking, past O'Connor, towards Henry Kamau's room.

'Um, sir, you can't—'

'Can't what, Detective Constable?' Porter turned back to face him.

'The boss, he told us the super didn't want you distracted from your Greenwich case.'

'All done and dusted,' said Porter. 'Three arrests and a press conference at noon, so no harm, eh?'

He left O'Connor lost for words, something the staff nurse would probably thank him for, and pushed open the door to Henry Kamau's room. The dressings that had hidden a good amount of his face were gone, swelling almost disappeared, and the face left behind looked too young, too far removed from the kind of one Porter had pictured these last few years.

'Henry? My name is Detective Inspector Porter. How are you feeling?'

It was as if the mention of rank, confirmation he was another copper, flicked a switch. Kamau's expression went from curious to something harder, like slipping on a mask.

'Fine.'

'You recognise my name?'

'I ain't never seen you before.'

'That's not what I asked,' said Porter. No time to sit and shoot the breeze to warm him up, win him over. Pittman could come back any minute, making any real conversation nigh on impossible. 'My name, Porter, that mean anything to you?' he asked, pulling up a chair, sitting down and leaning in.

Kamau wrinkled up his nose like Porter had hit him with a bad case of garlic breath.

'Man, I don't know you.' The deep voice didn't fit. It belonged to a man years older, but he somehow still sounded like a scared kid to Porter. Only playing at being a gangster.

'That car you were in, the one that killed the woman almost four years ago. Holly Porter, she was my wife.'

Flash of fear in Kamau's eyes, like he expected Porter to lunge at him.

'I already told your man, I didn't drive no car.'

'I know, I know, you were just seeing what you could nick. Here's the thing though, I know you're not telling us everything. You sure you weren't driving?'

'Man, that's bullshit. That other copper, he already told me you got my prints on the passenger side.'

'And no trace of anyone else in the car, Henry. How do you think that's going to look to a jury? Then they hear about you trying to rob that old fella. Not exactly a model citizen, are you?'

'You ain't pinning that shit on me,' he said, more animated now, sitting up a touch, shaking his head, his IV drip rattling against the side of his bed.

'If you weren't driving then who was?'

'Yo, you can't do this, man. I want a lawyer.'

'You'll get one soon enough, Henry, but you don't owe Tyler a thing. You're the one going to do time, for the burglary at least. You're just a kid. Don't give up the next ten years of your life for them, maybe more.'

Porter glanced back through the door, saw O'Connor on his phone, looking like he was on the wrong end of a dressing-down. Must be Pittman on the other end. Not much time.

'We can protect you, Henry. Just tell me who was driving.' Porter leant in closer, hearing the edge in his own voice, borderline growl behind the words.

Kamau shuffled an inch over, trying to preserve personal space.

'Just give me a name, Henry. One name and I go away. You don't, and I'll be there when you get out. I'll be there every time you look over your shoulder. She was my wife. You think I'm gonna let this slide, then you're stupider than I thought.'

If he gripped the side rail of the bed any harder he fancied it might snap off. Kamau seemed to shrink away from him, wedging up against the far side.

'What about your brother? What will he tell me?'

'Ben? What's he got to do with this?' said Kamau.

'You tell me. Went to see him yesterday and he scarpered pretty quickly.'

'This is nuffin' to do with him.'

'Then give me a name, or I'll have him in an interview room next door to yours.'

'I can't give you a name,' Kamau said, all trace of bluster having fled the room.

'Can't or won't?'

''S the same thing. You don't understand, man. You don't just—'

'Detective Porter, a word, please.'

Pittman stood framed in the doorway.

'With you in a minute,' Porter said, turning back to glare at Kamau.

'Now would be better.'

Porter huffed out a loud breath, stood up and shot one last hard stare at Kamau before joining Pittman in the corridor.

'What the hell do you think you're doing?' Pittman hissed.

'What does it look like? He was about to give me something until you barged in.'

'Barged in, on my own suspect? Really?' Pittman asked, eyebrows raised.

'You could have told me he was awake at least, Isaiah.' Porter felt the anger leeching away. Pittman wasn't wrong. Didn't stop him from feeling hard done by.

'Super's orders, and looks like he was right if this is how you go on. Look, mate,' he said, patting a hand on Porter's shoulder, 'for what it's worth, I don't believe this bollocks about robbing the car after it got ditched any more than you do. But that shit story is mine to break. You got a result yesterday. Go enjoy that. I promise when he gives up a name, you'll be first to know after the super.'

Porter sighed, nodded. 'You're right. Sorry, mate. I'll leave him to you. Look, I'd appreciate it if the super didn't hear about this.'

Pittman shrugged. 'Milburn's a prick. Gives us all enough grief without us grassing on each other.'

He held out his hand, and they shook. Porter checked his watch. Couple of hours before he needed to be at Paddington Green. Enough time to swing by the community centre to catch Benjamin Kamau unawares. Pick up where they left off. He was through the ward doors and out into the corridor when he felt the buzz of a text in his pocket. Not a number he recognised. Short and to the point.

You want a name, you got one. Ben Kamau.

CHAPTER SIXTY-FOUR

Porter burst through the door, seeing Pittman and Kamau jump. If it wasn't for the bedrail, Henry could well have fallen out the far side. Pittman's face turned grim.

'What the—?'

Porter didn't give him a chance to finish. 'He was there, wasn't he? Your brother?'

'Porter, you need to step back outside.'

'Not this time, Isaiah. His brother, he was the driver, and this piece of shit has known all this time.'

'That's bollocks, man. I already told you. I just grabbed a few CDs and some cash.'

'That's not going to fly, sunshine,' said Porter.

Pittman was on his feet now, hands on Porter's shoulders, pushing him backwards, towards the door.

'You're not out of here in five seconds, then you're not giving me any choice about Milburn.'

'Fuck Milburn,' Porter snapped. 'I know it was him, Henry. I know it was Ben.' He was shouting over Pittman's shoulder now, taking begrudging steps back. 'Next stop the community centre, and we'll see how long he holds up when we get him to the station.'

'What makes you think it was his brother?' Pittman asked, level with the door frame now.

'I don't think. I know.'

'You know that how?'

No simple way to explain the link to Jackson Tyler. Easier for Porter if how the information came to light stayed buried, but he spat it out before he could stop himself.

'Tyler gave him up, Henry. Tyler named Ben.'

Pittman stopped guiding him out, frowning. Behind him, Henry's face was all circles, wide eyes, wide mouth.

'And why would he give that information to you?' Pittman asked, words coated with a healthy dose of cynicism.

Kamau looked close to tears now, running both hands across his head, IV tube tapping out a rhythm again.

'Doesn't matter. What matters is I've got it, and if you won't follow it up, I will.'

'When did he tell you?' Kamau's voice was practically a whisper.

'Just now, in a text. So it's true then?'

Henry shook his head. 'He's gonna kill him. If he's told you that, he's gonna kill him.'

'Kill who, Tyler?'

'Eh? No. JT, he's gonna kill Ben.'

'Why would he do that, Henry?'

'Cos Ben weren't driving. It was him, Tyler. Said if anyone ever found out, he'd take the hammer to the pair of us.'

CHAPTER SIXTY-FIVE

'Jesus, didn't see that one coming,' said Styles. 'We sure he's telling the truth?'

'He looked petrified. He thinks Tyler is going to come for the pair of them now, make sure there's nobody left who can put him in the car. The fear he puts in his men, can't see Kamau flipping on him for nothing. Maybe he wouldn't have for his own sake, but he was practically gnawing through the cuffs to get out when he found out Ben might be in danger.'

'What about Tyler? Why put you on to Ben in the first place if he can put Tyler in the car?'

'I think Henry's right. He needs to clean house. He takes care of both brothers, he can tell people it was payback for Henry talking to us. If he's gonna kill Ben anyway, then he loses nothing by giving us the name. Rather that than give up anyone else in his crew and risk it coming back on him.'

'He'd have to be pretty confident of scooping up Ben to give you the name though.'

'What's to say he hasn't already. I'm heading there now.'

'I'll meet you there.'

'No, you finish up with Finch. Send Gus instead, he's half involved from yesterday anyway. No need to drag anyone else in.'

Porter signed off, weaving through reception and out into his car. Should take him ten minutes to get to the community centre. Normally he wouldn't call ahead. Chances are whoever he was going to see would make themselves scarce. In this case though, a call could save a life.

A bored female voice answered after three rings.

'I need to speak to Benjamin Kamau, please.'

'Ben's reffing a match at the moment. Can I take a message?'

'No, I need to speak with him now, please. It's urgent.'

'He should only be a few minutes. He's a popular lad today. If you leave a number, I'll have him call you back.'

'Wait, what do you mean, popular lad?'

'Had a few people in asking for him just before, and I told them the same. I can either take a message, or you can come and wait for him to finish and see him yourself.'

'These other men, what did they look like?'

'I'm sorry, sir, but I don't see as that's any of your business.'

'My name's Detective Inspector Porter, Met Police. I'm on my way there now, but Ben may be in danger. Can you get a message to him now?'

Porter weaved through traffic, background noise coming through his speakers as he waited. Why was it always the way, when you needed to be somewhere fast, everyone else seemed to have their cruise control set at ten miles an hour. To hell with it. He hit the blue lights and traffic parted like the Red Sea.

'Hello, Detective?' the woman's voice came back over the car speakers. 'I'm afraid I can't find him.'

'I thought you said he was refereeing a game?'

'He was, but apparently he started feeling poorly and had to step out. Not sure where to, but his car's still here.'

Felt poorly, or spotted whoever the someone was that came looking for him? Porter thanked her and left his number in case she spotted Ben. Where would he head? Somewhere he'd feel safe, but Porter didn't have the foggiest where to start. He dialled another number. Pittman answered, sounding far from pleased to hear back from him so soon. Porter explained what had just happened.

'I need to know where Ben might go. Can you ask Henry?'

'I'd love to, if I knew where he was.'

'Eh? What's that supposed to mean?'

'Exactly that. After you left, he started complaining about stomach cramps, said he was going to shit himself. Begged me to take the cuffs off. Little fucker was playing possum, chucked a full bedpan of piss at me and left me rolling in it on the floor while he did one. Managed to crack my head off the sink when I went down. Even bloody apologised on his way out the door.'

The absurd mental image made for a blink-and-you-miss-it smile. 'Bloody hell, you OK?'

'Course I'm not. There's gonna be bedpans left on my desk for the next ten years.'

'We'll get him back, and when we do, Milburn doesn't have to know.'

371

'How the hell are we supposed to find him that fast?'

'He's got to be either looking for his brother or looking for Tyler.'

'And?'

'And I might have an idea where we can find Tyler.'

CHAPTER SIXTY-SIX

The warehouse on the Camberwell Trading Estate didn't look anything special. If Nuhić was to be believed, this was the hub of Jackson Tyler's little empire. Pittman and his team of three sat in the car behind, Tessier having joined Porter in his. They'd spent an uneventful hour, both he and Pittman avoiding calls from Milburn. Porter had given Styles a heads up, asking him to stand in for the press conference, fobbing Milburn off with talk of a bad head from yesterday's scrap. Possible concussion even.

Traffic in and out had been practically non-existent, until five minutes ago. A silver Range Rover Evoque glided to a stop in front of a double-width roller door. It cranked a noisy tune as it opened, impossible to make anything out inside, but Porter had seen the unmistakable figure of Jackson Tyler in the passenger seat. Just him and the driver. No way of knowing how many others were already inside. Pittman's name flashed on his phone. They'd agreed to keep in contact via mobile rather than airwave radio. Pittman now had a vested interest in a quick and quiet resolution to this to spare his blushes, so no sense broadcasting for all to listen.

'What you thinking? Go in now or wait?'

'I say we give it ten more minutes. If Henry's here, he's seen Tyler going in just like we have. If he isn't, we see what Tyler has to say. I'll be amazed if there's nothing in there we can't take him in for.'

Turns out they didn't need ten minutes, only two. Up ahead, a figure appeared from behind a parked van. It wasn't until he got closer that Porter recognised Henry Kamau, now wearing baggy trousers, the sort that looked like the arse was hanging halfway down his thighs, and a hoodie big enough to fit Tessier. He had his hood pulled up, but glanced both ways as he cut in towards the warehouse. He'd lost the young, scared look from the hospital ward. It was more determined now. The face of a man with a purpose. He picked up his pace, trotting across the concrete forecourt and through the side door before Porter could get out of his car. Pittman and his crew followed suit, and they went through the ritual of pulling on stab vests, grabbing batons and tasers from cars. Porter spoke, concise, no words wasted.

'Tyler is priority number one as the biggest threat. Henry number two, Ben number three. Anyone else, we play by ear.'

'You never said how you found this place,' Pittman said, fastening the last strap on his vest.

'That's right, I didn't,' said Porter, then seeing Pittman's face twist, added, 'Anonymous tip.'

Pittman looked unconvinced, held his gaze for a second, but let it drop. Bigger fish to fry. No visible CCTV, so they double-timed it across the open concrete quadrant. A couple of the neighbouring warehouses were in use, curious faces framed in doorways. Porter was pretty sure one of them whipped out a phone. Everyone's a reporter these days. The roller doors were dead centre but offset to the right was a single PVC door, set into the brick lower half of the structure. Opened inwards from the looks of it. Porter approached, fingers curling slowly around the handle, holding fingers up for a three countdown with the other.

Seemed like the six of them held their breath for the count. The door opened with a click that seemed far louder than it should be. It opened straight into a space that resembled a mini aircraft hangar, and as deep as two of the five-a-side pitches at the community centre laid width ways. The Range Rover sat towards the far end, two white transit vans parked side by side a little further in. Both sides were lined with racking, the kind you saw in Costco, pallets and boxes stacked as far as the eye could see. Nothing Porter could see that hinted at contents. No sign of Henry, Tyler or anyone else for that matter. Porter felt the others bunching against him and moved in, one hand on the taser strapped to his chest.

He motioned for the others to fan out, Pittman pointing at the Range Rover. Porter held up two fingers, pointed at Pittman and O'Connor, and the pair slinked across until they were crouched behind the boot. Ayla and Manfredo followed suit, taking up position by the left-hand racking, Porter and Tessier covering the right. A place this size would only allow an unseen approach for so long.

Right at the far end, beyond the transits, was what looked like a single storey, built out from the wall, Portakabin size.

Dull lights glowed behind dirty panes like old headlights in the gloom. Muffled voices, hard to say how many, seeped out into the cavernous belly of the warehouse.

Pittman and O'Connor peered through both sides of the vehicle, shaking their heads. All six walked cautiously towards the far end, Porter resisting the urge to check any of the storage boxes they passed. There'd be time for that later. The volume coming from inside the shed-type structure was punctuated by shouting, faded away, then rose again, at least two voices, maybe three.

Porter picked up the pace and was about thirty feet from the door, when a figure began to back out. He recognised Henry Kamau's hoodie straightaway. Something off about his gait though, then it hit him. Two sets of feet, two pairs of legs. Kamau was dragging a second figure out with him. Two more faces appeared at the door, following him out.

'You're a dead man walking Henry, you hear me,' the first face out of the door snarled, arm outstretched. Porter clocked the claw hammer, held out like an extension of the hand.

It was as if the whole set-up freeze-framed. Henry glanced behind, checking his position versus the vans, locking eyes with Porter. Angry face one and two looked over his shoulder, left and right, seeing the advancing men. Kamau's hostage tried to twist free, managed a half-turn, showing a side profile. Jackson Tyler. The movement also showed Porter something that made goosebumps pop. Kamau had a gun under Tyler's chin. Real or not wasn't up for debate at the moment. There was a split-second pause, then the volume cranked up. Tasers drawn. Shouting all round, high metal ceilings bouncing it back at them at a rate of knots, echoes adding ghostly extras to the cast.

'Police! Drop your weapons!'

'On the ground. Do it now!'

'Dead Henry. Fucking dead.'

Kamau pulled Tyler around a quarter-turn. A rock and a hard place between Tyler's men and Porter. Breathing heavy. He should still be hooked up to a drip, resting up. His eyes seemed impossibly white, round like an owl under the shade of his hood.

'Henry. This isn't the way.' Porter shouted the name to cut through the noise, though dropped back to firm but conversational for the rest. 'You do this, you're no better than him.'

'You wanna listen to him, Henry. Young lads like you are prime real estate in prison,' said Tyler.

'Put the gun down and let's talk,' Porter tried. 'There's six of us here. You put that down, he's going nowhere.'

'He's got Ben,' Kamau's voice was husky, thick with emotion, like he'd been crying. 'All I've done for you? Where's my brother?' The last three words shouted point-blank into Tyler's ear.

'Why would I have your brother?'

The two thugs wielding hammers started to edge out, only inches, but too far for Porter's liking.

'That's far enough,' he warned them. 'You so much as bend to tie a shoelace and you'll be on the business end of fifty thousand volts.'

'He knows it was you,' Kamau snarled at Tyler. 'You killed his wife.'

'What? Cos you told him? What you been snorting, son?'

'Yeah, I told him, cos you told him it was Ben. You said Ben did it, then you sent two blokes round to grab him before the coppers could. Figured I'd be next, that way there's nobody left to say you were even there.'

'Come on, son,' Pittman echoed Porter's calm tone. 'There's plenty of ways left out of this for you.'

He might as well have not spoken. Henry only had eyes for Tyler.

'Where is he?' Kamau stage-whispered into his ear.

'I. Don't. Know.' There was space between each word, but the confidence wasn't there. That cocky tone Porter had heard too often over the last few days was fading.

'Where is he?' Louder this time.

'Fuck you, Henry. I don't know.'

'Where is he? Where is he? Where is he?' Each louder than the last, the final one a roar. No chance for Tyler to answer. Definitely not third time lucky for him. It happened so quick that Porter didn't even have a chance to discharge his taser. Kamau took a half-step back, creating just enough distance to pull the gun around and away from Tyler's chin, swinging it around to the side of his head, and fired.

CHAPTER SIXTY-SEVEN

The noise was deafening, a thunderclap with an aftershock that ricocheted from wall to wall. Every single one of them instinctively flinched. It was a fraction of a second, but long enough for Kamau to drag Tyler another quarter-turn around, backing towards the outer wall of the office. Six tasers pointed at him, plus two hammers within ten feet, but not a one of them had a clear line thanks to his human shield.

Even at this distance, Porter could see dark crimson specks around the lobe of Tyler's ear, a single crimson punctuation marking spotting the white cotton shirt, as the gang leader's face contorted with the agony of a newly perforated eardrum. Porter heard a crackle to his right, as the two Triple H thugs reacted differently. One tried to spin away, worried about a second shot, the other had seen it as an opening, lunged forwards and fell short. Literally fell, twin taser probes embedded, trailing back to Tessier. He went down hard falling into his mate, taking him down with him. Two hammers clunked to the floor.

'Where is he?' Kamau screamed into Tyler's only functioning ear.

'You shot me, you fucking shot me,' Tyler shouted, almost as loud, no sense of volume thanks to the thunder still rolling around his eardrum.

'You don't tell me where he is, next one's for real.'

'Henry! Henry!' Porter shouted. 'We'll help you find Ben. Just put the gun down, and you have my word I'll not rest until we do.'

Tyler moaned in pain, head tipping towards his shoulder, like he was trying to scratch an itch. 'In the boot. He's in the bloody boot.'

Henry glanced at the Range Rover, then across at Porter. Started to drag Tyler in the direction of the vehicle, but Porter held out a hand. If Ben Kamau was in there, and anything apart from perfectly healthy, there was no telling what effect that might have on his brother, what it might make him do.

'Stay there, Henry. Let us check that for you,' he said, gesturing for O'Connor to take a look. The young officer glanced at Pittman, who nodded, and they watched as he walked around to the boot, casting nervous glances back at them.

The boot opened with a soft whirr. Porter held his breath, shifting his weight, ready to dive towards Kamau if needed.

'He's here, boss. Bashed up, but alive.'

Pittman jogged across, helping lift a dazed Ben Kamau out, peeling a strip of duct tape off his mouth. His hands looked secured with a cable tie, and they brought him around to the passenger side, easing him into the seat.

'Ben! Ben! You OK, bro?'

The older brother's head bobbed up at the mention of his name, and Porter saw the damage to his face. One eye closed, swollen shut, Blood from a split lip had tricked down his chin. He managed a nod, but nothing more.

'Now, tell him,' Henry snapped, turning his attention back to Tyler. 'Tell him who drove the fucking car.'

Tyler said nothing, cheeks puffing out loud breaths, blinking like he'd had sand kicked in his face.

'Tell him!' Henry shouted again, clubbing the injured ear with the butt of the gun.

Tyler howled this time, sagging, eyes rolling with the pain. A second blow landed. Same spot, same force.

'All right, all right,' he said, mini grenades of spit bubbling at one corner of his mouth. 'Me. It was me. You happy? I drove. I did it.'

The confession bellowed out, any sense of volume lost no doubt thanks to the perforated drum. The echo bounced back from the ceiling, whispering a ghostly *did it, did it* to Porter, just in case he missed it first time around.

Being told it back at the ward was one thing. Hearing it said out loud by his wife's killer was another. One of the most surreal moments in Porter's life, beaten only by the split second after he'd been told about the crash over three years ago. He stared at the man who had taken a wrecking ball to his life, and all he could think of was how much he'd love Henry to pull the trigger.

Tyler's admission was like a pin to Kamau's angry bubble, one long, loud exhale escaping the young man's lips. Porter saw his shoulders sag, gun starting to follow suit, bobbing down a few millimetres with each breath.

Porter kept his tone neutral, took baby steps forward, sliding his taser back into its holster, hands held out for Kamau to see. The very definition of calm. Inside, his stomach knotted, twisting in on itself, feet away from his wife's killer.

'You've won, Henry. Ben's safe. Tyler's just confessed. You've won. I need you to put the gun down now though. Let me take him in.'

'You don't understand, man. I got to do this. I don't, how long you think I'll last?'

Porter shook his head, six feet away now. Five.

'Doesn't have to be that way, Henry. Don't chuck away the rest of your life for scum like him. Let me take him in.'

Edging nearer. Close enough to reach out and touch, but he held off.

'Yo, H,' a tired voice came from behind, and Porter turned to see Ben Kamau out of the car, holding onto the door for support. 'Enough's enough, man.'

'You know I'm right,' Henry said, 'He ain't gonna let this go, not now they know.'

'He ain't gonna be walking the streets for a long time,' said Ben, shaking his head slowly. 'He's finished. Just doesn't know it yet.'

Henry's hand twitched up again, barrel pressed right up to Tyler's damaged ear, making his captive hiss in pain. Henry held it there for a few seconds, before he let out a frustrated growl, hand sagging back down, gun resting on Tyler's shoulder now, pointing a few degrees away from his body. Porter exhaled slowly, looked around at the others, seeing postures relax despite faces full of tension.

Tyler moved fast for a man swimming in pain. As the

gun lowered, Henry's grip around Tyler's shoulder and chest relaxed, and the gang leader drove a heel down into Henry's foot, reaching up at the same time with his left hand, clamping onto Henry's wrist. A second kick, this one square on the shin bone, and Henry released his grip on the gun as Tyler's right hand closed around it.

Porter reacted out of instinct, lurching forwards to close the gap, seeing with startling clarity as Tyler took possession of the gun. Two feet and closing. Tyler turned the gun around, settling the grip into his palm just as Porter hit him. He dipped as he made contact, shoulder catching Tyler square in the ribs, feeling the flare of pain from his own already broken ones.

A cacophony of shouts behind him as they went down. No sense of where the gun was. Porter landed on top, Tyler half twisted around, and a second supernova of pain washed through Porter, ribs on fire as he straddled Tyler across the hips. The younger man's head bounced off the floor with a loud double tap, and Porter clocked his outstretched right arm holding the gun. Tyler gave a loud groan, initially trying to push Porter off with his left, but jerked his head towards the gun, as if seeing it for the first time. As it swung back up, Porter grabbed the wrist with his good hand, pushing and pinning to back to the floor as he slid off Tyler to the left, swinging a leg around, trapping Tyler's forearm. Something crunched, although could just as easily be Porter's knee. Tyler's fingers spasmed open, and Porter lunged for the gun, stripping it from scrabbling fingers and turning it back on Tyler, breathing hard like he'd just crossed the finish line at a marathon.

'Jackson Tyler, I'm arresting you on suspicion of assaulting a police officer, and for the murder of Holly Porter.'

Those last five words nearly didn't make it out, forcing their way past almost four years of grief and anger. Porter heard someone else reciting similar words off to one side. He looked over to see Pittman cuffing Henry Kamau.

He felt, rather than saw, Tyler move. Hips arching up, trying to throw Porter like a rodeo bronco unseating its rider. At the same time, he reached up, grabbing for the gun, but bucking up the way he had sent Porter's hands up six inches, and the best Tyler managed was scratching against Porter's fingers. Porter clenched his thighs, clamping tight to Tyler, letting his weight bear down again. A white-hot wave of anger came with it, losing all sense of any spectators. This man, this piece of shit, was the sole reason Holly wasn't here now. His gun hand swung down, hammer-fist style, butt smashing into Tyler's nose, bursting it like an overripe strawberry. Porter pointed the barrel back down at him, hating the tiniest of tremors he saw in his own hands.

Tyler yelped in pain, eyes rolling back for a split second, before snapping back into focus and hitting Porter with both barrels of pure hate.

'Do it!' Tyler snarled, lips pulled back from his teeth, looking borderline feral. 'Go on! Do it!'

His trigger finger tightened. Half a pound of pressure closer to making a broken nose and burst eardrum the least of Tyler's worries. He'd imagined this moment so many times. Dreamt about how satisfying it would feel.

'Fucking do it!' Tyler spat up at him, wet spray speckling Porter's hands with streaks of saliva.

He heard Tyler's words reverberated in his head, except it was his own voice shouting them back at him. Half a pound more. It'd be the end of him, never mind Tyler, but right here, right now, that felt a fair trade.

Shadows played across Tyler's face. Someone moving in behind. Strong hands reached past Porter's face, clamping over his, lifting the gun skywards. It had only travelled inches when the shot rang out. Porter saw the puff of grey dust where it did a Dam-Busters off concrete flooring, punching a hole in a nearby crate. He looked up, seeing Tessier take the gun from him. Ayla came across, flipping Tyler over onto his back as Porter stood up, clicking on cuffs.

'I didn't . . . That wasn't . . .'

''S OK, boss. My fault. Must have caught your finger. My fault.'

Tessier nodded, just the once, holding Porter's gaze long enough to show he had Porter's back if anyone tried to spin it any different. He looked back down at Tyler, the gang leader lying cheek to the floor, bad ear to the concrete. Ten feet beyond him, a groove in the concrete where the bullet had struck. Inches. If his aim had been inches lower, life as he knew it would be over.

He closed his eyes for a second, feeling the trigger click, unable to separate the feel of his own finger from Tessier's hand. Not sure which version he wanted to believe.

CHAPTER SIXTY-EIGHT

Milburn looked from Porter to Pittman and back again, looking for holes to poke.

'And that's your story as well, Pittman, is it?'

'That's how it happened, sir. Henry Kamau fingered Tyler for the hit-and-run and gave us a location. DI Porter had called me for an update, being as that it's my case, and you'd told him to let me run it my way. I didn't want to go in after Tyler short-handed, so took the opportunity to ask DI Porter and DC Tessier to join us.'

Muscles bunched in Milburn's jaw, not wanting to accept being spoon-fed a version that sat as awkwardly as glasses on a one-eared man.

'You were supposed to be at the Henderson press conference with me,' he said finally. 'What do you think that made me look like, sat next to a stand-in with my lead detective missing?'

Pretty safe bet that it made him look like the centre of attention, but best not poke the bear.

'And you,' he said, looking at Pittman, 'could have called in any one of a dozen others. Don't think for a minute I believe this crap.' Milburn gave the pair of them his sternest headmaster-style stare for a five count, then sat back down. 'As if that wasn't bad enough, Sally Ashbrooke came along. She was wanting to present you with a cheque.'

'Sir?'

'That reward that was put up. You know, that anonymous extra fifty K. Told her you couldn't accept anyway. Said she could donate it to the Benevolent Fund. She's insisting on handing it over to you personally for some reason, so you need to call her office and set that up.'

'If it's all the same, sir, I'd rather she just popped it in the post.'

'She could end up being your Prime Minister at this rate, so no, you will not ask her to pop it in the post. You'll arrange to meet her. You'll actually turn up this time, smile, shake hands and play the hero she thinks you are.'

Not a battle worth fighting, Porter thought, so he nodded and let it drop. Never one to stand on ceremony without a camera about, Milburn sent them both packing, muttering again how this wasn't the end of the conversation. Two massive wins in the space of twenty-four hours and the man still had his nose turned up like he'd trodden in the world's biggest turd.

His team were all waiting for him back in the incident room, Taylor Bell included.

'Rogered?' she asked, one eyebrow bobbing up.

'Well and truly.'

'You need a drink,' Styles said, pushing to his feet. 'Come on, after a result like this, you're buying.'

Porter's head felt like a shaken snow globe. He'd expected more of a sense of victory, Tyler behind bars and likely to stay that way. As it was, it felt like an anti-climax. Something that had built up over the years to the point of feeling like an impossible goal that didn't exist any more. Now what? Just all felt a bit . . . flat. He dug in his pocket, pulled out three tenners and handed them to Styles.

'Think I'll take a rain check, mate. I should get home and see Evie, but here, get a round in on me.'

'Gonna be a lonely evening for you then,' Styles said. 'She's on her way in for a drink.'

'Eh? How's that?'

'I called her. Said you needed to get drunk, and that I wasn't responsible enough to look after you.'

Twenty minutes later, Porter was weaving his way across from the bar in The Green Man to their table, carrying a tray with enough bottles to rack up a frame at a bowling alley. Wasn't until he'd handed the last drink over to Bell that it hit him. Shit! Evie hadn't exactly been Bell's biggest fan when she'd found out about the one drink that Porter had kept from her. Last thing he wanted was confrontation. Not with everyone here. Not today. He pulled out his phone to text her, ask her to meet him back at the station when he saw her picking her way between pockets of people. He made his way over, meeting her halfway.

'Hey, I was just about to drop you a line. Buy you a drink?'

She held up a bottle of Corona. 'Already been via the bar. You can get the next one though.'

So much for his delaying tactic to give him a chance to at least mention Bell's presence rather than Evie just stumble into her. He was about to suggest they got that second drink in now before they joined the group, but Evie had already started heading across. She managed to squeeze her way through gaps he couldn't and made it across a full ten seconds ahead, standing on tiptoe to give Nick a peck on the cheek, and as Porter caught up, Evie turned to Bell, introduced herself and fell into a conversation with her and Sucheka.

Styles sidestepped past her, sidling up to Porter. 'What's up, boss? You look a bit peaky.'

'Hmm, oh, nothing. I just thought . . .'

'That the girls were going to have a cat fight over you?' Styles said, aiming for poker face, but Porter spotted the corners of his mouth twitching. 'Oh, come on,' Styles said, 'didn't take a genius to spot she was pissed at you for having a drink with Taylor. Don't worry though, I sorted it.'

Porter frowned. 'Sorted it? What do you mean, sorted it?'

Styles shrugged. 'Just helped her see that she had nothing to worry about. You're not Taylor's type.'

'How do you know what Taylor's type is?'

'Love that you're now getting arsey at the suggestion she might not be interested. Let's just say you're not the one in the team she's got eyes for.'

'Oh, here we go, it's all about you,' Porter said with an eye-roll. 'I'm grassing you to Emma.'

'Not me, you fool,' Styles said, nudging Porter, inclining his head towards the trio.

'What? Kaja? Really? I thought she was already spoken for?'

Styles shook his head. 'They broke up two weeks ago.'

Porter soaked in the new info, realising how far off the mark he'd been with Bell.

'Some bloody detective I am,' he muttered, annoyed that he hadn't known about Kaja's break-up to ask how she was doing. Too wrapped up in his own shit to notice. That was one thing that had to change. Now Styles had pointed it out, it was like someone had whipped the blinkers off. Glances between Kaja and Bell, a coy smile as Kaja fiddled with a stray strand of hair. He took another swig from his bottle.

'Mmm, forgot to ask, how did the follow-up with Finch go?'

Styles rolled his eyes. 'You'd get more conversation on a coma ward. Just sat there doing his strong, silent type impression for most of it.'

'Still bothers me,' Porter said. 'If it's all about some idealistic notion of what he wants the country to look like, you'd think he'd be singing that crap from the rooftops non-stop. That and the fact he tried to stitch up his boss. You'd have thought he'd want Winter to keep stirring things up as well.'

'No idea,' Styles said. 'To be honest, the more we looked into him, I'm surprised he was slumming it with the likes of Winter. They might have a similar world view, but the firm he works for, Sentinel, have got a hell of a client list. I'm talking actors, footballers, proper politicians, party leaders, not the likes of him who just play at it.'

Styles pulled out his phone, hopped onto the Sentinel page, scrolling through a who's who of familiar faces on the testimonials page.

'Guess he just pimped himself out to someone with more cash than sense.' Porter shrugged.

'Turn it up, mate, can you turn it up?'

Glenn Waters chased after a retreating glass collector, pointing at a screen on the wall. The poor young lad looked positively harassed, glasses with assorted dregs in, tightly crammed onto his tray. He shook his head, zigzagging through gaps in the early evening crowd.

All heads in their group swivelled mid conversation, fixing on the screen. Volume wasn't essential as it happens, blocky white subtitles popping on screen, overlaying Roger Milburn's face. Shame he couldn't be muted more often. The screen cut to footage of a previous press conference, Porter's own face, gravely serious as he addressed the camera. Subtitles popped along the bottom.

Witnesses say Detective Inspector Jake Porter tackled Leo Finch single-handed after Finch tried to fight his way out of the Victory Services Club, on Seymour Street in Central London yesterday.

A chorus of cheers and repeated pats rained down on Porter's back as the group gathered around him. More subtitles. A mention of Holly brought a soberness to those around him. He disappeared from screen, replaced with a series of talking heads, chipping in their ten cents. Politicians spouting soundbites, the Mayor praising the restraint shown by the majority, condemning those who had borderline rioted these past few days. The fuss around him began to die down, and he lifted his bottle to drain the remainder, when he glanced back at the screen. The words floated under the speaker's face, hovering, snapping away, replaced by the next sentence, but stayed front and centre in his mind. A ghost of a memory floated forwards, solidifying, crashing into any notion of this being over.

'Boss? You all right?' Styles's words seemed to come from far away, but when Porter looked round, he was only a couple of feet to the side.

'Can't believe I missed it.'

'Missed what?'

'Need to check to be sure, but we've got to go. Tell you on the way.'

CHAPTER SIXTY-NINE

Postman's Park was deserted at this time of the evening. Less than half an hour to go before the gates would be locked, the usual flow of city workers seeking solace from offices long since dried up. A mini oasis of green squeezed between buildings that loomed over it, the park, more of a garden really, was a tranquil little treasure, tacked on to the side of St Botolph's Without Aldersgate Church. There'd been a church of one type or another here for over a thousand years.

Porter shuffled along the line of plaques on the wall, the park's main attraction. Each was a memorial to an ordinary member of the public who had lost their life trying to save another's, the brainchild of George Frederic Watts, a nineteenth century artist. Some of the everyday heroes had only been children, as young as ten, saving a sibling from drowning. He paused for a moment by the last, a quote from Watts himself.

The material prosperity of a nation is not an abiding possession; the deeds of its people are.

There were plenty that had fallen well short of that ideal this past week. The path wound its way around a circular dot of grass, a green punctuation mark in the paved yard, and he made his way across to one of the last benches before the exit out onto King Edward Street.

He could still be wrong about this, about all of it. There was still time to walk away. He could head home to Evie and away from a fight he didn't have to pick. Except walking away didn't feel like a genuine option. Not this far in. If he was right and he walked, the repercussions could be a lot more serious than the events of the last few days.

Porter sank down onto the wooden bench, feeling perspiration blot his shirt as he leant back and opted for sitting forwards, elbows on knees, flicking through his phone to kill time. He didn't have long to wait though. He'd barely had a chance to click into his emails when he heard footsteps approach from the left. He looked up to see a familiar face heading towards him. Not one he'd seen in person before, but one he knew well nonetheless.

'Detective Porter,' she said, the barest hint of a Yorkshire accent lurking beneath the surface. From what he'd seen, she played on it when it suited her, hid it when it didn't.

'Mrs Ashbrooke,' he said, standing to greet her.

'Oh, there's just you and me here. Call me Sally,' she said, choosing not to count the bodyguard who waited just inside the King Edward Street gate as part of the gathering.

'In that case, I'm Jake. Nice to meet you,' he said, shaking her hand, gesturing towards the bench. 'Shall we sit?'

The seat was divided in three by half-height armrests. The leader of the British Independence Party left the middle vacant, plumping herself down in the far seat. She seemed softer than her on-screen persona, more of a youthful grandma vibe about her than politician. Late fifties, hair more white than grey. Eyes the colour of Arctic water, behind thick black frames.

'I know you can't accept my reward personally, but I must admit, I thought it would at least make for some positive press for the Met. Are you sure your superintendent wouldn't rather do this with a few more people present?'

Porter shook his head, thinking to himself, *Of course he would*, poker face giving nothing away.

'He's not one for pomp and ceremony, ma'am.'

'I've told you, it's Sally, and that's exactly what I thought he was. Oh well, makes no difference to me. Anyway, it's not as if there's a giant novelty cheque to change hands. I'll have my people transfer the money to the Met first thing tomorrow. We could have done this over the phone I suppose, but I did want the chance to meet you, say thank you in person. Your stopping Finch, hopefully that can bring the city back from boiling point.'

'That's very generous, thank you.'

'And this man, Finch, he's confessed?'

Porter shook his head. 'He's not saying much, but to be fair, we've got enough without a confession.'

'Mm, yes, Superintendent Milburn mentioned something about recorded calls and matching his voice to the awful Facebook video.'

Typical Milburn, oversharing to ingratiate.

'Can't really go into detail, ma'am . . . Sally.'

'Of course.' She nodded, showing a smile that said she could find out exactly what she wanted whether he liked it or not. 'I hear Damien Winter has managed to crawl out from under this though. He's a dangerous man, that one. Even more so for having gotten away with this.'

'We can only go where the evidence leads us.'

'I suppose if that stops with Leo Finch, your hands are tied.'

'Not exactly,' Porter conceded.

'What do you mean, not exactly?' she asked, narrowing her eyes. 'Your hands aren't tied?'

'They might still be, but it doesn't stop with Finch.'

'But you just said there was no link back to Damien Winter?'

'Not to Winter, no.'

'To whom then?'

'Leo Finch, he served with your son. Did you know that?'

'I'm sorry,' she said after a beat, 'what does that have to do with anything?'

'His dishonourable discharge, turns out he was beating information out of a local who they suspected was protecting the man that ordered the attack that killed your son.'

CHAPTER SEVENTY

Ashbrooke just stared at him. He waited her out for the five seconds it took her to respond.

'And what's your point?'

'I just find it peculiar that you've never mentioned the connection.'

Stern features dissolved into a smile that creased the corners of her eyes. 'You know us politicians, we try and stay downwind of anything that makes us look bad. Anything other than shaking hands and kissing babies, people look to twist things into something they're not.'

'And what are they, then, when they're not twisted?'

'I'm not sure I like your tone, Detective,' she said, saccharine sweet, but the smile had left her eyes. Dropped the first names too he noted. 'Leo did what he thought was the right thing, just went the wrong way about it. Made some bad choices.'

'That's putting it mildly,' Porter said.

'Well, it's been a pleasure meeting you, Detective,' she said, standing up, straightening her jacket. 'If you'll excuse me, I've got a Party event this evening, so I'll leave you to enjoy the peace and quiet.'

'Probably best you give me five more minutes,' Porter said, making no move to stand himself.

'Excuse me?'

Anger twinkled in her eyes, warning him he'd walked to the edge of a very short plank.

'Five minutes, and I'll be on my way. If not, I'll have my super on the phone before you've left the park. See what he thinks about what I've got to say.'

'You've got three,' she said, but stayed standing.

That should be enough, he thought, peering past her to where the bodyguard had clearly picked up on the shift in atmosphere, edging a few feet closer without looking too obvious.

'Finch wasn't just your son's friend, was he? Did a stint as your CP, your Close Protection, a few years back?'

'There were threats,' she admitted. 'Not enough for the police to act, but back when I was campaigning for the removal of troops from Afghanistan. Enough that I wanted to feel safe. Leo gave me that feeling.'

'And the company he works for, Sentinel, that's part-owned by your son's former fiancée, isn't it? Didn't twig at first, different surname, but Companies House lists you as a director as well. They've even got a nice glossy pic of you on their website in the testimonial section. Now I know what you're thinking, where am I going with this?'

'Two minutes left,' she said, sounding bored, with a hundred better places to be.

'Here's the thing, when we arrest a suspect, like Leo Finch or Damien Winter, we dig deeper than a miner on speed. I'm talking finances, known acquaintances, phone logs and locations, the works. Know what we found?'

'Do hurry up, Detective. I don't have time for a full show-and-tell.'

'Turns out Finch and Winter were regular visitors in your neck of the woods. Not your office, your home. Not actually at your house, but nearby, along the river path. Their phones pinged there four times in the last six months. Not only that though, Finch, he came calling solo as well, and he did come to your house. Here's the kicker: so did Ross Henderson.'

She'd worn a stony mask up until that point, but the mention of Henderson cracked through the icy veneer. More of a micro expression, but enough to confirm it had struck home somewhere. Porter pressed on.

'Ross liked to record things. Had all sorts of gadgets. Buttonhole cameras, drones, you name it. We've already got one death threat from Winter on tape, and it got me thinking, what if it wasn't only Winter that Henderson wanted to expose? You've publicly spoken out against Damien Winter, Mrs Ashbrooke, so why was he a regular around your way? And why was Leo Finch even more of a regular?'

'If you've got something to accuse me of, Detective, why don't you just spit it out? That way I know exactly what slander I'll be suing the Met for. What exactly are you saying?'

Stick or twist time. He'd played this part through in his

head a hundred times since Finch's arrest. No going back.

'It's not really slander if it's true though, is it? Finch called you three minutes after he pretended to be Winter to get handed Henderson's location on a plate. I'm saying Finch was working for you, not Winter. I'm saying Finch did what he did with your blessing. I'm saying he's your attack dog. I mean, come on, he even talks like you. All this talk of tidal waves sweeping the nation, wiping the slate clean, starting again. Like I said before, Mr Henderson was a cautious man. Voice recordings, drone footage. More than enough to expose the who and the what. That much I know. What I'm a little hazy on is the why.'

Ashbrooke studied him intently, as if seeing him for the first time. A glance back at her bodyguard, another past Porter towards the far gate. Still only the three of them, and only two party to the conversation.

'And you're saying what? That I'm part of some kind of conspiracy? That I'd risk my reputation, my freedom, just to shut one bleeding heart liberal up? What I'm hazy on, Detective, is if you have what you say you have, why we're having this conversation here, just the two of us, and not at Paddington Green?'

'My gaffer reckons you might be in charge of all this soon enough,' he said, looking around the park.

'Maybe,' she agreed. 'Who knows?' A pause. A shift in her expression. 'You know, if you were ever to leave the Met, Sentinel could use a man of your skills, your . . . tenacity.'

'You offering me a job?'

'Would you accept if I did?'

'Depends who I'm working for. If you do win, what do you actually want?'

'You're ex-army,' she said. 'You know what it's like to serve your country. To keep our enemies at a distance, only for someone to slip through the net at home. They walk into an arena wearing their IED on their back, next thing you know we've got casualties on our own soil.'

She took her seat beside him again, eyes fixed ahead for now on a wall of plaques.

'Sacrifices need to be made to keep our country safe. They all understood it,' she said, nodding towards row after row of those who'd given their lives so that someone, often a stranger, could live. 'My son understood it.'

'Part of the job,' he said simply.

'Leo understands it. Men like Ross Henderson, they do not.'

'And Winter?' Porter asked. 'Does he understand it?'

The EWP leader was still a shifting piece in this jigsaw, couple of possible slots he could slide into.

'Damien,' she said, with a slow shake of her head. 'Damien means well, but we can't very well have him running rampant. This last week has proved that beyond a shadow of a doubt. He overstepped the mark a while back with that poor delivery boy his men left for dead.'

'Allegedly.'

Sally Ashbrooke swivelled around in her seat so she was facing him, the hint of a smile.

'There's a reason why they're called the far right,' she said. 'They're too far away from what your average middle-Englander is comfortable with. Don't get me wrong, he spins a good yarn, but he's not going to be picking out a colour scheme for Downing Street any time soon. All he had to do was stoke up the fires a little, then let me smooth things back over.'

'A safe middle ground,' Porter added. 'More appealing than the Tories, less extreme than the in-your-face racists.'

'Something like that. Ross Henderson was the opposite of Damien. As liberal as a man could get. All this talk of borders open like a twenty-four-hour Tesco.' She shook her head at the thought of it.

'He had evidence against Winter,' Porter said. 'Threats on camera.'

'So I heard.' She nodded.

'Winter, he genuinely didn't know about Finch, did he?'

She pursed her lips. 'That's a bit of leading question, Jake, don't you think?' Ever the politician. Answer a question with a question.

'If that job offer is real, I need to know what I'm hitching my trailer to.'

She sighed, seeming to wrestle with something. That's the trouble with politicians though, he thought. Ask them for a straight answer and they clam up.

'And there's the sticking point. Trust. I hear good things about you, but I don't know you. Trust is something you have to earn.'

'Like Leo did?'

'We all have to at some point, Jake.'

'And how exactly would I be able to earn yours?'

'These recordings you say Henderson made. You know how the press love to twist things in the name of headlines. Words get taken out of context, and the next thing you know, good people get their names dragged through the mud. As you said before, there's a chance I could be in charge soon enough. Do some real good for this country. Our country. If there was anything on those that put that at risk, however innocent, anyone who could make them disappear would be someone I could trust.'

As politicians went, she was as slick as any he'd seen. Using a hundred words, when ten would do.

'You're asking me to destroy evidence?'

'You're asking me how to win my trust.'

'Here's the thing, Sally. I can still call you Sally, can't I? You can dance around it all you want, but I know you ordered Leo Finch to kill Ross Henderson. I know you wanted it to look like Winter was behind it. I know you think you're some kind of white knight riding in to save the country, that you're better than the likes of the EWP. But, when it comes down to it, you're worse. At least they're upfront about what they believe in.'

'We're done,' she said, flashing a look that could cut glass and rising from her seat.

'We're a long way from that. Once what we have goes public, the closest you'll get to Downing Street is Google Maps.'

She took quick steps towards him, anger hissing out with every word. 'Big mistake, Detective. You have no idea what it takes to make the kind of decisions needed to keep our country safe. What's one death if it saves thousands? If it stops the next Manchester bomber from entering the country, then I can live with that.'

'And that's why you're not fit to run the country.'

That one lit an already shortest fuse. 'I'd choose my next words carefully if I were you,' she said through gritted teeth.

'Or what, I'll end up like Ross Henderson? Good luck with that now your Rottweiler's in jail.'

'If that's what it takes. There's plenty more where he came from that'll follow my orders every bit as well as he did.'

And there it was. No more going round in circles.

'How can you stand there and say what you did was right?' He wrinkled his nose in disgust. 'You're no better than the people you're trying to keep out.'

'I did what had to be done, to put me where I need to be. The PM's taken a hammering. I'm two points off him and closing after this week. If anyone had had the guts to do what I did, to stand up for this country a decade ago, my boy might still be alive.'

'This isn't going to bring him back, Sally.'

'No, but there'll be plenty more saved that don't have to go through what I did. Now if you'll excuse me, we really are done.'

She turned on her heel and strode away towards her bodyguard.

'You've just admitted conspiracy to murder, Mrs Ashbrooke. You don't get to walk away from that.'

'And who's going to believe you?' she said, whirling to face him. 'If whatever recordings you had were enough, you'd have used them.'

Porter stared her down for a slow three count in head. 'Actually, we didn't have any,' he admitted. 'Until today.'

Confusion flickered behind anger. 'What the hell is that supposed to mean?'

'Elliott,' Porter called over his shoulder. 'You can come out now.'

After what seemed like an eternity, over towards the east gate, a face peered out from the church doorway. Elliott Kirk looked almost embarrassed to be there as he made his way across.

'What the hell is this?' Ashbrooke muttered, then louder, 'And who the hell are you?'

The sound of footsteps approaching fast. Porter turned back to see the bodyguard making a beeline for them, sliding himself between Ashbrooke and the unknown quantity, even though Kirk couldn't have looked less threatening if he'd walked out in a priest's robes.

'This is Elliott, Ross's friend. Elliott, we good to go?'

Kirk nodded. 'All ready when you are.'

'Ready? Ready for what?'

'Mrs Ashbrooke, we should leave, now,' the bodyguard urged.

'Do it,' said Porter, talking to Kirk, but his eyes not leaving Ashbrooke.

Kirk lifted his phone, tapped out something on the screen, then nodded to Porter.

'What now, you're going to try and trick me into saying something incriminating on camera?'

Porter shook his head. 'No tricks needed. We got what we needed.' He walked over to the bushes by the side of the bench, arm disappearing up to his elbow, far from empty when he pulled it back out. Smartphone and tripod. Just like the kit Ross Henderson's murder had been filmed on.

'This is entrapment,' she gasped, then to the bodyguard said something inaudible. The man's arm shot out, grabbing the tripod, wrenching it from Porter's grasp, handing it to Ashbrooke. She looked smug, the kind of level reserved for schoolyard bullies after they've rifled the weaker kid's pockets.

'Nice try, Detective. I might even use this one to make my call to the commissioner asking for your suspension.'

'You might want to have a look on this one, before you do,' he said, borrowing Kirk's handset, turning the screen so she could see. Her face went from irritated, cycled through confused as she processed what she was seeing, to something bordering on terror.

405

He angled his head around so he could watch. Saw the footage from minutes ago. Blue and white Facebook banner. That same profile picture, a rolling bank of clouds, one that he'd first laid eyes on a week ago. Dead centre, a screen within a screen, still muted but unmistakably Sally Ashbrooke approaching him minutes ago. One tap, and voices started.

'Don't worry, we didn't share it live, just in case I was wrong,' he said. 'Elliott here is a dab hand with the tech though. Set up a private page to let it run live to an audience of zero. He's just shared that link to the Stormcloudz page though. You wanted a soapbox to shout from, you got one.'

CHAPTER SEVENTY-ONE

The next week was a blur. Milburn was unsurprisingly pissed off at not having had Porter's suspicions shared in advance. That soon faded with each new headline about the Met ruthlessly exposing corruption. Plenty of press conferences for him to preen like a peacock. Ashbrooke had continued to rant about being set up, going as far as to smash the spare smartphone he'd used to film her, even ordering her bodyguard to intervene as Porter had arrested her. The man had seen sense. Whether that had anything to do with Tessier and Styles walking through the west gate at that stage, was anybody's guess.

After the first twenty-four hours, Porter made it his mission to avoid the press, keeping news off the TV. Better things to do than watch Westminster tear itself to pieces, parties fighting for moral high ground, which after Ashbrooke's video went viral was somewhere below sea level in the public's eyes if you were a politician.

Winter tried to beat the EWP war drums again, but after several anonymous posts on the Stormcloudz Facebook page about his trips to Peterborough, plus a copy of the threats he made against Henderson, he was speaking to empty venues within days.

Ashbrooke lawyered up, said very little, scuttling out the back door when she made bail, avoiding the mosh pit of paparazzi waiting outside. That silence continued throughout subsequent interviews, guarded by high-priced lawyers in high-priced suits. They were still peddling entrapment, saying comments were taken out of context, claiming she had simply spoken about her efforts to get elected. That she'd do what she had to on the campaign trail, but of course she hadn't *actually* ordered Ross Henderson's death.

A spokesperson from the British Independence Party said she had the entire party behind her. But after a week's worth of mauling in the press and a twenty-point gap opening between her and the PM, Sally Ashbrooke stepped down as leader of the BIP, for the good of the party, and so she could 'attend to personal matters'. Equivalent of saying the *Titanic* had sprung a bit of a leak.

Amongst the whirlwind of white noise surrounding the Henderson case, Jackson Tyler's arrest and subsequent charging with Holly's death barely made a splash as far as any press was concerned. That suited Porter. He wasn't the sort to have his life paraded in public. The man responsible would pay, although for how long remained to be seen, and that, he hoped, would be enough. Felt like a weird way to describe it when he rolled the words around in his mind, but the sense of unresolved grief, a need for answers, had followed him around like a shadow for years, matching him step for step. Constant, conjoined, it had taken on a life of its own, a weight.

Jackson Tyler's arrest seemed to have cut it loose, but he'd become so used to it, he didn't quite feel himself. Milburn insisted Porter took a few days off, and for once, Jake didn't fight it. Some were calling Sally Ashbrooke's arrest a career-defining moment, but truth be told, he couldn't think of anything more important he could have achieved than getting justice for Holly.

He toyed with escaping London with Evie for a few days, but when he mentioned it to her, she reminded him of his promise to spend Saturday at Kat's for a barbeque and a kick-around with the boys. And so, as Sally Ashbrooke started to slide from the front page and disappear from headlines, at least until the trial, Porter found himself in Kat's garden, trying to stifle his competitive nature so as not to wipe out the twins with an overzealous tackle. Their dad, Tony, handed over barbeque duties to Kat, to even up the sides, and for half an hour, Jake's world consisted of a square patch of grass and some dubious shirt-pulling by Tom and James when it suited them.

By the time Kat called them over to eat, Jake had a sweat on and matching grassy stains tattooed on the knees of his jeans. Egged on by the twins, he built his own tower of a sandwich. Burger, cheese, tomatoes, mushrooms, pickles, plus a few sausages for good measure. Any more and he'd need planning permission, much to Kat's feigned horror, and the twins' delight.

He looked up from his construction, seeing the ear-to-ear grins on the twins' faces, both boys egging Evie on to do the same, if not bigger. A memory slipped in between frames of the present, the blink-and-you'll-miss-it type. Little over four years ago, Holly sat at the exact same table, cutting crusts off cheese sandwiches for the boys, promising she and Uncle Jake would take them to the park later so they could feed the scraps to the ducks.

Past and present spliced, spacing him out, only for a moment. He blinked and he was back in the here and now. Evie looked up from her plate, as if she'd sensed something in his gaze. She gave a smile that started from the mouth, radiating all the way out like ripples on a pond. He couldn't help but respond with one of his own, very much back in the moment. This last week since Postman's Park, and the last few days in particular, he'd felt cast adrift somewhat. Time away from the job, the thing that had been his focus for so long since Holly, coupled with the shadow of her case, had left an oddly empty feeling somewhere in the back of his mind. Not a bad empty though, more a feeling of roominess. Headspace he'd been without for too long.

He hadn't managed a second bite of his house-sized burger, before Evie was out of her seat, dragged under fake protest by the boys back out onto the makeshift football pitch, to have shots pinged in at her. Tom tried to dribble around her, and she knew she was beaten, ignoring the ball, grabbing hold and tickling as he tried to go past. James tried valiantly to rescue his brother, suffering the same fate, but only for a few seconds, until they, with a little leniency from Evie, double-teamed her, one tickling each armpit. Right there, in that moment, present trumped past. Even offered a sneak preview of a future that could be his, filling up that empty space the last few years had hollowed out. Theirs. One that made him smile. One he wouldn't just be settling for. One he wanted. One he was pretty sure Holly would want for him just as much.

ACKNOWLEDGEMENTS

Four books on, and the novelty of being in a position where I get to write these still hasn't worn off. *End of the Line* was written exclusively in lockdown, which might sound like perfect conditions – stuck in the house with fewer distractions. The reality is though that's been possibly the busiest year of my life, personally and professionally. My day job is in HR, so has been insanely busy throughout, and it's meant more late nights than ever to hit my deadline. This one has felt a little different for other reasons too. My first three have felt more insular when I look back on them. By that, I mean I hear other writers talking about reflecting social themes in their books, and I've just been head down, focusing on the idea I've had. For this one though, I wanted to explore some pretty divisive issues. It's been a weird few years, and events like Brexit have brought out the worst in way too many people, at a time when we need a sense of unity and inclusivity more than ever. The research into far-right groups, and some of the dialogue I had to write for those characters associated with them, genuinely left a bad taste in my mouth, but I'm hoping that's just a reflection on how realistic the people who speak those words come across.

As ever, it's not just about me scribbling words down. There's a whole army behind the scenes that make my grubby drafts a whole lot prettier. Big thank you to all the team at A&B. It never ceases to amaze me how much better the finished product is because of you folks, and any errors left behind are entirely mine.

Lockdown hasn't been all doom and gloom. I've actually come out of it with more friends than I went in with. Thanks to the miracle of Zoom, and a weekly dose of lockdown episodes of Virtual Noir at The Bar, I've gone and found myself a new group of pals – my circle of trust buddies – you know who you are. You guys have helped make lockdown more bearable, one Zoom call at a time. Rockstars, every last one of you.

Shout out to my fellow Y-Files crew for always being there as a sounding board, givers of advice, shoulders to vent on and just generally being all-round legends.

I want to give a shoutout to a couple of charity anthologies I was lucky enough to contribute to during lockdown, and to all the other authors who contributed. First up is *Afraid of the Light* (all profits going to Samaritans), followed by the sequel, *Afraid of the Christmas Lights*, (all profits shared between East Surrey Domestic Abuse Services, providing help and outreach in East Surrey, and Rights Of Women, a national charity that helps women understand their legal rights and access a range of support services to which they are entitled. Lastly, Virtual Noir at the Bar, with all profits going to NHS charities. Lockdown really has brought out the best in some people, and it was an honour to take part and give a little back.

To Jude and Malc, the best in-laws a bloke could wish for. Your support and encouragement mean a lot, especially bearing in mind I still haven't taken all of Nic's stuff from your loft like I promised I would when I married her.

My own mam and dad have literally been a never-ending source of encouragement and support my whole life, and these books are borne out of that. I wouldn't be writing these were it not for you two. Took me a while to persuade my mam to read past the opening scenes in this one. Apparently, she was disturbed that her son could dream up such things.

To my kids – Lucy, Jake and Lily. Only one of you is old enough to read this right now, but hope your old man makes you proud from time to time.

To my wife, Nic, chief proofreader, toddler wrangler, BFF and partner in crime. There's nobody I'd rather have been locked down with. Every day is just that little bit better for having you in it, even though you never finish a single cup of tea I make for you.